Praise for *Zone*

"The novel of the decade, if not of the century."

—Christophe Claro

"A modern *Iliad*. . . . You turn the pages as if it were a great thriller. . . . A great novel. You must read it!"

—François Busnel, TV5, France

"*Zone* is a major and compelling work, a work that will keep you in its grip from its first utterance to its last."

—Brian Evenson

"A powerful read, a novel for the ages."

—François Monti, *Quarterly Conversation*

ZO

Mathias Énard

Translated from the French
by Charlotte Mandell

Introduction by
Brian Evenson

Originally published in France as *Zone* by Actes Sud, 2008

First edition, 2010

This work, published as part of a program providing publication assistance, received financial support from the French Ministry of Foreign Affairs, the Cultural Services of the French Embassy in the United States, and FACE (French American Cultural Exchange). www.frenchbooknews.com

(French Voices logo designed by Serge Bloch)

Library of Congress Cataloging-in-Publication Data:

Enard, Mathias, 1972-
[Zone. English]
Zone / Mathias Enard ; translated from the French by Charlotte Mandell ; introduction by Brian Evenson. — 1st ed.
p. cm.
ISBN-13: 978-1-934824-26-9 (pbk.)
ISBN-10: 1-934824-26-7 (pbk.)
1. Intelligence officers—France—Fiction. 2. Croats—Fiction. 3. Mediterranean Region—Fiction. I. Mandell, Charlotte. II. Title.
PQ2705.N273Z6513 2010
843'.92—dc22

2010029057

Text set in Caslon, a family of serif typefaces based on the designs of William Caslon (1692-1766).

Design by N. J. Furl

Open Letter is the University of Rochester's nonprofit, literary translation press:
Lattimore Hall 411, Box 270082, Rochester, NY 14627

www.openletterbooks.org

To the world of A's

Introduction

I first learned about *Zone* in September of 2008 when I was in France for a literary festival. Looking for something new to read, each time I'd meet with a journalist or reviewer, I'd ask what they'd read recently that they'd liked. The book that came up most often, and most enthusiastically, was one published just a few weeks earlier, Mathias Énard's *Zone.*

On first glance, *Zone* seems an unlikely choice for best-loved novel, even among critics. Not only is it not a plot-driven book, it's a book that takes place entirely during a train journey from Milan to Rome. In one sense, very little actually happens: a man boards a train on his way to Rome after having a deranged individual hold out his hand to him and say "comrade one last handshake before the end of the world." Shaken, he proceeds on to Rome. While in transit, he smokes in the bathroom, he goes to the bar and has several drinks, he watches people get on and off the train, he dozes a little. But, most of all, he thinks, turning over and over in his head the details of his own life as well as very specific and often very troubling obscurities from the wars and conflicts of the twentieth century. This, in fact, is where the action and the tension of the book lie: within a single human skull. The man is, we quickly learn, an amateur historian of atrocity—or, rather, someone able to pass as an amateur historian. In actuality he is an ex-soldier from the Balkans, where he both witnessed and participated in atrocity, and a spy for the French intelligence service. Or, as he phrases it, a "warrior, spy, archeologist of madness, lost now with an assumed name between Milan and Rome, in the company of living ghosts . . ." He is bringing to Rome a briefcase full of secrets that he intends to sell and, afterward, to abandon his real identity for good. Along the way, his mind will touch on Ezra Pound and Dalton Trumbo, Eduardo Rózsa and the song "My Way" (in multilingual versions), the Spanish fascist Millán-Astray and the autoerotic asphixiator William Burroughs, the Armenian genocide and the crimes of Croat terrorists, the Black Hand and the Holocaust, on girlfriends and comrades he left behind. Indeed, his time on the train is the moment in which Francis Servain Mirković, exhausted and drunk and a little frantic, begins to take all the different things that have led him to this moment and synthesize them in a way that is at once brilliant and terrifyingly disturbing.

The swirl of information, the confusion of Francis's own mind, is augmented by the way the novel represents his thoughts; *Zone*, 517 pages long, is written as a single run-on sentence in which everything is allowed to jostle up against everything else. Énard does show a little mercy: this sentence is broken up into twenty-four chapters (not un-coincidentally the same number as in *The Iliad*—"I wanted to do a contemporary epic," Énard told Robert Solé in *Le Monde des Livres*) and in addition is disrupted three times by excerpts from a Lebanese book that Francis is reading. But what's remarkable is how quickly a reader's mind can adapt to this, how the rhythms of Énard's text and his sometimes slightly eccentric use of commas end up carrying one swiftly forward. There's a remarkable flow and rhythm to the sentences, partly imitating the rocking rhythm of a train, which almost allows you to forget that you're reading a book that's a single sentence long. *Zone* rarely if ever feels artificial; its form, as Beckett suggests of Joyce's "Anna Livia Plurabel," *is* its content, its content its form: "His writing is not *about* something; *it is that something itself*." (Beckett, "Dante . . . Bruno . Vico . . Joyce").

Zone owes something to Michel Butor's *La Modification* (1957), a novel in which a man takes a train from Paris to Rome to unexpectedly visit his lover, intending to inform her that he is leaving his wife for her but changing his mind along the way. Like *Zone*, the frame of the story proper is the train ride, though the nature of each narrator's thoughts are rather different. In addition, Butor writes in second person using standard punctuation and paragraphing. One might think as well, in passing, of other *nouveau romanists* such as Claude Simon (for the non-paragraphing he uses in *Conducting Bodies*, not dissimilar to Énard's own non-paragraphing) or Alain Robbe-Grillet (because of his interest in detectives and spies and because of the importance of a train journey in *La Reprise*). Yet at the same time it would be as appropriate to mention either Samuel Beckett's trilogy or Thomas Bernhard's *Gargoyles* in the place of Simon, or Javier Marías's *Your Face Tomorrow* in the place of Robbe-Grillet. Not to mention Patrik Ouředník's *Europeana*. Or countless other books. Indeed, *Zone* is a book aware of, and carrying on a conversation with, many different literary traditions.

On a political level, *Zone* is engaged but very far from being partisan—it's a very different book from, say, Peter Handke's polemical *A Journey to the Rivers: Justice for Serbia*. Francis is neither wholly reliable nor wholly unreliable, and it is difficult for the reader to ever feel fully at ease with him. He is implicated and not particularly trying to hide it, but he can reveal himself only gradually, only slowly, as a way of trying to free himself from himself so that he can start over. In his mind, the line between victim and murderer comes to seem as confused and arbitrary as the lines we draw between nations and then fight to the death to protect. For him "there are lots of innocent men among the killers in the suitcase, as many as there are among the victims, murderers rapists throat-slitters ritual decapitators . . ." Strains of innocence and guilt run through both sides. Someone's views can shift as easily as a gun can be aimed, and individuals begin to fall into roles out of fear or hate, almost against their will. This is a book about trying—and probably failing—to escape the aftershocks of one's own trauma, about trying to shake one's ghosts.

Indeed, for me, *Zone* is ultimately a book about collective and individual trauma, the way trauma bleeds its way up and down between the individual and the larger collective groups to which he belongs. It is at once about bad faith and about the absurdity that terms such as bad faith take on in the face of decapitation, atrocity, and overwhelming fear. A little push, almost nothing—a bullet that breaks one's car window, say—may well be enough to tilt the scales and make one begin to become inhuman.

After its publication *Zone* went on to win several major prizes, including the *Prix du Livre Inter*, the *Prix Décembre* (whose other recipients include such greats as Pierre Guyotat, Pierre Michon, and Jean-Philippe Toussaint), and the *Prix Initiales*, and to be a finalist for several others. "What is amazing in this horrible and sublime book," Anne Brigaudeau suggests, "is the magnificent use of language, an uncommon erudition, a meticulous know-how for narrating the worst atrocities of the century, down to little known or forgotten details." Does *Zone* live up to such praise? I think it does. It is a profoundly (and complexly) ethical book, satisfying both as a work of prose and in its incisive interpretation of our times. *Zone* is a major and compelling work, a work that will keep you in its grip from its first utterance to its last.

Brian Evenson
2010

ZONE

Milestones

And then went down to the ship,
Set keel to breakers, forth on the godly sea, and
We set up mast and sail on that swart ship,
Board sheep aboard her, and our bodies also

—Ezra Pound

Jerusalem and I are like a blind man and a cripple:
She sees for me
As far as the Dead Sea, as far as the end of days.
I carry her on my shoulders
And, under her, I walk in the shadows.

—Yehuda Amichai

I

everything is harder once you reach man's estate, everything rings falser a little metallic like the sound of two bronze weapons clashing they make you come back to yourself without letting you get out of anything it's a fine prison, you travel with a lot of things, a child you didn't bear a little Czech crystal star a talisman beside the snow you watch melting, after the re-routing of the Gulf Stream prelude to the Ice Age, stalactites in Rome and icebergs in Egypt, it keeps raining in Milan I missed my plane I had 1,500 kilometers on the train ahead of me now I have six hundred still to go, this morning the Alps sparkled like knives, I was trembling with exhaustion in my seat couldn't close my eyes like an aching drug addict, I talked to myself out loud on the train, or under my breath, I feel very old I want the train to go on go on let it go to Istanbul or Syracuse let it go to the end at least let it know how to go to the end of the journey I thought oh I should be pitied I took pity on myself on that train its rhythm opens your soul more deftly than a scalpel, I let everything flow by everything flees everything is more difficult these days along rail lines I'd like to let myself be led simply from one place to another as is logical for a passenger like a blind man led by the arm when he crosses a dangerous street but I'm just going from Paris to Rome, and to the main train station in Milan, to that Temple of Akhenaton for locomotives where a few traces of snow remain despite the rain I turn round and round, I look at the immense Egyptian columns supporting the ceiling, I have a little drink out of boredom, at a café overlooking the tracks the way others overlook the sea, it doesn't do me any good it wasn't the time for libations there are so many things that divert you from the path, that lead you astray and alcohol is one of them it makes the wounds deeper when you find yourself alone in an immense freezing train station obsessed by a destination that is in front of you and behind you at the same time: but a train isn't circular, it goes from one point to another whereas I am in orbit I gravitate like a chunk of rock, I felt like a measly pebble when the man approached me on the platform, I know I attract madmen and deranged people these days they rush into my fragility they find a mirror for themselves or a companion in arms and that is truly crazy, priest of an unknown divinity he has an impish cap and a small bell in his left hand, he holds out his right hand and shouts in Italian "comrade one last handshake before the end of the world" I don't dare shake it afraid he's right, he must be forty, no older, and he has that keen prying gaze of fanatics who ask you questions because they've just discovered an instant brother in you, I hesitate before the outstretched arm terrified by that screwy smile and I answer "no thanks" as if he were selling me a newspaper or offering me a smoke, then the madman rings his bell and begins laughing in a big doleful voice and pointing at me with the hand he offered me, then he spits on the ground, moves away and an immense almost desperate solitude sweeps the platform at that moment I would give anything for arms or shoulders even the train taking me to Rome I would give up everything for someone to appear there and stand in the middle of the station, among the shadows, among the men without men the travelers clinging to their telephones and their suitcases, all these people about to disappear and give up their bodies during the brief digression that will take them from Milano Centrale to Fossoli Bolzano or Trieste, a long time ago at the Gare de Lyon a deranged mystic had also announced the end of the world to me and he was right, I had been split in two then in the war and crushed like a tiny meteor, the kind that have stopped shining in the sky, a natural bombshell whose mass according to astronomers is laughable, the madman in the Milan station reminds me of the gentle screwball in the Gare de Lyon, a saint, who knows, maybe it was the same man, maybe we grew at the same rhythm each on his own side in our respective madnesses and find each other on platform number 14 in the train station in Milan, a city with the predatory Spanish military name, perched on the edge of the plain like a glacial crust slowly vomited by the Alps whose peaks I saw, flint blades ripping the sky and setting the tone of the apocalypse confirmed by the demon with the bell in that sanctuary of progress that is the Stazione di Milano Centrale lost in time like me here lost in space in the elegant city, with a patch on my eye like Millán-Astray the one-eyed general, a bird of prey, feverish, ready to rip vibrant flesh to shreds as soon as the light of flight and danger is found again: Millán-Astray would so have liked Madrid to become a new Rome, he served the Iberian Franco Il Duce his bald idol in that great warring prelude to the 1940s, that one-eyed belligerent officer was a legionnaire he shouted *viva la muerte* a good military prophet, and he was right, the fugue of death would be played as far as Poland, would raise a tall wave of corpses whose foam would end up licking the shores of the Adriatic, in Trieste or in Croatia: I think about Millán-Astray and his argument with Unamuno strict high priest of culture while travelers hurry to the platform to take off for the end of the world and the train leading them straight there, Unamuno was such a classical and noble philosopher that he didn't see the massacre on its way, he couldn't admit that the one-eyed general was right when he shouted *long live death* in front of his flock for that hawk had sensed (animals tremble before the storm) that the carrion would increase and multiply, that death would enjoy years of plenty, before also ending up in a train, a train between Bolzano and Birkenau, between Trieste and Klagenfurt or between Zagreb and Rome, where time stopped, as it stopped for me on that platform lined with railway cars, furious, panting engines, a pause between two deaths, between the Spanish soldier and the train station with a similar name, as crushing as Ares god of war himself—I light a last cigarette mechanically I have to get ready for the journey, for moving like all the people pacing up and down the platform in Milano Centrale in search of a love, a gaze, an event that will tear them from the endless circling, from the Wheel, a meeting, anything to escape yourself, or vital business, or the memory of emotions and crimes, it is strange that there are no women on the platform at this precise moment, motivated by the memory of Millán-Astray and his bandaged eye I climb into the trans-Italian express that must have been the zenith of progress and technology ten years ago for its doors were automatic and it went faster than 200 kilometers per hour in a straight line on a good day and today, a little closer to the end of the world, it's just a train: the same goes for all things like trains and cars, embraces, faces, bodies their speed their beauty or their ugliness seems ridiculous a few years later, once they're putrid or rusty, once up the step now I'm in a different world, plush velour thickens everything, heat too, I left winter by getting into this train car, it's a journey in time, it's a day unlike the others, it's a special day December 8th the day of the Immaculate Conception and I am missing the Pope's homily on the Piazza di Spagna as a madman comes and announces the end of the world to me, I could have seen the pontiff one last time, seen the spiritual descendant of the first Palestinian leader the only one who got some results, but it wasn't easy for that skinny whining Levantine who didn't write a single line during his lifetime, outside on the next track a train is stopping and a pretty girl behind the window has intriguing eyes, I think she's talking to someone I don't see, she is very close to me actually a meter away at most we are separated by two dirtyish windows I have to be strong I can't linger over the faces of young women I have to be resolute so I can gather momentum for the kilometers ahead of me then for the void and the terror of the world I'm changing my life my profession better not think about it, I placed the little suitcase over my seat and I discreetly handcuffed it to the luggage rack better close my eyes for a minute but on the platform policemen mounted on two-wheeled electric chariots like Achilles or Hector without a horse are chasing a young black man who's running towards the tracks rousing surprise and concern among the travelers, blue angels, announcers of the Apocalypse maybe, astride a strange silent azure scooter, everyone gets out to take in the scene, Pallas Athena and the son of Tydeus rushing at the Trojans, a few dozen meters away from me one of the two policemen reaches the fugitive and with a gesture of rare violence aided by all the speed of his vehicle he hurls the man at bay up against one of the cement posts in the middle of the platform, the captive flattens against the concrete his head bangs into the column and he falls, he falls on his stomach right in the middle of the Milano Centrale station just in time for the second angel to jump on his back and immobilize him, sitting on his lower back the way a farmer or a wrangler ties up a fractious animal, then, back on his machine, he drags the criminal stumbling at the end of a chain to the admiring murmurs of the crowd, ancient scene of triumph, they parade the chained conquered ones behind the chariots of the conquerors, they drag them to the gaping galleys, the black man has a swollen face and a bloody nose his head held high a little incredulous everyone gets back into the car the incident is over justice has triumphed just a few minutes before departure, I glance at the suitcase, I'm afraid I won't manage to sleep or I'll be pursued as soon as I doze as soon as I lower my guard they'll interfere with my sleep or get under my eyelids to raise them the way you open shutters or Venetian blinds, it's been a long time since I thought of Venice, the green water by the Dogana, the fog of the Zattere and the intense cold when you look at the cemetery from the Fondamente Nuove, back from the war, hadn't thought of the shadows, in Venice they're made of wine and drunk in the winter starting at five o'clock in the evening, I see again the Slavic violinists who played for the Japanese, the French in full carnival masquerade, a rich hairdresser from Munich who bought himself a palace on the Grand Canal, and the train suddenly gets underway I lean my head back we're off over 550 kilometers till the end of the world

II

I let myself fall under the spell of the flat cadence of the suburbs of that city with the name of the predatory Spanish soldier, outskirts of a Northern city like so many others, buildings to cram the proletariat in, immigrants from the 1960s, vertical concentration camps, to the paradoxical rhythm of the cross-ties—I am in Venice in that tiny damp apartment where the only light was in the kitchen the floor was sloping, you slept with your feet in the air which apparently is good for the circulation, it was at the entrance to the Ghetto opposite the bakery in front of the big synagogue where I sometimes heard psalms and songs, sometimes the name of the neighborhood made me afraid, the Old Ghetto, especially at night when everything was deserted and silent, when the *bora* blew the icy wind that seemed to come straight from the Ukraine after freezing the Czechs the Hungarians and the Austrians, in my Old Ghetto it was impossible not to think of Łódź of Cracow of Salonika and of other ghettos of which nothing remains, impossible not to be pursued by the winter of 1942, the trains to Treblinka, Bełżec, and Sobibor, in 1993 a few months after my own war and exactly fifty years after the extermination, in the Venetian Ghetto shrouded in fog and cold I imagined the German death machine not realizing that one of its last cogs had turned right nearby, a few kilometers away, but if I am thinking now again of Venice in a railway torpor it's mostly because of the one who had joined me there, the body she so often refused me forced me into long nocturnal walks sometimes until dawn, with my black cap, I passed the Square of the Two Moors, I greeted Saint Christopher on top of the Madonna dell'Orto, I got lost among the few modern buildings that they have over there as if they had been purposefully hidden in secret recesses, as if they weren't hidden enough by the lagoon, and how many times have I found myself back again having a coffee at daybreak with the pilots and skippers of the vaporetti I didn't exist for them, Venetians have that atavistic ability to ignore anything that isn't them, not to see, to make the foreigner disappear, and this sovereign scorn, this bizarre superannuated grandeur of a recipient that lets him completely ignore the hand that feeds him was not unpleasant, on the contrary, it was a great frankness and a great freedom, far from the commercial chumminess that has invaded the whole world, the whole world except Venice where they keep ignoring you and scorning you as if they didn't need you at all, as if the restaurant owner had no need of customers, rich as he is with his whole city and sure, certain, that other more easily pleased guests will soon come to fill his tables, whatever happens, and that gives him a formidable superiority over the visitor, the superiority of the vulture over its carrion, the tourist will always end up fleeced, dismembered with or without a smile, what's the use of lying to him, even the baker across from my apartment admitted, without blinking an eye, that his bread wasn't very good and his pastries overpriced, this baker saw me every day every day for months without ever smiling at me his strength was his certainty of my disappearance, one day I would leave Venice and the lagoon, whether it was after one, two, three, or ten years he belonged to the island and not me, and he reminded me of this every morning, which was salutary, no delusions to maintain, I associated only with foreigners, Slavs, Palestinians, Lebanese, Ghassan, Nayef, Khalil, and even a Syrian from Damascus who ran a bar where students and exiles gathered, he was a former sailor who had jumped ship during a stopover, a rough guy you'd never associate with any sea or any boat, he had a sturdy landlubber's head with very big ears that I remember as being on the hairy side, he was very pious, he prayed, fasted, and never drank the alcohol he served to his customers, his weakness was girls, whores especially, which he justified by saying that the Prophet had had a hundred wives, that he loved women, and that in short fornication was a fine sin, in Venice I didn't fornicate much, the winter was endless, damp and cold, hardly favorable to fornication in fact, I remember that the first night in the Ghetto I had no blankets and I was so frozen I rolled myself up in a dusty oriental rug, fully dressed, with my shoes on because the rigid carpet was like a tube and didn't cover my feet, I read some stories about phantom boats by William Hope Hodgson before falling asleep like a failed fakir or a dead sailor ready to be returned to the sea sewn up in his hammock, far from the eroticism that some attribute to Venice, a guy rolled up like a dusty threadbare cigar, on his own bed, with his shoes and a hat, why wasn't the heat working, I am incapable of remembering in any case in this train now it must be about 75 degrees, I took my sweater off at the same moment as my neighbor opposite, he looks like a white New York rapper, he is reading *Pronto* with a superior air, I wonder what it is going to announce, certainly not the end of the world, probably the end of a couple of Hollywood actors or the cocaine overdose of a thirty-year-old Italian businessman, the nephew or grandson of Agnelli the Fiat mastermind, I manage to read his first name on the cover, Lupo, that's strange, I must be mistaken, how can one be a businessman and be called Wolf, I picture him handsome, his hair shiny, his teeth white, his eye keen and just slightly bloodshot, they probably found him unconscious in a luxury apartment in Turin, maybe in the company of some classy escort, his Lamborghini nicely parked down below, with who knows a little blood or bile on his unbuttoned Armani shirt, and I picture the agitation of the women in the lobby who are mostly the ones who read these papers, my God this wolf is so handsome, so rich and well-born, what a waste, he could have had the decency to crash into a security gate at 300 kilometers an hour, a helicopter or even a jet-ski accident, end up cut to little pieces by one of the propellers of his own yacht, even shot in the face by a jealous husband or a Mafia hit man but drugs, drugs, it's as if he had caught smallpox, it's a shame, it's not possible, unfair, for a little while he seems almost pitiable this young Turin wolf who is plunging his great family into scandal, I hope he'll get out of the hospital before the end of the world, my neighbor looks condescending and disapproving, he shakes his head emitting little noises with his tongue as night falls outside, we are in the plains, the sad plains of Lombardy the darkness is invading thank God the twilight will be brief the bare frozen trees standing next to the electric lines will disappear soon you'll be able to make out nothing but their shadows and the moon might emerge from the clouds from time to time to illumine the hills before Bologna, then we'll glide towards the southwest in the Tuscan softness to Florence and finally in the same direction to Rome, still almost five hours before the Termini station, the churches, the Pope and the whole kit, the Roman caboodle: religious trinkets and ties, censors and umbrellas, all lost among the Bernini fountains and the cars, there where, on the stinking streets and the putrid Tiber, float Virgins with Child, the Saints Matthew, the Pietàs, the Depositions from the Cross, the mausoleums, the columns, the policemen, the ministers, the emperors, and the noise of a city resurrected a thousand times, gnawed by gangrene beauty and rain, which rather than some beautiful woman evokes an old scholar with superb knowledge who forgets himself in his armchair, life is leaving him in every way possible, he trembles, coughs, recites the *Georgics* or an ode by Horace as he pisses himself, the center of Rome empties itself in the same way, no more inhabitants, no more eating places, clothes clothes and clothes enough to make you lose your head billions of shirts hundreds of thousands of shoes millions of ties of scarves enough to cover Saint Peter, to circle the Coliseum, to bury everything beneath endless gear, and let the tourists make the tour of the antique shops in this immense religious secondhand store where gazes greedy for discoveries shine, look, I found a magnificent Borromini church under this fur coat, a ceiling by the Carracci brothers behind this hunting jacket and in this black leather boot the horns of Michelangelo's *Moses*, if they weren't waiting for me I'd never go back there, if in man's estate everything were simpler I'd never have made this journey, never have carried this last suitcase, *better my Gallic Loire than the Latin Tiber*, Du Bellay's verses learned by heart in high school, *happy who like Ulysses* and so on, I too have my *Regrets*, Ungaretti said that the Tiber was a deadly river, Ungaretti born in Alexandria in Egypt lived there until he was twenty before setting off for Rome then settling in France, there is an Alexandria in the Piedmont not very far from here, I've never been there, I remember in Venice I had asked in a travel agency if there were any boats to Alexandria and the employee (a blonde Venetian, a kind of barrette held in her mouth like a toothpick) had looked at me stunned, to Alexandria but there's a train, and in that immediate confidence one has in professionals I had pictured, for a second, a train that would go from Venice to Alexandria in Egypt, direct via Trieste Zagreb Belgrade Thessalonica Istanbul Antioch Aleppo Beirut Acre and Port Said, a challenge to geopolitics and to the mind, and even, once I had understood her confusion, Alessandria in Piedmont, I began to dream of a train that would unite all the Alexandrias, a network connecting Alessandria in Piedmont Alexandria Troas in Turkey Alexandria in Egypt Alexandria in Arachosia, possibly the most mysterious of them all, lost in Afghanistan far from railroads, the train would be called the Alexander Express and would go from Alexandria Eschate in Tajikistan to Piedmont through the lips of Africa in thirteen days and as many nights, Alexandria in Egypt another decadent city a decadence that does not lack charm when it rains or when it's dark, I remember we had a hotel there on the Corniche the first time we spent hours on the balcony facing the Mediterranean until a big block of cement broke off and came within two inches of killing a guy sitting on the terrace below, he barely raised his eyes, an Egyptian used to the sky almost falling on his head every day, in that double room I slept with Marianne, she got undressed in the bathroom, she had a body, a face to rend your soul and mine asked for nothing but that, in the scent of the Alexandrian rain and sea I got drunk on Marianne's fragrances, our hotel was not the Cecil, nothing of Durrell in our stay, at the time I didn't know any of his books, or Ungaretti or Cavafy that sad little employee in one of the immense banks still there in Ramleh, or in the cotton market, leaving work he visited the giant bakeries where he dreamt of Antony the vanquished one of Actium as he watched an Arab waiter sway his hips and the sun set on the Mameluk fort, at night everything looks alike, I could be in Alexandria, in that hotel on the Corniche beaten by sea spray just as my window now is streaked with rain, it was sad out and it rained, one night, slowly now, almost at a walking pace like the Italian train I join Marianne in that frozen hotel where we shivered, I close my eyes to remember this contact, the sort of crude, quick coitus, did it take place, did she just let me kiss her, I don't think so, she had kept her sweater on her scarf the room was full of drafts but in the morning there was a big sun the sea was very blue Marianne soon left for Cairo I stayed a few more days walking around in the city and in alcohol, "Ricardo the real Alexandrian pastis" terrible Egyptian anisette I drank without ice in a plastic glass as I watched the sea, glorious solitude, in the morning a tea in one of those bakeries near the Ramleh train station with a cement croissant weighing at least a pound, watching the streetcars rattle by, in a leather armchair that might have known the idle asses of Tsirkas, of Cavafy, of Ungaretti, ghosts in this city gnawed by poverty, with its back to the Mediterranean the way you have your back to the wall, filthy and unhealthy as soon as you leave the downtown neighborhoods that are already filthy, a fine place to wait for the end of the world while you eat fried fish under a big winter sun in the hollow of the sky scoured by the wind, it's very warm in this car, I'll doze off, I'm already half asleep rocked by Marianne with the white arms, her face changes, deformed by the twilight elongated by the trees passing by, I went back to Alexandria I often went back there and not always in dream, to carry out more or less secret transactions with Egyptian generals whose importance was measured not by the number of their stars but their Mercedes, those generals who fought against Islamic terrorism by conscientiously rubbing their foreheads with sandpaper every night to imitate the abrasion of skin against the prayer rug until they got a callus from it and seemed more pious than their enemies, in Egypt everything is always excessive, I took down names addresses networks the traces of activists from Afghanistan or the Sudan, and the military men, each one fatter than the next, peppered their talk with *in sha' allah, allahu a'lam, la hawla*, they who, with the same devotion, vigorously tortured and shot bearded men in the rear courtyards of overcrowded prisons along the Nile valley, I was indeed in Alexandria, twice I managed to go there by sea, in the summer, a ferry made the crossing from Cyprus, you could go from Beirut to Alexandria by changing boats in Larnaka which is not the most unpleasant of stopovers and, for someone carrying sensitive material as I was, was more practical than the Beirut airport swarming with Syrians, of course Marianne had stopped being there a long time before that the instant Ras et-Tin emerged from the morning fog, you felt as if you were seeing the city from behind, secretly, without any affectation, the way you surprise a naked woman at dawn in her bathroom, and the sea was so clear that, from the rail, you could count the jellyfish in the warm water: on every trip I pictured Marianne, the flash of her underwear in the freezing bedroom, the two seconds of silence facing her bare legs on the edge of the bed, which she had too quickly hidden under the sheets, outside the storm was raging, wind blew against the shutterless bay window, what were we doing in the same bed, she was probably complying with modernity, she saw in this sharing a pallet an innocence laced with danger whereas I, steeped in desire, saw only a magnificent opportunity, the rosé wine called Ruby of Egypt I had filled her with was still, along with the Ricardo, my Alexandrian madeleine: at a table with the soldiers or police officers who sipped

Johnny Walker at lunch without removing their sunglasses I downed Ruby of Egypt and Omar Khayyam in big swigs happy at the memory of Marianne in front of their horrified gazes, as if the Prophet had authorized only British whisky, and I even knew someone close to the president of the Republic who stuffed himself with fried red mullet and washed it down with single malt, a symbol of status, of power, all the while telling me in detail the fate of such-and-such a person, dead under torture or in who knows what torments—why did I so rarely go to Cairo I don't remember anymore, we were given assignments to meet in Alexandria or in Agami at the entry to the Libyan Desert, maybe because it was summer, in winter everything was different, the winter of 1998 something important was being negotiated in the capital, right against the Nile at the edge of Garden City with businessmen who looked like the Communist activists in novels by Tsirkas, boastful talkative men the kind who can put you to sleep as surely as this train at night, cautious but also pleasant, Salomé made into a snake, far from the seedy simplicity of the soldiers and cops, people who took off their tinted pince-nez so as the better to look you in the eyes, assess you, sound you out as the train rocks me, puts me to sleep as in Alexandria where I fell asleep shivering and counting Marianne's unattainable breaths, now despite myself I count the vibrations of the train as it goes over the crossties, one by one, I become aware of my body on the seat, Egyptian, Lebanese, and Saudi businessmen all educated in the best British and American prep schools, discreetly elegant, far from the clichés of colorful, rowdy Levantines, they were neither fat nor dressed up as Bedouins, they spoke calmly of the security of their future investments, as they said, they spoke of our dealings, of the region they called "the area," the Zone, and of their safety, without ever saying the word "weapon" or the word "oil" or any other word for that matter aside from *investment* and *safety*, I wondered, as now the exhausted landscape is hypnotizing me, just as the French say dusk is "the hour between dog and wolf," who were the dogs and who were the wolves, these people who were so courteous, I watched, I listened to my boss, that's what I called him, I listened to my boss convince these pleasant predators, some had sold weapons to the Croats in Bosnia, others to Muslims, still others in Africa before changing over to smuggling with Iraq—the lords of the Zone in that sumptuous hotel in Cairo were present at an informal meeting during which we tried to convince them to go along with us, we informed them of the situation, of the help we could offer them in selling Iraqi oil at the best price, they owned whole tankers full of it, black gold is voluminous and it floats, the Syrians charged them fortunes to send it as if it came straight from their dried-up wells on the Euphrates whereas it had been loaded in Latakia, strange route, everyone had tons and tons of crude oil to sell, so much that a few years later French diplomats coming from Baghdad strolled about Paris in broad daylight with thousands of barrels to sell as if they were pots of jam, they reminded me of the trafficking of the Blue Berets in Bosnia, who sold their rations, their gasoline, and rented out their armored vehicles like taxis for Split or Zagreb, as naturally as anything, happy, with a good conscience and the pocket money these services got them, but still complaining about the danger, just as our businessmen from the Zone didn't see the threat behind the outstretched hand, the deadly games that would play out in the course of the years to come, and of course I was unaware that all that would end up propelling me like a cannonball towards Rome at 150 kilometers an hour over the frozen plain streaked with trees from the landscape, this landscape eroded by the Lombard twilight illumined suddenly by the Lodi train station: the Lodi bridge over the Adda must not be far away, during the first Italian campaign, not long before going to Egypt, Bonaparte too fought there—Bonaparte maybe the greatest Mediterranean soldier along with Hannibal and Caesar, the somber Corsican beloved of Zeus faced my Croatian ancestors serving under the Austrians lined up neatly in front of the bridge on the other shore of the Adda, 12,000 soldiers, 4,000 horsemen with their cannons, their heavy muskets with the endless bayonets and their military music, Napoleon lent a hand, he helped aim the weapons, he was an artilleryman, right beside his men, he breathed courage and determination into them as Athena did for the Greeks, they will cross, against all expectation they will attack a wooden bridge on which bullets and grapeshot are raining down, a column of 6,000 grenadiers charges on the carpet of their own corpses fallen to the rhythm of the Austrian salvos, in the middle of the bridge they hesitate Lannes the little dyer from Gers advances shouts and with sword drawn at the head of his men emerges onto the opposite shore facing the enemy gunners seized with panic the French forge a path for themselves through the lines with their swords as the cavalry having forded the river upstream massacres the panicking Croats, 2,000 killed and wounded,

2,000 Hapsburgians fallen in a few hours lie strewn across the river's shore, 2,000 bodies that the Lombard peasants will strip of their valuables, baptismal medals, silver or enamel snuffboxes, in the midst of the death rattles of the dying and the wounded on that night of 21 Floreal 1796 Year IV of the Revolution 2,000 ghosts 2,000 shades like so many shapes behind my window, the poplar trees, the factory chimneys, we're heading for the Po the countryside is becoming darker, the Grande Armée which is not called that yet enters Milan the day after the battle of the Lodi bridge, the Little Corporal is born, the myth is underway, Bonaparte will pursue his adventure into Russia, passing through Egypt—he will land in Alexandria two years later with the idea of carving out an empire for France like that of British India, and the dead will be strewn not along the shores of the Adda but around the slopes of the pyramids: 15,000 human corpses and a few thousand Mameluk horses will rot at the entrance to the desert, the ripples of worms will give way to swarms of shifting black flies, on the channels of blood absorbed by the sand, there where, today, it's tourists that succumb to the blows of vendors of postcards and all sorts of souvenirs, in Egypt the flies are innumerable, not far from the Fertile Valley, on the slaughtered cows hanging in the covered markets, irrigated by putrid ditches where the blood of sacrificed animals calmly flows, the smell of dead flesh must have been the same after battle, the flies always win, I rest my head gently against the window, pressed by the speed in the half-light, sleepy from the memory of the dense heat of Cairo, of the dusty mango trees, the shapeless banyan trees, the dilapidated buildings, the pale turbans of the porters and the boiling fava beans that made the dawn stink as much as the livestock hanging in the sun, a stone's throw away from the British embassy where in the 1940s spies swarmed the way stoolpigeons do today, in a nameless boarding house on the top floor of a building whose elevator shaft served as a garbage chute where there piled up, as far as the second-floor landing, ripped-open mattresses and rusty bikes, my room had by some miracle a little balcony and at night, in the entirely relative calm of the city that never sleeps, I looked out on the dark strip of the Nile with the smell of catfish, streaked by the plunging lights of the new opera house on the island of Gezira, magnificent silurid with long luminous mustaches, I read Tsirkas's *Drifting Cities*, without really understanding it, without recognizing in the schemes of the shadowy figures in his pages my own steps as an international informer, just as today, sitting below my suitcase, motionless at over a hundred kilometers an hour, I let myself be carried through the twilight without perhaps really being aware of the game I'm taking part in, of the strings that are pulling me as surely as this train is carrying me towards Rome, and in that gentle fatalism that weariness and insomnia push you into my eyes get lost in the middle of the December evening among the frost fireflies the train illumines at intervals on leafless trees, life can seem like a bad travel agency brochure, Paris Zagreb Venice Alexandria Trieste Cairo Beirut Barcelona Algiers Rome, or like a textbook of military history, conflicts, wars, my own, the Duce's, Millán-Astray's the one-eyed legionnaire or else before that the one in 1914 and so on ever since the Stone Age war for fire, a good soldier I arrived at the Gare de Lyon this morning right on time, what a funny idea I hear myself saying on the phone, what a funny idea to come by train, I guess you have your reasons, I don't have any, I think, I simply missed the plane and in the train that brought me to Milan, half asleep, I dreamed—how long has it been since I took a train—about the Spanish War and the Polish ghettos, probably influenced by the documents in my briefcase, whose computer ink must have flowed onto my seat and penetrated my sleep, unless it was Marianne's diaphanous fingers with the bluish veins, in this point of inflection in my life, today, December 8th, I dreamed, sitting between two dead cities the way a tourist, swept along by the ferry that carries him, watches the Mediterranean flow by under his eyes, endless, lined with rocks and mountains those cairns signaling so many tombs mass graves slaughter-grounds a new map another network of traces of roads of railroads of rivers continuing to carry along corpses remains scraps shouts bones forgotten honored anonymous or decried in the great roll-call of history cheap glossy stock vainly imitating marble that looks like the twopenny magazine my neighbor folded carefully so as to be able to read it without effort, the drug overdose of the Italian businessman, the scandals of actresses and call girls that aren't very scandalous, the deeds and gestures of unknown people, actually quite close to the contents of the suitcase, secrets I'll resell to their legitimate owners, fruits of a long investigation in the course of my activities as an international informer: in 1998 between two meetings I was walking through the city in the still-clear winter of Cairo, when the dust is possibly less abundant than in summer and above all the heat is bearable, when the Egyptians say it's cold, a strange idea in a city where the temperature never goes below 70 degrees, on the Avenue Qasr el-Ayni at the edge of the decadence of Garden City the eminently British, crumbling neighborhood where my hotel was there stood a liquor store run by Greeks, I went there from time to time to stock up on Ricardo the real pastis of Alexandria, in the window so as not to shock Muslims one saw only mountains of boxes of tissues, blue, pink, or green whereas inside old wooden shelves were bent beneath the Metaxa, the Bordon's gin and Whack Daniels *made in the Arab Republic of Egypt* probably all made from the same source alcohol the immense majority of which was then used as additives in cleaning products, to polish metals or clean windows, the Egyptians didn't risk it, my military men drank only imported drinks bought in duty-free shops, the Greek poisoners must not have made much, in fact they sold mostly beer to people in the neighborhood and a little anis to adventurers either idiotic or amused by the labels, they wrapped the bottles up in the pages of an old issue of *Ta Nea* from Athens, then in a pink plastic bag taking care to explain to you in flowery French that *it was better not to use the handles*, always without a smile, which instantly reminded me of the Balkans and the old joke according to which you needed a knife to make a Serb smile, Hellenes are without a doubt Balkan, if only for the stinginess of their smile—among the Greeks of Qasr el-Ayni there was always an oldish man sitting there in a corner of the store on a wooden chair bearing the effigy of Cleopatra, he spoke French to the shopkeepers with a strange accent, he held a quarter liter of Metaxa or "Ami Martin" cognac wrapped up in newspaper and thus discreetly and methodically got drunk while making conversation with his hosts, the first time I heard him he was copiously insulting Nasser and the Arabists, as he said, twenty-five years late, Nasser had died a long time ago and pan-Arabism with him or mostly, it was quite surprising to hear that old drunkard with his face marked by the sun of Cairo, thin in a dark-grey suit that was too big for him, seeming like a local, to have such vindictiveness against the father of the nation, he reminded me of the grandfather of my wartime comrade Vlaho, an old Dalmatian winegrower who spent his time bad-mouthing Tuđman and calling him a fascist bigot, because he had been a partisan, the grandfather, and had fought on the Neretva with Tito, he insulted us freely, calling us little Nazis and other nice things, he must have been part of the seven or nine percent of the population who called themselves "Yugoslavs," and was probably the only peasant in that fraction, the only peasant and the only Dalmatian, and in that Greek liquor store in Cairo I remembered the old man this strange guy calling Nasser a thief and a pimp without pulling his punches as he knocked back his firewater that had apparently not managed to make him blind, but maybe mad, he was Dutch, his name was Harmen Gerbens, he was seventy-seven years old and had lived in Egypt since 1947, a force of nature, as they say, to have so long resisted adulterated drink, born in 1921 in Groningen—he might be dead now, as a few drops of melted snow streak the Milanese countryside behind the window, did he die in his bed, by surprise, or after a long illness, a diseased liver or a heart that gave up, or else run over by a taxi as he crossed the Avenue Qasr el-Ayni to go visit his Greek friends, who knows, maybe he's still alive, somewhere in a home for old people or still in his immense gloomy apartment in Garden City, what could he live on, he got a little Egyptian pension fund as mechanical "engineer," a big word for someone who had been enlisted in 1943 as a mechanic in the 4th Brigade of *Panzergrenadier* SS "Nederland" the last elements of which surrendered to the Americans in May 1945 west of Berlin after two years on several fronts, Gerbens is a talkative man, one afternoon he tells me his life story, in his dark, empty lair on the second floor of a dilapidated building, above all he tries to explain to me why Nasser was a son of a bitch—what made me think of the old cantankerous Batavian off Lodi, at the time I didn't know the "Nederland" brigade had been posted for a few months in Croatia to fight against the partisans after the Italian surrender in fall 1943, maybe he had fought against Vlaho's grandfather, maybe, maybe I thought about Harmen at a time of choice, of my own departure for another life like him after a year of privations and indignities in a country destroyed ravaged by war had gone to seek his fortune elsewhere through the intermediary of a cousin who since the days before the war had been working in the port of Alexandria, now that Egypt is one of the images of poverty it seems strange that anyone would emigrate there as a supervisor to improve his lot, I ask Harmen if his past in the *Waffen-SS* had something to do with his decision to leave, he says no, or yes, or maybe, after the defeat he had spent many months in a military prison, after all I was just a mechanic, he said, and not a Nazi, I repaired caterpillar tanks and trucks, that's not what gives you the *Ritterkreuz*, is it? I don't remember anymore, they let us leave pretty quickly, it was the first time I'd been in prison—for three years he worked in the port of Alexandria, repairing and maintaining the cranes, the fork-lifts, and all the harbor machinery, he had two children, two daughters, with a woman from Groningen, in the beginning she liked Egypt fine, he said, at the outset, and I think of my mother also displaced, growing up far from her country she almost doesn't know, my neighbor with the *Pronto* has folded up his magazine, he gets up and goes to the bar or the toilet, who knows where his own parents were born, maybe they emigrated from Naples or Lecce, still young, to try their fortune in the prosperous North, Harmen Gerbens had gone to the prosperous South—he had then left Alexandria for a better job in Helwan near Cairo in the brand-new weapons factory that made Hakim rifles, heavy 8mm adapted from a Swedish model, all the equipment and the machines came directly from Malmö, including the engineers: I got on well with them, Harmen says, I was in charge of maintenance, the Hakim was a wonderful rifle, better than the original, almost without recoil despite the immense power of the Mauser cartridge, it could even survive sand getting in the ejection mechanism I was very proud to make it—after Nasser's revolution everything began to go "sideways" Harmen tells me, I was the only foreigner left in the factory, everyone left, the Greeks, the Italians, the British and then one day war broke out: the English, the French, and the Israelis intervened in Suez—they arrested me for espionage on October 31st, 1956, the day after the bombing of the airport, and locked me up in the "foreigners' section" of the Qanater prison, Harmen never knew either why or how, or for whom he was supposed to have spied, Harmen Gerbens was already seriously drunk when he told me this story, he was drooling a little, tea stuck to his drooping mustache then streamed into the corners of his mouth, his accent was increasingly pronounced and his chin trembled as much as his hands as the setting sun plunged the empty apartment into shadow, empty of the wife and two daughters who had been "deported" back to Holland soon after his arrest, Harmen Gerbens the alcoholic Batavian stayed in Qanater for eight years, forgotten by the gods and his embassy, afterwards I knew why, eight years in the foreigners' section next to the jail where my Islamists rotted forty years later, he was the appointed mechanic of the prison director, Gerbens spits on the ground at the mere mention of his name, he pours a swig of hard stuff into the dregs of his tea utters terrible Dutch curses and I wonder if this story is true, if it's actually possible that this man spent eight years in prison for some obscure reason, isn't he just some lost guy, some old madman gnawed by solitude and rotgut—why don't you go back to Holland, I can't he replies, I can't and that's none of your business, I say nothing I take my leave of the old drunkard he has tears in his eyes he accompanies me to the door—the stairway is strewn with trash and I go down back into the red death throes of Cairo evenings that smell of mummies

Harmen Gerbens the Cairo Dutchman rests now in the briefcase above my seat—a name and a history, chronologically the first on the list, without my knowing at the time that the list had begun and that I'd end up carrying it to Rome five years later, all trembling with a terrible hangover exhausted feverish unable to sleep, would I have chosen the Vatican if Alexandra weren't waiting for me at Trastevere, in that little ground-floor apartment by a pretty courtyard, Alexandra called Sashka a Russian painter with the face of an icon the worst is over now, the worst leaving everything behind quitting leaving my strange employer, ever since Venice after my two years of war I've never been so free, I own nothing now, not even my real name—I have an appropriated passport under the name of Yvan Deroy, born almost at the same as me in Paris and locked up a long time ago now in an institution for psychotics in the suburbs, he never had a passport and his doctors would be quite surprised to know that he's wandering around Italy today, I got this document in the most legal way in the world with a record of civil status and a doctored electric company bill at the 18th arrondissement town hall: I've had so many different names these past years, on identity papers of all colors, I'll become attached to Yvan Deroy, tonight the mute psychotic will sleep in the Grand Plaza in Rome, he reserved a room at an internet café on the Champs-Elysées, Yvan Deroy won't go see his Roman lover right away, he'll hand over his last suitcase to whomever has a right to it, as they say, someone will come visit him in his room they'll proceed with the exchange before Yvan Deroy disappears more or less for good, Yvan has had a new life since last month even an account opened in a big branch of an ordinary bank, which is a big change for him from his postal savings account where his parents regularly deposit the price of his little extras in his "residence," today he owns an international credit card—Yvan bought himself two pairs of pants and as many shirts in a big department store, withdrew cash paid in advance for one night in the Plaza and an airplane ticket he didn't use and now he's playing at making out the landscape in the gathering dusk, far from Venice from Alexandria from Cairo from Marianne with the white breasts a little closer to the end of the world thirty kilometers from Milan where Bonaparte rested for a few days in the middle of his first Italian campaign, in a magnificent palace confiscated from I forget whom, Milan whose train station so resembles the pharaonic temples that the same Bonaparte conquered before launching ever further into the Syrian expedition and the disaster of the siege of Saint Jean d'Acre, Yvan Deroy the mad or catatonic schizophrenic interned in a specialized institution in L'Haÿles-Roses, in the asylum they used to say—Yvan emerges from his lethargy only to shout and assault the staff and the other patients violently, to try to kill them for they are his enemies, he shouts, they want to hurt him he is simply defending himself nothing more no mystical flights of fancy no voices no hallucinations Yvan emerges from his semi-comatose state only into the pure violence of a wild animal according to the phases of the moon or the changing course of his treatment, and this has been the case for almost twenty years despite the quantity of medication he has taken he resists his sickness resists therapy, he is me now Yvan had a shaved head the time he raised his right arm in salute wanted to put an end to democratic corruption the servants of Bolshevism and international Jewry, he went to church on Sundays to hand out pamphlets to middle-class housewives whom he frightened more than anything else, he read Brasillach and every February 6th visited his grave with the other militants to celebrate the martyr and promise revenge for the victim of Gaullist injustice and Jewish hatred, Yvan and I visited Maurice Bardèche official fascist who offered us a volume of his pro-Franco history of the Spanish War written in collaboration with Brasillach—Yvan Deroy went mad, I forgot him as I went through normal military training then paratrooper military training and finally all possible military trainings before going to serve France, volunteer for a long period of service they said at the time, months slogging around in the mountains, team spirit songs weapons marches nighttime commandos grenades light artillery a hard happiness shared with comrades I was more than a little proud to come back on leave and share my naïve martial exploits, the kid from Arès was still just a puppy on parade, in training, on maneuvers in the South of France, on maneuvers in the North of France, on maneuvers in the Alps always happy to have a life so full of weapons honor and fatherland, sweating in the mountains on the Saint Bernard Pass with Hannibal and Bonaparte who didn't get blisters, mounted on their elephants or their horses, Hannibal the Tunisian was inches away from succeeding, Rome trembled, Bonaparte succeeded, Austria capitulated—Yvan Deroy remembers today in this train that his parents were proud of him, that those fervent Catholics thought of his army as a scout camp that would fortify body and soul, his mother whispered in his ear, prophetically, *don't forget, your homeland is also Croatia*, I wanted to go into politics enroll in Sciences-Po once my time of service was over I had a knack for contemporary history tenacious and hardworking everything would smile down on me even Marianne who without sharing my right-wing opinions came from a good Christian family, Yvan Deroy has just crossed the Alps one more time while his actual body languishes, waiting for the end of the world prostrate in a wheelchair—now I'm traveling incognito while still being "legal" a good suitcase-carrier invisible in the crowd of identities and minor bank transactions, Yvan Deroy, impossible to sleep effect of the half-amphetamine I took this morning to hold out after having snored for two hours good and drunk like an imbecile I missed the plane and even more stupidly I rushed over to the train instead of waiting for the next flight, now I'm hungry, a little, maybe I should go eat or drink something we're traveling very fast it's drizzling a little this December evening I remember the long nights of the Croatian autumn, the corn fields are the same the rain too in Slavonia around Osijek in 1991 we were freezing in our hunting jackets and despite all my military training and my alpine exploits I was afraid, I was the most experienced of my companions and I was afraid, in the name of well-greaved Achilles I trembled from fear clinging to my Kalashnikov the best weapon in our squad that they'd entrusted to me because of my military experience my Croatian was rudimentary I said little cannon for mortar shell bullets for cartridge group for section not to mention regiments battalions units that I still mix up, fortunately there was Andrija, Andrija the lion had courage to spare, he was a farmer from around Osijek he fished for pike and carp in the Drava and the Danube with which his mother cooked a mean terribly spicy fish stew smelling of mud—I must be hungry to be thinking of that now, the best meal I ever had I still owe to Andrija, one night around Christmastime, we were exhausted and chilled to the bone in the mostly destroyed farm that served as HQ for us we began drinking *šljiva* to get warm 400 meters away Chetniks were snug in their shelters nothing very new on the front not many shells a few explosions as if to keep us warm—no one likes handling mortars in the cold and the rain the cartridge cases slip from your gloved hands you flounder in the mud the barrel always sinks down into it a little and makes the shot go wrong, better stay snug inside despite the leaks and the drafts, we drink then drunk two hours later we're dying of hunger, no desire to eat canned food, a desire for a celebration, Andrija takes my hand he says come come I know where there's a fantastic dinner and suddenly we're out in the rain slogging between the mines in the middle of fields in the dark holding our assault rifles, he leads me to the western end of the sector almost in front of our lines—stop they'll mistake us for Serbs, we'll get ourselves blown away, shh, he replies, he points to a ruined farm on the other side, the Chetnik side: there are pigs there beautiful pigs what can we do with a pig I said, we'll eat it you idiot we hear an explosion and the night lights up and whistles, the night lit up blue, we dove into the mud—our own people had spotted us, God knows how, and logically thought we were Serbs, demented Serbs strolling about in the rain in the midst of enemy mines, they were probably going to fire one or two more shells to be safe, Andrija began crawling toward the pigs, the Chetniks, and dinner, fortunately the mine field was ours up to the road, we were pretty much in familiar territory, the earth was soaking it stuck to our stomachs a little 40mm mortar exploded somewhere behind us how could there still be pigs in a bombarded farm by the edge of the road that separated us from the enemy, I heard them when we set the mines Andrija replies, having reached the asphalt we wait a few minutes, the silence is complete, we cross, on the other side about 200 meters away are the Serbian positions—we can see a few vague lights between the hedges, we swig some liquor to warm ourselves up and full to the brim of *šljiva* not worrying about the landmines the enemy might have put there we approached the ruined farm, listened for a long time and in fact we heard the snorts and grunts of animals that had smelled our presence, and now what, how are we going to find a fucking black pig in the dark? Andrija began laughing, uncontrollable laughter his hand on his mouth, unable to stop, he tried to control himself and his hiccups sounded like a pig's squeal, which made him laugh even harder, they must have heard his animal-like *hiiic hiiic* kilometers away in the silence—stop, your noises are going to make the Chetniks hungry, I said, and Andrija almost crapped in his pants from laughing, we were there in the dark drunk as pigs in the middle of no man's land stretched out in the mud in the rain in front of a bombed farm the Serbs 200 meters away at most, so drunk we didn't even hear the Croatian shell set off that fell a scant twenty meters away, the sudden abrupt explosion flecked us with dirt, Andrija's laughter suddenly stopped, come on, he said, we'll go get the fucking animal and we'll get back, the Serbs began to return fire, we spotted mortars being fired just in front of us, 80s, we'd end up stuck there between two lines of fire with no dinner, it must have been almost midnight we carefully went round the shack and in the flash of a nearby explosion we discovered an enormous sow stuck in an improvised corral, mad from the shells she was turning round in circles like a goose Andrija began laughing again, laughing uncontrollably, how are we going to carry this colossus we'll have to cut it up on the spot, he went over to the animal took out his bayonet the sow tried to bite him and began squealing when the knife slashed her fat, I was seized with mad laughter too, despite the bombardment, despite the Chetniks who must have been thinking about preparing an attack I had in front of me a soldier black with wet mud dagger in hand in the process of running after a crazy animal in the roar of explosions, a machine gun began firing on the Serbian side, Andrija took advantage of it to shoot a bullet from his Kalashnikov into the animal 7.62 too small caliber to drop the pig he'd have to hit it in the head it went on squealing even louder as it limped Andrija the bloodthirsty madman ended up knocking it onto its back knife between his teeth like the Bolsheviks in the Nazi propaganda posters, Andrija straddled his pig like a pony I felt sick to my stomach I was laughing so hard, he ended up reaching the carotid with his blade the sow fell grunting in a gurgling puddle of black blood, around us the battle was raging, an exchange of artillery and machine gun volleys—we finished off the flask of *šljiva* and the dying animal before hurling ourselves onto it bayonets in hand to cut ourselves a thigh apiece which took us at least a quarter of an hour of steady effort especially to detach the bone from its socket, in the meantime the artillery duel ended in a scoreless tie, we just had to go back and crawl for a good half of the way dragging the animal's legs that must have weighed almost fifteen kilos each—we arrived soaking wet exhausted stinking of shit so covered in mud manure and blood that our comrades thought we were fatally wounded, finally when we fell from exhaustion into a dreamless sleep, on the ground, Andrija still amorously clinging to a sow's ear like a child with his rattle—the next day it was pouring out we roasted the two thighs in a fire of damp wood and the gods were so happy with this porcine burnt offering that they protected us from the shells that the Serbs rained down on us all day, enticed by the smell: the smell in the wind cruelly reminded them that we had relieved their mascot of its two hind legs, Andrija all throughout the war kept "the Chetnik ear" dried and hairy in his pocket, so that new recruits thought with horror that he actually possessed a monstrous human relic torn from the enemy, Andrija I miss you, two years we lived together two years from Slavonia to Bosnia from Osijek to Vitez and Herzegovinan Mostar, Andrija funny brutal great soldier a crummy shot it was not the archer Apollo who guided your shafts, your protector was Ares the furious, you had strength boldness and courage: Apollo protected the Serbs and Bosnians, Athena with the seagreen eyes watched over us as well as she could—in that great fight between East and West the goddess appeared in Šibenik, in Medjugorje, Virgin at the edge of the Catholic West, just as Ghassan told me in Venice that the statue of the Virgin of Harissa, perched on her mountain 600 meters above sea level, had turned towards bombarded Beirut, a sign of pity or encouragement for the combatants, she too at the edge of the western world, in the same way the Virgin of Medjugorje had pitied her children grappling with Muslims and inscribed her messages of peace in the sky of Herzegovina: no apparition at my window where darkness is settling in, summer sunsets over the sea near Troy were much more beautiful—Apollo the archer of the East also guided the Turkish artillerymen near the well-guarded Dardanelles, on the banks of the Scamander, facing Cape Helles where the monument to unknown soldiers of the battle of Gallipoli stands, white as a lighthouse, you can read over 2,000 British names there for as many bodies whose remains are scattered throughout the peninsula along with the dusty bones of 1,200 unidentifiable Frenchmen from the years 1915-1916, before the Eastern Expeditionary Corps gave up and went to try its luck near Thessalonica in support of the Serbs against the Bulgarians, leaving the Dardanelles and the Bosporus inviolate after ten months of battle and 150,000 French, Algerian, Senegalese, English, Australian, New Zealanders, Sikh, Hindu, Turkish, Albanian, Arab, and German corpses, like so many Boeotians, Mycenaeans, brave Arcadians, or magnanimous Cephallenians against the Dardanians, Thracians, Pelasgians with the furious javelins, or Lycians come from afar, guided by the spear of blameless Sarpedon, but the Allies didn't have the patience to wait ten years, the battle of the Dardanelles or of Gallipoli was savage and quick, it began with a naval attempt to force a passage through the Dardanelles on March 18th, 1915 at 10:30 in the morning: British and French ships began advancing in three lines and shelling the Ottoman forts port and starboard, blindly, to try to put their mobile batteries out of operation, the giant marine cannon shells—305 millimeters, 200 kilos of explosive—were so powerful that the houses in neighboring villages collapsed from the concussions, Hephaestus himself was breathing on his forge, the earth trembled and Seyit Çabuk Havranli the Turkish artilleryman, from the height of the fort of Rumeli Mecidiye, watched the heavy vessels immobilized at every volley on the impenetrable sea, he saw the battleship *Bouvet* strike a floating mine and disappear with all hands in less than six minutes, 550 men carried down in an armor-plated coffin, eighty meters deep among the jellyfish, the gunner Seyit and his comrades hammered the seaboard with huge shells until a volley aimed at the *HMS Ocean* damaged the gun: the handcar that brought ammunition up to the breech is hit, impossible to transport the warheads, but artilleryman Seyit is a lumberjack from the slopes of Mount Ida, a descendant of the Mysians of Troy, he takes the 200 kilos of metal and explosives on his back he suffers he bends beneath it Zeus himself helps him and encourages him Seyit carries his burden into the still burning soul of the cannon loads the gun that the firing officer points at the *HMS Ocean* motionless in the middle of the strait, it too has just hit a mine: Apollo guides the Turkish arrow towards the British destroyer, the 400 pounds explode on the stern of the English battleship which loses its rudder and springs a giant leak, the entire aft is flooded in a few seconds: drifting, threatened by mines, the *Ocean* would sink a few hours later, making *Koca* Seyit from Havran lumberjack of Mount Ida a hero—*Koca* the giant has served since 1912 as a simple soldier, he fought the Serbs and the Bulgarians in the Balkans, his head shaved, with a proud mustache, the Turkish army desperate for glory immediately promoted him to *onbaşi*, corporal, I wonder what the giant of Mysia thought when the journalists from Istanbul arrived to photograph him, in a photo from then he looks embarrassed, modest, not very big either, the propaganda reporters want to immortalize him with a mortar shell in his arms, they try but Seyit can't manage to repeat the exploit, Zeus is no longer there to help him, the shell weighs too much, fear not, they make a wooden replica that the little corporal takes on his back, the photographer triggers his apparatus and forever humiliates Seyit of Havran by transforming him into a liar for posterity, into a circus strong man: demobilized in 1918 Seyit returns to his forest, now they call him Seyit "Çabuk," "swift-footed"—he goes on to work in the somber coal mines where he will come down with what is probably lung cancer from which he will die at the age of fifty, absolutely forgotten, until a beautiful bronze statue is erected in his honor near the fortress of Kilitbahir, his burden on his back, 200 kilos of explosives on its way to send destruction onto the battleships of the Argives—it was nice out and the sea was beautiful, from the Gallipoli peninsula on a clear day you can see as far as the hills near Troy, Asia, the narrow sea wound of the Dardanelles opens onto the Sea of Marmara a few leagues away from Constantinople, with Marianne on vacation in a resort in July 1991 I stay glued to the TV, trying to get news of Croatia, this vacation was an engagement gift from her parents if I remember right, in the end we didn't get engaged I left to hunt pig and meet Andrija in Osijek I got engaged to death as the marching song of the Spanish legionnaires says, *soy el novio de la muerte*, but Marianne still wore a ring with a diamond and gold earrings I had given her maybe the same as Helen of Lacedaemon's under her veil, in that boring resort one could take advantage of organized excursions, one to the Dardanelles one to Troy that's all Marianne managed to get me to agree to, the statue of Seyit the army bearer was brand new the guide told us the story with sobs in his voice, then he had us visit the house where Mustafa Kemal lived father of the Turks when he commanded the defense of the peninsula I remember I had an erection in the tour bus I began caressing Marianne under her skirt she blushed but went along, the Italian tourist across the aisle didn't miss a thing, he had taken umpteen pictures of the corporal and the shell and the Atatürk Museum I wondered if he was going to get out his camera to immortalize the taut thighs of Marianne who was looking out the window as if nothing were happening, the return trip on the ferry seemed very long to us and scarcely had we arrived back than we threw ourselves on each other in the bedroom, I saw the sea the sunset through the white curtains and Marianne too leaning over bent double her chest on the bed maybe she said *how beautiful it is*, it was certainly beautiful, pleasure seized us, a beam over the blazing Mediterranean—the expedition to Troy was an ordeal of dust and heat, walls, stones, pathways, no guided visit to the tomb of Achilles or Hector's pyre or Priam's treasure, tourists, not a spot of shade to be alone with Marianne in, I remember a very ugly giant wooden horse that would have made Ulysses ashamed, I remember too the adventures of Heinrich Schliemann the passionate, the Arsène Lupin of archaeology smitten with women, foreign languages and mythical narratives: poor, self-educated, son of a pastor in the duchy of Mecklenburg on the Baltic, perhaps it was because he was a man of the North that he passionately loved money and the Mediterranean—the little herring merchant sets off for California to make his fortune selling supplies to gold dust miners, then tired of America he becomes a smuggler and arms trafficker during the Crimean War, using his Russian wife to make the necessary contacts, finally his fortune made he develops a passion for archeology and takes as his second wife a Greek woman of great beauty they say, he buys a palace in Athens and travels the ancient world in search of lost cities, Ithaca, Mycenae, and then Troy: in 1868 he acquires the hill of Hissarlik where his faith in the blind poet makes him situate the site of Ilion with solid walls, he begins to excavate it with the help of a hundred or so Turkish laborers, comes across the traces of several superimposed cities and an immense treasure of vases and jewelry, the treasure of Priam and the jewels of Helen which he quickly steals to bring back to Athens, thinking thus to close the circle begun 3,000 years earlier when Paris carried off the woman of unbearable beauty with the sweet sojourn in Lacedaemon, he is restoring to Attica and Menelaus these jewels that the Ottomans, by his lights, had no right to—before offering them to the brand-new Germany in exchange for various influences and favors, especially because Schliemann had understood that these pieces, beautiful as they were, post-dated the Trojan War by quite a bit, that the "mask of Agamemnon" had never touched the rough skin of the king of the Achaeans, that Helen with the beautiful *peplos* had never placed these fabulous necklaces on her perfect neck, which caused a scandal when people realized it, Schliemann died soon after in Naples, near Pompeii whose paintings he had admired, the gods had assured his posterity as they had for the Turkish artilleryman a few leagues to the east, his name will remain linked to the Scaean Gates along with Homer's, both inspired by the goddess who protects smugglers poets workers of the night warriors and I see again all the names in my briefcase, the photos, the documents the thousands of pages contained on the computer disks carefully arranged in their covers classified by date and number, year of investigation, of theft, of more or less secret pillaging of the archives, done on the fringes of my job as informer, case officer as they say, my job as secret pen-pusher, poet with the silent epos, *sing, goddess, of the memories of the wanderers among the shades in the depths of Hades*—Casalpusterlengo, strange name, we're going at top speed through the white neon-illuminated station, the well-wrapped travelers watch the express go by my neighbor glances absentmindedly out the window then continues his reading, I could read a little too, I have a little book in my bag, three stories by a Lebanese writer named Rafael Kahla recommended to me by the bookseller on the Places des Abbesses, a handsome book on slightly ochre laid paper, barely a hundred pages, how much time would I need to read them let's say a page a kilometer that would take up a good part of the 500 milestones left to travel, the little book is about Lebanon, the back cover situates the three stories at three distinct times of the civil war, another cheerful book, it's strange the bookseller recommended it to me, she couldn't have known about my connections with the Zone and armed conflict, maybe it's an omen, one more demiurge placed there in Montmartre like a sign, I put the little book on my fold-out tray, don't have the courage, I feel feverish exhausted by the drugs and the day before, I have a pain in my right temple, I'm sweating and there's a slight trembling in my hands—I close my eyes, might as well return to the Dardanelles or to Venice, to Cairo or Alexandria, I wonder what has become of Marianne where could she be now I picture her as a mother of five children who made her quit teaching, almost ten years after our separation I'm on my way to Sashka now better not think about the painful interval between one and the other about Stéphanie the sorrow of Stéphanie the headache intensifies, it's normal go forward go forward with the train that carries you eyes closed blindfolded like a hostage by his kidnappers Yvan Deroy confined in a railroad car by his alter ego prey to the hangover of the century, yesterday I celebrated the departure the end of a life I so want this interlude to be over, the kilometers that separate me from my new existence to have already traveled, everything comes to him who knows how to wait says the proverb, Marianne's body haunts me despite the years and the bodies that succeeded hers, when I see Sashka before I kiss her I'll say shh, my name is Yvan now, she'll wonder why a researcher who specializes in the ethology of insects suddenly changes his name, maybe Sashka's body is like Marianne's, her underwear always virgin white on the dark skin of her slightly heavy breasts the top of the back of her neck hollowed out like a second sex with the fine hair of a newborn child Marianne was *serious*, as she said, she took her time before she slept with me, at the time I saw it as a proof of commitment, a truth a passion in Turkey it was the explosion of desire the experimentation of pleasure the pelagic plain was very blue very erotic very salty it gave off a warm smell at nightfall in that vacation club there were games organized by the residents, after the dinner buffet there was multilingual bingo, the MCs announced the number first in Turkish then repeated it in English German French and Italian, *yirmi dört, twenty-four, vier und zwanzig, vingt-quatre, venti quattro*, this absurd and regular threnody slid over the sea for hours on end, hypnotic interminable poem I didn't miss a thing from the bedroom balcony, I watched the international incantation shine on the Aegean, *on yedi, seventeen, siebzehn, dix-sept, diciasette*, I conscientiously repeated all the numbers, which made Marianne furious, once is already unbearable enough, she said, close that window we'll put the air-conditioning on, night was not her time, what with the bingo, the heat, and the mosquitoes I remember she read a lot, I read nothing at all, I meditated, I mentally played bingo I sipped Turkish Carlsbergs as I thought about Croatia, Slovenia had just declared its independence on June 25th, 1991—on our side the Krajina Serbs had seceded in mid-February, the Yugoslav army didn't seem in a mood to withdraw despite Tuđman's declaration of sovereignty and things seemed to be going from bad to worse, I would have liked to bring Marianne to Opatija, Šibenik, or Dubrovnik but her parents preferred taking things into their own hands and sent us far away from the Adriatic, to the other side of the Balkans the tip of which, Thrace, we could glimpse on a clear day—the booklet about Troy explained in broken French that the Trojans were actually a tribe that originated in Kosovo, *a province of Yugoslavia* said the brochure, why not, that the Dardani with the beautiful mares were Albanian isn't unlikely if you think about Skanderbeg, about the Mamluks of Egypt and other valiant warriors, with the swift sabers and the two-headed eagle, so by the shores of the Sea of Marmara I was closer to Yugoslavia than I thought, thanks to the belligerent Illyrians: listening to the Turkish MCs chanting bingo results in five languages I was far from imagining that I was about to go fight for a free and independent Croatia, then for a free and independent Herzegovina, and finally for a free and independent Croatian Bosnia, *Za dom*, *spremni*, said the pro-Nazi Ustashi government motto during the Second World War, *for the homeland, always ready*, without knowing it I was ready, I was ripe, Pallas Athena was about to whisper into my ear, and ten years later I would find myself in an overheated railway car holding my head in my hands my eyes closed under a borrowed name can one put an end to something really change your life as for Andrija he is quietly decomposing in Bosnian soil, thousands of white worms maggots bacteria are making sure he disappears, I survived the war and the Zone that followed, but I almost didn't leave Venice, I was about to put an end to my days there as they say before Marianne sort of suddenly threw in the towel I drifted along the lagoon to the bitter end in the fog, I ended up falling drunk into a frozen canal, in the dark water severed limbs and faceless skulls were waiting for me, the crazy smile of a broken face bit my stomach a cut-off hand grabbed my hair torn-off filaments of skin slices of decomposed flesh sank into my mouth I instantly rotted in the briny liquid carried off towards the thick black mud and finally everything stopped, I stopped struggling, there were no more ripples on the surface, nothing but the movements of rats that threw themselves by the dozen onto my inert body in the Venice lagoon city of noble rot and rickety palaces, I never went back there, even when I was filling my suitcase in Trieste or Udine I carefully avoided it, I changed trains in Mestre so as not to be tempted to leave the Santa Lucia train station and return to the Ghetto, return to the Square of the Two Moors or to the well-named Quay of Oblivion where I knocked myself out on alcohol with Ghassan, you don't forget much in the end, the wrinkled hands of Harmen Gerbens the Cairo Batavian, his trembling mustache, the faces of Islamists tortured in the Qanatar Prison, the photograph of the severed heads of the Tibhirine monks, the reflections on the cupolas in Jerusalem, Marianne naked facing the sea, the squeals of Andrija's pig, the bodies piled up in the gas trucks of Chełmno, Stéphanie the sorrowful in front of Hagia Sophia, Sashka with her brushes and paints in Rome, my mother at the piano in Madrid, her Bach fugue in front of an audience of Croatian and Spanish patriots, so many images linked by an uninterrupted thread that snakes like a railroad bypassing a city, the possible connections between trains in a station: back from my investigation in Prague not long ago I take the night train for Paris via Frankfurt, last car, last compartment, a man in his fifties is already sitting there, he's eating a sandwich, it is eight o'clock at night, his head is round and bald, he's wearing a grey suit he looks like an accountant, he greets me politely in Czech between two mouthfuls, I reply just as politely, I settle in, the train leaves the Prague station on time, I mechanically play with a little crystal star prettily wrapped in red tissue paper, souvenir of Bohemia—once he's finished his sandwich my companion extracts a thick paperback volume from his luggage, a kind of catalogue he begins consulting feverishly, jumping from one page to the other, one finger on columns of numbers, then back to the previous page, he looks at his watch before looking angrily out the window, it's dark out, he can't see anything, he goes back to his book, he often looks at me, questioningly, he's burning to ask me a question, he asks me do you know if the train is stopping in Tetschen? or at least that's what I understand him to say, I jabber in German that I have no idea, but it probably will, that's the last Czech city before the border, on the Elbe, the man speaks German, he agrees with me, the train must stop in Tetschen, even if it doesn't take on any passengers there, *wissen Sie*, he says, if we got out in Tetschen, we could get on the freight train that left Brno this afternoon a little before five o'clock, it would leave us in Dresden around two in the morning and we could catch this very train which isn't supposed to leave before 2:45, it's incredible, don't you agree—I agree, the man continues, his catalogue is actually a giant railroad timetable, there are *all* the trains here, do you understand, *all*, it's a little complicated to use but when you get the hang of it it's practical, it's for railroad professionals, for instance we've just passed a train going in the other direction it's 9:23 well I can tell you where it's coming from and where it's going, if it's a passenger train or a freight train, with such a book you never get bored when you travel in a train, he says seeming very happy, how come he doesn't know if the train is stopping in Tetschen, well it's very simple, very simple, see, the stop is in parentheses, which means it's optional, but the stop is indicated, so we have the *possibility* of stopping in Tetschen, we had another possibility for a stop a few minutes ago and you never realized a thing, you didn't even notice that we *could* have stopped there, *wir hatten die Gelegenheit*, you see this book is wonderful, it allows you to know what we could have done, what we could do in a few minutes, in the next few hours, even more, the little Czech man's eyes light up, all eventualities are contained in this schedule, they are all here—the train's engineer has only to consult it, I'll give you an example, I know you're going to Paris and so you are going to change in Frankfurt to take the 8:00 A.M. Intercity, in the meantime you'll have eaten *Brötchen* and a sausage in the train station, then when you arrive you'll certainly go to your home on 27, rue Eugène-Carrière in the 18th arrondissement of Paris where you'll arrive tired at 3:23 in the afternoon, you'll set down your bags take a quick shower and two options will then occur to you, go to the office immediately or wait till the next morning, each possibility will have its advantages and its disadvantages, if you go to the Boulevard Mortier you won't be home when someone rings your doorbell at 5:48 P.M., but if you stay, the intervention of this young person and the news she brings will make you forget one part of the information to be included in that secret file, that list of dead people you've been gathering for some time now by using more or less illegally the means that Foreign Security puts at your disposal, you see everything is written here, pages twenty-six, 109 *et passim*, in either case, whether you're there or not, the next connection will be on page 261 in the timetable, the Venice-Budapest express, where you'll get drunk and sing "Three Drummer Boys," then on page 263 you'll get into a freight car headed for the Jasenovac extermination camp on the Sava river, then on page 338 into a Benghazi-Tripoli train, you see, the Tangier-Casablanca express is on page 361, all that will bring you to page 480 and the loss of a kid you won't know, and so on, your whole life is there, many connections will bring you quietly, almost without your knowing it, to a final Pendolino train *diretto* Milano-Roma that will carry you to the end of the world, expected at the Termini station at 9:12 P.M., I listen attentively to the little man's train litany, he is right, this catalogue is a magnificent tool, the train professionals are lucky, I think, the man puts the book down and takes out another sandwich, he eats it with great appetite as he looks me in the eye, all of a sudden I'm hungry—the Czech smiles at me, offers to share his meal with me, I have the sensation of imminent danger, deformed by the obsequious smile his face is suddenly horrible, he insists, holds out half of his sandwich to me and I understand that he wants to poison me, that this guy who looks like an accountant is dangerous, Death is a German-speaking Czech with a railroad timetable, the end of the line always comes by surprise I'm going to die I'm afraid, I'm afraid and I wake up with a start my heart is pounding absurd dream I must have given a violent jump maybe even shouted out loud for my neighbor is staring at me, the Czech accountant who looks like the madman in the Milan train station, I realize it now, horrible nightmare, bad omen, I could have had a nice little erotic dream with some unknown woman, but no, I had to have a dream of the railway grim reaper, in Prague I did in fact buy this little star carved from a block of crystal, it came from the Theresienstadt camp, Jewish children locked up in that ghetto had polished it for days, in one of the Nazi workshops, the antique dealer who sold it to me had a deceitful face, he said imagine the little hands of the poor kids who made it, I don't know why but I believed him—night has definitely fallen now you can only make out a few lights in the distance, in one of the dreams in *Johnny Got His Gun* who is driving the train, it's Christ I think portrayed by Donald Sutherland, who knows who is at the controls of this train, what demiurge is calmly driving me to Rome, according to the Great Timetable of the Parcae, I'd like to go have a drink at the bar, I'm thirsty, it's too early, at this rate if I begin drinking now I'll arrive in Rome dead drunk, my body is weighing me down I shift it on the seat I get up hesitate for an instant head for the toilet it's good to move a little and even better to run warm non-potable water over your face, the john is like the train, modern, brushed grey steel and black plastic, elegant like some handheld weapon, more water on my face and now I'm perked up, I go back to my seat, seeing the *Pronto* cover I spare a thought for the young cocaine-addicted wolf who is vomiting blood in his clinic in Turin, may the gods be merciful to him—in his hospital the character in *Johnny Got His Gun* is caressed by the sun and a beautiful nurse, Johnny whom they don't let die despite his prayers in Morse, Johnny the little soldier destroyed by a land mine dreams of the landscapes of the Midwest and of driver-Christs, the little Lebanese book winks at me on the tray-table, why not go there after all dive into it go out of myself for a bit enter the imagination of Rafael Kahla and his stories, for lack of Dalton Trumbo and *Johnny Got His Gun*, the slightly textured paper is pleasant to the touch, let's see if the bookseller on the Place des Abbesses was mocking me or not:

Intissar raised her right fist. She shouted, cried, angrily wiped away her tears and leaned on her rifle like a cane.

Defeat begins with the feet.

It insinuates itself first into the same boots that were supposed to lead to victory, the ones you'd gotten ready, for years, for the last parade. Defeat begins with the boots that you polished every morning, the ones that grew misshapen, covered with dust, the ones that kept the blood from your toes as well as they could, that crushed insects, protected you from snakes, withstood stones on the path. Physical at first, like a cramp that makes you limp, defeat is a weary surprise, you begin to stumble, in war you totter on fragile feet. Suddenly you feel what you'd never felt before, your feet can no longer run, they refuse to carry you into the attack—suddenly they're paralyzed, frozen despite the heat, they no longer want to serve the body that owns them. And then the rifle, Intissar's cold staff, no longer fires straight, instead it gets jammed, begins to rust in the soldier's imagination; you hesitate to use it from fear of breaking it completely and finding yourself without any support in a world that is starting to sway dangerously because your feet, inside the shiny boots, are beginning to bemoan their weariness and their doubt.

Suddenly your comrades avoid looking at each other, their eyes no longer settle on anything, they sink to the ground, their heads lowered to their weird feet and the mute sensation of defeat that fills their entrails, from the bottom up, from the legs, and then you see many of them dying, sadly, for no reason, whereas they used to die handsome and sleek and gleaming in the sun: now you know, you feel that from here on everything is pointless, if your feet, your legs, your stomach, your rifle yield to the defeat that is seeping in everywhere and is suddenly replacing the rightness of your cause, the songs, the anthems, the sharing of food and caresses, you'll never be able to cross the mountain, never reach the top of that hill; the wounded are unbearable mirrors and the dead become strangers about whom you wonder, day after day, defeat after defeat, what will become of them—they're no longer heroes, brothers, just victims, conquered people that history will hide on its bad side in that earth pounded now by the heavy feet of deserters, the boots of abandonment and fear. Everything follows quickly after that: after walking slowly at the front you find yourself walking silently in town, under the betrayed stares of civilians who blame you for their desperate grief, those women in front of their empty houses, those men, who recently, too recently, used to cheer you on, now they all are getting ready to cheer the new conquerors as from the ground they watch the fierce shadows of planes, doing their funereal work and finishing the defeat.

Tonight, Marwan died, boots on his feet, near the airport. He must have smelled the scent of the sea as he died. The heat is unbearable. Apparently Arafat is negotiating. In Hamra, turbulence is at its height. No one understands a thing. The ones who were supposed to be fighting are no longer fighting. The Lebanese left is still defending West Beirut. Marwan is dead. If he had died the day before yesterday, or in May, Intissar would have collapsed. But today she has a ball and chain on her feet, conquered by heat, thirst, and the bombs. The city is suspended in air, no one knows on which side it will fall.

This morning in headquarters there was motionless turmoil. The planes have destroyed a whole group of buildings in Chiah.

It's unfair and no one can do anything about it. The Russian clodhoppers are so heavy that Intissar feels as if she's glued to the ground.

She plays at loading and unloading her rifle as she thinks about Marwan. The well-oiled mechanism is reassuring, it's still working perfectly. A little after noon. At dawn Beirut smelled not of thyme but of burning trash. Yesterday too. She slept in a stairway. Abu Nasser woke her gently around six in the morning. He said: Marwan has fallen.

Now he's the martyr Marwan. They'll print posters with his photo and paste them onto the walls of the city. If there's still a city left. If there's still anything left to print posters with. If they still have time. If time still exists.

The sea is everywhere. Beirut is an island. Where could they go? Intissar has never left Beirut. She has never slept anywhere but in Beirut. No, that's wrong, once she slept in Tripoli and, when she was little, a few days in the mountains. Beirut is her island.

Defeat is all the more obvious when no one wants to acknowledge it. Their possible exile is proclaimed as a victory. The Palestinians have gloriously resisted the Israeli army. The resistance continues. The glorious fight for the liberation of Palestine continues. In the stench spread by the bombardments, Intissar wonders whether Palestine really exists. Whether something besides the Palestinians themselves (a piece of land, a homeland) exists, Palestinians who scatter their dead throughout the Middle East like wheat. There are Palestinian graves all over the world, now. And Marwan lying dead somewhere. Intissar closes her eyes to keep back tears of impotent rage. Despite herself she sees again the most horrible corpse of the siege—in Khalde, a combatant crushed by a tank on the road, as easily as a rat or a bird. His faceless head was a flat puddle of reddened hair. The first-aid people from the Red Crescent had had to peel him off of the asphalt with a shovel. Around the body, a circular pool of viscera and blood, as if someone had stepped on a tomato. Palestinians cling to the land.

She goes on playing mechanically with the rifle. Marwan is dead. When she asked Abu Nasser how he had died, he didn't know what to say. He said: I wasn't there, Intissar. Abu Nasser has four sons. He was born in Jerusalem. He has a fine greying beard and lives in a big apartment in Raouche.

She'd like to know how he fell. *Ya Intissar, ya Intissar, istashhad Marwan.* That's all she knows. She hears the bombings, it's like everyday music, a drumbeat or heartbeat. The planes are tearing the sky apart. She wishes Marwan a fine death. Without pain, without anxiety, a sudden flight, a disappearance into the sea or into the sun. She sees again Marwan's hands, Marwan's smile, feels the absence of Marwan's mouth, his chest.

She goes out to go to the main command post. Fighters are running, shouting, calling to each other, the battle is still raging, she discovers. At the southern entrance to the city. In the mountain. Everywhere. The Israelis are making statements on the radio, on television. In the South the Shiites welcomed them as liberators. Villages tired of supporting Palestinian fighters. Tired of being poor, bombed, and despised. Cowards. Traitors. Abu Nasser hesitates to send Intissar to the front. She insists. I want to know what happened to Marwan, she says. Did . . . Did they bring back his body? Abu Nasser doesn't know. His voice catches in his throat. Everything's going badly, my little one, everything's going badly. Look for Habib Barghouti and the others, they were with him yesterday. Take care of yourself. I'll come soon.

Without Marwan she'd never have taken up arms. Defeat would have another taste. She'd be looking desperately for water in the midst of rubble. Or dead at home in Borj Barajne, in unbearable heat, in the burning wind from the bombs. How much time now? Soon nothing of the city will be left. The sea, that's all. The indestructible sea.

She sees a Jeep full of comrades leaving for the front. The front. That's a funny word. You defend yourself. You're besieged. Finally being as close as possible to the Israeli tanks is an enviable position, you don't risk a napalm bomb or a phosphorus shell. Near the southern part of the city the streets are strewn with debris, charred cars, the heat from explosions drew waves in the asphalt, like a rippling black rug. The civilians are hiding. To the east Israelis are in the museum, where they've been fighting for weeks, she thinks. Or maybe just a few days. By the airport too. Yesterday she drank half a bottle of water for the entire day. Bread is rationed. Just thinking about the smell of canned tuna or sardines makes her nauseous.

The only Israeli she ever saw was the corpse of a soldier, fallen in a skirmish. Brown-haired, young, not many things distinguished him from the Palestinian fighters, once he was dead. Only once he was dead. On the other side they have things to drink and eat, weapons, ammunition, tanks, planes. Here there's nothing but a city stuck between the sky and the sea, dry and burning. They already have Palestine. Beirut is the last star in Palestine's sky, flickering. And about to go out, to become a meteor and sink into the Mediterranean.

•

"Intissar? Marwan is . . ."

"I know. Abu Nasser told me."

On the ground floor of a half-destroyed building, fortified by the rubble and fallen rocks from the upper storeys, in the midst of anti-tank rockets and two 30-caliber machine guns, the four Fatah fighters smoke joints, bare-chested. The smoke makes you thirsty. The smell of hashish softens the smell of sweat a little. From time to time one of them looks out onto the street through an opening in the wall. Intissar sits down on the floor. Habib makes as if to pass her the joint, but she shakes her head.

"We're waiting. No one knows what's going to happen."

"How . . . how did he . . . ?"

Habib is a giant of great gentleness, with a childlike face.

"Last night. A little further away, there, at the front. With Ahmad. On reconnaissance just before dawn. Ahmad is in the hospital, lightly wounded. He told us he saw Marwan fall, hit by many machine-gun bullets in the back. He couldn't bring him back."

The possibility that Marwan might still be alive makes her heart skip a beat.

"But then how can you be sure?"

"You know how it is, Intissar. He's dead, that's for sure."

"We could call the Red Crescent maybe, so they could go look for him?"

"They won't come this far, Intissar, not right away in any case. They'll wait to be sure, to have authorization from the Israelis. There's nothing to do."

Habib breathes in his smoke, looking sad but convinced. She knows he's right. Now the front is calm. Defeat. She imagines Marwan's body decomposing in the sun between the lines. A burning tear trickles out of her left eye. She goes to sit down a little farther away, her back to the wall. Here the smell of urine has replaced that of hashish. The comrades leave her to her pain. The silence is terrifying. Not one plane, not one explosion, not one tank engine, not one word. The crushing sun of midday. Marwan a hundred meters away. Maybe the Israelis have picked him up. No one likes having bodies decomposing in his camp. Ahmad. He had to have fallen in the company of Ahmad the coward. Treacherous, cunning, vicious. He might have been lying to cover himself. Maybe he shot himself in the foot. Maybe he killed Marwan. She mechanically loads her Kalashnikov, all the combatants turn around, surprised. The metallic click of the breech resounded like a knife on cement. She wishes the fighting would begin again immediately. She wants to shoot. To fight. To avenge Marwan stretched out over there. At this moment Arafat and the others are with American envoys negotiating their departure. To go where? 10,000 Fedayeen. How many civilians? 500,000 maybe. To go to Cyprus? Algiers? To fight whom? And who is going to protect the ones that stay? The Lebanese? This silence is unbearable, maybe just as unbearable as the heat.

Habib and the others have begun playing cards, without much enthusiasm. The weight of defeat.

Most of the fighters are nomads. Some are escapees from Jordan, who settled in Beirut in the late 1970s; others took part in operations in the South; still others joined the PLO after 1975. All of them nomads, whether they're children from the camps or refugees from 1948, or from 1967, whom war surprised far from their homes and who were never able to go back. Abu Nasser crossed the Lebanese border on foot. He never returned to Galilee. Marwan neither. Intissar was born in Lebanon, in 1951; her parents, from Haifa, had already settled in Beirut before the creation of Israel. Often, watching the old railroad tracks in Mar Mikhail, she thinks that the trains used to come slowly down the coast to Palestine, passing through Saida, Tyre, and Acre; today the space has grown so much smaller around her that it's impossible for her to even go to Forn El Chebbak or Jounieh. The only ones that can travel through the region without difficulty are the Israeli planes. Even the sea is forbidden to us. The Israeli navy is patrolling and firing missiles. Habib and the *shabab* are children of the camps, sons of refugees of 1948. Palestinians from the outside. Palestinians. Who resuscitated this biblical term, and when? The English probably. Under the Ottomans there was no Palestine. There was the *vilâyet* of Jerusalem, the department of Haifa or Safed. Palestinians had existed for barely thirty years before they lost their territory and sent a million refugees on the roads. Marwan was a militant as soon as he was old enough to speak. Marwan sincerely thought that only war could return Palestine to the Palestinians. Or at least something to the Palestinians. The injustice was intolerable. Marwan was an admirer of Leila Khaled and the members of the PFLP who hijacked airplanes and kidnapped diplomats. Intissar thought you had to defend yourself. That you couldn't let yourself be massacred by fascists, then by F16s and tanks without reacting.

Now Marwan is dead, his body is turning black under the Beirut sun near the airport, a scant hundred kilometers from his birthplace.

Ahmad. Ahmad's presence next to Marwan disturbs Intissar. Ahmad the cruel. Ahmad the coward. What were they doing together? Ever since the incident they were joined solely by a common cause and a cold hatred. But the first time she saw Ahmad something in her trembled. It was on the front line, a year earlier, when some combatants were returning from the South. Ahmad was almost carried in triumph. He was handsome, crowned with victory. A group of Fedayeen had gotten into the security zone, had confronted a unit of the Israeli army and destroyed a vehicle. Even Marwan admired their courage. Intissar had shaken Ahmad's hand and congratulated him. Men change. Weapons transform them. Weapons and the illusion that they produce. The false power they give. What you think you can obtain by using them.

What earthly purpose can the Kalashnikov, which is lying across her thighs like a newborn child, serve now? What can she get with her rifle, three olive trees and four stones? A kilo of Jaffa oranges? Vengeance. She will get peace for her soul. Avenge the man she loves. Then defeat will be consummate, the city will sink into the sea, and everything will disappear.

half-starved wretch sublime those Palestinians with the heavy shoes what a story I wonder if it's true Intissar pretty name I imagine her beautiful and strong, I am luckier than she is, I went to Palestine, to Israel, to Jerusalem I saw paralyzed pilgrims one-armed people one-legged people people with no legs weird people bigots tourists mystics visionaries one-eyed people blind people priests Catholic and Orthodox pastors monks nuns every kind of habit all the rites Greeks Armenians Latins Irish Melchites Syriacs Ethiopians Germans Russians and when they weren't too busy "fighting over cherry stems while ignoring the cherries" as the French saying goes all these lovely folk mourned the death of Christ on the cross the Jews lamented their temple the Muslims their martyrs fallen the day before and all these lamentations rose up in the Jerusalem sky sparkling with gold at sunset, the bells accompanied the muezzins at top volume the ambulance sirens drowned out the bells the haughty soldiers shouted *bo, bo* at suspects and loaded their assault rifles one finger on the trigger ready to fire at ten-year-old kids if they had to, fear strangely was in their camp, the Israeli soldiers sweated from fear, at the checkpoints there was always a sniper ready to fire a bullet into the heads of terrorists, staked out behind bags of sand a twenty-year-old conscript spent his day keeping Palestinians in his sights, their faces in his cross-hairs: the Israelis know that something will happen sooner or later, the whole point is to guess where, who, and when, the Israelis wait for catastrophe and it always ends up coming, a bus, a restaurant, a café, Nathan said that was the most discouraging aspect of their work, Nathan Strasberg the one in charge of "foreign relations" for the Mossad took me around Jerusalem and stuffed me with falafel, don't believe the Lebanese or the Syrians, he said, the best falafel is Israeli, Nathan was born in Tel Aviv in the 1950s his parents, survivors from Łódź, were still alive, that's all I knew about him, he was a good officer the Mossad is an excellent agency, never losing sight of its objectives, cooperation with them was always cordial, sometimes effective—out of dozens of Palestinian, Lebanese, American sources they were the best on international Islamic terrorism, on Syrian, Iraqi, or Iranian activities, they kept watch over the traffic in arms and drugs, anything that could finance Arab agencies or parties at close range or from a distance, all the way to American and European politics, that was the game, they readily collaborated with us on some cases while trying to block us on others—Lebanon especially, where they thought that any political support for Hezbollah was a danger for Israel, Hezbollah was for them hard to penetrate, nothing at all like the divided, greedy Palestinians: the sources on Hezbollah were fragile not very reliable very expensive and always liable to be manipulated from above, of course with Nathan we never spoke about that, he showed me thrice-holy Jerusalem with a real pleasure, in the old city you heard dozens of languages being spoken from Yiddish to Arabic not counting the liturgical languages and the contemporary dialects of tourists or pilgrims from all over the world, the Holy City could duplicate all joys and all conflicts, as well as all the various cuisines smells tastes from the borscht and *kreplach* of Eastern Europe to the Ottoman *basturma* and *soujouk* in a mélange of religious fervor commercial buzz sumptuous lights chants shouts and hatred where the history of Europe and the Muslim world seemed to wind up despite itself, Herod Rome the caliphs the Crusaders Saladin Suleiman the Magnificent the British Israel the Palestinians confronted each other there argued over the place in the narrow walls that we watched grow blanketed with purple at sunset, over a drink with Nathan at the King David Hotel, the sumptuous luxury hotel that also seemed to be at the heart of the world: famous for the attack of the Irgun Zionist terrorists who had killed a hundred people in 1946, the hotel had also welcomed exiles, unfortunate monarchs dislodged from their thrones by one conflict or another, Haile Selassie pious emperor of Ethiopia driven away by the Italians in 1936 or the disastrous Alfonso XIII of Spain put to flight by the Republic in 1931 who ended his days in the Grand Hotel on the Piazza Esedra in Rome, for a few weeks

Alfonso XIII occupied a suite on the fifth floor of the King David in Jerusalem where he had a view over the gardens and the old city, I wonder what the Iberian sovereign thought about when he contemplated the landscape, about Christ probably, about the Spanish monarchy that he saw go out in one last golden reflection on the Dome of the Rock and that he hoped to see come to life again: they say that Alfonso XIII collected slippers, he had dozens of them, plain, embroidered, or luxurious and all those wools those furs those felts around his feet were his real home in exile, in Jerusalem Alfonso XIII bought sandals which he was still wearing when he expired in his Roman luxury hotel without having seen Madrid again, condemned to international hotels those chateaux of the poor—at the King David bar that British jewel I sip my bourbon in the company of Nathan without knowing that Jerusalem would soon catch fire, we spoke about the end of the Israeli-Palestinian conflict not knowing that violence would very soon resume on the Temple Mount, you could make it out in the distance, that's where my collection begins, in Jerusalem talking with Nathan in the golden-brown twilight, the man of the Mossad an accomplice despite himself gives me some pieces of information, the first, about Harmen Gerbens the alcoholic Cairo Batavian, out of kindness, without questioning me about my interest in this forty-year-old affair, wanting to please me, just as he offered me falafel in the old city and whiskies at the King David he told me that Harmen Gerbens had of course never worked for Israel, but his name appeared in an old file on the Suez expedition that Nathan had gotten from the Shin Bet, cleared of ever-embarrassing military considerations four decades later—why this interest in the old Dutchman, in the "foreigners" rounded up in Egypt in 1956 and 1967, in the Qanatar Prison, maybe it was the effect of Jerusalem, a yearning for penance or a way of the cross, do we always know what the gods are reserving for us what we are reserving for ourselves, the plan we form, from Jerusalem to Rome, from one eternal city to the other, the apostle who three times denied his friend in the pale dawn after a stormy night perhaps guided my hand, who knows, there are so many coincidences, paths that cross in the great fractal sea-coast where I've been floundering for ages without knowing it, ever since my ancestors my forefathers my parents me my dead and my guilt, Alfonso XIII driven out of his country by history and collectivity, the individual against the crowd, the monarch's slippers for his crown, his body versus the function of his body: to be both an individual in a train crossing Italy and the bearer of a sad piece of the past in an entirely ordinary plastic suitcase wherein is written the fate of hundreds of men who are dead or on the point of disappearing, to work as pen-pusher man of the shadows informer after having been a child then a student then a soldier for a cause that seemed just to me and that probably was, to be a string on the bobbin that the goddess spins as she proceeds on a straight path among passengers each one in his body pushed towards the same terminus if they don't get off along the way, in Bologna or Florence, to meet one of those madmen who haunt the station platforms announcing the end of the world: my neighbor has turned on his Walkman, I hear sounds but can't really tell what he's listening to, I can make out a high-pitched rhythm superimposed over that of the train tracks, Sashka can't live without music either, CDs galore Russian or Hebrew airs melodies ancient or modern when I met her the night was very dark, a glance is stronger than a ship's mooring says a Dalmatian proverb one look and you're pulled out to sea—in the little Roman streets painted with ivy, perfumed by rain, stricken too with the sickness of history and death like Jerusalem Alexandria Algiers or Venice, I cling to lies and to Sashka's arm, I pretend to forget Paris the Boulevard Mortier violence and wars the way, when I was a child, a ray of light would always slip beneath the door to reassure me, the distant conversations of the adults lulled me with indistinct murmurs pushing me little by little into the world of dreams, Sashka is the nearby body of a distant being, surrounded as we are by all these ghosts my dead and hers whom we resist by putting our arms round each other's shoulders near the sad Tiber great carrier of refuse, it's over, I left Paris my civil servant's studio apartment my books my souvenirs my habits my lunches with my parents I filled lots of trash bags threw it all out or almost all got loaded one last time by accident in my old neighborhood slipped into the skin of Yvan Deroy and farewell, on the road to the end of the world and a new life, they all float past the window in the darkened plain, Nathan Strasberg, Harmen Gerbens, and the ghosts of the suitcase, the torturers of Algeria, the executioners of Trieste, all that foam on the sea, a white slightly sickening froth made from the putrescence of a load of corpses, I needed patience to collect them, patience, time, intrigues, leads, not losing the thread, consulting thousands of archives, buying my sources, convincing them by following the rules of information-gathering I'd learned haphazardly through the years, sorting through the information, compiling it, organizing it into a file that can be consulted easily, by name, date, place, and so on, personal stories life stories worthy of the best Communist paranoid administrations, archives such as there are by the millions records traces—maybe it was in The Hague that I began, in 1998 before Jerusalem I take a few days' leave to go to the International Court of Justice where the trial of General Blaškić was taking place, the commander in Vitez of the HVO the army of the Bosnian Croats, in his box at the beginning of the hearing Tihomir Blaškić recognizes me and nods to me, after becoming brigadier-general he is facing twenty major charges, among them six infractions of the Geneva conventions, eleven violations of the laws and customs of war, and three crimes against humanity, committed in the context of "grave violations of humanitarian international law against Bosnian Muslims" between May 1992 and January 1994, I left Bosnia on February 25, 1993, I had gotten there from Croatia in April 1992, and after a few months' stay on the front near Mostar I joined Tihomir Blaškić in central Bosnia, his headquarters had since November 1992 been located in the Vitez Hotel, he was an efficient, respected officer, I felt bad when I saw him in the midst of that multilingual administrative circus of the ICJ where a large chunk of time was lost in arguments over procedure, in misunderstandings of the American prosecutor's quibbles, in countless witnesses and hours and atrocities while I knew perfectly well who had committed them, I could see again the places, the flames, the battles, the punitive expeditions until my departure after Andrija's death: at bottom

I hadn't been attached to anything, theoretically I was answerable to the Croatian army but we were supposed to have resigned and left for Bosnia so as not officially to embarrass Croatia, I went to see the captain then the major I said *I'm leaving I can't stand it any more* they replied *but we need you* I said *think of me as having fallen in battle* Blaškić gave me a funny look and asked me *are you OK?* I answered *can't complain*, then he gave the order to sign my travel papers and I left, I crossed the lines to go back through Mostar then Split whence I reached Zagreb, I moved into a shabby boarding house I bought sneakers that were too small for me I remember I had only combat boots, I didn't know where to go, I remember calling Marianne crying like a baby I don't even know anymore if I was drunk, I felt guilty for abandoning my comrades, guilty for my share of the destroying, the killing, I dreamed for hours and hours on end without really sleeping, I dreamed of funeral ceremonies where Andrija blamed me for having abandoned his body I walked for kilometers in the mountains to find him to put him on a tall wooden pyre and burn him, his face was outlined then in the smoke that rose to the heart of the spring sky—all that came back to me all of a sudden as I saw Blaškić in his box at The Hague among the lawyers the interpreters the prosecutors the witnesses the journalists the onlookers the soldiers of the UNPROFOR who analyzed the maps for the judges commented on the possible provenance of bombs according to the size of the crater determined the range of the weaponry based on the caliber which gave rise to so many counter-arguments all of it translated into three languages recorded automatically transcribed 4,000 kilometers away from the Vitez Hotel and from the Lašva with the blue-tinted water, everything had to be explained from the beginning, historians testified to the past of Bosnia, Croatia, and Serbia since the Neolithic era by showing how Yugoslavia was formed, then geographers commented on demographic statistics, censuses, land surveys, political scientists explained the different political forces present in the 1990s, it was magnificent, so much knowledge wisdom information at the service of justice, "international observers" took on full meaning then, they testified to the horrors of slaughter with a real professionalism, the debates were courteous, for a time I would have volunteered as a witness, but neither the prosecution nor the defense had any interest in having me appear and my new occupations imposed discretion on me, for a long time I thought about what I would have said if they had questioned me, how would I have explained the inexplicable, probably I too would have had to go back to the dawn of time, to the frightened prehistoric man painting in his cave to reassure himself, to Paris making off with Helen, to the death of Hector, the sack of Troy, to Aeneas reaching the shores of Latium, to the Romans carrying off the Sabine women, to the military situation of the Croats of central Bosnia in early 1993, to the weapons factory in Vitez, to the trials at Nuremberg and Tokyo that are the father and mother of the one in The Hague—Blaškić in his box is one single man and has to answer for all our crimes, according to that principle of individual criminal responsibility which links him to history, he's a body in a chair wearing a headset, he is on trial in place of all those who held a weapon, he will be condemned to forty-five years in prison then to nine years on appeal and today he must be taking advantage of his early release near Kiseljak, not very far from the villages where the burnt bodies of civilians for whose deaths he was blamed lie, those people who are still waiting for a justice that will never come, in the very Dutch Hague there was such a procession of ex-Yugoslavs that it was a headache to arrange their court appearances without all those people meeting each other in the planes, trains, or cars before finding themselves all together in the luxurious cells of the detention building or the antechambers of the hearing rooms, the vanished country was reconstituted one last time by international law, Serbs Croats Bosnians of all kinds Montenegrins fell into each others' arms or pretended they didn't recognize each other, they were there to speak about their war to air their dirty linen in front of judges who of course could be neither Serbs nor Croats nor Bosnians nor Montenegrins nor even Macedonian or Albanian or Slovenian, only their defenders were, and this international community that judged them indirectly watched with a remote air all these barbarians with unpronounceable names, hundreds of thousands of pages of trials became a distressing ocean, a tidal wave of justice in which the victims who had come to testify floundered, the displaced the tortured the beaten the raped the plundered the widows usually cried behind closed doors in a room with lowered blinds and their stories didn't leave the glassed-in cages of the interpreters, consigned to court reports in English or French for posterity, without the judges hearing the accents the dialects the expressions of their voices that traced a real map of pain—they all took the plane home afterwards with a taste of bile in their mouths for having returned seen their enemies their torturers or their memories without their hatred or their love or their loyalty or their suffering serving any purpose at all, characters in the Great Trial organized by international lawyers immersed in precedents and the jurisprudence of horror, charged with putting some order into the law of murder, with knowing at what instant a bullet in the head was legitimate *de jure* and at what instant it constituted a grave breach of the law and customs of war, referring endlessly to the rulings of Nuremberg, Jerusalem, Rwanda, historical precedents recognized as such by the status of the court, retracing *customary international law* in the interpretation of the Geneva conventions, peppering their verdicts with flowery, apposite Latin expressions, devoted, yes, all these people were very devoted to distinguishing the different modes of crimes against humanity before saying *gentlemen I think we'll adjourn for lunch* or *because of repairs in Hall 2 the Chamber requests the parties to postpone the hearings planned for this afternoon until a later date, let's say in two months*, the time of the law is like that of the Church, you work for eternity, at least all this palaver offered a distraction to the defendants, they listened for months on end to the story of their country and their war, interested as you'd be by a good film, or maybe bored by its repetitiveness, I stayed for three days in The Hague I wondered if someone was going to recognize me and shout *police! police!* when they saw me but no—my name must have appeared somewhere in an investigative report though, buried there with the others, lying black on white among the dead and the survivors of our brigade, maybe with the list of our civilian victims on the facing page, intentional or accidental, as accidental as a mortar shell can be when it buries a family under rubble, I feel as if I'm floating all of a sudden, the train is passing over a series of switches and is dancing, the lights of the countryside pirouette around us in a random ballet that makes me nauseous or is it the memory of the war, I took advantage of the trip to The Hague to go as far as Groningen, to see the multicolored houses lining the canal that surrounds the city center, the main square had a magnificent tower, the sea and the islands quite close, Germany a few kilometers to the east, an average quiet city with a glorious past, I strolled at random in the streets downtown before finding a very handsome hotel near the canal in a seventeenth-century building with the evocative name *Auberge du Corps de Garde*, Inn of the Guard Corps, just like that, in French, which led me to think that they spoke that language, the first thing I did after settling in was to rush to the phone book, there were two Gerbens, initials A.J. and T., one living a little outside the city and the other near the venerable university south of the center, according to the map, if Harmen Gerbens the old Cairo-dweller had had two daughters they had probably gotten married and taken the name of their husbands, the receptionist at the Guard Corps was nice but suspicious, what did I want with these Gerbens, I asked her if the name was common she replied no, not really, I decided to explain the story to her, in Cairo I had met an old man from Groningen named Harmen Gerbens who had asked me to say hello to his family for him, a white lie the old drunkard would rather have spat on the ground, she suddenly looked moved and decided to help me, to pick up the telephone and ask for me if the first Gerbens in the phone book knew a Harmen residing in Cairo, I couldn't understand a scrap of the conversation but the young woman was smiling at me and nodding her head as she spoke, before putting her hand over the receiver and explaining to me—it was his nephew, he in fact did have an uncle named Harmen who left for Egypt after the war, she was all excited about it, ask him if I can meet him, please, she took up the telephone again and her Dutch conversation—this first Gerbens in the phone book was a doctor and received visits in the afternoon, I made an appointment for four o'clock and went to eat herring in a passable restaurant by the water, fortunately the weather was nice, a pale autumn light and a sea breeze perfumed the landscape, what questions was I going to ask this doctor, what attracted me in Harmen's story, in the shadiness I thought I discerned in it, my head full of war memories rekindled by The Hague, pursued by the impenetrable face of Blaškić on the accused bench, heroes, fighters, the dead, feats of arms, it's time I kill as I walk along the canal, a few moored canalboats remind me that from here you can reach the Rhine then the Rhone leading to the Mediterranean and thus reach Alexandria, the Venetian tradesmen brought back furs from Holland that they exchanged for spices and brocades, according to my illustrated guide Groningen was a prosperous trading city where they imported tobacco from the colonies, it's almost time, the pleasant receptionist showed me how to reach the nephew's office: as four o'clock strikes I'm facing a man in his fifties in a white lab coat, he knows English, he is polite, somewhat surprised to hear about a relative he's never met, I thought he was dead, he says, if I remember right my aunt said he was dead, she died a few years ago, my cousins are married and they live in Amsterdam—my father is no longer in this world, carried off by tobacco and alcohol, so far as I know after the war he was never very close to his brother, they weren't on the same side, you see, my father was a resistant and my uncle, hmm, *not so much*, I think they fell out with each other, at the Liberation my uncle was forced to flee to avoid the death penalty, he escaped from the military prison not long before his execution, what had he done to deserve such a sentence? I asked, I don't know, the doctor stammers, I don't know anything about it, he'd been a Nazi I guess, I confess I never tried much to find out, you understand, my parents never spoke about it, it's strange to think he's still alive, over there in Egypt, it's just as strange that the British didn't arrest him when he arrived in 1947, I thanked the doctor and left imagining Gerbens's two daughters, they the daughters of a traitor and he the son of a hero, maybe they're both murderers but for different causes, the two children of Harmen the Cairo Nazi probably bore the mark of the absence of a father despised by his homeland whom they had never tried to see again, just as they had never seen their father's family again, they had changed cities, changed their name by marriage and left this gap in their genealogy to their descendants, when she returned to Holland Gerbens's wife must have declared her husband in Egypt dead, and had condemned him to keel over alone and far away in the exile of Garden City and alcohol which was one of his many prisons, probably the strongest one, along with his past, Harmen Gerbens the old Nazi locked up so many times, in Holland, in

Qanater, at his place in Garden City, in Metaxa, and in Egyptian brandy, condemned to watch himself die as he remembered perhaps the death's head on his SS collar, which had not stopped accompanying him all throughout his existence like an invisible tattoo—did he remember the people he had loaded into trains headed east, the women he had raped in the Westerbork camp, how far back did memory go, Harmen Gerbens took his place in the list in the suitcase—I went back to the Guard Corps hotel, it started to rain, I thanked the receptionist warmly, I told her *mission accomplished* and she smiled at me as she handed me the key to my room, and tonight in the Plaza when the unknown man comes to take possession of the briefcase and hand over my cash I'll toast the health of the receptionist and the doctor in Groningen, of Gerbens's daughters, of Nathan Strasberg the Jew from Łódź who in Jerusalem translated the appendix to the Shin Bet report for me, he thought it rather ironic that Israeli intervention had the effect of sending a former Nazi to prison in Cairo, it was a kind of relief for him, Nathan was also compiling lists, endless lists of targets, of men to kill, of Palestinian personnel hostile to the Oslo agreements, PFLP, DFLP, Hamas, Islamic Jihad, the new "refusal movement" constituted a major risk for the Mossad, and Nathan was gathering information on their schemes, not knowing that very soon after the beginning of the second Intifada he was going to have to murder most of these people, according to the nice doctrine of preventative murder, with air-to-ground missiles over Gaza or Merkava tanks in the West Bank camps, Nathan was a little chubby smiled a lot and was full of good humor I wonder where he is today, a little closer to the end of the world, as the train is crossing the Po almost without slowing down, a factory slips by in white neon lights behind brick walls, a tall structure, metal girders lit here and there by red lamps like a boat—in Venice Ghassan Antoun worked in Porto Marghera in a similar petrochemical establishment, an immense jumble of tubes and storage tanks also lit at night by red lamps that appeared out of the fog, he went home in the early dawn by bus, over the bridge called the "Freedom Bridge" that joins Venice to terra firma and commemorates the end of Austrian domination, Ghassan always gave off a strange smell, like peanuts or grilled corn, washing didn't do any good this strange chemical smell never left him, it only diminished a little according to his distance from the factory, without ever completely disappearing: the night shift stole his body from him without ever entirely returning it to him, contaminated by familiar and unsettling effluvia, the way a soldier on campaign smells of sweat and grease, I met him at dawn in a bar where daybreak freed me from my walking insomnia, we were both going home like exhausted frozen vampires, he with an anorak over his blue overalls I with my eternal hat shoved down to my eyebrows, he reminded me immediately of Andrija the Slavonic, go figure, there was nothing similar in their features, aside maybe from an unsuitability of the body for its clothes, Andrija always badly dressed the uniform never fit him, either too big or too small, his outfits were stained and his kit dangled oddly he always looked awkward, weighed down by the bag, the ammunition, the weapons and Ghassan in his blue worksuit crammed into the anorak had the same ungainly walk that went with his eternal smile and the little mustache he was so proud of, Andrija killed in central Bosnia near Vitez was reincarnated in the damp cold dawn of a café in Venice, a proletarian café by the lagoon not far from the romantic island cemetery of San Michele—Stravinsky, Diaghilev, Ezra Pound the old madman—which I hadn't deemed it wise yet to visit, Andrija's absence, I was probably looking for a replacement for him, a substitute in the great solitary boredom of La Serenissima: Ghassan lived a stone's throw away in a damp dark apartment that he shared with his cousin head waiter at a luxury hotel Riva degli Schiavoni, that morning we had coffee side by side without exchanging a word, at least that's what I remember, maybe our countless breakfasts at dawn in the course of the months that followed are superimposed over that first meeting, I forget at what instant exactly I spoke to Ghassan for the first time, I don't think our friendship was immediate, as they say, in the yellowish lighting of the Piacenza station and the air-conditioning of the train that keeps me from smelling his factory odor, friendship or camaraderie needs time, experience, and if in love the union of bodies gives each the illusion of profound knowledge of the other, so the effluvia of fighters, their sweat and their blood, gives the illusion of intimacy, Ghassan and I observed each other for a long time without sharing anything, despite (or maybe because of) the similarity of our personal stories, the strange points in common that were immediately guessed, the empathy and the resemblance, real or imagined, with Andrija and his mustache, just as in this overheated train I don't speak to my neighbor, despite the points of contact that could link our existences together, of which this motionless journey is an example, what is he going to discover, where will he get out, Bologna, Florence, or Rome, he looks like he's bored stiff, his *Pronto* in his hand, he too is looking out the window Piacenza is fading away and the industrial zone is starting up its intermittent lights, which the night of this flat fertile countryside hides from us at the border of Emilia, crossed by the train—soon Ghassan will be forty, if he's still alive despite the recent avalanche of corpses in Beirut: did he become one of the bodyguards for Elie Hobeika or some obscure Christian second-in-command, did he take up the weapons he had abandoned in 1991, fleeing the arrival of the Syrian Great Brother in his corner of the mountains, who knows, I left Ghassan when I left Venice, and afterwards, in Trieste or during one of my trips to Beirut on business as they say, I didn't seek him out, he had told me though where his family lived, right in the middle of the hill of Achrafieh that overlooks the eastern side of the city, he had said that from the roof of his building you could see the sea, much bluer than in Venice, much more sea-like than that interminably flat lagoon: the eastern Mediterranean its colors marked by the seasons like a tree, from grey to turquoise, beneath the immense sky of Lebanon that the mountains make even vaster by limiting it, in the reflections of the summits, Ghassan vanished like Andrija, finally disappeared in his turn and maybe helped by age didn't I try to replace him too, to fill the void left by the end of that cold friendship that began in a bar at dawn facing the island of San Michele the floating cemetery of Venice with its corner for foreigners, we saw each other every morning or almost at daybreak, Ghassan was emerging from his factory of fertilizers or God knows what putrid residue and I from my nocturnal wanderings, a way to escape the woman who had joined me in Venice whom I no longer wanted to see, I think, unless the opposite was true, she obstinately refused to go to bed with me arguing that Venice made her depressed, which was probably true, she was always cold, she didn't eat much, but today I realize that she was my reflection, that I was the depressed one, most likely, motionless in Venice as I am now in this train, on my way to recovery, to oblivion, to two years of war I lost roaming through Croatia and Bosnia, I had wanted Marianne to join me but I preferred solitude and the company of Ghassan, Nayef, and the others, we didn't meet often, she slept at night, whereas I slept during the day, exhausted by insomnia—maybe that was the consequence of two years of amphetamines, two years of cultivating the body, two years of fear of dying in the mud, huge hangovers two years of bullets bombs alcohol and drugs it was a miracle I thought that Marianne waited for me, that she came to join me in Venice which was not a romantic choice but a way of disappearing, an island outside of time and outside of space, a tomb for me and for Andrija who was rotting in my memories as he was decomposing in the earth, on weekends Ghassan and I got drunk—often he told me stories about the civil war in Lebanon, his own war, he was on the side of the Lebanese Forces, of course, on the side of the flag and the crucifix that was so similar to us Croats, he was sixteen at the fall of West Beirut, in 1982, when Intissar and the Palestinian fighters left Lebanon, Ghassan had thought the war was over, he had enlisted a few months later when the massacre had started up again, inspired by his elders who told him about the glorious years in the 1970s, when the other side was leftist, long-haired, and wore an upside-down Mercedes symbol for a badge, later the enemy was Druze, then Syrian, then Christian during the last great confrontation that put the mountain to fire and sword for nothing, the city was burning, he said, the bombings were more intense than ever, Geagea's Lebanese Forces were fighting against General Aoun, in that mixture of pride, power and money that summarized his country so well: he might have fought against Marwan, Ahmad and Intissar, maybe even against Rafael Kahla the author of the story, who knows, every time I went to Beirut I thought about Ghassan's stories, and the new contacts in my new profession told me more stories of war and espionage, *Lebanon is a market stall by the sea*, said Kamal Jumblatt, *and everything's for sale*, everything's for sale, especially information and the lives of the undesirable, Kamal the father of Walid Jumblatt prince of the Druzes the funniest the cleverest the cruelest of the lords of the Lebanese war, secluded in his palace in Mukhtara to escape the Syrian bombs and the car bombs, Walid the killer of Christians from the Shouf is a witty, cultivated and very wealthy man, his warriors were the toughest, the boldest, the craziest, the bloodiest, they infuriated their leader because they were incapable of marching in step, but they had no equals in leaving 200 dead on a village square in less time than it takes to say so, and in that tiny country where everything is known or everything happens among family they tell the most unlikely stories about the warlord Walid, they make you smile and tremble at the same time, like all of Lebanon, country of laughs and shudders: one night he invited a cousin and his wife Nora to dinner, up there in his mountain, and at the end of the meal, as the couple was about to leave, Walid, without even getting up from the table they say, told his relative that he could leave but that his wife was staying, and so there were two possible solutions, either she got an immediate divorce, or she became a widow, this Helen of Phoenicia, always the passion for the wives of others, just as frequent among the kings of Lebanon as those elsewhere, witness Ghazi Kanaan the Syrian colonel who used all the terror of power in Damascus not only to get rich, but also to sleep with well-placed ladies in high Lebanese society, and they say—of Kings, of Warriors—that he was capable of summoning a minister in the middle of the night and telling him to send his mistress straightaway, so she could come give him head, him the leader of the Syrian forces, his revolver at his minister's temple: ogres want everything, take everything, eat everything, power, money, weapons, and females, in that order, and these stories of monsters reminded me of my own ogres, Serbian, Croatian, who could unleash all their rage and quench all their thirst for mythic humanity, violence and desire, these stories were the delights of the man in the street, the children, the meek, happy to see the powerful get humiliated in turn in front of someone more powerful, lose their honor their wives as the poor had lost their houses their children or their legs in a bombardment, which after all seemed less serious than dishonor and humiliation, the defeat of the powerful is tremendous, beautiful and loud, a hero always makes noise when he collapses, a hundred kilos of muscle strike the ground in one huge dull thud, the public is on its feet to see Hector tied to the chariot, see his head wobble and his blood spurt, the ogre conquered by an even bigger ogre: Ghassan couldn't help but be fascinated by these heroes, the Jumblatts, Kanaans, or Geageas, admire their feats of arms and their escapades that he recounted like good jokes, slapping his thighs, smiling from ear to ear, over a *spritz* or a Campari and soda on one of those Venetian squares that themselves seemed the opposite of all violence, on the other side of the world, a piece of history floating on the motionless lagoon, one of the centers of the political and economic Mediterranean cut off from reality and eaten away by tourists as well as by vermin and moss, slowly but surely, the army of underlings has taken the city, they stroll among the dead palaces, invade the sumptuous churches, happy to contemplate the corpse of the giant up close, the empty shell of the dried-out snail—with Ghassan we were absolutely insensitive to all the beauties of Venice, he the emigrant, the worker, I the depressive who in La Serenissima probably appreciated only the silence of the deserted streets invaded by night and fog, disoriented, incapable of making a step towards firm land, Marianne had to leave me one fine morning on the Ponte delle Guglie for me to wake up, we were coming back drunk from a night of endless talk, Ghassan and I, it must be six or seven in the morning, I almost haven't seen Marianne at all the two or three preceding days, she in light and I in darkness and there she was on the bridge, in the grey dawn, pajamas on under her coat, her hair loose, pale, rings under her eyes, and when I go up to her worried she lands me a furious kick right in the balls which doubles me over cuts off my breath and she disappears, she leaves right in front of the dumbfounded eyes of Ghassan who doesn't even dare laugh for a few minutes, astonished as I clutch my abdomen my head against the parapet not understanding what's just happened not realizing that my aching testicles are sounding the alarm, that this unexpected shot from Marianne is propelling me out of Venice, I'll never see her again, she took the first train, she left, and I did too, shaken all of a sudden by her despair the pain makes me come to my senses, at daybreak, Ghassan stunned watches Marianne walk away without believing it, what was she doing outside at that hour half dressed I guess she was looking for me, she was looking for me to tell me she was leaving, it was over, she couldn't say anything she aimed her shoe at my privates I hurt all the way up to my ears, my eyes full of tears, I took note: I took note, I woke up, shaken, pulled out of waiting and drunkenness, I packed my bags in the shadow of Marianne's vanished perfume, Achilles the proud warrior gathers his spoils, his shining greaves, and his bronze weapons into hollow vessels, I said goodbye to Ghassan knowing full well I probably would never see him again and three days later, more than six months after my arrival, I took a train almost like this one headed north passing through Milan: there are geographical points about which you realize, once the route has been traveled, that they were crossroads, cruxes perhaps, detours, required passages without your being able to guess—trains and their blind progress always lead you there—that they harbor an important part of the journey, that they define it as well as contain it, modest, those train stations you travel through without ever going outside them, for me it's the

Milan station, a city actually unknown but where, at every change of my existence, I passed through to get into a new train, from Paris to Zagreb, from Venice to Paris, and today from Paris to Rome to go deliver—like any merchandise, pizza, flowers—fifty-year-old secrets and other more recent ones to trembling prelates, in return for hard cash, I set the amount at $300,000, thinking that the irony wouldn't escape men of the Church, thirty pieces of silver, they didn't breathe a word, agreed without a murmur, without daring to bargain with the sinner over the price of treason, Rome is still Rome, whoever its master is, I turn round in my seat and close my eyes, Milan, at every bend in life, without ever really pausing there: I've never seen the Duomo, or da Vinci's *Last Supper*, or the Victor Emmanuel Gallery, or the gallows where they exposed the dead Mussolini, hanging by the ankles like a common pig, giving his porcine face the homage due to it, that face with the immense forehead that today adorns so many weird objects in all the markets in Italy, T-shirts aprons playing cards penknives with engraved handles collectible matchboxes alcohol flasks or soccer balls, the economy of fascism seems to be doing well and just recently I saw, after a meeting at the Vatican, on the other side of the river, on People's Square, a Mussolini ceremony in proper form, for some kind of general election maybe, the new fascists were there with the old fascists, brown shirts, black, songs flags arms raised eagles unfurled Latin inscriptions shouts into microphones authoritarian loudspeakers violence cars swerving tires screeching around the square and immediately I thought of Croatia of course but especially of the end of Salò, the Italian Social Republic, worn away little by little by the partisans who themselves were exterminated en masse from Bolzano to Mauthausen, sent by train beyond the Brenner Pass to die in Teutonic land, whenever the SS didn't bother finishing them off themselves by clubbing them to death in cells from La Risiera to Trieste—trains carry soldiers and the deported, murderers and victims, weapons and ammunition and for now in the darkness of the countryside that I guess at by dint of the movements of the car behind my closed eyes, the desert of factories sky of fireflies of apocalypse in the dust of the immense industrial zone that hides, to the west, the foothills of Piedmont, rocked by memories as well as by the rails, I left Venice as Marianne left me and I fell asleep, I fell asleep in an Intercity train that was going to Milan to bring me to Paris, everything's mixed up everything's muddled I get younger in my sleep disturbed by the memory of Marianne I see again her underwear always white sometimes lacy her curves heavy at the hips and breasts the simplicity of her smile her slightly naïve generosity or the naïvety that we attribute today to generosity, the abyss between us dug with the soldier's shovel of my departure for Croatia, the first night in Alexandria that always returns with the vividness of a beacon, in that room facing the Mediterranean, it was raining, a yellow lamp illumined the streaks of rain that was the only light she got undressed in the dark, she was on vacation with her parents at the Cairo Club Mediterranean and had treated herself to an excursion to Alexandria on her own, treated herself to adventure, I met her by chance in the train that goes from Cairo to Alexandria, in a luxurious first-class and extraordinarily slow car, a real cliché of Oriental laziness, and along the Nile delta, so green, I ogled the sheer white of her cotton blouse, already, more moved by lust than by any real interest in her soul, drawn by her prehistoric Venus curves, seeking a refuge in tender shapes, the way a child sucks his thumb, a maternal baby bottle in those breasts of hers I couldn't manage to tear my eyes away from, we lived in the same neighborhood in Paris, bought our bread at the same bakery, and although we had never seen each other there this coincidence seemed, in an Egyptian train jolting along 4,000 kilometers away from the Rue de la Convention, like a divine sign and triggered our complicity, the immediate friendship of people foreign countries push towards each other, corralling them in closeness thanks to the circle of otherness and the unknown that surrounds them: she was on vacation, and so was I, I was seeking in adolescent flight a sense to my life that I thought I could find in Marianne's imposing breasts, in her white lingerie that illusion, that gift of Aphrodite the dissembler, it hides from desire itself the identity of the flesh it covers, its banality, a false transparency a game of hide-and-seek and asleep daydreaming outside of what I imagine to be Piacenza I see her again once more undressing in the pool of humid half-light, I leave her she leaves me with a resounding kick in the balls, in those organs the cause of our meeting, the circle was closed, my testicles source of my passion ended up getting their comeuppance, crushed under Marianne's shoe until they shot up and hid at the bottom of my throat, she had punished the ones responsible for the initial mistake and we each took a different train a much faster train than the one that gamboled through the Egyptian countryside between those thin downy cows called *gamous*, in the midst of dovecotes and farmers whose swing-ploughs and hoes haven't changed since Ramses, one more train, in Venice I had begun reading, reading passionately, withdrawing from the world and burying myself in the pages, whereas in two years of war I hadn't held one book in my hand not even a Bible in Venetian apathy I stuffed myself with adventure novels, maritime novels, stories about corsairs pirates naval battles whatever the Francophone tourists abandoned in hotels on the lagoon and ended up at the little bookseller's behind the Campo Santa Margarita, thrillers, spy novels, historical novels and aside from my nocturnal expeditions and my conversations with Ghassan I spent the best part of my time lying on the sofa reading, Marianne was obsessed with the war, more than me maybe, she wanted to know, questioned me endlessly, read treatises about the former Yugoslavia, she had even started learning Croatian which infuriated me, I don't know why, her accent, her pronunciation irritated me, I needed silence, I needed her body and silence, the only person I managed to talk about the war with was Ghassan: indirectly, little by little, by commenting on the qualities of some rifle, a certain brand of rocket-launcher we began, the way lovers create intimacy little by little, exchanging anecdotes, war stories, and comparing our lives as soldiers, they were nothing alike—Ghassan the handsome warrior, sunglasses, new outfit, M16 in hand, sat in state at a roadblock or hung out at the beach in Jounieh with his comrades, the confrontations were violent and quick, the war lasted for ten years and was well-run, as he said, the only real battle in which he took part was against the Lebanese army in February 1990 in the Metn and at the Nahr al-Kalb, bloody final butchery, from one hill to the other the artillery massacred the fleeing civilians, the fighters threw themselves at each other in a furious melee: Ghassan told me how he had killed his own cousin, a private in the army, with a grenade thrown at his Jeep that was transporting ammunition, the three occupants were blown away in a spray of flesh, metal and fire, over there no one knows that I'm the one that threw that grenade, said Ghassan, how am I supposed to talk normally to my aunt after that, he remembered hurtling down hills shouting to give himself courage, pissing on the barrel of a machine gun to cool it down, without success, putting an armored vehicle out of commission with a LAW 200 meters away and seeing the commander of the tank manage to extricate himself from the carcass but burn like an old blackened shoe bent double over the barrel, crying for hours on end (he said laughing) after a horse died, accidentally knocked down by a volley of fire, and above all, above all he told how he had been wounded, how he had thought himself dead, cut up all of a sudden by dozens of pieces of shrapnel after a bomb exploded, he had seen the jacket of his uniform burst open with machine gun fire, he was suddenly covered in blood pierced from ankle to shoulder by countless bites, a foul viscous substance covered his entire right side, Ghassan had collapsed in spasms of pain and panic, convinced it was the end, the shell had fallen just a few meters away, the doctors removed eight foreign teeth and seventeen bone fragments from his body, debris of the poor guy in front of him volatilized by the explosion and transformed into a human grenade, pieces of smoking skull propelled in a plume of blood, the only metallic shard of which was a gold premolar, Ghassan did come out of it, he still got shivers up his spine and bouts of nausea from disgust, he said, *just thinking about it gives me the creeps*, I didn't know if I should laugh or cry at this story, Ghassan transformed into a living tomb the martyr's relics enshrined directly in his skin, the union of warriors married by the magic of explosives, Ghassan's story wasn't a unique case, strange as it may seem, in Syria Larrey surgeon of the Great Army tells of having removed from the stomach of a soldier a piece of bone stuck straight in like a knife, *sharp as a bayonet, horrified we thought for a moment*, he says, *that the cannons of the place had been loaded with bones, before learning from the very mouth of the wounded man that this fragment came from the dried corpse of a camel, scattered by a cannonball*—Marcel Maréchal the cellist also relates, in his Memoirs of the War of '14, that a pocket watch from Besançon, a baptism medal, and two fingers (forefinger and middle finger, still attached to each other) landed on his knees after the explosion of a torpedo in the embankment, and that he didn't know what saddened him more, the flesh or the two objects, infinitely more human, in the midst of the butchery, than the simple bloody knuckles—Ghassan still had under his skin, in his neck mainly, minuscule fragments of bone that were invisible or practically invisible to X-rays which, no one knows why, years later, manifested from time to time in the form of cysts and boils that he then had to have lanced, what annoyed him most was having to explain to the doctor why his body was vomiting ossicles the way others do shards of glass from a windshield: poor warriors' bodies, I had been lucky, aside from a few scrapes, superficial burns, and a sprain I had gotten out of it pretty well, my flesh didn't remind me of the war all the time, I have two little scars but they're in my back and behind my shoulder, I never see them, I'd need two mirrors to examine them at leisure—Sashka caresses them with her finger, I know, when I'm lying on my stomach, she never asked me where they came from, unlike Marianne and Stéphanie who questioned me so often, the story of Ghassan's wounds reminded me of my seafaring novels, on the ships the wounded were crammed with wood shards, from the gunwale, the pulleys, the tackle, the masts, the cannonballs, or grapeshot chopped up the deck hurling thousands of splinters, so many savage needles that stabbed the crew, like the ones that landed in the left hand and thorax of the arquebusier Miguel de Cervantes Saavedra at Lepanto on October 7, 1571, on board the vessel *Marquesa*, held in reserve in the rearguard of the Christian fleet and engaged in combat around noon to counter the bold attack of Uluj Pasha the brave, he was trying to turn the center held by Don John of Austria the commander of the Holy League who had gotten up in a good mood that day they say, at dawn around six in the morning, one fine fall morning, and this even though the season was already advanced, in the revolting stench of the galley where over 300 people lived piled on top of each other, Don John of Austria had put on his breastplate and his armor when, around seven in the morning, the first Turkish vessels were sighted, within range in two hours more or less, which left the young twenty-five-year-old bastard time to organize his fleet, the day will be long, the opening of the Gulf of Patras sparkles due east in the rising sun, it has become a deadly trap where 208 Turkish galleys and the

120 light vessels that accompany them are enclosed, carrying 50,000 sailors and 27,000 soldiers, janissaries, spahis, volunteers, in twelve hours 30,000 corpses or over 1,800 tons of flesh and blood will have joined the fish in the peaceful blue water, I told Ghassan about the Battle of Lepanto when we visited the arsenal of Venice the tranquil warrior, which without a qualm would negotiate a separate peace with the Ottomans a few years later, thus putting an end to that famous Holy League commanded by Don John of Austria the first bastard of Charles V, hard to imagine the foul smell spread by 500 galleys and their slaves, the illnesses, the parasites, the vermin they transported, the first cannon thunder around nine in the morning, average speed five knots, let's not rush ourselves, let's try to preserve marching orders, in the rearguard on board the *Marquesa* Cervantes is feverish, in bed, he insists on taking part in the battle, on deck—better to die standing up in the open air than be drowned or burned alive in a fetid forehold, Cervantes goes back to his arquebus, the enemy galleys are a few miles in front of him, behind the center of the Christian camp where the Austrian's flagship sits in state, it fires a cannon and raises its flag to identify itself, the Turkish standard-bearing vessel the *Sultana* with Ali Pasha on board does the same, customs are chivalrous, men less so, before long they'll massacre each other forgetting all the courtesies of war, already the Venetian galleys, veritable battleships of the time, loftier and better armed, break the Turkish central lines and cause terrible damage, it is 11:15 in the morning, the Christian left wing is under fire and seems on the point of being turned round, Barbarigo its commander is hit with an

arrow in his eye, his nephew and officer Contarini is already dead, sunk with the *Santa Maria Maddalena*—on the right, facing Andrea Doria the clever condottiere, Uluj Pasha moves to the south, so as not to be outmaneuvered Doria follows him, leaving a void in the line of defense, the galleys of the rearguard advance to fill it, from his arquebus Cervantes sees Don Álvaro de Bazán give the orders: the oarsmen strike the flat sea, the speed increases to ten knots, in a few minutes there will be a confrontation with the Turkish galleys that have detached from Uluj Pasha's squadron, already the arrows are flying, grapeshot too, at the very instant Cervantes fires his arquebus at the Turkish soldiers fallen into the sea I empty my glass of wine, like Captain Haddock right in the middle of the adventures of the knight François his ancestor, and Ghassan begs me to continue, how was Cervantes wounded, what was the outcome of the battle, despite being Christian he can't help but be on the side of the Ottomans, which after all is understandable but soon the Turkish center will collapse, the head of Ali Pasha will adorn the galley of Don John, that of Murat Dragut will follow, already their right flank is nothing but a memory, the galleys are captured one by one by the Venetian fleet, boarded in a wild melee, driven against the coast and bombarded from the shore, the Turkish archers confront the muskets and cannons of La Serenissima and Don John of Austria, from the height of his twenty-five years and all his nobility, sees with pleasure the fire and battle on the *Sultana* whose escort his galleys destroy vessel by vessel, the Christian slaves suddenly freed gather together the scuttling axes and massacre their former masters with fury, Uluj

Pasha the infidel has seized the standard-bearing vessel of the Knights of Malta, Don Álvaro de Bazán's squadron launches forward to free it, on the *Marquesa* Cervantes the artilleryman loads his weapon in the company of five soldiers, he aims it at the galley of Saïd Ali Raïs the pirate from Algiers, without knowing that a few years later their fates would cross again, conversely, that Cervantes would be imprisoned and at the mercy of the corsair noble, already near the center of the battle cries of victory resound, the surviving Turkish galleys are trying to escape, one of the vessels opens fire on the *Marquesa* to free Saïd Ali, a volley of grapeshot sweeps the top of the deck where the weapons are in battery, and a shard of wood penetrates Cervantes's wrist, slices a nerve and deprives him forever of the use of his left hand, *for the greater glory of the right*—what would have happened if the Muslim gunner hadn't had the noon sun in his eyes, if Cervantes had passed away, anonymous on a forgotten galley, erased by the Glory of Don John of Austria, he would no doubt have been replaced, if there is always someone to take over a cannon there will also be someone to take up a pen and a knight of mournful countenance, his brother Rodrigo who knows, his brother whom the subsequent good fortune of the author of *Don Quixote* has crossed out of history, I imagine he would have related his elder brother's death with panache, and today, on the ferries that go to Patras from Italy, Bari, or Brindisi, loudspeakers would point out to passengers the monument to the older brother of the one who imagined the old sailor crazy with pirate tales, *on board a galley whose name I prefer to forget*, and so on, soldiers are for the most part unknown, where are the names of the 30,000 drowned, burned, decapitated men of Lepanto, where is the name of the one whose teeth and skull almost killed Ghassan, who knows the name of the Turkish soldier who was on the verge, without realizing it, of changing the course of Western literature and who died in Smyrna or Constantinople, still trembling with rage about the memory of the disaster of Lepanto, mustache in his gruel—at 7:00 p.m. on that October 7, 1571 the Turkish spoils and the Christian armada are sheltered in the cove of Porta Petala, Don John of Austria has an immense *Te Deum* chanted in the starry night, the Muslim is defeated, the Turk conquered, the allies of the Holy League sing of the glory of God and their captain, that young twenty-five-year-old imperial bastard who has just won the most important naval battle since Actium in 31 BC: a few miles north of Lepanto, in those same waters ruled by Poseidon, the fate of the world has already been played out once before, the divine Antony and Cleopatra the Egyptian confronted Octavian the landowner, the two former triumvirs threw their fleets and their gods into battle, Isis and Anubis against Venus and Neptune, another battle between East and West, between North and South, without anyone knowing very clearly who the barbarians were: all these stories fascinated Ghassan, he swallowed Christian propaganda and was pleased to believe that the Lebanese were Phoenicians, descendants of worshipers of Astarte and Baal, originally from Byblos he imagined his ancestors like himself, cultivated, cosmopolitan, tradesmen, great founders of cities, Carthage and Leptis Magna, Larnaka and Malaga, great navigators and formidable fighters, whose elephants crossed the Alps: Hannibal son of Hamilcar the tamer of warriors first conquered the Romans in Ticino and wounded Scipio the horseman his enemy—out the window, as the Po plain stretches out to the outskirts of Piacenza, a hundred kilometers from Milan, I wonder if I'll see one of Hannibal's elephants, who died of cold and of their wounds after having crushed the Roman legions a few kilometers away from here, in Trebbia, in the course of that Battle of Trebbia where 20,000 legionaries and foreign auxiliaries of the Roman army perished, 20,000 corpses looted by the locals—beneath the sediments of the river, beneath the dead of one of Bonaparte's first battles in Italy, beneath the tons of dust borne by time are the skeletons of pachyderms who were victorious over the Romans but conquered by snow, abundant this year too, I want to ask my neighbor if he knows that there are elephant bones buried right next to us, he never looks out the window, he is content to drowse over his magazine, one December day similar perhaps to this one in 218 BC, the day of the winter solstice says Livy the scholar, 80,000 men 20,000 horses and thirty elephants clashed: Livy the precise counts the legions, centuries, cohorts of horsemen, names the leaders of each troop, the ones who won glory for themselves and the ones who deserved shame, he describes Hannibal the stubborn who, after over fifteen years of war on Roman soil, didn't manage to wrest surrender from the senate or the people of Rome, despite a series of massacres that are unique in ancient history: in Tunis near Carthage sitting in the Porte de France I order an espresso that they call here a *direct* as I read the paper, in 1996 I paused for a few days in Tunisia to meet Algerians in exile there, within the framework as they say of my new functions, I visit residential and seaside Carthage, cluttered with luxury villas, in Megara, Hamilcar's gardens are still planted with sycamores, vines, eucalyptus, and especially jasmine, with my source, a friendly reformed bearded man, we stroll along the beach, I think about the Carthaginian vessels come from Sicily, Spain, or the Levant that landed there, acceding to the war orders of the senate inflamed by the memory of the Roman dead at the Battle of Cannae, then they decided to reduce it to ashes, *Ceterum censeo Carthaginem esse delendam*, and nothing more, Cato the Elder the gravedigger of Carthage certainly wore a beard, like my repentant Algerian Islamist who rounded out his monthly paycheck by snitching, in the name of the Good, on his former comrades who had strayed from the path of God, on the wrong path, *Ceterum censeo Carthaginem esse delendam*, there are always Carthages to destroy, on the other side of the sea, from Ilion the well-guarded, in that to-and-fro motion, like a tide that gives victory by turns to Constantinople, Carthage, or Rome: on the beach of Megara you still find, washed up by the waves, tiles of mosaics torn from Punic palaces sleeping on the bottom of the sea, like the wrecks of the galleys of Lepanto, the breastplates sunk in the Dardanelles, the ashes thrown in bags of cement by the SS of La Risiera along Dock No. 7 in the port of Trieste, I collect these square multicolored stones, I put them in my pocket just as later on I will collect names and dates to file away in my suitcase, before reconstructing the entire mosaic, the full picture, the inventory of violent death begun by chance with Harmen Gerbens the SS-man from Cairo, locked up in the Qanatar Prison along with Egyptian

Jews suspected of collaborating with Israel, which gave Nathan a good laugh at the bar of the King David Hotel in Jerusalem, I wonder what those Egyptians could have been thinking, he said, how long did you say they held him? Eight years? They realized what he was, I guess, they didn't know what to do with him, finally they freed him just before the war of '67, the enemies of my enemies are my friends, and they granted him Egyptian citizenship, still under his real name, without anyone worrying if he'd be found one day, hidden under the dusty mango trees of Garden City, alcoholic prisoner of eternal Egypt, like the defeated Antony of Actium if he hadn't preferred death to prison and said farewell with one thrust of the sword to Alexandria, Alexandria that was leaving him forever, in 1956 and 1967 the Jewish community in Egypt had been forced into exile, today it counts fewer than fifty members—the great synagogue on Nebi Daniel Street in Alexandria is nothing but an empty shell now, the old custodian you have to bribe to visit it apes the prayers and ceremonies, he pretends to get out the scrolls, to read them, chant them, making the absence even realer by his sham, no one prays anymore in the synagogues of Egypt, except for a few, come from France from Israel or from the United States, they organize ceremonies for the celebrations, in 1931 however Elia Mosseri director of the Bank of Egypt, one of the wealthiest bankers in Cairo, owner of a magnificent Art Deco palace in Garden City, invested with his brother and friends in Jerusalem on a site located on the ancient Julian Way and built an immense luxury hotel there that would become the King David: strange to think that Harmen Gerbens's apartment is a few meters away from the former villa of the founder of the hotel where Nathan and I spoke about the Batavian SS-man relocated by the Egyptians at his release from prison to an apartment abandoned by a Jewish family, just as Nathan's parents, who landed in 1949 in Haifa after many sufferings, would occupy the house of a Palestinian family driven away to Jordan or Lebanon, in a strange Wheel of Fortune where the gods give and take away what they gave—Isabella of Castile promulgated the Alhambra Decree in 1492 and expelled the Jews from Spain, a decree abolished by Manuel Fraga with the pale-faced Minister of Tourism under Franco the Iberian Duce in 1967 when he offered passports to the stateless Jews of Egypt citing the fact that they were Sephardic and thus of Spanish origin, allowing by a fanatical stroke of nationalism the resumption of diplomatic relations with Israel: in the fall of 1967 the Egyptian Jews who had no ties with the Powers, France, Great Britain, or Italy, got off the boat in Valencia in the orange-freighted port where their ancestors might have cast off 500 years before, leaving behind them houses, gold, jewels, and above all the myth of that Andalusian culture of the three religions of the book, to be scattered from Morocco to Istanbul, on the shores of that sea that I walk along with my Algerian Islamist gathering Carthaginian tesserae in 1996, Lebihan my superior at the time often sent me to meet the "sources," you inspire confidence, he said, they'd hand over the good Lord to you without a confession, with that honest look you have, you'd better go yourself, also because he couldn't stand Arab food, lover as he is of blanquette of veal oysters Muscadet and celery rémoulade, what's more he couldn't bear chili pepper, for him Tunisia was a digestive and circulatory disaster, the fire of Baal—food considerations aside, with information of human origin contact is essential, confidence, especially when the "source" doesn't present himself first to collaborate, when you have to go to him circle round him stroke him the right way a game of fox and Little Prince, the animal knows it wants to be tamed, it lets itself be, it always steps back once or twice like a frightened virgin, you have to determine its motivations, whether they're ideological familial venal crooked or vengeful and always keep something up your sleeve for the master stroke, "serving the homeland" still works with some Frenchmen, especially in the sciences or economics, where the risks are all in all negligible, "fighting against the Reds" doesn't work anymore, people are suspicious of it, replaced by "fighting the rise of Islam," which comes down to pretty much the same thing, but in my experience the motivations of informers are most of the time pecuniary, money sex power that's the Holy Trinity of the case officer, it's better to carry a money clip than a weapon, even if, for obvious psychological reasons, the sources prefer to believe they're working "for the good cause," more rewarding than "I sold out": the nice bearded Islamic fundamentalist was serving the cause of God now by non-violence, as he said, I've seen too many massacres, too many horrors, it has to stop, he was a former member of the armed branch of the ISF, close to the Rome negotiators under the guidance of the Sant' Egidio community, St. Giles of Trastevere a stone's throw away from Sashka's place—in the winter of 1995-1996, when I was still a novice spy, thanks to this Catholic intervention the different political parties of Algeria had signed an agreement in principle, a platform of demands supposed to put an end to civil war, they were all there, except the army of course, from the historic Ben Bella to the Islamists, including the Kabylians, the liberal democrats, and even Louisa Hanoune the Red from the Workers' Party, the only woman in the meeting, they called for democracy for respect of the Constitution for the end of torture and of military machinations, all of that of course was doomed to failure but it offered a fine basis to negotiate a peace to come, at the same time in Algeria the ISA and the GIA were massacring infidels while soldiers were torturing and executing anything that fell into their hands, my source confided concrete information to me, my first source abroad, my first voyage into my Zone, names, organization rules, factions, internal tensions, which I tallied afterwards in my office with other files, other sources, to draw up a memo from it, a piece of paper included in a weekly report sent to the ministers concerned, to the office of the Prime Minister and the President of the Republic, weather forecasts of trouble, this week showers likely over North Africa, fair weather in the Balkans, threatening in the Middle East, storms in Russia, etc., a special service was in charge of compiling the information from the different sections for this secret regular publication, not counting the special memos or the precise requests from X or Y, economic, geopolitical, societal, or scientific anxieties are finished at last for me, the shadowy times are over, one last suitcase and I'll join Sashka with the transparent gaze, lie down in silence next to her and bury my lips in her short hair, no more lists no more torturers' victims investigations whether official or not I'm changing my life my body my memories my future my past I'm going to throw everything out of my sight out of the hermetically sealed window into the great black mass of landscape, purify myself, plunge, in Venice La Serenissima one December night I had been drinking, I was staggering home from the end of the Quay of Oblivion, north of Cannaregio I had 300 meters to cover to get back to my Old Ghetto, might as well be a hundred kilometers, or a thousand, I swayed from right to left, pitched forward, headed in the wrong direction, I turned onto the Square of Two Moors, I sprawled into the sculpted well in the middle of the little esplanade, then lifted my painful knees the way you extricate yourself from a trench in wartime, I saw myself again rifle in hand bent double I took three more steps towards the Madonna dell'Orto bridge, two to the left, one to the right, carried forward by my own weight, by the weight of my black cap or my memories in the frozen-mud smell of the Venetian fog, breathing hard as hard as possible to get my spirits up, my mouth wide open my lungs frozen, go forward, go straight ahead if you fall you won't get up you'll end up dead killed by the Chetniks behind you by the Turks by the Trojans with the swift mares I breathe I breathe I go forward I cling to the rail of the bridge it's a tree in the Bosnian mountains I climb, I climb in the night I climb down I see the tall façade of bricks on the church what the hell am I doing here I live on the other side on the other side I make a U-turn stumble miss the bridge and plunge into the dark canal head first, a hand grips me, I'm drowning, it's the conductor waking me up, he shakes me, asks me for my ticket I hand it to him mechanically, he smiles at me, he looks pleasant, outside it's still just as dark, I glue my eyes to the window, open countryside, it's stopped raining

VI

the route is predictable, despite the failing light there will be Reggio Emilia then Modena Bologna Florence and so on until Rome, its sweetness like overripe fruit, Rome, rotting flamboyant corpse of a city you understand too well the fascination it can exercise over certain people, Rome and the suitcase I'm going to hand over there the time I'll spend there maybe the choice has been made the choice has been made ever since the goddess sang of the wrath of Achilles son of Peleus, his warlike choice his honor the love that Thetis his mother bore him and Briseis his desire whom Agamemnon took just as Paris possessed Helen, the one waiting for me in Rome in her most beautiful *peplos*, maybe, the train is slowing down now approaching a station, boredom is holding me in its grip, on the other side of the aisle a man in his fifties is doing crosswords with his wife in a paper called *La Settimana Enigmistica*, the puzzle week or something like that, his wife looks much younger than he, in man's estate everything is harder, in the nothingness of indecision that is the world of rails and shuntings, she is waiting for me, I like to think Sashka is waiting for me, that her body is waiting for me, I think about the life we abandon and about the one we suddenly choose for ourselves, about the clothes we take off, the beautiful greaves, the breastplate, the leather sustaining the breastplate, the beech-wood spear cast into the fire, the shield, all those times when you get undressed, when you show yourself, naked with nothing else but the shivering of skin—those naked men taken by the hundreds out of trains blind their clothes piled up in a corner of the yard the air suddenly frozen the arms that cross the hands that cover the elbows to clothe with flesh the naked flesh marked in its center by the birthmark of the pubis: the enemy always rushes at the conquered to strip them, and we ourselves we strip our enemies for money for a souvenir for a rare weapon and our prisoners too before finishing them off, on principle, in the cold, we order them to get undressed sometimes so as not to stain or make a hole in the uniform, the jacket that could always be useful of course, but also to enjoy the power of man over naked animal, the man standing up against the shorn and trembling animal, laughable it was easier to take despicable life away from them, the gentleman with the *Settimana Enigmistica* seems very paternal, he explains the words, the letters that fit, his companion is looking through a little pocket dictionary, she's a brunette, her hair long and tied back, in man's estate you leave your suitcases, you cling to the youth of others, you strip your women, you undress them, it's been almost ten years since I left Venice since Marianne left and the other life that was beginning without my knowing it in the train from Milan by a dull pain in the testicles is coming to an end today, the resignation handed in, treason consummated, dread of the world now, I am entrusting my entire self to another train, one more, I'm no longer a kind of snitching pen-pushing nosey civil servant but a free man, and this cumbersome freedom fruit of my treachery I'll spend it in the company of Sashka who is waiting for me maybe, Marianne is so present now, close down one existence open up the one before, ten years later, livelier than ever, what could have become of her, I picture her a teacher in a Parisian high school, a mother, of course, she whose body and education were pushing her towards teaching and maternity, just like mine towards the war that for it was entirely natural, for a boy brought up in violence, used to the idea of weapons since childhood, primary school and cartoons, raised in the idea of God and the nation oppressed by his mother's wailing, finding himself one day with an assault rifle in his hand, near Osijek, propelled by his parent's tears and drawn by the summons of Franjo Tuđman the Savior, it's the bland but pleasant face of the crossword enthusiast that makes me think of him, dazed by the fruitless drowsiness of the train's rhythm, Tuđman whose photograph soon joined that of Ante Pavelić in uniform on my mother's patriotic altar, along with Christ and a weeping Virgin, Tuđman arrived in Zagreb as King of Kings, to transform my existence radically, save me or ruin me, who knows, and in front of our television in the 15th arrondissement, in the dark, religiously, we listened to his elegiac speeches only half of which I understood, which my mother translated for me with devotion, *on the day Christ arrived in Jerusalem, he was welcomed as a prophet*, shouted the newscaster, *today the Croatian capital is the new Jerusalem: Franjo Tuđman has come for his own*, Croatia was born again, it emerged completely armed from Tuđman's helmet, finally dragged itself out of its Titoist sleep, found in war wounds a strength a courage a youth and in the clash with its enemies a will a power a beautiful pain whose names were inscribed in letters of fire on television screens, Knin, Osijek, Vukovar, the hairy drunken Serbs were marching against innocence and beauty, they were massacring us, taunting us as they massacred us, in my entire Parisian quiet student's existence, those trips on the metro, those for me abstruse classes in public law, history, and politics, those daily meetings with Marianne all slipped into the void that I was discovering within myself the silent void of the summons of a homeland in danger, hunger desire appetite for a sense of struggle of combat of another life that seemed to me terribly true, real, you had to fight the injustice that was being unleashed on the young State all the bolts of the archer Apollo protector of the East, and the more images and speeches reached me, the more my mother cried both from joy and from pain, the more I slipped towards Croatia, the more I disappeared from Paris from the university I was escaping Marianne and the present, I was burying myself in news reports in Krajinas in surrounded Dubrovnik in the provocations of the Yugoslav army in patriotic songs that I was discovering and even the language even the language that I had half-forgotten never really learned scorned in fact for years even the language came back to me realer and stronger than ever to the great displeasure of my father I began speaking Croatian at home he who hardly understood a word felt excluded from this nationalistic madness as he called it probably rightly, you look like your grandfather said my mother, *podsjećaš me na djeda*, you look like your grandfather, it was a trap, I fell into it just as a train plunges into the night I followed in my grandfather's footsteps without knowing who he was, two years of war, two full years aside from three getaways, one to Trieste with Andrija and Vlaho and two in Paris, mostly to see Marianne again, to feel again what the *poilus* of 1914 told about, the incomprehension of people not at the front, the impossibility of telling about it, of speaking, like those children leaving school who don't know how to say what they did all day: when Marianne questioned me about the war, both of us lying in the dark in her tiny attic room I replied "nothing," I did nothing, saw nothing learned nothing I didn't know how to say it, it was impossible, I told my mother that we were fighting for the glorious homeland, that's all, I saw nothing in war and then I left, I took the night train from Italy or Austria and the next night I was in Zagreb, I thought about the *poilus* who left Paris, I imagined, in that civilized, comfortable train, that I was a Hapsburg soldier on leave who was returning to the front, who was returning to fight the Italians over there on the Isonzo in the foothills of the Alps in 1917 while on the other side of the aisle the crosswords are in full swing, the man older than his companion is talking to her like a professor, Hemingway and his nurse, Hemingway who came this way before going to play at being ambulance driver in the mountains, did he too feel the discrepancy, the impossible gulf hollowed out by the war, between those not at war and the soldiers, the ones who saw, who know, who suffer, the ones who have become dead or death-dealing flesh, and in that immense flat countryside extended by night I think of those who went up to the front on the Somme after seventy-two hours in Paris, after downing their little drinks after being very sad after having sadly and thoroughly fornicated they are like us silent in their car they don't exchange a word in the distance a few bright flashes announce the zone of the armies the zone we're coming close even if you don't hear the cannon you see it you're coming close, your throat contracts, you get out of the train, you walk through a group of wounded men who are waiting to be evacuated and they're moaning, you get into a truck driven by a slightly bad-tempered guy, just a bit abrupt, jealous of a man on leave, then you end up on foot, you greet the artillerymen whom you envy for being so cozily entrenched at the side of their howitzers, even if they all end up half-deaf that's not serious, you advance through the lines, through the half-buried networks following the directions written on wooden signs or on German helmets stuck in the clay, you hope that the first night will be calm, for now it's the English taking it on the chin over there towards Ypres, you forbid yourself from thinking about the girl you've just left, about the last load you shot in a furnished apartment, the last shot you drank alone in the Place de Clichy because all your friends are at the front or at work, the waiter at the café still too young to leave felt envy and respect for you the *poilu*, but his turn will come, when will he die, will he fall in a few months on the Chemin des Dames, cut in half by a machine gun, decapitated by barbed wire or disintegrated by a mine in his trench, will he cry as he holds his warm smelly guts in his hands, will he call for his mother, will he look like a ghost for his arm sticking up somewhere in the mud, you're in the ground, in the first lines that are made of dirt churned up by bombs, barely shored up, you reach the 329th infantry commanded by an officer you've never seen before, there's X, there's Y, they all know it's best to leave the man on leave to his silence, they're all muddy covered in lice starving it's been seventy-two hours since you saw them unconsciously you look for the missing ones you *see* the missing ones then you say nothing, the lieutenant makes a curt sign with his head you set down your kit you look for a position you clutch your Lebel sitting as if in a train you're back and a part of you most of you has remained behind, back there where you savor the end of the world, the pistol shot of Gavrilo Princip in Sarajevo marks the beginning of the race to horror, on June 28, 1914, Gavrilo nineteen years of age thin and tubercular weapon in hand cyanide in his pocket pieces together the destroyed world three empires and rushes me without knowing it into this train ninety years later, near Parma judging from the suburban lights, Gavrilo the Bosnian Serb believed in the Great Serbia that I did my share to undo, the little activist was lucky, like Jaurès's assassin on the Rue Montmartre he was in a café, the plans failed, the bomb that was supposed to make an end to Franz Ferdinand didn't explode beneath the right car, the archduke is still alive, for his misfortune Gavrilo Princip is beloved of Hera, the clever goddess will blind the Austrian chauffeur and the motorcade will come up to Princip, up to his café, Moritz

Schiller's café at the corner of the street facing the tiny bridge it's a fine day he just has to go out leave his cup half empty take the capsule of poison in his left hand the weapon in his right and shoot, did he have time to observe the Habsburg's surprised mustaches, the quivering lips of the beautiful Sophie his wife killed instantly, did he glimpse the millions of dead who gushed forth along with the Austro-Hungarian blood, was he happy with his shot, did the son of Leto guide his shots, was he proud of his four cartridges, did he hesitate, did he think it's nice out today I'm in a café I'll set off the massacre some other day, probably he didn't have time to reflect, he went out, and according to the police reports he fired from five feet away, eye to eye—Gavrilo Princip would die in turn in Theresienstadt, in the prison of the Czech city where the Reich would install a model ghetto in 1941, thus paying absurd homage to the man who indirectly allowed its advent, piling death on death, a ghetto for artists, for intellectuals, one of the worst concentration camps, it superimposed farce on horror, Gavrilo in his cell in the Theresienstadt castle died in 1918 without having seen the birth of the Kingdom of the Southern Slavs for which he had indirectly fought, and the cyanide capsule served no purpose, he died slowly from tuberculosis, which is why he had been recruited to begin with: a band of tubercular terrorists, condemned men doomed to die soon, that's the ideal thing, you feel much less remorse sending them to the slaughterhouse—the first time I went to Sarajevo I passed by the former Moritz Schiller café on the corner by the bridge, on the side of the embankment there's a proud plaque, what does it mean today, what did it mean then, at the height of the siege, along the river where every now and then Serbian or Bosnian mortar shells landed, to remind the international community that times were hard they didn't hesitate for long to shoot at each other, like the recruits of 1917, just as the waiter on the Place de Clichy gone to the Chemin des Dames would shoot himself in the foot to escape the slaughter, the Muslim army probably shot itself in the foot once or twice, in the agony of the city where Gavrilo Princip, coughing, spitting blood, had killed the brother of the emperor, a bomb looks like a bomb, it has no owners once it's thrown, the self-mutilations were countless during the war of 1914, some in the hand, others in the fat of the belly, and I understand those Bosnian artillerymen, exasperated by international indifference, who probably used the tactics of the exhausted *poilu*, hoping that the American planes circling around them would end up putting the Serbian batteries out of commission and I imagine, just as the young soldier points his Lebel at his shoe and pulls the trigger, that they must have hesitated for a long time before shooting at their own men, or not, maybe like Gavrilo Princip at nineteen they were determined, hardened by the certainty of death that was the ambiance of Sarajevo during the last war—the battalion of tubercular Serbs of the Black Hand presaged the number of desperate, suicidal, sacrificed ones that are the army of shades of the century, or of all of history, maybe there was something foundational in Princip's 32-caliber, was it really him who pulled the trigger, he was already dying, condemned, a ghost, a plaything in the hands of the wrathful gods, one instant of glory is given to Diomedes son of Tydeus, to the Ajaxes, to *Koca* Seyit Çabuk the artilleryman in the Dardanelles, Gavrilo had his moment of glory before going to rot in Theresienstadt, with his own hand he sets loose the thunder of war, the Terezín prison where he lumbers and suffocates will survive him, and will see many other condemned men, Jews, Czech communists, enemies of all kinds shot or hanged in a back courtyard by Gestapo agents, cousins of the SS who just across, on the other side of the river, were running one of the most terrifying ghettos, holding almost 50,000 detainees, Jews from Prague, from Germany, from Austria and elsewhere, in the complex geography of deportation a ghetto where you died in music, where you created, where you could reflect at leisure on your epitaph, inscribed in brown clouds in the sky over Auschwitz, most often, the great space of the sky after the filth and pain of concentration, Terezín model for the good conscience of the entire world, look how well-penned our animals are, how healthy and well-groomed our livestock is, and the Red Cross won't find anything to say to this sturdy model whose pictures, duly stamped "*Made in Third Reich Germany*," were broadcast throughout all of Europe, showing without showing what everyone knew without knowing, that concentration was the prelude to destruction, just as branding—of steer, of steer left free in the corral—was the beginning of the end, mark something to slaughter it, control it, separate good from evil the good from the bad your own from another's in order to construct yourself make the self stand out your shoulders thrust against difference against the Orthodox Jew the barbarian the titans order against chaos thus Gavrilo Princip builds his Slavic kingdom by killing the Habsburg: I've seen dozens of them over the years, in my files, martyrs candidates for martyrdom torturers enlightened ones desperate ones activists full of the cause or of God without really knowing which they were serving, whether it was Ares aegis-bearing Zeus or Pallas Athena, hooked on a single God who is all that at once, order and chaos the beginning and the end, who scatters their bodies with an entirely Olympian pleasure, Algerians Egyptians Palestinians Afghans Iraqis in my own zones of activity between 1996 and today how many have died I have no idea, they interest only a few, those victims who make victims the grandchildren of Gavrilo Princip the great instigator—the crossword enthusiast who looks vaguely like Hemingway because of his beard is having a coughing fit at this precise moment and I can't help but smile, history always has its winks, I turn round in my seat, I close my eyes not far from Parma pleasant city I recall I stayed there once on my way to Greece on my first vacation as a young bachelor agent, Marianne's kick had put me on the straight path I returned to political science I finally got my degree my war was described as "long-term training period abroad with the Croatian Ministry of Defense" and got me extra points I think, where could I have found the strength to sit on school benches again, the pain in my balls maybe, the long inactivity in Venice, or simply my share of fate—I could have tended my garden after a fashion like Vlaho the crippled near Dubrovnik, slowly decompose like Andrija, go into a factory like Ghassan the exile, or stay sitting in front of the television at my parents', never leave the 15th arrondissement, my mother had added a photo of me in uniform to the patriotic altar, Pavelić, her photo as a teenager with Ante Pavelić in Spain, the Pope, grandfather,

Tuđman, the flag and me, that's her world, but I wasn't in a hurry to go back home, on the contrary, I wanted to leave again, and I was preparing for exams with the most various and most exotic administrations: I saw my salvation in the beautiful crystal chandeliers in the Quai d'Orsay, in the gold cravats of plenipotentiaries, in the dark blue of diplomatic passports, and in the old-fashioned phrases of letters of credit, not knowing anything about the diplomatic service but what you could learn in Albert Cohen's *Belle du Seigneur*, which seemed an entirely enviable fate to me, even attractive, sparkling, in fact, in the heart of the world, with the highest salaries in all the civil service, with chauffeurs, receptions, and countries where you'd never have thought to settle, Mauritania, Guinea-Bissau, Congo, Bhutan, so I forced myself to learn, to train for these abstruse tests, law, synthesis, history, God knows what else, with no success, obviously—either because of my dubious soldiering past, or simply because my test results weren't up to that prestigious ministry the diplomatic corps turned me down after two different examinations, despite, at least this is what I was told later, *an honest oral presentation*, and my huge disappointment seems to me today, ten years later, in man's estate, in this train to the Vatican, hard to understand: I couldn't see what thundering Zeus was saving for me, a fate in a much more obscure administration than Foreign Affairs, on the Boulevard Mortier, Mortier marshal of the Empire survivor of all the Napoleonic campaigns where they employed me, against all expectations, as *defense delegate*, or so the title of the administrative exam delicately worded it, and I suppose the hundred candidates present in that absolutely commonplace exam room all knew what *defense delegate* meant, or at least they thought they did, information agent, more or less secret agent, an agent more or less from outside, for action wasn't in our purely administrative and linguistic program, an exam pretty much identical to the one for the prefecture, Social Services, or the Naval Command, and as Parma slides by the window I see again my first days at the Boulevard, the curiosity, the training, the strange ultra-secure building, without a coffee machine so as not to encourage idle conversation among the staff, armored toilets, soundproof offices, endless files, dozens of files to go through one by one, to synthesize, classify, tally with their sources, fill out forms to ask for information in one direction or another, under such-or-such a surname spotted in reports coming from "stations" or "correspondents" with code names, transmit, refer to the superior, write up notes, work for the defense of the nation, in the shadows, in the shadow of a stack of manila folders, and my only geographic expertise had obviously been ignored in purest military logic, no Balkans for me, no Slavs: I was thrown into the Arab world of which I knew nothing, aside from Ghassan's stories, the mosques of Bosnia and whatever history books wanted to say about it, I began in the Algerian hell as Chief Classifier in the third rank, in a world of child-slaughterers and polite mass-murderers with names that were all alike to me, in the madness of the 1990s the stench of medieval war, disembowelments, amputations, corpses scattered everywhere, houses burned down, women kidnapped, villagers terrified, bloodthirsty bandits, and God, God everywhere to control the dance of death, little by little I learned the names of the cities and hamlets, Blida, Medea, viciously, I began with seven decapitated monks' heads seven red roses their eyes half-open onto their advanced age the Tibhirine affair on May 21, 1996 which was the beginning of my two Algerian years at the Boulevard Mortier, the marshal with the long saber—he too had used it from Jemappes to Russia, maybe he had decapitated robed monks, women, children, in the imperial storm, every morning I thought of him, of his uniform, his epaulettes as I went to my ultra-secure hideaway to deal with my files, in the heavy grey atmosphere of that world of secrecy where I read my reports of throat-slittings and military operations without understanding a word, without talking to anyone about it, I burrowed into the Zone without passion but also without disgust, with an increasing curiosity about the dealings of the wrathful gods, patiently in my armored tent I guarded the hollow vessels, I defended Algeria from itself in the darkness, and just afterwards, as I took the metro, when I went home to Rue Caulaincourt, I always saluted Mortier on the boulevard plaque, my guardian angel, knowing that I was very likely being followed and observed by my own colleagues who had to make absolutely sure, all throughout my first year—civil servant trainee, beginning spy—that I was not in the pay of foreign nations or God knows what extremist movement, I could verify this recently when I read, almost ten years later, the report of the preliminary security investigation on me, a strange mirror, a dried-out life, a leaf in an information herbarium, dates places names suspicions psychological outlines relationships guilty or not family assessment of the case officer and so on up to codes references additions classifications assignments various notes absences requests for leave like those that led me to Athens passing through Parma to escape for a few days the Algerian horror and the dead monks they had dumped on me so I could archive the massacre out of sight so I could give a plausible version of the incredible confusion of the Algiers station, Parma I remember I had dinner there not far from the baptistery and the cathedral, thinking about the Farnese family dukes of Parma and Piacenza, about Marie Louise the empress, above all not about Algeria or Croatia or anything having to do with war, except for the pyre of a strange monk, Gherardo Segarelli burnt by the inquisitors in 1300, a preacher of evangelical poverty for whom it wasn't a sin to lie down naked next to a woman without being married, and to touch, Segarelli wanted to rediscover the beauty of apostolic love, poverty generosity and the caresses of female bodies, he paced up and down Parma with his followers preaching until an inquisitor got hold of him hauled him in for questioning and decided to condemn him to the stake, Segarelli did not fear death, he thought that the decadence of the Church was one of the signs of the end of days, that they were all going to die, all the prelates the bishops they'd all end up in hell, when the flames licked him Segarelli screamed, to the great delight of the spectators, his head fell onto his chest, his body burned for a long time, attached to the post, then the two executioners broke his bones in the still-smoking logs, threw his half-carbonized limbs on top of each other in a pile and covered them with another batch of wood, taking care to salvage the still intact heart of the monk of love in order to place it on top of the fire and thus be certain that it would burn completely, then the next morning, once the man was completely reduced to ashes, once they were sure that Gherardo Segarelli could no longer take part in the resurrection of the body on the Day of Judgment, the two sinister vergers scattered his grey powdery remains in the Parma River, tittering giddily—sitting on a terrace near the square where the eternal Church had tortured the monk who sought perfection in the coming together of bodies, my car parked in a garage nearby, I was crossing Italy seemingly the most civil country in the world to get a ferry in Bari to see the Acropolis before losing myself in the islands, eating squid salad and lamb kebabs, in the heat of the evening, the reflections of the fishing lamps on the Aegean and I'd happily go and forget myself in the windy winter of the Cyclades now change trains in Bologna go back to Bari cruise off Albania or go to Sicily island of the end of the world sit down in the Greek theater in Taormina and watch the bay of Naxos bathe the hillsides, but I have to finish the sale hand over the suitcase stay in Rome for Sashka with the angelic smile remake my life as they say with the price of treason which isn't much the money accumulated in my spy's account, erase everything empty myself of my man's life finish my share of existence leave trains journeys movement in general listen to the marine forecast far inland in a deep armchair, that's it for adventure without adventure files sources endless investigations into the networks of the world that continually meet and meet again, train tracks, fasces of spears, rifles with bayonets joined, *fascis* of lictors, whose rods whipped the condemned and whose axes decapitated them, those same fasces from which Mussolini would make his and his empire's emblem, the world surrounded by spikes rods and an axe, everywhere: I meet myself in Milan or in Parma, I check up on myself like my sources on the Boulevard Mortier, and yesterday, tidying up my desk for the last time before going to wander alone through deserted Paris and missing the plane, my empty desk in fact for you never leave anything trailing behind, the usage guide the dictionary a box of paper clips I thought of all the names I had encountered all the places all the affairs the files on site or abroad the long list of those I had observed for a while just as I am now observing the passengers in this oppressively hot train car, the crossword enthusiast and his wife, I could offer them my dictionary for their puzzles if they weren't Italian, my neighbor the *Pronto* reader, in front of me the heads I can glimpse, a blond girl, a bald man, further on boy scouts or something similar with scarves and whistles on a chain, I can still see them with my eyes closed, a professional habit maybe, when the first thing they teach you, in a spy's training, is the art of passing by unperceived while nothing escapes you, the theory of the butterfly net, said my instructor, you have to be transparent invisible discreet but with your net taut, information agencies are establishments of light-hearted and usually bucolic butterfly hunters, which greatly amused Sashka the first time she asked me my profession, I'm an entomologist, a natural historian, a hunter of insects I said, she replied laughing that I didn't have the build, that I was much too serious for such an activity, but it's a serious discipline, completely serious, I said, and I added that I divided my time between the office and research trips, like any good scientist, that I was a civil servant, like any good French scientist—she confessed that she hated insects, that they frightened her, an unreasonable fear, like lots of people, I said, lots of people are afraid of insects that's because they're not familiar with them I could have talked to her about the stick insect, the dormant kind that camouflages itself as a tree branch and waits for years before it acts, or about the Coleopteran, which you have to spot when it's still a larva, before it flies away and becomes much harder to catch, about the suitcase-carrying dung beetles, the midges, tiny informers, the big blue carrion flies, the ants with or without wings, the army of cockroaches, we call informers cockroaches too, that whole invisible world in my office but I said nothing, and now in this train near Parma, so much for insects but the specialist's reflexes still remain, the discretion of the professional observer, the information man, defense attaché, this Henri Fabre of shadows, who wants to hang up his net and his magnifying glass, stop seeing the faces of his travel companions, stop noticing the wine stain on the shirt of the crossword-solving Hemingway or the absolutely submissive air of his young companion, I can't wait to arrive, I can't wait to arrive now that I think of Sashka she's not waiting for me or else not really what will I say to her I'm still all sticky from the night before still shaky from the alcohol, a little feverish, last night comes back to me with a big wave of shame, the door closed on the darkness on Hades devourer of warriors life in parentheses on a train taking me to Rome, to her clear gaze—she'll look surprised when she sees me, seeing me in this state, transparent wide open from alcohol and night, from the meetings in the night, yesterday when I left the Boulevard Mortier for the last time I wandered from bar to bar in Montmartre until I ended up dead drunk ethereal like a soothsayer an oracle foreseeing the end of the world and all that follows, meetings hesitations wars global warming the cold colder the heat hotter Spaniards fleeing the desert to take refuge in Dunkirk the palm trees in Strasbourg but for now outside it's freezing it's raining the Alps were full of snow this morning I saw almost nothing I snoozed to the rhythm of the train from the Gare de Lyon after two hours of sleep a horrible awakening an aspirin and half an amphetamine to make the journey even harder—but I didn't know I was going to miss the plane, that I'd run to catch the nine o'clock train, just barely and without a ticket, my breath must have frightened the conductor, always these difficulties in leaving, after Marianne's kick in the balls ten years ago another kind of pain in my testicles today, shame makes me shiver, I squeeze my eyelids shut until I crush an angry tear of regret for last night, that night the absurd encounter of alcohol drugs and desire, at the Pomponette on the Rue Lepic the only bar in the neighborhood that's open until 4:00 or 5:00 A.M., old Montmartre joint that you always leave staggering, yesterday aside from the regulars there was a woman in her sixties very thin with a long angular face what came over me, she was very surprised by my interest, mistrustful, I broke loosely into her solitude, smiling, she couldn't make up her mind about me and I desired her, her name was Françoise, she was drinking a lot too, I don't know why I went over to her, I'd rather not think about it, night entomologist pinning that insect maybe, I could have told her I want to pin you violently if I had thought about anything but I just kissed her out of mischievousness in fact as a dare out of joy at my last Parisian night her tongue was very thick and bitter she was drinking liqueur I turn my eyes away from the window I observe the companion of the crossword-Hemingway, there's an elegant weariness in her features, she has lain her head on the man's shoulder her hair loose now is slightly covering the crossword journal—Françoise didn't talk about pinning, she said I want you to plow me, she talked to me about plowing her, in my ear, with a lot of modesty, she said I want you to plow me thinking it was a euphemism, because I want it she said, and that's what happened, a plowing, nothing more, her eyes wide open onto nothing like a blind person, her wrinkles became furrows in the half-light, in the weak oblique light from the street, she wanted to stay in the dark, ground floor former concierge box on the Rue Marcadet a plowing without any preliminaries she went to the bathroom quickly without saying a word or even turning back, and once the stupor of orgasm was over I understood that she wasn't going to come out again until I left, that she was just as ashamed as I was once desire was slaked I got dressed in a minute I slammed the door to take refuge in the fresh air under the rain that hadn't stopped, wet dog with his caudal appendage sticky in his trousers, the pitch-black night and the return to the bar all full of shame stupid and filthy, sent to the bottom with one more little humiliation, as I looked for my change I lightly nicked the pad of my index finger against the condom wrapper stuffed without thinking back into my pocket and now fifteen hours later there's a little diagonal wound on the finger that I crush against the cold window: I regret I don't know why I regret, you regret so many things in life memories that sometimes return burning, guilt regrets shame that are the weight of Western civilization if I had caught the plane I'd have been in Rome for hours already, I turn round once more in my seat my head facing right towards the great void outside, going backwards, I'm going backwards my back to my destination and to the meaning of history which is facing forward, history which is taking me directly to the Vatican, with a suitcase full of names and secrets: I'll find Sashka in Rome, her fat cat, the apartment, her short hair in my hands and that strange silence there is between us, as if through her ignorance I could erase the weight of remorse, the women, the insects, the traces, the war, The Hague, the ghosts of my Service files, Algeria first of all, then the Middle East, and recently I dreamed of a post to South America, for a change of polluted air, names, and languages, maybe that's the reason for this journey, moving through phonemes as if into a new world, neither my father's language nor my mother's, a third language, another one, and in the rhythm of this monotonous train rewrite myself to be reborn when I get out—the tired traveler invents idiotic games for himself, memories, daydreams, companions to pass the time since the landscape is completely invisible in the night, unable to sleep, I see again despite myself the photos of the Tibhirine monks faces without bodies I had a copy of them in my file, immortalized by the Algerian embassy, the first shock of my new life as a spy that all of a sudden brought me back to wounds to massacres to revenges to the cold rage of revenge the muddy blackened heads I was entering the Zone entering Algerian land that brought forth limbs and corpses more abundantly than Bosnia, then the long carefully recorded list only grew, Sidi

Moussa, Bentalha, Relizane, one after the other, stories of axes and knives in the shadows in the flames the scenarios all identical: a few hundred meters away from a post of the Algerian army a band of terrorists got into the village began systematically massacring the population women men men women children newborns their throats cut their bellies ripped open burned shot slammed against walls skulls burst jewelry torn from fingers from wrists with axes beautiful virgins carried off into the mountains as spoils the share of honor for the conquerors with no enemies in the night and the warriors killed killed killed villagers just as poor as they or farmers even poorer, there was nothing in our notes and our reports, nothing whatsoever aside from endless torrents of blood names of villages and emirs scrublands chaparral touched by the fury of Ares, bearded men who spoke more and more incomprehensibly, more and more abstrusely, who spoke of Satan and God of the vengeance of God of all those farmers those Algerians who were infidels and deserved to die, the translators transcribed into French for me the pamphlets the declarations of war the anathemas the insults against the West the army the government farmers women alcohol livestock life and God himself whom they ended up excommunicating because he was too forgiving in their eyes, they worshipped their saber their rifle their leader and when they weren't fighting amongst themselves they went cheerfully off to massacre and raid in darkness, in front of my civil servant's eyes, why didn't they provide night vision equipment in the Algerian army, that was their only excuse for not intervening, they were blind, night was night it belonged to the warriors and I knew better than anyone the terror of combat in the dark, in the midst of civilians between houses they could do nothing—but without provoking it terror suited them, turmoil favored them, Europe had no other choice than to support their dying regime against the barbarism and extremism to protect the oil the mines the villagers the workers the laypeople the infidels the liberals the region the quaking Tunisians and Moroccans, they had to hold firm, the Trojans were outside the ramparts, about to invade the camp and push us out to sea in our hollow vessels, the Islamists were the common enemy and this already before 2001, before the Great Accord that would have us exchanging terrorists galore, the Great Cleanup, suspects activists of all kinds sent off to Guantánamo, chucked out of planes in the middle of the Indian Ocean, tortured in Pakistani or Egyptian cellars, lists and more lists as long as possible until the Iraqi bone of contention, Troy took ten years to fall, and in my well-guarded office I began as an accountant of bodies, like someone who becomes a referee after having been a boxer and himself no longer touches the faces that explode beneath fists, he counts the blows, I gave Algeria beaten down by KOs several chances, and even raised high the arms of winners in my endless reports: Lebihan my boss constantly congratulated me on my prose, you'd think you were there he said, you are the all-round champion of notes, but couldn't you be a little drier, get a little more to the point, just think, if everyone were like you we wouldn't know if we were coming or going, but bravo my good man bravo—poor Lebihan, he constantly had health problems, never very serious, always very annoying, hives, pruritus, alopecia, all kinds of fungus, he was nice to me, he addressed me with the formal "vous," I never knew anything about him or almost nothing, aside from the fact that he came from Lille, which his name did not suggest (if that really was his name), and that he wore a wedding ring—he was a specialist in the ISF, the GIA, all sorts of more or less violent movements, we'd find their names and their members' names for years to come scattered throughout the four corners of the globe, sometimes with a different spelling or nickname, sometimes in a list of those "presumed dead," because of the problems in Arabic transcription there were guys with us who had three or four index cards that had to be grouped together, some died three times in a row in three different places and finding a man was not always easy, even if that wasn't our main objective, as Lebihan gently pointed out to me, the threats against internal security are the concern of the DST, the internal state security department, and cops didn't at all mind throwing a spanner in our works whenever they could, convinced that we'd do likewise, which was no doubt the case—in the incredible muddle of the affair of the Tibhirine monks everyone had taken credit for himself, Foreign Affairs, the Service, everyone, and afterwards, when the DST picked up an Algerian officer who had "gone over to France" or an Islamist who asked for asylum, they kept the information to themselves, carefully doling out what might be useful to us in dribs and drabs, like us, more or less, with the information the agent gathered, those false solitary diplomats, immured in their embassy whose only contact with the outside was their precious "sources": I went there one time, with an Agency passport and an assumed name, barely forty-eight hours, just enough time to meet the two guys we had over there and a local soldier whose name I forget, Algiers the white city was grey, dead after sunset, drowned beneath the unemployed and the dust, Cervantes the survivor of Lepanto had spent five years here in captivity, dreaming of escape plans just like the Islamists in the government jails, we had a meeting with the "source" in a magnificent villa atop the city, which I was allegedly supposed to be renting, an immense furnished villa, with a pool, property of a merchant who had taken refuge in Nice—the contact was brief, I remember his swaggering air, almost scornful of us, and the fear, the great fear we could still sense in his voice: the deal was clear, he wanted to go to Paris, get a residency permit and money for sensitive information, they all dreamed of the same thing, they thought they were selling themselves at a high price and didn't realize that for us the price was laughable, that any engineer in pharmaceuticals or biotechnologies was worth ten or fifteen times more than they, the third world remains the third world even in the most specialized transactions, the advantage of the cost of living, and I myself if I think about it carefully I could have sold myself for much more, who knows, if I had offered my documents elsewhere, that's the law of the trade, the seller fixes the price, I could have included my room at the Plaza in it and a piece of the true Cross and they would have agreed, what's a little money compared to Eternity—Cervantes was ransomed by a congregation of monks for 500 escudos just as he was about to be deported to Istanbul, in 1996 Algiers the white smelled of sweat burnt tires hot oil and cumin, I had put places and landscapes into my notes, faces, smells into my summaries, fear, the mustiness of fear that reminded me of the odors of Mostar and Vitez, the Islamists were afraid of the army, the army was afraid of the Islamists and the civilians were dying of fear of everyone, cornered between the saber of the true Faith and the combat tanks of the *toughât*, the "tyrants" of the government, Algiers the white where my father served, between 1958 and 1960, I see myself exchanging impressions with him, memories—of course against all the rules of security I had spoken to him about my trip, he was very surprised, in this day and age, he said, ever since my return from Croatia he looked at me suspiciously, always trying to stare straight into my eyes, maybe to find the traces of war there, I didn't understand why, I would understand later on, for now I was learning little by little to distinguish the parties, the emirs, the factions, and the tiny groups and I had my work cut out for me, as they say, to train myself in my Zone, I was sinking into it without realizing it, now I've become an expert, a specialist in politico-religious madness which is an increasingly widespread pathology, which is spreading the way the fungi or pustules spread on Lebihan's body, now there isn't one country that doesn't have its future terrorists, extremists, Salafists, jihadis of all sorts and Parma that's fleeing into the night with its Napoleonic nobility is giving me a headache, or maybe it's fear, fear panic of darkness and pain

everything is harder once you reach man's estate, living shut up inside yourself harried destitute full of memories I'm not taking this trip for nothing, I'm not curling up like a dog on this seat for nothing, I'm going to save something I'm going to save myself despite the world that persists in going forward laboriously at the speed of a handcar operated by a man with one arm, blindly a train at night in a tunnel the dark even denser I had to sleep for a bit, if only I had a watch, I just have a telephone, it's in my jacket hanging on the hook, but if I take it out I'll be tempted to see if I have any messages and to send one, always this passion for writing into the distance, sending signs into the ether like smoke signals gestures with no object arms hands stretching out to nothingness, to whom could I send a message, from this pre-paid phone that I took care to get a tramp to purchase for me in return for a big tip, as luck would have it he had an identity card and wasn't too wasted, the seller didn't cause any trouble, I left my apartment dropped off a few things at my mother's sold my books in bulk to a bookseller at the Porte de Clignancourt took three or four things, as I was sorting through things I of course came across some photos, I saw Andrija again in his over-sized uniform, Marianne in Venice, Sashka at twenty in Leningrad, La Risiera camp in Trieste, the square chin of Globocnik, Gerbens's mustache, I took everything, and I can say that everything I own is above me in a slightly scaled-down bag, next to the little briefcase that's going to the Vatican and that I plan to hand over as soon as I reach Rome, then tonight in my room at the Plaza on the Via del Corso I'll go drink at the hotel bar until it closes and tomorrow morning I'll take a bath buy myself a new suit I'll be another man I'll call Sashka or I'll go straight to her place I'll ring at her door and God knows what will happen, Zeus will decide the fate that's suitable to allot me the Moirae will bustle about for me in their cave and what will happen will happen we'll see if war will catch up with me again or if I'll live to be old watching my children grow up the children of my children hidden away somewhere on an island or a suburban condo what could I possibly be living on, what, like Eduardo Rózsa I could tell the story of my life write books and screenplays for autobiographical films—Rózsa born in Santa Cruz de la Sierra in Bolivia of a communist Jewish father a resistant in Budapest was the special correspondent for a Spanish paper in Zagreb before he became a commander in the Croatian army, I met him once or twice on the front and later in Iraq, an admirer of Che Guevara and war who founded our international brigade, a group of volunteers who spoke English among themselves Warriors of the Great Free and Independent Croatia who all arrived like me after the first images of the Yugoslav madness, Eduardo was already there, he landed in Croatia in August 1991 one month before me during Osijek and the first clashes, he came from Albania and before that from Budapest and Russia where he trained for espionage for guerilla warfare for comparative literature and philosophy, a poet—today he writes books collections of poems and plays himself in films, maybe Che Guevara would have ended up the same if he hadn't made Achilles's choice, if he had been given life he too might have become—weapons put away, life over—an actor, he was so good-looking: like Hemingway Eduardo Rózsa wrote fast, I picture him on an August night on the terrace of the Hotel Intercontinental in Zagreb where all the foreign press stayed, the *Vanguardia* from Barcelona reproached him for describing the fighting too much and for not talking enough about politics, he downed shots as he described the first battles, the Yugoslav tanks against the shabby Croats, his hotel room was transformed into a real War Museum, pieces of shrapnel ammunition the tail-ends of rockets maps relics of all kinds, Eduardo a funny character idealist warrior converted to Islam after having fought for the Catholic crucifix, vice president of the Muslim community of Hungary, formerly press secretary for the first free Iraqi government, men want causes, gods that inspire them, and in that scorching August of 1991 in front of the Intercontinental's pool his R5 riddled with bullets in the garage his pen in hand he thought about the Bolivian sierra about socialism about Che and his old hole-filled uniform, he had just been shot at by Serbs on the highway from Belgrade, he writes his article, it was the first time he was under fire, the half-open window shattered to pieces, the passenger seat opened up suddenly spitting out its stuffing with hisses and metal clangor, with the speed and distance he probably didn't hear the explosions, he swerved turned off the headlights instinctively and kept going straight ahead his hands damp clutching the steering wheel sweat in his eyes up to the suburbs of Zagreb, up to the hotel, up to the foreign colleagues the two French photographers who were sharing his room, they see Eduardo arriving dripping with sweat beside himself those two twenty-five-year-old journalists also came to Croatia to get shot at and to run around the countryside with Yugoslav tanks on their tail, to them Eduardo is a master, a man of experience and now he's arriving trembling and sweating, he says nothing, he takes out his notebook and quietly goes to get drunk on plum brandy by the pool watching the American reporters laughing in the water at their cameraman's jokes, that's where it happens, touched by Zeus Eduardo *Che* Rózsa chose his camp, the next day in Osijek he'll go see the Croatian officers, he'll enlist, join the Achaean ranks in a fine rage, a rage against the Serbs: the journalists saw him one fine day in a khaki uniform, a rifle on his shoulder and when I arrived at the end of September he had abandoned the pen to devote himself to war, he would come back decorated medaled honorary citizen of the new Croatia, a hero, godfather of I don't know how many children, and he would write his exploits himself, play his own role in the film—the first time I saw him it wasn't on the screen, he was sitting in the middle of the trench in which I was crawling in Osijek, I was scared stiff, absolutely clueless, the shells were raining down in front of us there was the Yugoslav army its tanks and its elite troops, I didn't know where I was going I climbed up the trench my nose in the autumn smell, in the humus, to escape, to go home, to find again the attic room and Marianne's caresses, I couldn't hear anything and I couldn't see much I had glimpsed my first wounded man fired my first cartridges at a hedge, the uniform of the national guard was just a hunting jacket that didn't protect much I was shivering trembling like a tree under the explosions Rózsa was sitting there I crawled right onto him he looked at me and smiled, he gently moved the muzzle of my gun away with his foot, had me sit down, he must have said something to me of which I have no memory and when our people began firing he's the one who propped me up against the parapet with a pat on the back so I'd start shooting too, before he disappeared, Athena comes to breathe courage and ardor into mortals in battle, and I fired calmly, I fired well before jumping out of the trench with the others, fear evaporated, flew away with the shells towards the enemy and the farm we were supposed to take, far from Zagreb, far from the Hotel Intercontinental from its covered pool its terrace and its sauna that I had never seen, far from Paris, *Che* Rózsa would continue his career, I heard his name many times during the war, heroic and other more mysterious deeds, like the murder of a Swiss journalist accused of espionage for I don't know whom, some people thought he had come to infiltrate the brigade: he was found dead by strangulation during a patrol, a dozen days before the British photographer Paul Jenks was shot in the back of the head as he was investigating the previous man's death, heroes are often wreathed in shadows, marked by Hades great eater of warriors, Eduardo as well as others, even though in those days journalists were falling like flies, in Croatia at least, or later on around besieged Sarajevo—in central Bosnia, between Vitez and Travnik, they made themselves much scarcer, aside from a few reporters from the television channel owned by the HDZ, the Croatian party in Bosnia, who had the strange habit of emerging from nowhere, like a jack-in-the-box, of appearing at the unlikeliest times and some British reporters clinging to the white tanks of the nuisances from BRITFOR—those photographers and journalists were plying a strange trade indeed, public spies in a way, professional informers for public opinion, for the majority, we saw them that way, high-end informers who hated us as much as Her Majesty's soldiers scorned us, frustrated by inaction their hands on the triggers of their 30-millimeter guns, perched on top of their Warriors painted white, ice-cream trucks they were called in Croatia, what possible use could they serve, they collected the corpses and negotiated cease-fires so they could go on leave to Split, where they swam, danced, drank whisky before returning to count the shots in Travnik, through binoculars at their windows, or to jog around the stadium—Eduardo *Che* Rózsa ex-secret agent ex-journalist ex-commander of one of the best-organized brigades in eastern Slavonia writer poet screenwriter turned Muslim and activist for Iraq and Palestine, in Budapest in his suburban house, is he thinking about the Chetniks he killed, about his first two dead, torn to pieces by a grenade in a barn by the Drava River, about his comrades fallen like mine, is he still thinking about the war, about Croatia, he a Catholic by his mother a communist by his father, a murderer by the grace of God, does he remember the freezing rain of the winter of 1991 in the outskirts of Osijek, Eduardo who grew up in Chile until the coup against Allende, deported to Budapest on a chartered flight of foreign "Reds" who couldn't be sent to the firing squad or tortured, Eduardo going in the opposite direction from me began in intelligence before he became a journalist, then a volunteer to fight with the Croats, by our side, and returned, enriched with wisdom's store, to live in Hungary through his remaining years, in poetry screenplays books strange missions, plus everything I don't know about him probably, Eduardo *Che* Rózsa who didn't recognize me when we met in Baghdad by the Tigris not long after the invasion, between a cheap restaurant and a peanut-vendor, during the fleeting euphoria of victory, of dictatorship overthrown, justice restored—the treasures of Troy were still burning, manuscripts, works of art, old men, children, while already the coalition forces were congratulating each other on the river's shores, not worrying about the first attacks, the signs of a catastrophe of the same caliber as the one in the 1920s, or even worse, Eduardo Rózsa was strolling in the company of a few officials by the eternal Tigris, I was eating a corncob from a street vendor with a guy from the embassy, I had just met Sashka and I didn't want war or peace or the Zone or to remember Croatia or Bosnia I wanted to go back to Rome even for just twenty-four hours to be with her, and then Commander Rózsa walks by without seeing me, a ghost, was I the ghost or him, I had already begun to disappear I was burying myself little by little in the contents of the suitcase, in Sashka whom I thought I'd seen for the first time in Jerusalem years before, in Iraq the heat was incredible, a damp vapor rising from the slow Tigris bordered with reeds where from time to time corpses and decaying carcasses ran aground like the Sava River in 1942 without perturbing the American patrols who were still strolling about like Thomson and Thompson in Tintin a blissful look on their faces as they observed around them the country they had just conquered which they didn't know what to do with, Baghdad was drifting, ungovernable like Jerusalem or Algiers, it was decomposing, an atom bombarded by neutrons, hunger, sickness, ignorance, mourning, pain, despair without really understanding why the gods were persecuting it so, destroyed, sent back into limbo, into prehistory the way the Mongols did in 1258, libraries, museums, universities, ministries, hospitals ravaged, Rózsa and I the ex-warriors come to share the spoils or inhale its remains, as specialists of defeat, of victory, of the New World Order, of the peace of the brave, of weapons of mass destruction that gave the soldiers a good laugh, they slapped each other on the back as they drank their Budweisers like after a good joke, in Basra the British were the same as in Bosnia, very sportsmanlike, professional and indifferent, they unloaded humanitarian aid trucks as I'd seen them do in Travnik, as Rózsa had seen them in Osijek, except this time they were authorized to use their weapons, which they weren't shy about using: they hunted former Ba'athists the way others hunt deer or rather wild boar in the Ardennes, the English soldiers were returning to

Basra, to the same place where their grandfathers had been stationed in 1919, after the Dardanelles, after the Hejaz and Syria, the exhausted Tommies rested their legs in the country of palm trees and dried lemons, by the edge of the swamps and meanderings of the Shatt al-Arab, they stuffed their faces with dates and lambs stolen from native shepherds, wondering how much longer the war would last, it lasts forever, almost a century after Gavrilo Princip's Balkan gunshot, the referee's pistol shot in a long-distance race, all the participants are already at the starting line, ready to dash forward into the world of Ares great eater of warriors, hoping to return loaded with treasure and glory: *Che* Rózsa commander covered in medals from the great patriotic Croatian war, Vlaho or me decorated with the order of the grateful nation, Andrija with a fine black marble tombstone with no corpse, *To our brother the Hero*, he no longer has a body, Andrija, no bones beneath his slab, no gold pin on his jacket he's a name a phrase a brother and a hero, I was thinking of him in Baghdad conquered humiliated subjected and pillaged as I passed Rózsa the Hungarian from Bolivia a convert to Islam and to international aid, president of the Muslim community of Budapest, or something like that, after having been a fervent defender of Opus Dei, was he informing for the Hungarians, or the Russians, or the English, were we still colleagues, colleagues of the shadows—in the night of war, of the Zone, of memories of the dead, we were living together, without seeing each other, we were sharing the same life, passing each other by the edge of the Tigris, that Styx like the Tiber like the Jordan the Nile or the Danube like all those deadly rivers running into the sea, river of urine along a wall, fluvial ways intersect each other like railroads and weave a spiderweb around the void, in the center the hollow sea abstract and moving, ink-black at night water-green during the day and steel-blue at dawn, I always wondered *why* Eduardo Rózsa had joined the Croats, why those volunteers, that international brigade of which I could have been a member, he says in his books that he was fighting for *Justice*, to help the weak against the strong, the Serbs though also felt their rights were being threatened, they were defending their land, which was their land because their houses and their dead were there, and volunteers came to their aid too, just as Rózsa and his people came to the Croats or the mujahideen came to the Bosnians, they all saw an international affair in it, a fight of right against wrong, aside from Rózsa's more or less apolitical comrades there was in Croatia a group of foreign fighters in the ranks of the HOS, the Croatian extreme right, neo-fascists who knew the Ustashi songs by heart, Frenchmen mostly, I knew a few of them by sight, glimpsed at a rally in Paris, it's a small world when it comes to that community, I saw them again in arms outside of Okučani then later in Zagreb, they were cheerful coarse soldiers, they were happy to be there—as Le Pen said the one-eyed nationalist ocular emulator of Millán-Astray *military experience is always good for the little ones*, he had had his own in Algeria, and the networks of international solidarity sent recruits to paint their faces green and learn the language in old songs from the 1940s, I could have been one of them, I could have been one of them that's for sure if I hadn't set out on a completely different tangent, at bottom we were all volunteers, even Vlaho who had deserted the Yugoslav army in the middle of his military service almost 700 kilometers away from home to join the ranks of the national guard right where he was, near Osijek, he had stayed with us, Vlaho the Dalmatian, despite the cold and the rain that froze his bones, and yet God knows he was fat when he arrived, fat, gentle, and funny, with a completely round, angelic face, Vlaho was a volunteer like Andrija like me like the French of the HOS like Eduardo Rózsa, like Orwell during the Spanish War, like Blaise Cendrars in Champagne in '14, just as Sashka's half-brother, Kolia, had fought at the side of the Serbs, Slavic Orthodox solidarity against Catholic Slavs, ex-communists against ex-fascists, she hadn't seen him for years she told me, Kolia the skinny mystic back from Afghanistan had wandered round aimlessly in too-confining Russia at the end of the 1980s before launching into a military adventure with the Chetniks, *sajkaca* on his head, probably whistling Tchaikovsky's *Marche Slave*, I can see Sashka lying on her blue sofa in Trastevere when she finds out I was a soldier in Croatia she says what a coincidence, my brother was at war with the Serbs, *was at war*, those are her words, *moj brat pobyval na vojne*, the paths of Slavitude meet in the lines of fire, *where* was he, I ask her, *gdje*, I might have seen him, maybe we sized each other up through our Kalashnikovs, maybe he killed one of my comrades, maybe one of his shells hurled us head over heels into the soft mud of the corn fields, she replies *in Serbia, konjechno*, the clear eyes of Sashka on her sofa don't understand the question, she doesn't see the war, she can't understand, I should be clearer, I know it's pointless—in the Slavic-Latin pidgin we speak there's no room for the nuances of war, we had so few words in common, old Slavic words and Italian terms that were transparent in French, too few to shed light on the motivations of international volunteers Russian French or Arab and that's all the better, imprecision the impossibility of going into detail, everything stays outside when I'm with her, the war, the Zone, the suitcase I'm filling, meaning passes through hands through hair through Sashka's immense gaze the coincidences that link us to each other the railroad tracks of the past that intersect, in Jerusalem, in Rome, like with Eduardo Rózsa my Hungarian double converted to poetry and international politics, what could I explain about my involvement—leaving for a noble cause, the cause of my Habsburg ancestors who had defended Vienna against the Turks, the cause of my maternal family, the bourgeoisie of Zagreb linked to Austria and Italy, Mama cried from sadness and joy when I left, I know she went to church every day to pray for me, and my father without admitting to praying as such thought again about his own war, his two years in Algeria, quite happy that my own *had some meaning*, as he said, even if that meaning escaped him a little, he knew almost nothing of Croatia, aside from a few of his wife's cousins, but respected passion for one's Country, himself a discreet French Catholic nationalist, an engineer without much curiosity about the world, a little self-effacing, but tender and attentive—I remember the huge electric train he had laid out for us, a whole network on giant wooden planks, patiently, dozens of trees, tracks, switches, signal lights, stations, and villages, all controlled by transformers, complex potentiometers that regulated the speed of the engines passing each other, waiting for each other, turning on their red headlights in the Christmas dusk, getting lost in tunnels beneath plastic mountains covered with a too-green, rough grass smelling of glue mixed with the ozone smell of all those electric motors functioning at once, from the switch-yard to the level crossing, meters and meters of little red and blue cables ran alongside the tracks nailed to the board, for the street lights, the gates, the houses, I remember there was a freight train with a steam engine, a grey German military transport, French passenger cars, for years in the basement of our house in Orléans we added tracks trees scenery trains to this fantastic assemblage built on the HO scale, I can imagine the fortune swallowed up little by little by this set that's sleeping in boxes today, since our move to Paris and the painstaking dismantling of the installation that put a precise end to childhood, farewell small-scale models make way for real trains like this one, somewhere between Parma and Reggio Emilia—Eduardo Rózsa writes in one of his books about the anger of his communist father when he learned that his son was fighting beside the Croats, fascists, he thought, descendants of the Ustashis of the NDH, *Nezavisna Država Hrvatska*, the Independent State of Croatia of 1941: the truth is there were loads of neo-Nazis, hooked on the mythology of victory over the Serbs, on the mythology of the single "independent" Croatian State scoured clean by the partisans, we all had Faith, we were all taking part in history rifle in hand feet in questionable socks with a fresh lungful of air our eyes full of pride for God and the homeland for vengeance for our dead for our children yet to come for the land for our ancestors buried in the land, against Serbian injustice, then for our comrades maybe also for the pleasure of it a taste for steel the pleasure of war the glory of honor fear danger laughter power our honed bodies our scars, and in the tiny apartment in Trastevere it was impossible for me to explain all that to Sashka, just as she couldn't explain the feelings of her half-brother, they didn't interest her, she hadn't seen him since she left Petersburg in 1993, just when Kolia came back from the war, she had left fled to Jerusalem City of Peace, of light and eternal violence, where I like to think I saw her, when she was painting fake Russian icons for American tourists near the Damascus Gate, an angel on her shoulder, I came across her there that's for sure just as I exchanged bullets with her half-brother around Vukovar, just as trains passed each other on two separate tracks on my father's plank table, just as I met Eduardo Rózsa ten years later in Baghdad without his seeing me, by the edge of the river—and the thousands of documents in the briefcase that the train is conveying across the Italian countryside are nothing but that, intersections, men glimpsed in Cairo in Trieste or Rome, it was simple, you just had to uncoil the lines follow the tracks wait to meet them at night in my own night gaining on the landscape and the food-processing plants in the region of Parmesan and pasta: the crossword enthusiast has gotten up to go to the bathroom, my neighbor is quietly snoozing, the car is silent, he is snoring or whistling, I don't know, according to the movement of the tracks, I close my eyes, where would I like to go now, to Beirut the blue to find the Palestinians again and Intissar in the little cream-colored book, not yet, or to Iraq country of hunger and death and Babel, to Troy maybe with Marianne, to the Homeric Dardanelles, to

Mycenae city of Agamemnon shepherd of warriors, it overlooks the plain of beautiful mares, far from the mounds and hills near Hisarlik, far from the trenches and ravines where the dehydrated bodies of English and Australian soldiers piled up in 1915, water had to be conveyed there by boat in immense metal vats, I'm thirsty all of a sudden, maybe the crossword enthusiast went to the bar not the toilet, from the Dardanelles to Iraq, from Troy to Babylon, from Achilles to Alexander, thinking again about Heinrich Schliemann the discoverer of Ilion the well-guarded, from Mycenae adorned with gold, to Arthur Evans knight of Her Majesty's Empire who until his ninetieth year pursued adventure in Crete at Knossos, pipe in his mouth, convinced he had discovered the labyrinth and sanctuary of the potent bulls, and I too, in a way I am an archeologist, brush in hand I search through and probe vanished, buried things, to make them rise up from corpses, from skeletons, from fragments, debris stories copied out on coded tablets, my own *Scripta Minoa*, begun by the excavation of Harmen Gerbens the brutal alcoholic rapist in Garden City, and followed by thousands of names of killers and victims, painstakingly annotated, delineated like the charred pottery of Troy VII the mysterious burned city, indexed, classified, without my understanding the reason for my passion, like Schliemann or Evans, pushed always further into endless research, standing over the huge charnel pit of history, feet in the void: when I arrived at the Boulevard Mortier, after having been recruited against all expectation despite my war-filled past and my foreign ancestry, plunged into my solitary Zone peopled with ghosts shadows living or dead in the middle of endless secret archives in those soundproof hallways, those tunnels under the boulevard, every night I walked across Paris up to the 18th arrondissement and my new civil servant's two-room-with-kitchen apartment, thirty square meters of disorder on the sixth floor with no elevator, as it must be, my head beneath the zinc of the Parisian ceiling, my elbow on the zinc of the bar down below, morning and evening, before and after the metro, coffee to go, draft beer on my return, little by little the regulars become the anonymous family of the café-owner patriarch, soldiers of the brewer officer, Jojo Momo Pierre Gilles and the others, madmen and not-so-mad men, alcoholic and sober, loners and family men, some were like cockroaches, impossible to get rid of, others disappeared from one day to the next, and Momo Pierre Gilles and their brothers in bottle speculated then about Jojo's disappearance, cancer, cirrhosis, or that second wound of the drunkard after his disease, the wife, the spouse who forbids you bar games and after-dinner drinks, it went without saying for all these barflies that you never willingly left a good bar once you'd found one, it was as unlikely in their eyes as leaving a comfortable inexpensive apartment to go live in the Salvation Army, Michael the owner reassured his flock about the fate of so-and-so, *I met him in the neighborhood, he's fine*—he was lying that's for sure so as not to frighten his parishioners, out of generosity, Saint Michael the owner had a great tenderness for his inveterate drinkers, and he regarded it as more than a business, an enterprise for public salvation rather, the fashioning of the social bond he willingly took part in by pouring himself a small whisky from time to time, cheerfully paying for a round when he lost at dice, he lavished affection and advice on matters of love, work, or finance, at the level of a small neighborhood bar, where those who managed to run up a tab were rare (*credit is dead, bad debtors killed it*) more out of a sense of education and morality, really, more than out of mistrust or greed, the bar in the 18th, might as well say a bar without a name, without anything special in the décor or the brown leatherette banquettes was a part of my life, every night a beer or two standing at the bar before climbing the well-polished steps to my woman-less and television-less home, during the ascent of my Parisian Olympus I slowly rid myself of the filth of the world of the Boulevard, of the Zone, to enter another—my photos of La Risiera di San Sabba on the wall, next to the picture of Globocnik in Trieste, the one of Stangl in Udine, now the snapshot of Sashka in Petersburg, and in its place, before, nicely framed, the image of Stéphanie on the Bosporus, which I found in a closet and threw into a trashcan yesterday morning, the glass broke immediately with a loud noise, for years every night the same ritual climb the steps get out the long bronze-colored key insert it in the old keyhole open the door smell the odor of cold tobacco sometimes of trash or alcohol go over to the window open the shutters watch the cars pass by in the street for a few seconds put away the empty bottles lying around the clothes scattered about then pick up a book sit down in my armchair with, according to my humor and my resources, a glass of wine or a beer in hand—curious this passion for reading, a remnant from Venice, from Marianne great devourer of books, a way to forget to disappear wholly into paper, little by little I replaced adventure novels with simply novels, Conrad's fault, *Nostromo* and *Heart of Darkness*, one title calls for another, and maybe without really understanding, who knows, I let myself be carried away, page after page, and although I've already spent a large part of my day as an ambiguous functionary reading—notes, reports, forms, on my well-guarded screen—there is nothing I desire more then than a novel, where the people are characters, a play of masks and desires, and little by little to forget myself, forget my body at rest in this chair, forget my apartment building, Paris, life itself as the paragraphs, dialogues, adventures, strange worlds flow by, that's what I should be doing now, going on with Rafael Kahla's story, finding Intissar the Palestinian again and Marwan dead on a corner in Beirut, a journey within the journey, to ward off fatigue, thoughts, the shaky train, and memories—warrior, spy, archeologist of madness, lost now with an assumed name between Milan and Rome, in the company of living ghosts like Eduardo Rózsa the Hungarian righter of wrongs dressed in black who went to Mass willingly, everything I was trying to forget as I read in my armchair in Paris, sinking into the Zone into Algeria of the beheading and the beheaded, the Zone land of the wrathful savage gods who have been clashing with each other endlessly since the Bronze Age at least and maybe even before, since the caves the stone hatchets and the flints that caused spectacular jagged wounds, not counting the maces, clubs, cudgels, bludgeons, ancestors of the hammer of the Stara Gradiška camp with which my Ustashi cousins smashed in Jewish and gypsy Serbian skulls as a boredom-dispelling switch from the knife, at the same time in Trieste at La Risiera the Ukrainian guards were finishing off the Croatian and Slovenian partisans with a fine weapon almost a medieval sledgehammer a cube of sharp metal attached to a thick steel cable with a comfortable wooden handle, who had invented this device, an engineer or a mechanic who knows, maybe his name is somewhere in my suitcase, somewhere, in the Trieste file, city of high winds and nightsticks, with the magnificent synagogue and two Orthodox churches, Serbian and Greek, Trieste port of the Habsburgs since the thirteenth century, through it the bodies of Franz Ferdinand and the beautiful Sophie passed on their way from Sarajevo, the city paid them one last homage, its farewell to the Empire, before sending them by train to Vienna via Klagenfurt, soon the Adriatic port would change hands and nations, would go over to Italy before rediscovering Germanness at the end of 1943, then being stormed by the new Slavs of the South for a few months in 1945: four countries in thirty years, an Austro-Hungarian Italian city annexed to the Reich then to the Yugoslav Republic of Slovenia finally governed by the Anglo-Americans before finding Italy again and falling asleep for a long time in the confines of democratic Europe, tired, deserted by the Jews the Greeks the Germans the Hungarians the Slovenians, cut off at the tip of the Julian Veneto, at the border of red Slavitude, at the edge of deadly Karst, near the gulf well-guarded by the ramshackle castle of Duino where Rilke took advantage in 1912 of the same hospitalities as, thirty years later, the officers of the German navy who set themselves up there, *hiersein ist immer herrlich*, Rilke received by Princess Marie von Thurn und Taxis mocked from afar the somber James Joyce, who at the time was being welcomed by the stiff professors of the Berlitz School and rebuked by his young wife every time he came home drunk, the little uncouth Irishman staggering in the wind, one of many visitors, many train cars that met there, on the endless jetties of a harbor that today is almost deserted, I went there for the first time on leave between two fronts with Andrija and Vlaho, I dragged them to Trieste then Zagreb going through Rijeka the grey and through Opatija the most respectable of Austro-Hungarian seaside resorts where we stayed for about an hour, just long enough to realize that the average age of those taking the curative waters was close to that in Vichy, Evian, or rather Karlovy Vary, it was the end of the winter of 1992, spring hadn't yet arrived, Vlaho, ill, was treating himself with *rakija*, he was vexed because a prostitute had refused to go to bed with him with the excuse that he was sick to death with a cold, he had caused a scandal in the sordid bar in Novi Zagreb, provoking general hilarity, *c'mon, it's just my nose dripping, not the rest, I don't have clap in my schnozzle*—since then he was grumpy, we mischievously suggested he take advantage of the sulfurous waters of Opatija and of the old ladies, surely less demanding than the professionals so careful of their health, what's more all these aged respectable German ladies were certainly there to take care of themselves too, they'd be understanding, Vlaho shrugged his shoulders saying *oh, very funny, very funny, so, where are we going?* and what with one thing leading to another we arrived in Italy, before leaving again for Herzegovina passing through Dalmatia, a two days' rest at the home of the more or less cured Vlaho, insulted all day long by his grandfather the Partisan who raised every glass shouting *smrt fašizmu*, Vlaho answered *heil Hitler* as he emptied his own to enrage him, in the middle of the vines a few kilometers away from Split where the UNPROFOR soldiers were dancing, their helicopters flew over us and we, we had to hitchhike soldier-style to reach Mostar—today these memories are a kind of old Yugoslav movie, the images seem to have aged, grown out-of-date, they're no longer mine, only the sensations remain: shame, fear, pleasure, danger remain, the smells too, the contacts, Andrija's face, Vlaho's hand, clutching his glass or his rifle, he was our dismantling and oiling champion, even the most exotic weapons, the most unlikely ones he could strip them bare almost with his eyes closed, arm a mine or a wire trap as easily as he scratched his ass or blew his nose, without ever realizing, we thought, what he was manipulating, with a dexterity of a rodent with a nut, rapid, precise, he ate in the same way, quickly, his fore-paws joined, his chummy face opened in an immense smile at the sight of drink or food or a new weapon: Vlaho is a field mouse, a dormouse or a rat, and above all a male child, war was his element, for it was simple, funny, and virile, in a world where *becoming a man* didn't mean growing up but sharpening yourself, reducing yourself, pruning yourself like a vine or a tree from which you take away the branches little by little, the female part, or the human part, who knows, a classic garden hedge sculpted into the shape of a warrior, you could just as easily say into the shape of a phallus, a rifle, the male archetype we were all trying to resemble, strong, skillful, prehistoric hunter free of a brain, capable of all kinds of boasts, swaggering, proud but submissive to anyone stronger and to his hierarchical superior, scorning the weak, women and homos, anything that doesn't look like him, in fact, Vlaho, Andrija, the others, and I little by little we were transformed into soldiers, into professionals, of course we squeezed out a tear from time to time, but it was soon hidden and erased disguised as sweat or smoke in the eye, an embrace and there you are, or at least that's what we'd have liked, sometimes everything collapsed, Achilles's shield pierced, the beautiful greaves torn off, the spear broken, and then he was just a naked child curled up calling for his mother or his brothers moaning crying in his sleeping bag or on his stretcher, I remember the day Andrija the invincible collapsed for the first time, the warrior of warriors whom we'd never seen without his shell: around Vitez, one morning like all the others in a village like all the others, when tensions were at their height with the Muslims, a warm morning, a little misty, a munitions transport going north, a few kilometers from Travnik the deadly beauty one fine morning with a smell of spring, with Sergeant Mile and Vlaho the crazy driver at the steering wheel, I don't remember why we stopped near that building, probably because there was a corpse on the threshold, an old man, an entire cartridge clip in his head and chest, machine-gunned from quite close up and his dog too, a Croatian house, the door was open, a smell of incense wafted out as from a church, a dark interior and wood furniture, shutters closed they must have been shot at night, the guy and his mutt, why had he opened his door, why had he gone out, Mile signed to us, a trembling orangey light was coming from a room in the back, a tiny fire, something's burning, all three of us move towards it, Vlaho remains behind to watch the entrance, a big bedroom with candles everywhere, dozens of candles still lit and on the double bed an old lady stretched out her hands on her chest a black or dark-grey dress her eyes closed and I don't understand, Andrija takes off his helmet as a sign of respect, he takes off his helmet sighs and mumbles something, Mile and I imitate him without understanding, all three of us are in the process of watching over an old woman who doesn't know she's a widow, that her husband who lit all these candles for her was shot with his dog on his doorstep by unknown men or neighbors, she has heard nothing, on her deathbed, not the machine-gun volleys outside, not the footsteps in her house, not the laughter of those who jammed that large crucifix straight upright into the middle of her stomach, its absurd shadow is dancing on the wall next to the lowered faces of Andrija and Mile, bare-headed, and it's Vlaho's voice that wakes us up, *u kurac*, he has just entered the room, *fuck, what the hell are you doing here, are we going yes or no*, he glances crazily at the grandmother at her desecrated body, I put my helmet back on, Mile puts his helmet on, and we leave like robots not saying a word we climb into the Jeep Andrija sits down next to me he remains silent his eyes gazing into space the tears are beginning to flow onto his cheeks he gently wipes them away with his sleeve, he doesn't sob he looks at the countryside the houses the trees I watch him he cries like a silent fountain without hiding it, why, he's seen lots of corpses, young, old, male, female, burnt black, cut into pieces, machine-gunned, naked, dressed or even undressed by an explosion, why this one, Andrija will die a few weeks later, he'll have time to avenge his own tears, to cauterize his tears in the flames, to ravage enemy bodies in turn, houses, families, exulting with Ajax son of Telamon, with Ulysses in the ruins of Troy, Andrija the furious was avenging that unknown grandmother he never mentioned again, I still have in my mind's eye the shadow of Christ on the flowered wallpaper, in the gleam of the candles, nothing had been disturbed, no vengeful inscription on the walls, nothing, it was a strange miracle this crucifix stuck God knows how into the flesh of this old woman, Andrija upset without showing it by this sign, Sergeant Mile didn't say anything either, Eduardo Rózsa cracked too one day, and Millán-Astray, and Achilles son of Peleus, one day one fine day when nothing prepared you for it, and I too, I cracked, fissured like a clay wall slowly drying, in Venice it was a collapse followed by ghostly wandering through the hallways of the Zone, you die many times and today in this train all the names in this secret suitcase draw me to the bottom like the cinderblock attached to the legs of a prisoner thrown into the Tiber or the Danube, in the middle of middle-class Emilia, a train where the travelers are all sitting nicely, a car of passengers ignoring each other, pretending not to see the fate they share, these shared kilometers entrusted to the Great Conductor friend of model railways of halberds and of the end of the world, some facing forward and others with their back to their destination, like me, their gaze turned to the rear, to black night, to Milan the departure station: Millán-Astray Franco's friend, the thin one-eyed one-armed general the Legionary responsible for splendid massacres in Morocco had a guilty passion for decapitation, he liked to slit the darkie's throat with a bayonet, that was his weakness, not to say his hobby, in 1920 he founded the Spanish

Foreign Legion, after a stay in Sidi Bel Abbès with the French who are always proud of their military cunning, a natural colonial mutual aid, the French Legionnaires made a great impression on Millán who was neither one-eyed nor one-armed at the time, just obsessed, fascinated with death, Millán formed his Legion in Morocco for Spain to which the poor, the hoodlums, the banished from all over Europe rushed, and he welcomed them singing them hymns—the Spanish Legionaries whom I came across in Iraq looked like young newlyweds dressed for their weddings, they sang while they marched quickly, *soy el novio de la muerte*, to their nuptials like those of their ancestors in Africa, to whom Millán said *you are dead, full of lice, vulgar, you are dead and you owe this new life to death*, you will live again by giving death, as good fiancés you will serve, pay court to the Reaper with passion, hand Lady Death the scythe, sharpen it buff it polish it brandish it in her place in Morocco first then after the beginning of Franco's anti-Red crusade on the very soil of the homeland, in Andalusia, in Madrid then on the Ebro in the last great offensive, in Morocco against the bloody Berbers tamers of mares, in the military disasters of the Spanish protectorate that allowed the ephemeral creation of the first independent republic in Africa, the natives' Republic of the Rif, the republic of Abd el-Krim el-Khattabi whose creased, yellowed bank bills you can still find at the second-hand stores in Tétouan, Abd el-Krim the hero, the gravedigger of Spaniards was on the point of losing Melilla after the disaster of the Battle of Annual in July 1921 where 10,000 poorly armed, malnourished Spanish soldiers perished, without leaders and without discipline, one of the most resounding military blunders after the Somme and the Chemin des Dames, which would make the liberal monarchy of Alfonso XIII the Roman exile tremble: did he know, in his room in the Grand Hotel on the Piazza Esedra, with his collection of slippers and his princely visits, that his enemy of the time, the Berber cadi with the ponies, had found asylum in Cairo, at the court of King Farouk the anglophile: I picture him smoking a hookah by the Nile, for years, until, one day in 1956, the new king of independent Morocco suggested he return home—he refuses, maybe because he likes Nasser and Tahia Kezem too much, or maybe because he prefers to have his blood sucked by Cairo mosquitoes rather than by a Sharifian king, he dies without ever seeing his country again or holding a weapon, aside from a 9-millimeter Campo Giro picked up from the mutilated corpse of General Silvestre, commander of the Rif Army, the buffalo-horn-plated butt of which, smooth and scratchless, bears the arms of Alfonso XIII sent into exile by the defeat of his general and his brand-new pistol, Silvestre the murdered with the undiscoverable scattered body, replaced by the brothers Franco Bahamonde and Juan Yagüe, eagles with poetic names, and their elder brother Millán-Astray with the absent eye, to whom his legionaries offered pretty wicker baskets garnished with decapitated Berber heads, to his great delight, just as before him, around 1840, Lucien de Montagnac, a colonel who was also one-armed, the pacifier of Algeria, staved off colonial boredom by decapitating Arabs like artichokes—I suddenly see Henryk Ross's photo of the Łódź ghetto, a crate full of men's heads next to another larger one where the headless bodies are piled up, that would have delighted Astray the one-eyed or Montagnac the ill-tempered, admirers of the samurais with the slender swords and of those saints who carried their own decapitated heads: long after his wars, Millán-Astray the bird of prey translated the Japanese *Bushidō* into Spanish, code of honor and of honorable death, of decapitation of the conquered soldier, law of the friend who slices your neck and thus saves you from suffering, just as the French revolutionaries adopted the guillotine for its democratic painless aspect, a king's death for everyone, the leader's rolling in a basket, whereas before the Revolution decapitation was reserved for nobles, with commoners dying in spectacular torments, drawn and quartered or burnt for the most part, if they survived questioning—in Damascus not long ago they hanged opponents from immense streetlights on the Square of the Abbasids, from the raised basket used in Paris to trim trees, I remember one day a hanged man who had stayed up too long ended up being decapitated from his body and fell his head rolled between the cars provoking an accident which caused one more death, an innocent little girl, probably just as innocent as the guy whose shoulderless face had frightened the driver, also innocent, just as there are lots of innocent men among the killers in the suitcase, as many as there are among the victims, murderers rapists throat-slitters ritual decapitators who learned to handle their knives on lambs or sheep, then Zeus did the rest, in Algeria my Islamists were the world champions of decapitation, in Bosnia the mujahideen killed their prisoners in the same way, the way you bleed an animal, and my own entrance to the Boulevard Mortier bore the sign of seven monks' heads abandoned in a ditch, I can't escape decapitation, these faces pursue me, up to Rome and Caravaggio with his head of Goliath David's fist closed in the bloody hair or in the so-refined Palazzo Barberini Judith with her sword in Holofernes's throat, the blood gushes so nicely, the beautiful widow looks both disgusted and resigned as she severs the carotid artery, the servant holds the bag that will surround the damp relic its eyes wide open, its hair sticky, a somber image among the religious scenes, the Saints Jerome, the portraits of bishops become popes, the innocent girls wild Judith neatly beheads the Babylonian general, to save her people in the same way Salome obtained the head of the Baptist, beheaded in his cell by a brutal guard, with a thick knife, as shown by Caravaggio, again, on the immense canvas in the cathedral of the Order of the Knights of St. John in Malta, summer of 1608, when the order was incorporated, a year after arriving in the impregnable island, forty years after the Ottoman siege when Jean de Valette shot Turkish heads out of his cannons like cannonballs, to frighten the enemy, Michelangelo Merisi di Caravaggio the Milanese would have liked to die beheaded, he died ill on a beach in Argentario, facing the grey sea that he had never painted, or that he had always painted, in the dark immensities where the bodies of beautiful boys and saints are born, of murderers prostitutes soldiers disguised as saints, Caravaggio great master of darkness and decapitation

the landscape of the Po plain is very dark also, little fireflies of farms and factories are disturbing ghosts, in Venice at the Santa Lucia station I had wondered for a while about going back to Paris, another night train was going south at around the same time, headed for Sicily, terminus Syracuse, a journey of almost twenty-four hours, I should have taken it, if there had been someone on the platform to guide me, a demiurge, or an oracle I would have taken the train to Syracuse to settle on the rocky island on the slopes of Etna home of Hephaestus the lame, who often sprinkles lava onto the peasants and Mafiosi taking cover in the countryside, maybe it's because of that volcano that Malcolm Lowry settled in Taormina in 1954, in that village that looks so pretty it seems fake, he had written *Under the Volcano* ten years earlier, maybe it was his wife Margerie who chose the destination, a change of air, Lowry the drunkard had definite need for a change of air, he joined the contingent of Anglo-Saxons who peopled the Zone, Joyce, Durrell, Hemingway, Pound the fascist and Burroughs the visionary, Malcolm didn't let go of his bottle as he watched the swordfish gleam in the Bay of Naxos, he got drunk morning to night with a serious steadfastness, their little flower-covered house is too beautiful for him, he says, it's all too beautiful, too brilliant, too luminous, he can't manage to write, not even a letter, his eyes dazzled by the too-blue Mediterranean, Margerie is happy, she goes for walks all day long, she visits the archeological sites, the steep inlets, she returns home to find Malcolm drunk, drunk and desperate, holding a copy of *Ulysses* or *Finnegans Wake* that he can't manage to read, even drink doesn't console him, the pages of his notebooks remain desperately blank, life remains empty, Margerie, fed up, decides to lock up all the alcohol in the house, so Lowry goes out to stroll through the little streets, he climbs up to the ruins of the Greek amphitheater and watches the spectacle of the stars on the sea beyond the stage wall, he feels a powerful hatred, he wants to drink, he wants to drink, everything is closed, he almost knocks on the first house he sees to beg for a glass of grappa, one drink, to drink one drink, anything, he goes back home, he'll try to break open the hutch where his wife has locked up the liquor, he works away at the little wooden door, nothing to be done, he's too drunk already, he can't manage it, it's her fault, it's his wife's fault, Margerie's who's sleeping after being stupefied by sleeping pills, she'll give him the key, she'll pay, Margerie who's pumping all the talent out of him, who's preventing him from writing, Lowry goes into the bedroom, his wife is stretched out on her back, her eyes closed, Malcolm goes over to her to touch her, he's standing up, he's thirsty, with an infinite thirst, an infinite rage, he stammers out insults, she doesn't wake up, he feels as if he's shouting though, the bitch is sleeping and he's dying of thirst, she'll see, he puts his hands around her neck, his thumbs against her Adam's apple and he squeezes, Margerie instantly opens her eyes, she fights Lowry, presses harder and harder, he squeezes, he squeezes the carotids and the trachea, he'll kill her, the more he squeezes the weaker he feels, he looks at Margerie's eyes rolling in terror, her arms thumping him weakly, he is strangling Margerie and he's the one who is out of breath, the harder he presses the more he observes his wife's face becoming purplish-blue the more he feels sick, he doesn't loosen his grip, despite her pummeling him with her fists and knees, he's the one he's in the process of killing, it's no longer Margerie's neck he has in his hands but his own, his own face as in a mirror, he is asphyxiated, he is asphyxiating himself, his fingers let go, his fingers let go little by little and he collapses on the floor, unconscious, while Margerie tries to cry and get her breath, in the saffron-yellow dawn that's showing through the Persian blinds: in Sicily deadly island Lowry and his wife lived eight months of hell under the shadow of their second volcano, every other day the villagers were obliged to carry Malcolm home on their back, when the fishermen discovered him, at dawn, collapsed in a street, conquered by the steep slope and by sleep, in the end maybe I did well not to take the train to Syracuse, who would I have strangled in the

Sicilian night, grappling with the bottle and my savagery—my father, whenever, as a child, I broke something or mistreated Leda my sister, always said to me you're a savage, and my mother intervened then to chide him, no your son isn't a savage, he's your son, and now a little closer to the end of a world I wonder if the great thin man my pater wasn't right, as the train is approaching Reggio capital of Emilia with the gentle name, I am a savage, brutal and coarse, who despite all the civilized threads that all the books I've read have clothed me in remains a wild primitive capable of slitting an innocent person's throat of strangling a female and eating with my hands, my father looked at me strangely the last few years, he saw the uncouth brute behind the functionary from the Ministry of Defense, he guessed, for almost ten years, to what point my savagery might have gone and even at his last hour, ill, pale on his sickbed, he couldn't keep from staring at me, scrutinizing me with his gaze to remove my jacket, my shirt, my highly civilized human shell and lay bare my hairy chest and my ritual scarrings, traces of crude and violent humor, and I averted my eyes, I avoided his nagging and silent questions, until the end—until precisely eleven o'clock in the morning at the Ivry cemetery, one spring day neither grey nor blue, where we buried my father's questions in a "family" vault as they say where the dead man is supposed to find a little warmth near his relatives, accompanied by the tears of the living all the way up to the welcoming arms of the dead, beneath a tombstone freshened with a new inscription in the Ivry cemetery the entrance to which I am looking for on this spring morning of the new millennium, late, I see in the distance a group bustling about a grave with a verger in full uniform, I hurry over, I almost run in the lanes I narrowly miss sprawling onto a gravestone as I take a shortcut through the plots, obviously this isn't the right funeral, I immediately realize the fatal error, I see an appropriately long-faced employee whom I ask for directions: section 43, he replies, is on the other side of the street, in the little cemetery and I can't stop myself from laughing to myself thinking that this man has a voice from beyond the grave, somber and almost inaudible, here everyone whispers, of course, and in this nervous state that only the act of arriving late to the burial of your own father can produce, of having already missed the Mass and joining the family right at the cemetery, ashamed, with rings under my eyes, my breath no doubt fetid, my eyes crusted with sleep reddened not by tears but by alcohol and lack of sleep, ashamed and guilty for having forgotten where the family vault is in which my grandparents already lie, I go out through a little gate cross a wall-lined street panting I get ready to confront the stares of the weeping women mother and daughter on the arm of the brother-in-law he has to be moved too now I'm late I enter the other part of the Ivry cemetery and it's there, I recognize it, the proportions, the lanes, to my right the Resistants of Mont-Valérien and then Manouchian and the bearded Resistants on the *Affiche Rouge* wanted poster, on my left I can see my family, my family's friends, my sister in black, my inevitable brother-in-law, but no trace of my mother, they're getting the casket out of the car, the body of Sarpedon, son of Zeus, carried towards his family, nicely washed, nicely combed, nicely embalmed, they strain to slide it into the hole—I arrive, my sister looks at me reprovingly, her husband looks away, the verger has a birthmark on his face, he officiates in a dignified manner, *now you may bid him a final farewell, touch the coffin or else toss in a handful of earth, as you like,* I'm late so I have trouble believing it's my father in this gleaming oak, the man of the electric trains, of 1,500-piece jigsaw puzzles, my mother appears suddenly and yells Francis, Francis to me, then clings to my arm, she is defeated, done in she pulls herself together straightens up stares at me searches out my eyes which I lower like a child, *say goodbye to your father*, suddenly serious stiff and powerful, *oprostite se od otsa*, so I turn to the brand-new casket, how can I say goodbye to him, I mechanically recite *our Father who art in heaven*, and so on, where Hypnos and Thanatos are carrying you, washed in the Scamander, locked in the flesh-eating coffin, you too were a warrior, in your own way, Leda is weeping in the arms of her husband the Parisian banker, I apparently have no more tears, I said goodbye to my father yesterday during a solitary funeral banquet at my place in the dark I thought about the electric train about Algiers the white about my wild childhood I collapsed drunk fully dressed as the clock struck 5:00 in the morning and now in the midst of my family encumbered by their presence all I can do is stumble through a belabored Our Father, the sweat on my forehead disguised as tears—who is it in this sarcophagus, who is he, is he the draftee sent to Algeria, the Catholic engineer, the husband of my mother, the lover of puzzles, the son of the locksmith from Gardanne near Marseille, the father of my sister, is he the same one, in the Ivry cemetery a few hundred meters away from soldiers who died in military hospitals in the First World War, there are even a few slabs for Serbian *poilus*, how did they end up here, maybe they were treated in a military hospital nearby, their faces smashed in, suffering from tuberculosis, infections of all kinds, far from Niš or Belgrade, very far, beneath a suburban cross, in the same cemetery where the bodies of the guillotined lie, hidden in a corner, those bodies that between 1864 and 1972 no one sought to claim, did they carry their heads in their hands in their graves, like Saint Denis patron saint of Paris, or beside them, or between their legs to reduce the size of the coffin—maybe they were cremated, those outcasts victims of prosecution and punishment, murderers who have turned grotesque beneath their marble slabs, next to my father assistant interrogator in a villa in Algiers, the Christian engineer specialist in torture by immersion, along with the steel bar and electricity, he never spoke about it, of course, never, but he knew when he looked at me, he had seen, spotted in me symptoms that he knew, the stigmata, the burns that appear on the hands of torturers—my mother is still clinging to my shoulder in silence, my father descends into the tomb, my sister redoubles her crying and my hangover becomes phenomenal, the crosses, the angels on the mausoleums are dancing, the verger waves his aspergillum of despair, the sanctimonious ladies cross themselves something sounds like endless bells or bees it's a bird that's begun to sing a bus at the Porte de Choisy or a train in the Italian countryside scattered with farms and factories, infinitely flat, in the outskirts of beautiful bourgeois Reggio, once my father was in the ground friends family colleagues filed by us to offer us their condolences, the old ones who were in Algeria too, I recognize a few of them, weeping companions in arms, surprised and frightened by how young the dead man was, they shake my hand warmly, *ah Francis, ah Francis, your father*, and they don't add anything else, they greet my mother in a dignified way, my sister, and then comes the turn of the Croats, my uncle traveled all the way from Canada to be by my mother's side during this ordeal, he kisses me on both cheeks, the bear from Calgary, giving way to endless cousins, then to unknown people, whom my mother moved greets and thanks indistinctly in Croatian, understood only by the Serbian and Montenegrin soldiers buried a few yards away, I can't stand still, I have a headache, my eyes are burning, I need to urinate, I'm thirsty, and the image of my father the abstemious, in the hospital, appears now on the train window with no other landscape than a few glimmers of light flickering in the dark, my neighbor the *Pronto* reader has a good torturer's head on him, I can easily picture him inserting blunt objects into a Muslim girl's vagina whose shaven sex made a whole company laugh, on the hills of Algiers the white where my father preceded me into the Zone, he landed on August 22, 1956, on a military transport from Marseille, a cadet in the Signals Corps, nothing that would predispose him to becoming a hero, student engineer then student officer radio specialist, sent after six months' training to the "events" that were taking a turn for the worse, conscripted to Military Intelligence, in other words to the organization of systematic roundups—did he remember, on his deathbed, the men the women the women the men who had filed by him that year, before he asked to be transferred to an obscure douar *to take a more active part in the pacification process*, as he wrote in the letter to his superior, and before finding himself chief of a radio section in a mountain deserted by its inhabitants who were "regrouped" lower down, I suspect he insisted on abandoning Algiers disgusted, tired of the rapes and the beatings, his military dossier, I was able to obtain a copy from the great spiderweb on the Boulevard Mortier, attests his summons to a regimental order obtained in April 1958 during a nice little operation nicknamed *Love* by a lyrical commander: a few villages burned down, some FLN rebels in full flight—no prisoners, unfortunately, no one to torture aside from some civilians discovered in a dark cave quickly cleared of rats, had my pater known pleasure for the first time in Algiers, in a basement where his comrades shouted *Virgin! Virgin! Virgin!* as he clumsily inserted his penis into the vulva of a Chryseis weeping from shame and pain, he didn't look at her, his eyes were fixed on her young chest with the black nipples, and urged by the shouts he quickly ejaculated, before withdrawing his bloody instrument to bravos and cheers, *she was a virgin, she was a virgin, maiden! maiden!* the basement smelled nicely of rancid alcohol sweat fear blood gun lubricants used to lubricate anuses forced open with a bottle of anisette, a training grenade, or to conduct electricity and prevent the flesh from burning too quickly, when the electric-shock torture is no longer manual, of course, but a transformer of the same kind (coils and elements) as the one that delighted me when I was little, to vary the speed of the trains just as my father, in his day, varied the intensity of the shouts and contractions of the muscles strained to breaking point—I remember in high school I had related a biology experiment to my parents, we applied a continuous current to the nerve endings of a dissected frog and it moved, its feet contracted obedient to the experimenter and his 4.5 volt battery, I had explained this experiment in detail and my mother had said "what cruelty, poor animal," I remember my father hadn't added anything, he had taken refuge in silence, he had looked away without commenting at all on the fate of the frog or on electric barbarity, he was silent, once again, just as he was silent once and for all that day in his grave, victim perhaps of cancer remorse or guilt, and I arrive at his funeral after having spent hours sifting through files and papers about him, after having learned that for a year he had been assigned to "special interrogations" for military information described in the secret reports of the Intelligence Service, after having retraced his glorious escapades in remote douars and hamlets, the son followed the shadow of the father, the grandfather and many others without realizing it, as I bury my progenitor I think of the dead who are accompanying him into the grave, tortured, raped, killed unarmed or fallen in combat, they flit about in the Ivry cemetery, around us, can my mother see them, does she know, of course, *he did what he had to do*, that's her phrase, like mine *I did what had to be done*, for the homeland, for *Bog* our God for the cemeteries who call out—I see again the monumental cemetery in Vukovar, its white crosses on one side and its black gravestones on the other, a cemetery stuck in time, frozen, fixed in November 1991, in Vukovar death seems to have gone on vacation on November 21st exactly, after three months of hard labor, tired and sated: I went back there not long after my father's Ivry funeral, to see eastern Slavonia again Osijek, Vinkovci and especially to see Vukovar restored to the fatherland, Vukovar where I had never gone, which I hoped to free on my arrival in October 1991 and which fell a month later to the hands of the Yugoslav army and Serb paramilitaries, the taste of bile at the fall of Vukovar, Hector and Aeneas inside our lines, the camp invaded, the hollow vessels threatened, and fear, the fear of losing, of being conquered, of disappearing of going back to the vacuity of things our useless arms broken against the bronze of T55 tanks, I put my black hat on again and once my father was in the ground I left to travel around Croatia, alone, I wanted Vlaho to go with me but he was too busy bottling or casking or something, and also he didn't much want to go back there into the humidity of the Pannonian autumn, to see Vukovar, the place of wolves, well-named—the draftees from Vojvodina and central Serbia tucked into it wholeheartedly, those mustached wolves who looked as if they'd come straight out of a poem by Njegoš, they genially massacred everything they could, at the fall of Vukovar we had gone mad, Andrija had gone mad, rigid, crazy with pain, furious, dangerous, in a rage, full of hate and brave, indomitable, for if the city was a sad symbol for us for him it was much more, perch, pike, friends from bars from familiar houses a first kiss by the Danube and everything that attaches you to a city, I passed through his village I had never seen before either, his parents who had been relocated to Zagreb suburbs had never gone back there—their house was still in ruins, with its little garden, its gate and a big shell hole in the front wall, obscene eye, I then headed for Vinkovci before turning left towards Vukovar, on my way between Osijek and Vinkovci I didn't recognize anything, none of my battlefields, no wolves in sight despite the late hour, Vinkovci looked placid and sleepy, the suburbs were dotted with wrecked or razed houses, abandoned, burned, bombed factories: I was driving through what had been Serbian lines at the steering wheel of my brand-new Golf from Avis, in the rotten evening under a freezing drizzle, and I saw the cemetery, a few kilometers away from Vukovar, what was left of the sun went away quickly and I stopped, a big flat field a parking lot roomy enough for thirty tour buses, flags, a monolithic monument, it didn't take long for memory to settle here I thought, the nation had reasserted its rights to its martyrs, the brand-new cemetery on a territory that had just recently been reconquered where death held sway ten years earlier, all the tombstones bore witness to this, died October 20, 1991, died October 21, 1991, died November 2, 1991, and this family, husband wife and son surprised probably by a shell all died together on November 5, 1991, and so on, up to November 19, the apogee, massacre, crosses—a little further on the cemetery for those who hadn't fallen during the war looked disordered, alive, almost, but here, in the field of black marble, I felt as if I were wandering round in a confused military necropolis, where all the soldiers were civilians, hastily dressed in the uniform of sacrifice, the Croatian flag flew to embrace the souls of its new children just as at the time it kept us warm on our fighting biceps, the shield Checquy Argent and Gules caressed 938 white crosses, night was falling gently, I was alone in the middle of all these dead bodies, filled with a dull and tenacious sadness I got back into the Golf, I drove to Vukovar, to the Hotel Danube a decrepit red tower by the river's edge, I walked along the bank, caught sight of another monument, a huge cross by the water's edge, the center of town stank of ghosts death and mud, I passed the door of a bar in the famous street of baroque arcades completely rebuilt, young people with shaved heads gave me strange looks, I downed two, three *rakija* almost all at one go which won me the bartender's respect, I felt very empty, I had just lost the battle of Vukovar a second time, the battle against sadness and despair, I passed near the old covered market burned bombarded abandoned, I bought a bottle of local plum brandy in a grocery store a package of peanuts I went back to the Hotel Danube to collapse on the bed my eyes turned towards Novi Sad and Belgrade on the surface of the majestic river and I drank, I drank as I thought of Andrija's anger of his tears after the city fell, Andi a toast for you, for your rage that day or the next I forget when Fate sent us two prisoners after an ambush, one was wounded, the other unhurt was trembling with fear he said *my father has money, my father has money, if you let me go he'll give you a lot of money*, he was too afraid to lie, we had picked them up when they were trying to desert, I was tempted to let them run, I was about to hand them over to a grunt so he could take them to Osijek, but Andrija arrived, *are you out of your mind? You forgot Vukovar already? Not one of them should escape*, and he machine-gunned them at length, right away, without hesitating, looking them in the eyes, fifteen cartridges each in the chest, on my bed in the Hotel Danube a toast for Andi great shepherd of warriors, a toast for the stupefied gaze of the two little Serbs when the brass pierced them, a toast for the Vukovar cemetery in the falling night, for the Ivry cemetery one spring morning, for the soldiers of '14, the Resistants the ones condemned to death and a toast for my pater probably a murderer neither a Resistant nor a man condemned to death who is keeping them company today, as the train slows down to enter Reggio in gentle and beautiful Emilia, luminous for those coming from the darkness, an Italian city where the churches the squares and the arcades have not been demolished with mortar fire, the train station is small, all length and no width, streaked with white neon lights, a few travelers are waiting on the platform muffled in coats, scarves, on the opposite track a train is passing, a freight train, headed for Modena, loaded with tanks of milk—there was probably no need for a train for the ten Jews rounded up in Reggio at the end of 1943, they must have transported them by truck, right nearby, twenty kilometers away, to the Fossoli camp antechamber of Poland, but there is a plaque, in town, near the big synagogue in the heart of the former ghetto, which lists the names of these ten people who were eliminated 2,000 kilometers away from their home, whereas just ten Carabinieri bullets would have sufficed to spare them the torments of the journey, and would have earned them a burial, secret no doubt, but a place in the earth where, like the massacred ones in Vukovar, they would wait for someone to find them again, they didn't have that luck, they were offered a piece of cloud in the heavy sky of Galicia—Fossoli transit camp through which passed, from autumn 1943 to August 1944, most of the Jews deported from Italy, before the camp was moved to Bolzano near the Austrian border, strange perseverance, the war was mostly lost, Mussolini's Italian Social Republic in Salò was taking on water everywhere and yet the German administration went to the trouble of organizing convoys, transports for the partisans and the last Jews from Bologna or Milan, to Fossoli then Bolzano and finally to Birkenau, one final effort to make Italy *Judenrein* or *Judenfrei*, according to the nuances of the time, the ten Jews from Reggio who hadn't gone into exile were perhaps caught at home, near the synagogue on the Via dell'Aquila, maybe denounced, maybe not, and went to join the Resistants behind the barbed wire, before being shoved into one more train, towards the Polish terminus, where there arrived, that year of 1944, the Jews from Hungary and the 60,000 last inhabitants of the Łódź ghetto, among them the relatives and grandparents of Nathan Strasberg the Mossad officer, at least the ones that hadn't already been gassed in Chełmno in 1942—Birkenau, where all the tracks join, from Thessalonica to Marseille, including Milan, Reggio, and Rome, before going up in smoke, my train has windows, some were deported in passenger cars, the Jews from Prague, the Greek Jews who even paid for their ticket to Poland, they sold them a ticket for death, and the community leaders negotiated bitterly over the price of the journey with the German authorities, strange cynicism of the Nazi bureaucrats, Eichmann, Höss, Stangl, calm men, quiet family men, whose tranquility contrasted with the virile belligerent hysteria of Himmler or Heydrich, Franz Stangl loved flowers and well-ordered gardens, animals, during his trip to Italy in Udine and Trieste he loved the gentle landscapes of the Veneto, and the sea, then he loved the old city of Damascus and its odors of cardamom, and his wife, and his children, the little Austrian cop who wasn't very smart the murderer of several hundred thousand Jews denied having beaten a single one, he even convinced himself that their death was easy, piled up between four concrete walls asphyxiated with the exhaust gas of a diesel engine it took twenty minutes to die, *when everything goes right*, when everything went right he said in twenty minutes it was in the bag, but of course Bełzec, Sobibór, or Treblinka were amateurish compared to Auschwitz, his colleague Höss had set up his business well, his compartmentalized factories of pain functioned to perfection, until the end they worked on bettering the machine, they were even planning to make it bigger, big enough to welcome all of Europe if necessary, all the Slavic vermin and all the subversives, without hatred, without anger, just solutions to problems, for a problem requires solutions just as a question calls for a response—my father son of a Resistant participated actively in the resolution to the Algerian problem, submachine gun in hand, and lies today in the Ivry cemetery, beside the gunned-down men of Mont Valérien, a torturer despite himself, a rapist too probably despite himself, executioner despite himself, of course nothing to do with Höss, Stangl, and the others, my father born in 1934 near Marseille believed in God in technology in progress in mankind in education in morality, the train gets underway again, slowly leaves Reggio Emilia with a grinding noise, how slow it is, how ominously slow, I suddenly feel as if the names in the briefcase are dripping onto me like the putrefying fluids of a corpse forgotten in a train car, I'm tempted to open it but it contains nothing visible, digitalized documents on shiny disks, five years of voracious obsession ever since Harmen Gerbens the Dutch camp guard, five years playing a historian of shadows or a spy of memory, now it's over, in a manner of speaking, I could just as well have gone on for ten more years, but there's Rome that's waiting for me and the new life, the money from the Vatican, beginning again, beginning everything again under the name Yvan Deroy, goodbye Francis ex-warrior Defense Delegate, after my father's death my mother shut herself up in widowhood, she's a very dignified widow, she's a professional at mourning, accompanied by her friends and my sister at Mass twice a week and at the cemetery Sunday morning after service, she lives for her dead husband in the same way she lived for him when he was alive, and when she isn't at the church or at Ivry she plays Beethoven and Schumann on her piano until she has cramps in her fingers, *how well you play, Mama*, Leda spends her days at home listening to her, she goes back to her place just in time to prepare dinner for her husband, she lives 200 meters away, she badgers my mother from dawn to dusk so she'll take on students again, *at my age*, she replies, *at my age*, my mother however is barely sixty years old, I forget when exactly she stopped teaching, when those well-mannered teenagers stopped coming to the house who, for me, were an unattainable dream, I remember one more precisely, she must have been three years older than me and came twice a week at around five or six o'clock, I was just getting back from school—she always wore a skirt, she was a little plump, with a round face, long blond hair tied back, she greeted me nicely when I hurried to open the door to her, I took her duffel coat as I observed her breasts, they seemed giant to me, I breathed in the smell of her coat as I hung it up, and I watched her walk into the study, the piano room which we called the study, her music scores and notebooks in hand, I spied, with the door ajar, on the girl approaching my mother to see how she settled down by the piano and lifted her skirt sometimes to position herself on the stool, a mechanical gesture, a terribly erotic second for me, I thought I could glimpse her underwear through her wool stockings, I felt the friction of her buttocks against the burgundy felt, the movement of her thigh when she leaned on the pedal, and I got a terrible erection, an immense desire that drove me to the bathroom as a Liszt etude or a Chopin Polonaise (she was gifted) resounded, the rhythm of her fingers on the keyboard must have been, I imagine, my own on my personal instrument, in desire and in music, while I hated Liszt, Chopin and all those horrible maternal notes I came terribly, too quickly, the desired student was made to start again because of her tempo and it was my mother's voice more than once that interrupted my pleasure, with her *no, no, no, not so fast, not so fast*, from the neighboring room she seemed to be directing my masturbation herself, *start over, start over*, with that martial tone that had the gift of making me enraged beyond belief, with a rage mixed with shame, as if she had surprised me with my thing in my hand, as if she couldn't leave me alone with this student, she took her away from me and the girl left once the lesson was over I gave her back her coat, usually my mother called me immediately, *your homework, stop gaping, your homework, your father will be home soon*, obviously my sister had already settled down pen in hand, so I took a malicious pleasure in shoving her elbow to cause a nice blot on her impeccable page, which could provoke tears of sadness or, according to her humor, a frustrated anger similar to my own and we'd start fighting until my teenage strength got the better of her, she ended up on the bottom I immobilized her with my knees on her arms and tortured her as I threatened to let my saliva fall onto her face, she twisted around in horror, I caught the thread of spit at the last instant, she sobbed, conquered, that was my vengeance over those women of the family who prevented me from having pretty women from outside and usually at that exact moment my father arrived, alerted by Leda's shouts as soon as he crossed the threshold into the apartment he said to me *you're a savage, leave your sister alone*, which provoked the immediate intervention of my mother, *no, your son is not a savage*, etc., I belonged by rights to my mother, I was her kid she defended me against the male's intervention, I then had to apologize to the little tattletale pest erase the ink stain on her notebook and start my homework dreaming about the breasts the buttocks of the young pianist until dinner—in our family alchemy my father ruled from his silence and his reserve my mother was an authoritarian regent who saw the world like a music score, hard to interpret, but able to be deciphered with order effort and application and that's how she brought us up, order, effort, work, she the exile who hadn't known her own country had constructed herself in exercises, in Scriabin's etudes which are the hardest thing in the world, and even though she had given up her career as a concert pianist when she met her husband she preserved that power, that arid ability to rule over, to direct, to make an effort, in the same way she made an effort to control her fingers on the piano by an iron discipline, my mother would have made an excellent soldier, like Intissar the

Palestinian, enduring, obedient, giving herself the means to fulfill her mission, at least as much as my father: his sober, even austere, nature predisposed him to the barracks as much as to the monastery, as at ease in the Port-Royal Abbey as at the École Militaire, Catholic, respectful of the Law more than he was a lover of order, with an idea of the homeland and the Republic that came to him from his modest family where no one ever studied beyond high school, for him my mother represented culture, culture and the bourgeoisie, a bourgeoisie brought down by exile of course, but for that very reason accessible, on the other hand I wonder how my mother, for whom social origin and even *race* are so important, could have fallen in love to the point of defying the prejudices of her family to marry him—maybe she had seen in him his Christian virtues, guessed his patience, his resignation, maybe also glimpsed that crack behind the silence, the wound from fierce Algeria, which so resembled that of her own father, nonsense after all an engineer with a promising career wasn't such a bad catch and, even if he had the immense drawback of not being Croatian, this son-in-law was altogether suitable, fear not, they'd teach him to dance the *kolo*, provided he's neither Orthodox nor Jewish nor communist, that's what counted, besides hadn't my uncle the bear from Calgary married a girl from Zagreb of an excellent family, they could allow this eccentricity for the youngest girl—that's what I imagine, but I suppose my mother didn't leave them the choice, tired of her tours as a child prodigy, a teenage prodigy then an average concert performer, she chose her existence with the same determination she had at the age of seven when she learned the sonatas of Scarlatti by heart to play them blindfolded to audiences of old people, the greatest Yugoslav pianist of all time was the *France-Soir* headline, which made my grandfather mad with rage, *Yugoslav, they said Yugoslav, why not make it Serbian while they're at it*, my mother decided, she didn't make Achilles's wager, she preferred a home to a hypothetical glory, she carried out the destiny for which she had been prepared for years, to be a wife, a mother, and even a mother of one of the fighters who would liberate the homeland from the Titoist yoke, and her piano was a gentle pastime for a lady, giving concerts was perfect but it wasn't an accomplishment, it wasn't *her place*, her place was with us at home, my mother made that choice, without regret, weighing the pros and the cons, she chose my father and great silence—how much I too would have liked to decide, to have been offered Achilles's choice, instead of letting myself be carried into the darkness from cellar to cellar, from shelter to shelter, from zone to zone, up to this train that's crawling in the infinite straight line of the Po plain, between Reggio and Modena, with the thousands of names in my suitcase and an Italian Adonis lover of gossip as my sole company, is it really my own doing, this departure, it could be some kind of machination of the Boulevard, of the Agency, a conspiracy hatched with my already suspicious recruitment, now I'm becoming paranoid, it's the effect of the drug and of years of espionage, let's call a spade a spade, in 1995 I swapped the Kalashnikov for deadly weapons that were much more subtle but just as effective, chases, hideouts, interrogations, denunciations, deportations, blackmail, haggling, manipulations, lies, which ended up in assassinations wrecked lives men dragged in the mud twisted fates secrets brought to light, could I leave all that behind me, leave behind me the war and the Boulevard the way you forget a hat in a bar, where could I take refuge, in the hard resolution of my mother, in the silence of my father, in the bodyless grave of Andrija, in my own suitcase, in the briefcase of the Vatican light of the world, a little place for my father the lover of electric trains, a little place in the suitcase for my bitter silent pater

aside from murdering my neighbor strangling him maybe like Lowry and his wife there's nothing to do just remain silent close your eyes open them search for sleep December 8th today at this instant in Rome on the Piazza d'Espagna the Holy Father is making his speech he keeps kicking the bucket this pope maybe he's immortal as well as infallible that would crown it all, all of a sudden a man refuses to die, he does not pass away like his brothers, he survives, despite it all he hangs on, bedridden, trembling, senile but he hangs on, he reaches his hundredth birthday, then his 110th, then his 120th, everyone takes bets on his demise but no, he reaches 130 years and one fine day people realize he's not going to die, he'll remain suspended between life and death stuck there with his Parkinson's, his Alzheimer's, mummified but alive, alive, for ever and ever and this discovery saddens his potential successors so much that they of course decide to poison him, the eleven o'clock broth for the cumbersome old man, no luck, just like the first Christian martyrs he survives the poisoning, he loses his sight but his heart is still beating, from time to time he whispers some words into his visitors' ears, in Latin, thousands of pilgrims stand in line to catch a glimpse of him, his hair is sold strand by strand like so many pieces of eternity, one of the last eternal locks of the blessed man who keeps dying, just as the end of the world keeps arriving, imputrescible locks like the corpses of those saints who never decompose and then in the end they're forgotten in a corner of the palace, with servants all of whom they outlive, little by little dust covers them over they disappear from memory, from the present they're a tableau vivant a bust a statue to which not much importance is granted—I can't complain about the Holy See though I owe my new life to it, money in exchange for the briefcase, to that papal nuncio in Damascus who introduced me to the curial secretary concerned in my affair, in secret of course, Damascus city of dust almost as much as Cairo, city of dust and whisperings, of fear and police informers, where they bury you alive in a grey prison in the middle of the desert, Syrian oubliettes are deep, you don't often climb back up out of them, how many Syrians or Lebanese are still missing in action, caught at a roadblock or arrested at home no one knows what's become of them, if they're still rotting at the bottom of a dungeon or if they were shot down with a bullet in the head in Mezzeh or Palmyra, hanged a stone's throw from the ruins of Queen Zenobia's city the Temple of Ba'al and legendary tombs, beneath the palm trees you sometimes see an open truck full of guys with shaved heads, everyone turns his eyes away then so as not to see them, they're detainees being transferred from Damascus or Homs, they'll be thrown into Tadmor prison for eternity: looking at them brings bad luck, like looking at men condemned to death, the prison is a few kilometers away from the palm grove at the entrance to the endless stone steppe, I went to see it out of curiosity, at a respectable distance, an old French barracks, they say, surrounded by a grey wall and barbed wire, no daylight no walkway no air or sky, the prisoners spend most of their time blindfolded, I thought about Rabia, one of our sources at the Syrian Ministry of Defense, the son of a good family who loved money too much fancy convertibles drugs and danger, he disappeared one fine morning and his contact told us airily *he's in Switzerland*, a euphemism used in Syria to designate that penitentiary in the middle of the rocks a few feet away from one of the most famous ancient sites in the Middle East, so beautiful when the saffron dawn illumines the white columns and the Arab castle like their shepherd on its hill, Palmyra-Tadmor caravan city today peopled with caravans of tourists and prisoners, city of sheep butchered in the middle of the street in front of the terrified eyes of passing Europeans, capital of the Syrian steppe where that same Rabia whom I never saw must still be rotting if he survived, in Switzerland, that's to say in Tadmor in Sadnaya in Homs or formerly in Mezzeh in one of those military prisons Meccas of torture and summary executions where all throughout the 1980s and '90s the Syrian members of the Muslim Brotherhood were hanged, by the dozen, by the hundreds, their corpses buried in mass graves nestled in desert valleys, along with the bodies of those dead from torture or disease, tuberculosis, all kinds of abscesses, blood poisoning, malnutrition, piled up hundreds to a barracks, no visits allowed, Muslim activists were rounded up in Hama, in Aleppo, in Latakiyah and sent, blindfolded, to Palmyra in Arabic Tadmor the well-named, where they stagnated for ten, fifteen years until they were set free, paranoid, delirious, malnourished, or crippled, I met one of them in Jordan, one more source in my Zone, fourteen years in a Syrian prison, between 1982 and 1996, from sixteen to thirty, his youth tortured, broken, one eye missing, a leg lame, he told me that his main pastime in prison was *counting the dead*, he kept track of the hanged men in the prison yard, the ones who disappeared amid shouts in the middle of the night, in the beginning I tried to remember their names, he said, but that was impossible, so I just kept count, I clung to that as if it were my life, to know if I died what number I'd be, day after day, in fourteen years I counted 827 dead over half of them by hanging, usually by a chain, at night—I was arrested in front of my house in Hama during the events of 1982, I knew nothing about Islam or the Koran, I was an ignoramus, they arrested me because one of our neighbors was with the Brotherhood, I had just turned sixteen, they put a blindfold over my eyes and they beat me, I don't know where I was, in a barracks I guess, I spent two days without drinking a drop of water and I was transferred to Palmyra in a truck, no one knew where we were going, we arrived at night, they made us get out with blows from a cudgel—the soldiers tortured us until dawn, that was the custom for newcomers, they had to break us, make us understand where we were, they broke my leg with an iron bar, I fainted, I woke up in a barracks like a giant dormitory, my leg was purple all swollen I was thirsty, I didn't know what was more painful, if it was the thirst or the fracture, I couldn't speak, one of the prisoners gave me some water and made me a sort of harness with an old crate that's the only medical care I got, the bone didn't reset right and ever since I've limped I can't run anymore, no more soccer but in prison you didn't think about soccer, the yard was mostly for hanging people, thank God I got out, I learned the Koran by heart, books were forbidden, pens too, but the Koran circulated by word of mouth, whispers, I learned sura after sura beginning with the shortest ones, I learned them from the mouths of the older prisoners, in the dark, a continuous almost inaudible flow pressed against each other we all prayed together, so the guards didn't notice anything we bowed down to God by bending just the pinky finger, as is permitted for the ill, God willed that I survive, when I counted the 492nd death one of my eyes got infected it turned into a big suppurating painful ball and never opened again, I had a good constitution I was young, time passed in Palmyra they never called you except for one reason, to hang you, the guards hardly ever spoke to us, sometimes after midnight they called out names, that was the day's list of men to be hanged, we saluted them everyone was used to executions, the first thing I did when I arrived in Jordan was go to the mosque to pray standing up, finally, to be able to kneel down even though my leg hurt, to thank God for having gotten me out of that hell, he ended his story and I thought he should have thanked God too for having put him there, in that hell, but for him the Baathist Alaouites in power in Syria were infidels, agents of the devil, Hasan (we'll call him Hasan) readily informed me about the Syrian opposition and their clandestine activities that he still followed closely but was much more reluctant to talk about the Jordanians or the Palestinians, he ended up being killed by the Mossad in 2002, during the Great Purge, when the CIA sent endless lists of "individual suspects" all over the world the luckiest of whom ended up in Guantánamo their eyes blindfolded tortured once again for many of them had already fallen into the clutches of the Jordanians the Syrians the Egyptians the Algerians or the Pakistanis for different reasons but with the same results, they ended up on the island of rum and cigars and mulatto women sculpted by the sun and by dictatorship, they sweated in Cuba in their high-security orange jumpsuits much more visible and pleasing to the guards' eyes than the striped or plain pajamas of Palmyra the magnificent: Hasan didn't have that luck, if you can call it that, he died hit by a little radio-controlled Israeli missile that completely destroyed the vehicle in which he was traveling along with his young wife and their two-year-old daughter, he died because of information I'd supplied, I'm the one who sold him to Nathan Strasberg in exchange for information about American civilian contracts in Iraq, as proof of good will I sacrificed a source that was in any case a little outdated by then, Hasan the lame had taken part in organizing two attacks on Jerusalem and another one against Israelis in Jordan, he was becoming less and less communicative, lied too often, farewell Hasan survivor of Tadmor, farewell Rabia the son of the dignitary fallen in disgrace after the death of Hafez al-Assad the old lion of Damascus who had managed, against all expectations, to die in his bed, or rather on the telephone, on the day of his death you couldn't find a single bottle of Champagne in Syria, Beirut, or Jerusalem, the Old Man of the Mountain had played Middle-Eastern poker for thirty years and he was unbeatable, he had played with Kissinger, with Thatcher, with Mitterand, with Arafat, with King Hussein, and many others, always winning, always, even with a pair of sevens, because he was clever possibly but above all because he didn't have any useless scruples, ready to sacrifice his pieces to go back on his alliances to murder half his compatriots if need be, Hasan the lame owed fourteen years of prison to him, lucky compared to the perhaps 20,000 dead from the repression in the 1980s, lucky Rabia, his dignitary father an Alaouite minister let him get rich off his fellow citizens and experience a few years of abundance before he ended up in the slammer for a while: whenever I went to Damascus, Aleppo, or Latakiyah I always felt as if I were putting my head in the wolf's mouth, in that country of informers where half the population was spying on the other half you had to be twice as careful, the only advantage being that the other half was by the same token perfectly willing to work for foreign countries, in return for cold hard cash, I went to Damascus "as a tourist" and so as not to blow my cover too quickly I had to see the sights, in Palmyra, in Apamea, visit the museum in Aleppo, go see the Church of Saint Simeon Stylites the saint chained on top of his pillar the base of which still exists today, explore the old city of Damascus, marvel inside the *cortile* of the Umayyad Mosque where there is, they say, one of the severed heads of John the Baptist, and above all eat, eat, drink, and get bored watching the fine winter sleet fall on the city of sadness and dust, of course the French embassy was a forbidden zone for me, that's too bad, I would have liked to see the beautiful Arabic house where Faysal settled in 1918, Faysal the sharif of Mecca whom Lawrence of Arabia had made King of the Arabs, before the French and General Gouraud threw him out of his new capital and the British recovered him to place him on the throne in Iraq by giving a Hashemite legitimacy to that country newly founded by the joining of three Ottoman provinces that had no intention of cohabiting peacefully within a puppet state, even to please Churchill or Gertrude Bell the archeologist spy, in that Near- or Middle-East that the French and English had shamelessly divided among themselves in 1916, what could be left of Faysal in the residence of the powerful French ambassador to Syria, the first velvet armchair in which the Bedouin king had sat, maybe, the tired springs of the bed where he had slept, did his ghost come to disturb the sleep of a charming ambassadress, causing dreams of horses galloping through the scorching desert, nightmares of thirst, or erotic dreams of frenzied Arabic nights—nights in Damascus or Aleppo were not very conducive to lust or Capuan luxury, the very prudish Syrian dictatorship preferred a martial austerity, Aphrodite passed only rarely through the mountains of Mount Lebanon, on the shores of the almost dry Barada River there were a few cabarets where drunken Saudis showered banknotes on fat, wrinkled belly-dancers with acid music accompaniment, a very ugly gentleman armed with a red plastic bucket collected the carpet of notes while these ladies continued shaking their breasts into the mustaches of emirs who immediately ordered another bottle of Johnny Walker to make their hard-on go away, in Aleppo in a side-street between two spare-parts stores there was a similar kind of establishment but full of Ukrainian and Bulgarian women in swimsuits who raised their legs French-Cancan-style for a few beer-drinking soldiers with mustaches, after each number they'd go sit on the clients' laps, I remember one of them had lived in Skopje and spoke a passable Serbian, she said she'd visit me in my hotel room in exchange for the modest sum of 200 dollars, at that rate the Syrians must not have screwed much, she told me that she had arrived in Aleppo in reply to a job offer for dancers, she loved to dance, she said to herself that dancing in a Syrian troupe would be a beginning I didn't know if I should believe her or not, and also the salary was good, it wasn't prostitution, she said, it was dancing, she seemed as if she were trying to convince herself, she was just on twenty, a smiling face she was blonde as wheat, they were all blonde as wheat, she got back on stage for the next number, she looked at me as she jigged up and down, the five girls took sensual poses to "My Way," they mimed kisses with depressed little pouts I left to go back to my hotel and to the solitude of my room very happy not to need to succumb to the charms of the swimsuit-wearing dancers, I remember the next day I had a "meeting" with a man about whom I knew nothing on a café terrace facing the incredible Citadel of Aleppo, I was supposed to sit on a terrace with a red sweater and a wool scarf placed on the back of the chair opposite me—sometimes reality becomes a spy movie from the 1960s, probably this honorable correspondent had read too many Cold War spy novels, in the

Zone things were very different, still I was a little worried, I didn't much want two Syrian secret service agents to sit down at my table and say "so, red sweater and wool scarf, eh?" and kick me out of Syria after giving me a beating, or worse, the most likely thing would be for them to keep me in secret somewhere while they waited to exchange me for someone or something, and even if there is in fact a share of risk in my business it always seems very remote, in the Agency I never carried a weapon or anything of that sort (I did have a little 7.65 Zastava at my place but that was an unusable war souvenir) but that morning when I went to the meeting at the Citadel I wasn't entirely at ease, because it was Syria, because Syria is the country of informers, because in Syria there aren't many tourists and it's not as easy to melt into the crowd as in Cairo or Tunis, I walked through the endless Aleppo souk on foot, I bought three knickknacks for Stéphanie the brunette (to hell with secret trips), some bay-leaf soap, a silk scarf, and a little copper hookah probably impossible to smoke but at least I looked like a perfect tourist when I emerged from the covered market onto the Citadel square, I settled onto a café terrace, I asked for *coffee, coffee, café, please,* I placed my scarf on the chair in front of me, and I waited as I contemplated the glacis of the impregnable fortress, a masterpiece of Arabic military architecture said the *Lonely Planet* open on the table to give me the look of a solitary adventurer, I had finished my coffee when a man about sixty, quite tall, with white hair, came up to me and asked if I spoke French, I replied yes, of course, and he said in French *it's a pleasure to meet you*, he added *come, we'll go visit the Citadel,* he paid for my coffee before I could even react and took me by the arm as if I were a lady, he didn't let it go for the entire visit, and I confess that this unaccustomed tenderness gave our strange couple an entirely natural look, he insisted on paying the entrance fee, he pointed out the machicolations, the hallways that twisted to foil invaders' attacks, the iron grates on the ceiling to bombard assailants, and it wasn't until we emerged from the central donjon onto the immense mound in the middle of the ramparts that he began to speak in earnest, I didn't say anything, I wanted to listen first, feel, try to make out if it was to my advantage to do business with him or not, as Lebihan the chief said *you have a gift for human relations*, the contact had spoken of a *source of exceptional interest*, which justified my presence, I grew doubtful when I realized that it was impossible to settle this business through the mail, a real exceptional source doesn't take risks, normally we never meet, it's a Syrian network that forwards the information but here the nice source held my arm as if he were my father, at the windswept summit of the Citadel of Aleppo the grey, from which we could see the whole city, the big mosque below, the countless pigeons whirling around the minaret, the black rooftops of the souk, the little cupolas of the caravanserai, the modern buildings in the suburbs all the way out to the countryside where the earth looked red in the winter sun, *my name is . . . um . . . my name is Harout*, his hesitation was not very professional, I began to sense a base trick, my contact's mistake, I sighed internally, sheesh, all that for this, I said Harout, fine, whatever you like, on my passport at the time my name was Jérôme Gontrand, with a *d*, I just said "Jérôme," I was patient you have to know how to wait to be calm

I had my butterfly net in hand I waited for Harout to relax a little before I caught him and added him to my collection of Lepidoptera, he was the one who was going to capture me I didn't know that of course, it was he who would hurtle me into this train five years later, look a city already, probably Modena, just forty kilometers or so until Bologna, the Pendolino slows down, at night all Italian suburbs look alike, during the day too probably, it is Modena, I just caught a glimpse of the sign announcing the station, Modena, pretty little city, sister of Reggio with two specialties, charcuterie and luxury cars, pork and Maseratis that's a very Italian way of putting it just like my neighbor the *Pronto* reader he probably wouldn't turn up his nose at either one, with his Ferrari cap, he should wave it out the window, we just passed close by the Scuderia factories, I remember the historical center of Modena, magnificent, squares, churches, Duomo, just a year ago on Thursday, December 11th Mohammad el-Khatib blew himself up at 5:00 in the morning at the corner of the Piazza Mazzini a few meters away from the synagogue, one of the most beautiful in Italy, the Palestinian born in Kuwait had a Jordanian passport he set fire to his white 205 Peugeot he parked it in front of the synagogue, the policemen on duty tried to intervene with a fire extinguisher but without success, Mohammad waited at the steering wheel in the burning vehicle its doors and windows closed, he waited until the LPG gas exploded and ripped the car apart scattering his body to the four winds, he was possibly already dead carbonized when everything blew up, the synagogue was very slightly damaged, there were no victims, aside from Mohammad and a very old Yorkshire terrier with a heart condition which died from fear in its urine on the second floor of the building across the way, a few broken windows, nothing more, the dog was named "Pace," peace, strange coincidence that no newspaper revealed—without knowing it Mohammad el-Khatib set off all the anti-terrorist alarms in the world, we all tried to find out if the poor fool was connected to a known cell, if his name was already listed somewhere, in a file, in a report, until the Italian services confirmed the police version, a suicide, not a suicide bomber, just a suicide: Mohammad el-Khatib, unknown, depressive, psychotic, violent, on tranquilizers had set fire to himself maybe without even thinking about the explosion that would follow, he wanted to die in front of the synagogue, maybe die like the Palestinian martyrs in Jerusalem or Tel Aviv, in glory and flames, or maybe sacrifice his life to protest against the occupation, peacefully, or else maybe simply to die, in the heart of a grey December night, when Hades is calling—still the fact is that there were no more Jews to kill in Modena, the synagogue is open only for the high holidays, and at 5:00 in the morning not many people are to be found in the city streets, the carabinieri and the assistant public prosecutor patiently collected the crimson ruins of Mohammad's body, they gathered them into black plastic bags, the municipal services hurried to make every trace of the death disappear, they cleaned the asphalt, repaired the streetlights, replaced the broken windows and then burned, in a dump, the remains of the old dead pooch whose mistress didn't know what to do with it, I thought about Attila József, the Hungarian poet who stretched out on the railroad tracks near Lake Balaton to get himself cut into three pieces by the first train, or into two lengthwise by the sharp wheels, Attila József had a twofold influence in Hungary, poetic and deadly, if I can put it that way, dozens of *poètes maudits* or over-lucid teenagers came down to die on the tracks at the same place he did, or, when the railroad administration, alarmed, decided to fence off the place, a little further up on the same line—in the same way Mohammad was following the example of the Palestinian martyrs those little solar Christs who cut their bodies in half at the waist with a belt of explosives, Nathan Strasberg told me that their heads were propelled dozens of meters high into the air, like a plastic bottle by a firecracker, I imagine their final moments, they contemplate Jerusalem one last time, from so high up, in a final blink of their eyes they see the Dome of the Rock shining, at the top of their final ascension, at the point of equilibrium, as when you throw a ball into the air, their bleeding heads freeze for a split second in the sky before falling back down—there are traditions in suicide, groups, fraternities: hanging, somewhat rustic, firearms and knives, more warlike and manly means of transport, resolutely modern, that of poison or bleeding into your bath in the old style, of gas with or without explosion, of being burned alive, for my part I belong to the category of the drowned, water signs tempted by the total disappearance of their bodies in the dark stream, Mohammad el-Khatib demonstrated as he died, he made one final gesture, maybe the only one that counted for him, that December morning a few hundred meters from the train station that we're hurtling through, he was taking his place with the most famous deaths of his people, joining them despite his Italian exile, his suicide didn't stop Luciano Pavarotti from getting married two days later at the Teatro di Modena (*the theater is the artists' church*, he would say) a few hundred meters away, with 700 guests, among them Bono the U2 singer and Zucchero who sang "Stand By Me" in the midst of Armani dresses, policemen on horseback, jewels, male and female socialites, the tenors Placido Domingo and José Carreras, a gospel choir, and a string ensemble surely to help Mohammad el-Khatib and the dead dog climb to paradise, there are so many ways to react to suffering and injustice, Pavarotti put a list of humanitarian organizations on his wedding register, the Palestinian of Modena set fire to himself in front of an empty synagogue and Harout in Aleppo held me by the arm as he tried to explain something to me that I did not understand, on top of the citadel, on the big windswept terreplein, something to do with eighty-year-old massacres, with death marches in the middle of the desert, and I couldn't see what this had to do with our negotiations, after half an hour I finally interrupted him, I was freezing and wanted to get straight to the point, he replied *don't worry*, don't worry you'll get your information, you'll know everything you want to know, and even more, at the highest level, you can find out the color of Hafez al-Assad's boxer shorts if that strikes your fancy, you'll get special channels to negotiate with the Syrians if necessary and an attentive ear at the presidential palace, everything you want finally in Syria and Lebanon, but on one condition: that France officially recognize the genocide of the Armenians—I was stunned, I couldn't believe my ears, this guy was definitely off his rocker, what could I do about recognition of the Armenian genocide, he smiled at me very calmly, I said to him listen, you should really speak with someone at the embassy, it's diplomats you need I think, in any case I'll see what I can do, Harout interrupted me and said don't worry, there's no hurry you know, it was already so long ago that it can wait a few more years, Harout was in fact only the representative of "honorable correspondents" whose services and information would possibly turn out to be so useful to France that despite the damages produced in Franco-Turkish relations the National Assembly on January 18, 2001 finally adopted the bill recognizing the Armenian genocide whereas in 1998 a similar initiative had not fared so well, the text having been "lost" in the Senate, where it was never placed on the agenda, and I don't know to this day if the man or rather men that Harout represented had something to do with that business or not, in Aleppo in 1997 in any case official recognition of the genocide by France seemed entirely unlikely, and one year later the Assembly voted unanimously for the act the first time, what's more a big historic conference was organized at the Sorbonne, the Turks were seething with rage and burned the tricolor in Ankara, the French presented themselves once again as the Just and France as the homeland of human rights, the deputies all embraced each other as they left the chamber, some had difficulty holding back their tears as if they themselves had just saved thousands of men from the massacre, forgetting that the bodies had been sleeping for almost a hundred years already in Deir ez-Zor in the Syrian desert, around Aleppo or in Eastern Anatolia, that little historic Armenia where the best proof of the destruction is the absence of Armenians today, where have they all gone, they disappeared,

disappeared from Van, from Diyarbakir, from Erzurum—in May 1915 the prefect of Jezireh complained about the corpses carried along by the Euphrates, linked two by two, killed with a bullet in the back or by the long knives of the Circassians or the Chechens whom the Ottomans recruited as stalwart executioners, Harout told me all this in Aleppo, at the bar of the Baron Hotel where the Young Turks had slept, come from Stamboul to supervise the butchery, the caravans of deportees coming from the north spent some time in the concentration camp of Bab a few kilometers away from the city, *everyone has forgotten*, said Harout, *everyone has forgotten that the death camps were here, around Aleppo, in Rakka on the Euphrates, in Deir ez-Zor, in Hama, in Homs, as far as the Djebel Druze*, almost a million Armenians passed through here on their long march to death and those who survived in the camps were always sent further away, on foot or by wagon, until their numbers were so reduced that it became feasible to kill them by hand, to burn them alive, to blow them up with dynamite or drown them in the river, the witnesses talk about cannibalism caused by famine, children feeding on animal excrement, Arab Bedouins who raided the columns of deportees, kidnapping the nubile young women, a brief apocalypse, a few months, between 1915 and 1916, at a time when the British and French soldiers were falling like flies on the hills of the well-guarded Dardanelles facing the soldiers commanded by Mustafa Kemal who wasn't called Atatürk yet, Harout told me, over a glass of arak in the shiny old leather armchairs in the Baron Hotel, about the killing of the Armenians and how the community of Aleppo, present in the city since the Crusades, had been ransomed but more or less spared, he told me about the end of the most brilliant Ottoman Empire, the most beautiful empire in the Mediterranean and the Balkans as far as Libya, which still had protected its Christian minorities for centuries, in exchange for a tribute—Harout Bedrossian born in 1931 showed me photos of his family around 1900, the men in tarbooshes and the women in black dresses, he took me to taste *the best soujouk and basturma in Aleppo*, his French was impeccable and distinguished, colonial, with a beautiful strange accent, we did not speak about work, of course, he was just an intermediary, like me, we were two suitcase-carriers, shady businessmen, on good terms and nothing more, the man or men he represented were businessmen close to government ministers whose palms they greased to get the right to deal with foreign countries, clients of Alaouite bigwig apparatchiks ruling over a country of countless varieties of police and information services in the country of cages and prisons with no exit, its desert littered with Armenian bones that the government glorified mostly to annoy the Turks their hereditary enemies, the Turks spearhead in the fight against the Axis of Evil, with whom military cooperation was in full swing, France was training Turkish officers in military schools, French officers left to train in Turkey, materiel was exchanged for expertise as well as information mainly about Iran and the Russian Caucasus, despite appearances our bilateral relations were entirely cordial and a few hundred thousand dead and forgotten Armenians were not going to jeopardize the geo-strategic equilibrium of the post-Cold War, we would go on working together, nothing stops, even when the deputies legislated *for Turkey's own good*, to bring it, they said, *to look its past in the face* or something like that, which made the ex-Ottomans in the wings laugh out loud, France would do better to set its own corpses in order, the France that in 1939 evacuated the last Armenians during the Alexandretta affair, with the cynicism proper to the Republic, after having put down the Syrian revolts it sold part of the Syrian territory to the enemy, France enraged and violent bombed the civilians of Damascus furiously in 1945 as it was leaving, a farewell gift, policy of scorched earth, I'll withdraw my guns but I'll use them one last time, leaving a few hundred unknown dead on the ground, nothing really serious, some Arabs, some treacherous and incomprehensible Orientals for General Oliva-Roget the one responsible for the gunfire, convinced that British agent-provocateurs were behind the riots that he suppressed before heading off with weapons and baggage for Paris to report to De Gaulle the great shepherd of warriors, France embarrassed Turkey in 1998 by throwing thousands of Armenian bones in its face, to which the Turks retorted with thousands of Algerian corpses, and this same Parliament of the Fifth Republic which had voted for the law of amnesty for war crimes in Algeria officially recognized the Armenian genocide, moved to tears, in 2001—the massacres of others are always less awkward, memory is always selective and history always official, I remember with Marianne in the Dardanelles the Turkish guide sang the praises of Atatürk father of the nation great organizer of the resistance on the peninsula, destined for a noble fate: that destroyer of the Empire had rehabilitated the Young Turks as soon as he came to power in 1923, after they had been tried in Istanbul in 1919 and condemned for the massacres of 1915-1916, to recognize the genocide today would be to betray the Sacred Memory of the mustachioed Father of the Turks, just as repealing the 1968 law of amnesty for Algeria is impossible and pointless, a betrayal of the Memory of the victorious General: Memory, that mortuary of texts and monuments, of miscellaneous engraved tombs, of textbooks, laws, cemeteries, handfuls of ex-soldiers, or dead soldiers rotting beneath rich gravestones, no paltry almost anonymous crosses in a cemetery of multitudes, but a marble vault, solitary like that of Charles Montagu Doughty-Wylie in Kilitbahir in the Dardanelles: the British officer fallen in April 1915 was probably the only one of his contingent who could speak Turkish fluently, who knew the Empire he was fighting against intimately, where he had resided as consul between 1906 and 1911, in Konya and Cilicia, Charles Doughty also mustached had then been a military attaché to the Ottoman troops during the Balkan war, in charge of organizing aid for the wounded, he even won a decoration for his bravery and his selflessness, the sultan pinned a crystal rose onto his jacket lapel, ironic medal, Charles Doughty would get a Turkish bullet full in the face on top of a remote hill in the Mediterranean, without being able to enjoy the sublime view over the Aegean, the Trojan hills he knew so well, torn apart by naval cannons—and he certainly did not know, at the moment of death, that the Armenians that he had saved in 1909 in Cilicia were in the process of being massacred yet again, this time without anyone being able to intervene, neither the American consul nor the few witnesses to the massacres, in 1909 in Konya Charles Doughty-Wylie and his wife receive a visit from a British traveling archeologist, Gertrude Bell, who photographs them in their garden, in the company of their servant and their huge black poodle, Mrs. Doughty-Wylie in a white dress, wearing a hat, with an unattractive face, hard features, jealous, perhaps, of the adventuress' success with her husband, with reason—Gertrude is in love with the handsome Charles, the first female "intelligence officer" in Her Majesty's government is taken with the elegant soldier diplomat, she will go pay her respects in secret to his grave, in the Dardanelles, a few years later, when she is plotting the formation of modern Iraq and offers the throne to Faysal King of the Arabs, Gertrude Bell the archeologist spy is surely responsible for many of the woes of the region, I thought of her in Baghdad in front of the museum she founded that had just been pillaged, they would find Mesopotamian cylinder seals as far away as America, everyone offered you ancient relics, the people from the UN left with their pockets full of ancient coins, statuettes and medieval manuscripts, the disemboweled country was losing its riches from its bowels and Gertrude Bell's grave, green and silent, was still there in Baghdad where no one remembered her anymore or her role in the birth of the country, her intrigues or her friendship with T. E. Lawrence of Arabia, or her mysterious death, suicide or accident, of an overdose of sleeping pills on July 12, 1926: I slept in Gertrude Bell's room at the Baron Hotel in Aleppo, thinking about Charles Doughty-Wylie and the Armenians, before going on with my tour, as a good carnival tourist, I went to Latakiyah, by train, from the Aleppo station where the Istanbul Express used to arrive after having made the tour of the Taurus Mountains—the

Syrian train that crossed the mountains had no windows, I was absolutely frozen in the compartment, now I'm suffocating, I have a terrible hangover, I'm all shaky, blurry, sticky, in Latakiyah the sky was purple after the rain, the immense sea an unsettling grey I booked a room in a hotel with the absurd name of "The Gondola," I had dinner in a restaurant run by Greeks, the fish was quite good as I remember it with a sesame sauce, there was nothing to do in Latakiayah aside from drinking in a pretty sordid bar where Russian pilots were on a binge, drunk as only Slavs can be, two giants from the Urals with uniforms and caps were dancing a grotesque, monstrous waltz, tenderly clasping each other their huge paws placed on their shoulders, they swayed from one foot to the other as they sang some Russian song, they were drinking undiluted arak straight from the bottle to the great disgust of the owner, a tanned slightly overwhelmed Syrian, the two ex-Soviet bears tumbled over a table provoking the hilarity of their comrades who offered me a drink, the boss wanted very much to throw them out but didn't dare—I went back drunk to my not very cheerful hotel room, on the wall photos of Venice plunged me into depression I felt more alone than ever Marianne had left me Stéphanie was about to leave me my shadowy profession was one of the most sordid there is I looked at the ceiling or the reproductions of gondolas as I thought about Harout Bedrossian's dead Armenians, about the Kurds and Arabs duped by Gertrude Bell, about the Dardanelles about Troy the well-guarded about the secret lagoon in the winter fog about death everywhere around me I thought about the Syrian prisons the hanged men the tortured Islamists about all those wasted existences thrown into the sea like the rain that was pelting hard on the window and now a fine Italian drizzle streaks the night horizontally in the outskirts of Bologna, and despite the suitcase the decision the new life before me I am in no better shape than in that hotel room in Latakiyah on the Syrian coast the profession of solitude despite the contact of bodies despite Sashka's caresses I feel as if I'm unreachable as if I'm already gone already far away locked up in the bottom of my briefcase full of torturers and the dead with no hope of ever emerging into the light of day, my skin insensitive to the sun will remain forever white, smooth as the marble gravestones in Vukovar

the papal nuncio ambassador from the Holy See to Syria was a charming cultivated man from a good Italian family, it was Harout Bedrossian the Armenian Catholic who introduced me to him—curious the detours Fate often uses to land on its feet, once the suitcase was full I had to sell it, empty those thousands of documents of names and stories patiently gathered all around my Zone starting with Harmen Gerbens the Dutch torturer, documents collected over five years of endless investigations, of thefts of secret archival papers of cross-checking of testimonies, why those thousands of hours patiently creating this list, to fill the terribly empty life of the Boulevard Mortier and Paris, to give a sense to my existence perhaps, who knows, to end with a flourish, to win forgiveness for my dead, but from whom, to obtain the Holy Father's blessing, or simply the money that's worth any number of pardons, to settle down somewhere under the name Yvan Deroy my double shut up in his madness and violence, my papers are legal, real, like the ones I used to use to move around in the Zone, the Pierre Martins, the Bertrand Dupuis so simple that they immediately became real, I think little by little I left my identity behind in those pseudonyms, I split myself up, little by little Francis Servain Mirković dissolved into the real false papers to reconstitute himself like an atom in the thousands of names in the suitcase, regrouped into a single one, Yvan Deroy poor lunatic who has probably never seen the sea or caressed a woman, locked up forever, it's so easy to appropriate an identity, to put your face in place of another's, to take his life, born the same year as me, he had the same adolescence fascinated by violent ideologies, oscillating between the extreme right and the extreme left with a disconcerting ease, without any opinions, in fact, aside from his friends', Yvan Deroy if he had gotten out of his hospital would have put up neo-Nazi posters, seduced by martial order and hatred, piling military training on top of military training and enlisting before being called up finally to become a man, a real man, as they say, eliciting admiration from his parents and fated for a splendid destiny, military service training in weapons, humbling oneself to the esprit de corps, the same esprit de corps that so fascinated Millán-Astray the founder of the Spanish Legion during his visit to the French in Sidi Bel Abbès in Algeria, the fortified village on the Oran plain deeply inspired the one-eyed general, the legionaries from all over Europe remade themselves in the barracks, they found a family a country in the Legion and more than France they served the

Legion itself, my military service was instructive, slogging along while singing, my kit, my rifle and my comrades, camps, night marches, I liked that rhythm, that full life, the illusion of importance and responsibility a rank gives you, a Velcro patch on your chest, a command, a power, in the Joffre camp in Rivesaltes we bivouacked in pretty sordid barracks, having come down from the Larzac plateau in Corbières or somewhere with weapons and gear—target exercises, maneuvers, I of course didn't know where we were camping, what these run-down buildings were, and who had been harbored in February 1939, then in 1942, then in 1963, in short all the possible uses of a well-situated military camp, close to the road, to the railroad and to the sea, a camp whose archival images I saw much later, I slept in a khaki sleeping bag where Spanish Republican refugees had slept, soldiers or civilians, Red or Black, who so frightened Daladier's France that the French deemed it preferable to intern them then exploit their labor in weapons factories and hilltop fortifications until the Germans deported them to Mauthausen, most of them, among them Francesc Boix the photographer, born in Barcelona in the neighborhood of Poble Sec on August 31, 1920, interned in Rivesaltes then in Septfonds, enrolled in the Foreign Workers' Companies and captured by the Germans he arrived in Mauthausen on January 27, 1941, stayed there four years, the blue triangle fastened onto his chest: his photos, stolen from the SS, document camp life, death everywhere, Francesc Boix testified at Nuremberg and at Dachau, he died in Paris on July 4, 1951, two months before his thirty-first birthday Francesc Boix dies of illness at the Rothschild Hospital without having seen Barcelona again, in Paris he lived in an attic room on Rue Duc on the corner of the Rue du Mont-Cenis, five minutes by foot from my place, we passed each other at the Rivesaltes camp, we passed each other on the slopes of Montmartre, he worked as a photographer at the paper *L'Humanité*, of course, why anything but humanity, I went to see the house where he was born in Barcelona, a quiet neighborhood on the side of a hill, with trees, a building from the beginning of the century number 19 on Calle Margarit, his tailor father owned a shop in the corner of his building, today there's a bar, I drank a glass to the health of the young Spanish socialist who enlisted in the Republican army at the end of 1938, when the collapse was certain, when the Battle of the Ebro was lost and when Franco, Millán-Astray, Yaguë, and the others were hurtling towards Barcelona the invincible, propelling 500,000 soldiers and civilians onto the roads to exile, they crossed the border in Cerbère, in Le Perthus, in Bourg-Madame, many would end up going back to Spain or would choose exile in Mexico: Francesc "Franz" or "Paco" didn't have that luck, he left Barcelona once and for all with his companions in arms, the Republic is defeated, Paco doesn't lose his smile, he's seventeen, he has hope, humor, joy, a passion for photography, and a little camera given to him by the son of a Soviet diplomat, a 1930 Leitz, thanks to which he published his first reports in the journal *Juliol*, when the Front was still holding up and the revolution was on the march, Francesc Boix will be the reporter of Mauthausen, I picture him in a striped uniform, in the terrible cold of Austria, for four winters, four long winters of suffering sickness and death that he fills by hiding photos, organizing the resistance, until the liberation—the Spanish liberated the camp themselves and hung a banner to welcome the Americans, Mauthausen and Gusen were overflowing with corpses, but so few compared to the 150,000 or 200,000 deaths in the camp complex, among them the massacred of the granite quarry, the gassed of Hartheim, those dead from hypothermia, immersed in freezing water for hours, the victims of medical experiments, the electrocuted, the hanged, the shot, the sick, the starving, the ones worn out by work, the ones asphyxiated in the gas vans, the ones beaten to death, according to the long list of the Nazi modus operandi, I was eighteen I didn't know about Francesc Boix's fate when I played at war in the Rivesaltes camp, I don't remember dreaming of the deportations there, that of the Spaniards or that of the foreign Jews who passed through there, on their way to death, or that of the Harkis that France put there in 1963 some of whom stayed there for over seven years before permanent housing was found for them—in those rotting barracks that were falling to pieces one after the other, no plaque, no monument, no memorial, Francesc Boix the photographer of the *Erkennungsdienst* of Mauthausen, the very young man from Margarit Street in Barcelona, the witness at the Nuremberg trial, what was he thinking about, after he testified, back at the Grand Hotel, he saw Speer, Göring, or Kaltenbrunner in the accused box, he commented on the photos stolen from the SS, taken by the strange artist officer Paul Ricken, creator, besides the official camp photos, of almost a hundred self-portraits, full-face, in profile, in uniform, wearing civilian clothes, armed, on horseback—maybe it's him Boix is thinking about, that January 27, 1946, lying on his bed in Room 408 of the Grand Hotel in Nuremberg, he's thinking about one of Ricken's photos, one of the most disturbing, where the Nazi snapped himself lying in the grass, arms alongside his body, in a suit, with a nice tie and shoes, in the same pose as the poor guys shot by the guards when, according to the Germans, they were trying to escape: Ricken has offered himself as an imitation of violent death, he arranged himself as the corpse he had photographed the day before, what could be the reason, Boix has copies with him, he looks at them, lying on his bed, he is preparing the second part of his testimony, what will the lawyer for the defense ask him? bah, wait and see, he thinks of Marie-Claude Vaillant-Couturier, so beautiful, he took her portrait for page one of *Regards*, they met in the wings, did they talk about Spain, who knows, Vaillant-Couturier wrote an article on the International Brigades, she too testifies about the camps, they say she went through the monumental entrance to Birkenau singing the Marseillaise, she is truly magnificent, I wonder if Boix was in love with her, if he desired her, his head was probably elsewhere, did he still remember his barracks in Rivesaltes, maybe the same one I slept in, almost fifty years later, I too in uniform, almost as young as he but destined for another fate: the idea of the documents in the briefcase came maybe from Boix the photographer from Barcelona, in any case the 296 images by Paul Ricken are carefully filed, digitized, in my suitcase, not the Mauthausen ones, but the ones from Graz, a sub-camp to which Ricken was transferred at the end of 1944, the report on the death march of the evacuation towards Ebensee, hundreds of dying people finished off with a bullet the minute they dropped from exhaustion, the photos of Ricken the austere are clean and artistic, he took his time, never a shaky blurred badly composed snapshot, just the opposite, a morbid body of work, self-conscious and precise, maybe he was trying to pierce a secret, Ricken the mad SS artist was condemned to life in prison at the Dachau trial in 1946, the 296 photos remained secret—296 close-ups, almost always framed the same way, where you see the killer's face the instant he shoots, sometimes tense, sometimes relaxed, usually impassive, and the effect of the shot, at the same instant, a black cloud rising from the head of a man stretched out, a collection of executions documenting the massacre, how was Ricken able to convince the SS to let itself be photographed, I have no idea, Paul Ricken was a strange man, professor of art history member of the National Socialist Party from the very beginning, Boix and his Spanish comrades describe him as a pretty nice guy, not a brute, he never denounced his detainee "employees," never manifested any violence, he was just a wee bit deranged, I think he was documenting his own moral collapse in his hundreds of self-portraits, he saw himself falling along with the world around him, falling into the bottomless night and it's that night he photographed for a week during the death march, it's a journey, an itinerary, like my own from the Rivesaltes camp all the way to the train to Rome, the disappearance of a man into a fascination with violence, his own disappearance and others—Francis Servain Mirković disintegrated in the same way Paul Ricken did, maybe I too wanted to document the journey, disappear and be reborn with the features of Yvan Deroy, if that's possible, the train is moving forward, soon Bologna, then

Florence and finally Rome, I suddenly have the strange sensation that something is going to happen in this car, something tragic like during the march of Paul Ricken the Nazi artist in eyeglasses, my neighbor is sleeping, his head back his mouth open the crossword-couple is conversing in low voices nothing new beneath the railroad sun temperature constant speed more or less constant so far as you can judge it on the black screen of the window where, from time to time, a sinister hamlet comes to life, we went to Rivesaltes by truck, old canvas-covered trucks that squealed whined rocked on their ancient shock absorbers, the drivers were also conscripts trained on-the-job in a barracks yard, their notions of driving couldn't have been more military or abrupt, stand on the brakes on the descents, we were jostled like sacks on every turn, I felt these same sensations in other trucks in Slavonia or Bosnia except usually it was Vlaho driving, just as badly but with a smile, more than once the guy almost tossed us into the Neretva with our weapons and gear, stubborn as a mule it was as impossible to make him let go of the wheel as to teach him to use the engine for braking, for him shifting down would have meant demeaning himself, a kind of cowardliness, and even today, disabled, he descends Dalmatian hills at full tilt in a vehicle specially modified for his handicap, Vlaho the reckless Catholic wine-growing driver it's been a long time since I saw him last, I confess that's entirely my fault, too many memories, the shadow of Andrija, of our violent acts as conscripts, we'd talk about war, that's for sure, I wonder if Francesc Boix liked to see his companions in deportation again, he probably didn't want to be reminded of certain times, of the little daily base things of the concentration-camp world, you don't survive for four years in Mauthausen without some low actions, without entering the grey zone of the privileged, of the *Prominenten* fed better, beaten less than their comrades, docile subordinates, accountants, administrators or photographers at the service of the camp, who can blame them for having escaped the 186 steps of the stone quarry, the freezing baths or the pickaxe handles, for having come through and survived, the luxury prisoners were authorized to move freely throughout the camp, is there guilt in surviving, probably, in Venice by the edge of the black water when I was thinking about Andrija I was overcome with shame and pain, Andrija's sad death, I am carrying his absent corpse wherever I go, it's heavy, I move forward with his body on my shoulders suitcase in hand, all this is very heavy—in the beginning Lebihan my pimply boss thought my passion for archives and secrets was completely natural, he said to me you'll see, it will pass, beginners are always enthusiastic, it's normal, after all it's one of the advantages of the job, this kind of knowledge, he helped me get information I would normally not have had access to, old records that no longer interested anyone but were still classified "military-top secret," archive reports often microfilm, personal files, Lebihan said that this way of working was the best way to teach me the Service's real way of functioning, to know how to get some piece of information or other, etc., his motto was "archives are the compost that grows information," he was an old hand at the "human" touch, as they say, with him I was in good hands, when he retired he invited me out to lunch, oysters at the Brasserie Wepler, if you please, he was pretty happy, even though he told me he was going to miss it, all this, I picture him clipping newspapers in the countryside around Évreux or Vannes, checking the sources, filling binders with scissors and glue, unless he's given himself over solely to his passion for biking, Lebihan told me as he gobbled up his plump *fines de claires* oysters on the Place de Clichy that when he started out, *for another agency*, he liked investigating the cycling world, we all have our hobbies, he added referring to my own, mine was biking, the leftists and anarchists in bicycling—there's no such thing as a profession not worth examining, I thought, and many facets to national security—of course we didn't find many, pinkos on bikes, that's OK, but I dug up a few each time, especially sports journalists, heh heh, my bosses at the time would always say to me come on, Lebihan, go to the Sorbonne or Nanterre instead, that's where they're recruiting, so then I wandered around the university for a while to put up a front, but as soon as there was a chance to follow the Tour de France or a Paris-Roubaix race, I was there—today he must be caught up in the scandals and finances of his favorite sport, explaining the ins and outs of things to a wife with her mind on something else or to his buddies at the bar, of course I haven't heard any news about Lebihan since our last handshake after brandy at the Wepler, he was moved, the old cyclist, think of it, he had trained me, and trained me well, he had made the style of my notes and reports drier, had taught me all the secrets of the shadowy trades, records and archives, enough to fill the suitcase, he suspected something, of course, but he was too close to retirement really to bother about anything, no need to saddle himself with possible annoyances, the affair with Stéphanie would make the rounds of the Service, or almost, "intimate relations" between functionaries were not encouraged, even if, at bottom, they resolved a certain number of security problems, at worst the possible leaks would remain internal and pillow-talk wouldn't pass the Boulevard door: it was the end of the affair that got me a strategic "removal" into the distant reaches of the Zone for a while, so as not to see her every day, and this thanks to Lebihan's scheming with the personnel department, thanks to the paternalist bicycle-loving boss—Francesc Boix the photographer of Mauthausen loved bikes too, he covered the Tour de France from 1947 to 1950 for *L'Humanité* and *Regards*, on the back of a motorcycle, as required, Lebihan might have classified him as a "Red" at the end of the 1960s if he hadn't died in 1951, poor Francesc dead of a strange illness of poverty or remorse he had contracted in the camp, one of those inexplicable illnesses of which death is the only outcome, I can imagine where it can come from, one winter night in 1943 who knows Francesc Boix might have gotten a few bogus reichsmarks from the Mauthausen camp in exchange for his work, Paul Ricken has him for good, he got him to walk around the first barracks near the entrance, the brothel for prisoners, opened after Himmler's visit six months earlier, a pass costs two marks, a few deportees from Ravensbrück worked there they were chosen by the SS they are beautiful they say, Boix crosses the main yard at night, the first time he went to a brothel it was in Barcelona, near the Parallel, in a murky neighborhood of stinking alleyways, an old-fashioned cathouse, red, full of velvet, the tiny bedroom smelled of lust and Doctor

Cáspar's prophylactic ointment, he lay down with a pudgy Aragonese, much older than him, the business was finished off very quickly, he put his pants back on in a hurry to finish getting drunk with his friends, he should have taken a picture of the young woman, a souvenir of her milky thighs and abundant pubic hair, which grew up almost to her belly-button, he will remember her, but maybe not really the orgasm, at least not as much as he'd like to remember it, pleasure is a lightning-bolt that leaves no trace, he crosses the Mauthausen yard the deathplace to go find his friend Garcia at the brothel, final recompense of Nazi power for those who serve it well: Germany holds us by the balls, he thinks, Germany holds us by the balls and he laughs all alone, that morning fifteen Czechs and Yugoslavs were shot by the Gestapo right next to the identification office where he works, he was developing film when he heard the gunshots, he went out of his darkroom looked out the window saw the corpses sprawled against the wall there were four women among them, and now that night has fallen he's going to the brothel where there's a record-player with German songs, the "guards" of the cathouse are common-law criminals, sent here after the most terrible crimes, killers, rapists, these degenerates are the kings of the camp, their subjects the Jews, Poles, and homosexuals, the nobility are the German opposition parties, the Spanish Republicans, the typical Nazi hierarchy—Francesc Boix passes a few scrawny prisoners returning from a Kommando outside, he greets them with respect, he knows he's lucky, that the few Spaniards employed in the camp administration services are privileged, that the prisoners are succumbing one after the other, exhausted, broken down by slavery and the guards' sadism, he also greets Johannes Kurt the SS officer who's accompanying them, not one of the cruelest, not one of the best either, among the detainees there are also former SS officers deserters from the Eastern Front, they never escaped any chores any heavy labor, they won't last much longer, they have failed, they don't deserve to live, they have betrayed the homeland and its aggressive Führer, Francesc arrives at the door to the brothel, he goes in, takes off his beret, in the antechamber an ex-warder converted into a pimp is slumped in an armchair, his eyes are gleaming, the room stinks of potato-peel alcohol, there's music, *guten Abend, Spanier* says the man, he makes the sign to pass, in the women's room there are women in civilian clothes and men in striped uniforms, voices amiable conversations laughter in the midst of the noise of wooden clogs on the hard floor, a dozen whores, double the number of inmates, Boix catches sight of Garcia deep in conversation with one of the ladies, he goes over, cap in hand like a shy child, the women are speaking German, Garcia introduces him, he hastily tries *ich heisse Franz. Wir gehen?* in his contraband German, they make for one of the adjoining rooms, Francesc holds out his two reichsmarks, the girl takes them, lets her dress fall to the ground, her skin is covered in bruises and scars, she signs to him to go over to the washbasin, she lowers his striped trousers washes his private parts examining them carefully to make sure there are no lice, the water is freezing he feels as if his tool is retracting into the base of his pelvis, he's a little ashamed, he remembers Barcelona here he is silent, he catches hold of one of the woman's drooping breasts she gives him a frightened look he closes his eyes thinks about his Aragonese whore about the photograph he did not take the German woman pulls him by his member to the bed she lies down spreads her legs Francesc stretches out over her she stinks of sweat and barracks her name could be Lola or maybe Gudrun he moves as much as he can with no result she emits carnival cries he pretends to come gets up smiles at her she is ugly neither of them has fooled the other—Francesc Boix goes back to the main room a smile on his lips Garcia gives him a tap on the shoulder, that's better, isn't it, he says, and Boix replies without lying yes, that's better, that's better already and soon it will be even better, at what instant does he know he'll get out, he'll survive, at what instant does he make the decision to survive? they say that the prisoners knew, saw the ones that had a chance and the ones that were going to die, Manos Hadjivassilis one of the Greek resistants from ELAS who ended up in Mauthausen after quite a tour, escaped twice, recaptured almost a thousand kilometers from Salonika, in the neighborhood of Gorizia in the company of Yugoslav partisans, scarcely had he returned to the camp, while he was still waiting in the identification line, already destroyed by what he saw around him, seized with the certainty that it was the end, Manos suddenly broke out of rank began running towards the electric barbed wire fence to throw himself onto it, the electricity contracted all his muscles made him bleed from his nose and mouth in a smell of ozone and burnt flesh he was still alive when a guard finished him off with a reverent volley of gunfire, *exit* Manos Hadjivassilis the Greek communist from Macedonia who had traveled the Epirus and crossed the

Balkans on foot rifle in hand, the image of his corpse photographed by Paul Ricken will appear in Francesc Boix's developing bath, then it will be hung on a clothesline to dry, in the meantime Manos's body will already have disappeared into the crematorium, to end up in the heart of Austria's filthy sky, let's hope that Zeus the patient made that grey cloud rain down on Olympus, Boix will get out of the camp, and will even go to Greece to cover the civil war for communist publications, a respite, a brief reprieve before the Rothschild Hospital and the Thiais cemetery, Francesc was already dead, he was already dead in Mauthausen which you don't leave, he was dead in the arms of the German prostitute, one night at the brothel of Barracks No. 1, in impossible contact with that Gudrun or Lola, his soul fallen between their two bodies, that's where he contracted the illness, there, in the impossibility of finding anything but more or less putrid flesh, no other contact possible, no consolation, an eternal solitude caught hold of him, he would float over the world without touching anything, like Paul Ricken documentarist of deterioration, stricken with the same affliction—if I think about it, my attempts at escaping the Zone and memory are part of the same syndrome perhaps, what happened, in Venice with Marianne, in Paris with Stéphanie the brunette, in the harlot bars in Zagreb or the sordid cabarets in Aleppo, what happened in Bosnia, what is waiting for me at the end of this trip, in Rome, in the distant tenderness of Sashka and her apartment, what's waiting for me under the name Yvan Deroy the mad, will I be able to rid myself of myself the way you take off a sweater in an overheated train, in the black despair of the Bolognese night, suburbs without end, I tremble at the memory of Stéphanie's face, I see her portrait thrown out yesterday with the rest of the apartment's useless objects, maybe a homeless man will recover it for its frame or for the shoulder-length dark-brown hair, the few spots of red on the nose and cheeks, the very calm half-smile, sure of herself, the black polo-neck, a three-quarter-length portrait with the Hagia Sophia and the Bosporus behind her, from the window of our last hotel room, a portrait of a dazzling beauty, maybe the tramp going through the trash is also falling in love with her, he sees her and immediately he swoons, he'll keep the photo to keep himself company, he'll talk to it, invent a name for it a life a passionate love story, if he only knew, if he knew Stéphanie Muller the brilliant strong dangerous Alsatian, I saw her before she left on a job, before she went under the drainpipe, as we say in our jargon, to be under the drainpipe means to leave on a job abroad and hence to get a rain of cold hard currency on your head corresponding to three or four times a Parisian salary, Stéphanie destined for a great future is probably in Moscow at present, I'm supposed not to know where she is, I shouldn't have thought about her again, it must be very cold in Moscow, a little like in Alsace, not at all like here in gentle Mediterranean Italy, I shift in the seat, I want to get up, take a few steps to chase away the image of Stéphanie with the perfect body, the perfect voice, the keen intelligence, Stéphanie to whom I told the story of Francesc Boix the photographer of Mauthausen during our trip to Barcelona, how can you care so much about such stories, she said, she was reading Proust and Céline, nothing but Proust and Céline, which gave her, I think, the cynicism and irony necessary for her profession, she was rereading the *Journey* and the *Recherche* she called them by those abbreviated names, the *Journey* and the *Recherche*, both in the Pléiade editions, of course, and she filled me with jealous admiration, I hadn't managed to finish the *Recherche*, the stories of Parisian aristocrats and bourgeois bored me almost as much as their narrator's complaining, and the *Journey* depressed me terribly, even though the wanderings of those poor guys had something touching about them all the same, when we left on vacation or for the weekend Stéphanie put in her bag either one of the volumes of Proust or the first volume of Céline, you don't change perfume brands, she didn't change her book, her Chanel and her Marcel, and voilà, ready to go, her only concessions to novelty were books *about* Proust and Céline, separately or together, which she skimmed, critically, and these essays comforted her in her monogamy, encouraged her to return to the Text after the commentary: listen, she said, notes and reports land on me all day long, I write analyses, I have a right to a little relaxation, the right to read well-written things, it's a change for me, Stéphanie is a specialist in what we call the *risk-countries*, she worked for a while in the Strategic Affairs Department before passing the test for our magnificent barracks of shadows, before it was suggested to her that she pass the discreet administrative test instead—in Barcelona city of banks and palm trees I looked for the traces of Boix, republicans, anarchists, militants in the POUM, Stalinists from the PSUC, she talked about tapas, the Picasso Museum, Miró, she said it's *sweet*, this restaurant is very *sweet*, the neighborhood is really *sweet*, Gaudí is *sweet*, she was so beautiful, with her sunglasses by the harbor, watching the ferries leaving for Majorca and Minorca, her hair down to her shoulders, her hand in mine, I forgot my Zone, my suitcase, I became a tourist, which is the pleasantest of conditions when there are two of you, when you have money and you want to make love all the time, she told me again stop thinking about those war stories, why don't we go back to the hotel? we'd go back to the hotel and wouldn't emerge until nightfall, to plunge into the carnival of little streets in the center of Barcelona that looked as if they were made by the tourists themselves to make them *sweet*, the way an old whore puts on a purple wig if necessary, ready to do anything to please you, Barcelona whispered *fiesta, fiesta* in the ear of the man from the North ready to do anything to have fun, stuff himself with sun and paella, drown in liters and liters of red sangria thick as the blood of the bulls on the Monumental whose ritual deaths gave taboo shivers to the French, the English, the Germans convinced by such a well-performed spectacle of a savage and mysterious Spain that they alone knew, you could even find absinthe for the incurable romantics, I remember there was a joint called the *Marseille* at the bend of a sinuous alleyway peopled with very ugly streetwalkers, a bar run by a bald German man, obese and antipathetic, a tavern stinking of filth, anise and cold tobacco, I went in with Stéphanie blinded by love and the *Hitchhiker's Guide*, someone slid an absinthe over to us that would have made Van Gogh cry, along with a plastic bottle of water and a cube of sugar wrapped in paper, traditions are reconstructed, the tourists and native twenty-somethings stirred their sugar in the absinthe with a spoon like a café au lait, the magic green tasted depressingly of chartreuse, the music and voices were deafening, *sweet*, so alive, I thought about poor Francesc Boix and his Aragonese prostitute, the stars of the neighborhood were named Jean Genet and Pierre Mac Orlan, there was even a very chic seafood restaurant that prided itself in having welcomed them and proudly displayed the badges of tourist guides from all over the world, queer Genet the scrawny thief must not have eaten often in high-class restaurants, may his soul rest in peace, with his johns and his gypsies with their long gleaming knives, the smelly bald German ended up throwing us out because we weren't drinking fast enough for him, a liberation really, who knows the grandson of one of Boix's guards at Mauthausen might now be serving absinthe to the photographer's great-nephews, Stéphanie was a little drunk and enchanted by the experience, she didn't want to go back right away, we strolled around the harbor, where in 1569 Miguel de Cervantes had set off for Italy, two years before the Battle of Lepanto, for which they were building immense galleys in drydocks nearby, reconverted today into a Maritime Museum—Cervantes with his ruff sees the military ships on the beach pulled onto dry land, the slaves feasting not knowing that soon he'll be on board one of these vessels, maneuvering an arquebus facing the cruel Turk, he looks for a while at the bonfires on the sand, it's evening, he plunges into the little streets near the Church of Santa María del Mar to find a bar suitable for getting drunk in, where they serve the thick wine from the surrounding villages and, tolerably drunk, not long before midnight, he engages in an animated argument with a local gentleman: why they came to blows, I don't know, they decide to go out, inflamed by alcohol and insults they draw swords on a small square nearby, Cervantes is a swaggerer but he's drunk, the steel clashes twice, only twice and his foil flies away, leaving him disarmed at the mercy of the Catalan, who must have been a poet, who must surely have been a poet for instead of skewering him straightaway he decides to humiliate the man from Madrid, orders him to strip naked, at sword's point, before having a solid beating administered to him by his men in arms and leaving him half fainting on the uneven flagstones in the cruel night—exhausted, aching all over Cervantes drags himself over to the wall surrounding the harbor, he's still drunk, and he laughs, he can't help laughing out loud at his own bad luck, decidedly there are no more knights or chivalry, man is naked, now, in the maze of modernity, he puts on the long johns his adversary had the kindness to leave him not without having first dipped them in the gutter, puts them on and turns back to look for a welcoming tavern where he can go on laughing and forget his bruises, shirtless, as undressed as Don Quixote the inspiration for whom will come to him later on, thinking about the Barcelona brawl, a drunkards' brawl as is necessary in literature—with Stéphanie we went into quite a different bar, the modern, stylish side of the Catalan capital, a red-and-white place, sober, where customers drank standing up, in the artistic phantasmagoria of a video projector, cocktails in assorted colors: there were well-dressed men, elegant women, and the contrast was so great that we got the impression of a schizophrenic, or illusionist, city, on one side the squalid phony nostalgia and on the other the most avant-garde image of calm bourgeois modernity, far from Don Quixote, the two aspects each just as artificial as the other, it seemed to me, Barcelona's identity must be hidden somewhere between these two images, just as Beirut on exactly the other edge of the Zone swung endlessly between gleaming modernity and belligerent poverty, a reflection, a symmetry with Barcelona, if you fold the Mediterranean in two over the central axis of Italy the two harbors of the East and West will cover each other exactly, in Beirut when I went there on a mission our guys from the embassy often took me to a nightclub with the strange name BO18, a huge depot behind the harbor in the Quarantaine district, where one of the first massacres of the civil war took place, in 1976 the Phalangists had sent Intissar's Palestinians to the firing squad along with the Kurds who lived in this putrescent camp that was wedged between the containers on the docks and the town dump, and it's at this exact spot of butchery that the owner opened his establishment, where a pleasant alternation of world music and Arab pop roared, during its most crowded period the ambiance was incredible, magnificent young women danced on top of rectangular tables, on the endless bar, the décor and lighting were dark and in good taste, in the explosive atmosphere of the overheated club everyone drank B-52 cocktails set on fire with a lighter by an expert bartender, everyone was pouring sweat, everyone was moving, at times a loud siren sounded, like the ones used during air raids and suddenly, miraculously, the mobile roof of the depot opened, the stars and sky of Beirut appeared over the dancers and drinkers and the songs, shouts, music rose to the skies like a column of smoke, spreading celebration and joy into the Bay of Jounieh, into the early hours of the morning, the opening of the ceiling was regulated automatically by the ambient temperature and protected the last customers from the coolness of dawn by closing gently, like a vampire's sarcophagus, I was drunk at the BO18 it was almost 7:00 A.M. it was broad daylight sprawling in a corner I watched the employees start cleaning up, in the huge empty room I looked at the arrangement of the tables, in parallel rows, blocks of wood, about two meters long all lined up like in a cemetery, tombstones, I thought in my drunkenness, the tombstones of the massacred ones of the Quarantaine, I looked closer and in fact each table bore a little bronze plaque on the side, invisible in the dark, with a list of names in Arabic, the customers were dancing on the symbolic coffins of the dead of the Quarantaine, war sirens resounded in the night, Beirut was dancing on corpses, Beirut was dancing on corpses and I don't know if it was a posthumous homage or a kind of vengeance, a revenge on the war that prevented people from dancing in a ring, a kind of memorial also, a musical cemetery for those who had no grave, a smoking libation during a funeral banquet, funereal dances, one last cocktail before oblivion—the Lebanese are champions of design and interior decorating on that side of the sea, just as the Catalans are on the other, they put tragedy on display: in Beirut, you don't find many monuments to the civil war, not many plaques, no memorial, each person bears his share of memory as well as he can, as Rafael Kahla the writer bears the memories of the Palestinian fighters, Intissar and Marwan, legends abound, like the mythic tales of Ghassan in Venice, the ogres of the Lebanese war, their deeds of prowess, the host of one lord against another, the dead the disappeared all that gets carried individually, it's a personal story of tears and revenge, in Barcelona though on the other side of the sea the rediscovered democracy has proliferated homages and monuments, the streets were renamed, George Orwell the disillusioned Trotskyite militant even has a square in his name in the old city, true it smells of urine, but it's a pretty little square surrounded by slightly sordid bars, peopled with Italian neo-hippies playing *Bella Ciao, Bella Ciao* on the recorder, another place that Stéphanie thought *sweet*, like nearby Avignon Street where I like to think Picasso received Inspiration in a brothel, his demoiselles d'Avignon were frail prostitutes in a Barcelona whorehouse, now an inn for tourists—Stéphanie armed with Proust and Céline liked everything, the pretty neighborhoods with the wide avenues where characters from the Faubourg Saint-Germain or the Opéra might have strolled, and the somewhat downtrodden historic district where Bardamu's Iberian colleagues must have exercised, between twilight and dinnertime we'd stay at the hotel, after making love we'd read, *History of the Spanish War* by Brasillach and Bardèche for me, which the old fascist had given me when I was still in high school and which seemed to me the best book, along with Orwell's reminiscences, for an escapade in Catalonia, Stéphanie was beside herself, that makes me sick she said, you should be ashamed of lugging around those Nazi monstrosities here, I tried to explain to her that this version of history had been the official one in Spain until the end of Francoism, the bad ones were the Reds, the good ones the others, and that there were still a few "historians" who defended the argument according to which

Franco had saved Spain from Stalin and the anarchists, who were even worse, Stéphanie wouldn't budge, that's no reason, she said, to read fascists and Nazis, so I'd use another argument, a low blow, I'd say and what about Céline? wasn't Céline an anti-Semitic fascist? she'd get upset, would answer it's not the same, it's not that simple, I agreed completely, it's not that simple, and we left it there, it wasn't that simple, in fact it was quite complex, Stéphanie Muller brilliant French intellectual geopolitical analyst for our strange Service began tickling me in revenge, and the political argument would finish in feathers and mattress noises, I think she could have forgiven Brasillach if he had written one single great book, but for her he was a mediocre writer who didn't deserve any leniency, he had been pumped full of lead at the Liberation, and voilà, purified—France was purified, Stéphanie tickled me and Barcelona shone with all its modern European festive Catalan lights, and didn't want to remember that it had gotten richer especially in the 1960s, when Francoism was in full swing, that the local middle class had very quickly adapted to the dictatorship and had made a fortune exploiting tens of thousands of migrants from all over Spain: poor Orwell, in his hotel room near the Plaça de Catalunya, today a stone's throw away from the Fnac store, the local Galeries Lafayette, and a cosmetics store, pursued by the Stalinists after the war in the war of May 1937 that pitted them against the POUM and the anarchists, forced to flee to avoid repression, the handsome Orwell in his room understands the battle is lost, and this was almost two years before the end, before the long route that will lead Boix to Mauthausen, terminus, the North—Stéphanie the gentle loved revolutionary myths, the raised fists and *no pasarán* slogans, she preferred Orwell's memoirs to the ideological ravings of Bardèche and Brasillach, Brasillach the Catalan from Perpignan loved to go fishing by lamplight on the Collioure side, in his cousin's boat, gleaming anchovies, pudgy sardines, was he already anti-Semitic, had he even met a Jew yet, had he already succumbed to the ease of paranoia and conspiracy, he who often passed by the Joffre camp in Rivesaltes, where, after the Spanish soldiers, a good part of the foreign Jews rounded up in unoccupied France were concentrated, Brasillach approved of these deportations, according to him Jews had to be gotten rid of down to the children, but that's not why De Gaulle had him shot, that morning, February 6, 1945, in the freezing dawn of the Montrouge fort, Brasillach shouted *Vive la France* like the Resistants sent to the firing squad before him, De Gaulle the noble had rejected Brasillach's appeal for clemency for obscure reasons, hatred of homosexuals maybe, maybe to appease the communists, maybe out of laziness, or maybe, as Stéphanie thought, because Brasillach wasn't all that great a writer, but certainly not for anti-Semitism, if he had just been an anti-Semite Brasillach would have been pardoned, witness his brother-in-law Maurice Bardèche who was liberated after a few months in prison or Céline himself, repatriated after months freezing his balls in a cabin in Denmark: the bitter little doctor was a supporter of Zionism and the state of Israel, supposed to rid Europe of its cumbersome Jews, those hybrids, those unclean stateless people, and Stéphanie thought deep down inside that he was right, that actually exile was the only solution to the Jewish problem, the answer to the Jewish question and Israel was a practical closet to put away these cumbersome flotsam and jetsam from the Mediterranean, Central Europe, or France, these debates depressed me, I thought about Harmen Gerbens the Dutchman and about his apartment, about the Jews of Cairo and Alexandria who came through Spain in 1967, about all those movements in the Zone, ebb, flow, exiles chasing other exiles, according to the victories and defeats, the power of weapons and the outlines of frontiers, a bloody dance, an eternal interminable vendetta, always, whether they're Republicans in Spain fascists in France Palestinians in Israel they all dream of the fate of Aeneas the Trojan son of Aphrodite, the conquered with their destroyed cities want to destroy other cities in turn, rewrite their history, change it into victory, in other places, later on, I thought about a page from the notebook of Francesc Boix, the Barcelona photographer, one of the pages of the lost manuscript of his memoirs, *the path changed, the ruts were full of corpses and the shadows of corpses, the road no longer follows the same bends, the sky seems heavier as if the clouds were still grinding and chewing on who knows what ideas, ideas that want nothing more of us, with Estrella a long time ago, her fingers closed over my wrists like handcuffs made of flesh, the smoke-filled air of the crowded café didn't even make her eyes cry, not one tear, nothing, just that aquamarine clarity that you know promises more than it can fulfill, Miguel and Inés were there too that night, we had decided not to reshape the world but to add a few absurdities to it, spots of incongruity so as to shade its cruel leaden color, my pockets were full of bills that were no longer in circulation, I walked around with one finger over the flame of tenacious little candles, Estrella spoke to me about that illness that had almost made her into a little frozen body slipped under the earth, about the drunken doctor who had succeeded, by no one knows what chance, in diagnosing her ailment and giving her the means to recover from it, and as I listened to her I couldn't prevent myself from feeling each of her illnesses, from following the moving curve of her pain, I became the memory of each of the drops of sweat that appeared on her skin, I was the fever, her fire fed from the ice in her eyes, all this Estrella told me by half-hints, between sips, between sighs light as feathers, everything always being done in the space between, a parody of twilight, I understood then that I would spend the night in Estrella's arms, that it was not a question of either choice or desire, the city was bathed in an implacable glow, you heard engines growling and drunkards yelping, as if the city were dreaming it was the country, at night certain squares could have been fields, and suddenly Estrella got up, an ascension, a miracle, her chin showed me the door, Inés and Miguel followed us for an instant then disappeared, they stopped existing or returned to a state before existence, everything seemed to dissolve then Estrella's breathing became more irregular and I knew we were running, not really, but in our hearts, in our flesh, a staircase presented itself to us and ten minutes later she threw me on a bed, the city had the delicacy to absent itself behind the windowpane, all noises contracted into an infinitesimal echoing fist, I wanted to forget the seconds as they unfurled before my eyes, I couldn't have endured it if they'd accumulated, formed a deposit, conspired against me, I wanted to stay fragile and volatile, but Estrella was like mercury, she rolled over me, twisted around me, I couldn't manage to unfasten her clothes, my fingers got bogged down in the countless buttons on her sweater, my eyes were closed and I felt as if I could see the inside of my body, a landscape in constant transformation, peopled with panting machines and frightened monsters, it was the alcohol, of course, but also the exhaustion of a man dedicated to losing himself in the beauty of the other, there was a moment when I felt her taking me inside her, and the blood in my temples sang like a drumroll, my nails dug in, my teeth sought her bones, somewhere in a neighboring room a gramophone liberated an opera aria, a woman's voice conquered but furious began to speak to us, about what we would become if we made the mistake of changing these gestures into habits, these cries into promises, space into time, then everything shattered, everything stopped, I was by the harborside and I was smoking a cigar, I was old, very old, people passed in front of me floating, there were two suns in the sky, I think I had just perfected such a powerful bomb that even the seas would catch fire, a telegram told me at the last instant that my evil project had been found out, I had to give myself up to the authorities, but instead of that I tried to jump-start a stolen car, the starting crank refused to turn, children were making fun of me and anxiety ended up snatching me from that bad dream, Estrella was sleeping right up against me, she was smiling in her sleep, both her hands rested between her thighs, it must have been 5:00 in the morning, I went out without leaving a word, the seal of her lips on my neck, more whole than the day before, a little older, too, as if there were still unsuspected virginities to abandon to life,* said Boix, five years after Mauthausen remembering Barcelona today a pearl of the Mediterranean capital of triumphant Catalunya full of the arrogance, the haughtiness of the new nationalist conquerors, proud of their economic victory over Castilian oppression, where the *good ones* finally triumphed, obtained the posthumous revenge they wished for: hand in hand with Stéphanie we would stroll on the beach and the seafront that had been recently remodeled, modernized, rid of their greasy spoons, planted with palm trees, torn away from George Orwell and Francesc Boix, hustled towards Cannes Genoa or Nice with huge tourist investments, ready to receive the masses of Scandinavians coming to thaw on the sand, around 7:00 p.m. the Ramblas was covered with an inexorable wave of bikinis and beach towels wrapped around exhausted flesh red from the sun, hurried buses released their clouds of amateur photographers in front of the Sagrada Familia, tons of paella were defrosting in ovens, Stéphanie bought herself shoes, dresses, costume jewelry—I managed to convince her to go to the end of Diagonal Avenue, when it meets the sea so dear to promoters and modern town planners, to see an immense worksite, a vacant lot strewn with bulldozers and cement mixers, at the base of elegant buildings, with a view, among the most expensive and modern in the city, this lot swarming with workmen used to be called the Campo de la Bota, Boot Camp, and the Falangists picked it out for an execution place, where people were shot, 2,000 innocent men, anarchists, union members, workers, intellectuals, massacred under the windows of today's luxury apartments, summarily condemned by a distraught and overworked court martial, then handed over to a distraught and overworked firing squad, before their memory was once and for all buried by distraught and overworked immigrant workers: at the scene of the carnage with the 2,000 corpses the Barcelona town hall built its Forum of Cultures, Forum for Peace and Multiculturalism, on the very spot of the Francoist butchery they raised a monument to leisure and modernity, to the *fiesta*, a giant real estate operation supposed to bring in millions in indirect revenue, tourism, concession stands, parking lots, and once again to bury the poor conquered ones of 1939 forever, the downtrodden, the ones who can only resist the excavators and backhoes with the endless list of their first and last names, Stéphanie was suddenly indignant, but there's no monument? no plaque? I replied don't worry, a brilliant architect will find a way to hide a vibrant homage inside his work, even if it means putting a few false bullet holes in a concrete wall, today the Forum of Cultures is used mainly for concerts, they dance on corpses as in Beirut, as in BO18 on the Quarantaine in Beirut, but instead of a dance of memory it's that dance of oblivion that only state-controlled memory allows, which decides where it is good to remember and where it is better to put a parking lot, much more useful to a European city than cumbersome remembrances of people who are dead, in any case, dead today from old age, bedridden, insane or sick, their children and their grandchildren are happy, they have motorbikes tramways and bicycle paths, beaches to put tourists on, a few thousand Francoist bullets aren't going to change things, you can't live sitting there sniveling over corpses, it's the way the world turns, I thought about the cheap buildings that clutter the former Bolzano camp today, they don't beat their wives any more there than elsewhere, I suppose, ghosts unfortunately do not exist, they don't come to pester the tenants of the housing projects in Drancy, the new inhabitants of the ghettos emptied of their Jews or the tourists visiting Troy, they no longer hear the cries of children burned in the ruins of the city: in La Risiera in Trieste I passed a group of high school students on a field trip, in the middle of the barracks near the crematorium they were very busy murmuring sweet nothings to each other, furtively smoking, elbowing each other, under the severe gaze of an emotional history teacher, here so many people have suffered, she said, and this sentence had no meaning for them, or so little, that's normal, it will come to have less and less, just as today the monuments to the dead of 1914 in France don't affect anyone anymore, the *poilus* sit enthroned on flower-covered roundabouts in squares opposite solemn churches, leaning on their stone Lebel rifles their haversacks beside them their helmets on their heads a curiosity a decorative item, just as the Marathon column no longer wrings the heart of any tourist, no more professional mourners at Thermopylae in front of Simonides of Ceos's epitaph, *stranger, go tell the Spartans that we died to honor their laws*, Leonidas the Spartan is a Belgian brand name today, I'd happily devour a chocolate bar to the health of the king killed by the Persians, a little sweetness melting in the train that's approaching Bologna

like train tracks at night straight lines infinite networks of relays and us, usually silent, strangers who don't open up to each other any more than we do to ourselves, obscure, obstinate, lost in the countless tracks that surround the inextricable railroad knot of the Bologna station, endless shuntings, circuits, sidings, a station divided into two equal parts where unlike Milan the gigantic size of the building is replaced by the profusion of the tracks, the verticality of columns by the number of crossties, a station that has no need of any architectural excessiveness because it is in itself excessive, the last great crossroads in Europe before the Italian cul-de-sac, everything passes through here, bottles of Nero d'Avola from the slopes of Aetna that Lowry drank in Taormina, marble from the quarries of Carrara, Fiats and Lancias meet dried vegetables here, sand, cement, oil, *peperoncini* from Apulia, tourists, workers, emigrants, Albanians who landed in Bari speed through here on their way to Milan, Turin or Paris: they've all come through Bologna, they've seen their train slip from one track to the other according to the shuntings, they didn't get out to visit the basilica, they didn't take advantage of any of the charms of a pleasant bourgeois city, suave and cultivated, the kind of city where you like to settle, the kind that offers you an early retirement and where you awaken, without anything particularly special having happened, on the threshold of death forty years later, a city like Parma, a nice place to live, a place where you die pleasantly and in a civilized way, with enough distractions so that boredom becomes the habitual caress of a mother putting her child to sleep, a city whose labyrinthine train station protects you from the uncertain world, from outside trains from the throb of the irregular from speed and from foreign places, a station I'm entering now the platform is sliding by in an orangey light, the pneumatic locks wheeze, the doors open, my neighbor a little surprised a little sleepy gets up picks up a little suitcase takes his magazine and goes out, ciao now I'm alone, wondering if someone's going to sit down opposite me or if, when the loudspeaker announces a three-minute stop, I'll be left to myself for ever and ever, like the little medieval wooden crucifix that somehow survived the twelfth century lost in an obscure chapel in San Petronio the magnificent basilica not far from here, solitary in the midst of flamboyant suffering Christs, this one has a little half-smile, the first time I saw it it was pouring out the rain was coming down in buckets it was the deluge and the church was full of people taking shelter from the rain, including a group of Senegalese sellers of fake Versaces looking towards the door at the rain coming down without a care in the world for what there was behind them, the splendor of the Church and the magnificence of its history were nothing to them and they were right they were selling bags to tourists and African statues *Made in Indonesia*, what could this pagan temple overloaded with figurines possibly do for them aside from shelter them for a while from the storm, like me, who knows, probably I went into the temple so as not to get soaked, or out of curiosity, or out of idleness, I was in transit, I was headed for Bari to board one of those Greek tubs that crisscross the Adriatic, when the storm broke I found shelter in the cathedral facing the little polychrome wooden crucifix so simple and so contrite it looked like the fetish from Tintin's *The Broken Ear*, what did I do to see it, in that dark corner where you couldn't even turn a light on for a 500-lire coin, those light-up fixtures typical of Italian churches must pay all the electricity bills for all the churches including the Vatican, back then only about half of them worked, the length of time the light stayed on was in inverse proportion to the fame of the work of art, two minutes for a Caravaggio, five for a somber Virgin with or without Child, but my little crucifix stayed in the dark, it has the beauty of primitive things, the thick face, the almond-shaped eyes, and the craftsman I sense behind it—a cobbler, a carpenter—must have cherished this little magical being in the same way a child adores his doll, with devotion and tenderness, like the anecdote about Moses and the shepherd by Rumi the mystic from Konya: the little shepherd was singing for God, he wanted to caress Him, comb Him, wash His feet, cuddle Him, make Him beautiful, the severe bearded horned Prophet hooked on His transcendence scolded him for his disrespect before he in turn was reprimanded by the Lord Himself, *let the simple worship me simply* He said and I imagine the medieval sculptor scrubbing his little crucifix to paint it, singing hymns, smelling the red odor of the wood that's more alive than marble, God at that time was everywhere, in the trees, in the cabinetmaker's chisel, in the sky, the clouds and especially in the dense chapels dark as caves that you entered with terrified respect, where the thick incense penetrated a real curtain of smoke masking the beyond, and when you went home you were ready to have your feet nibbled by the devil in your bed, you were ready to be cured by a saint and blinded by the apparition of an angel, in San Petronio Basilica in Bologna the Italians not long ago thought they could avert one of the strangest Islamist attacks ever, an artistic one, the alleged terrorists supposedly wanted to destroy a fresco by Giovanni da Modena, painted in the early fifteenth century and representing hell according to Dante, a horrible demon devours and tortures sinners in it, and among them, in the ninth trench of the eighth circle, Mohammad the prophet of Islam, lying suffering on a rock, under Dante's eyes, as he tells it, in I forget which canto in the *Inferno*, "*cracked from chin to where it farts, between his legs hung his entrails; his heart and all around it showed, and the sad bag that makes shit from whatever is swallowed . . . He looked at me, and with his hands opened his chest, saying 'See how I rip myself apart. See how mangled is Mahomet,'*" poor Prophet, and the painter from Modena has represented him thus, his chest open, which must have aroused the wrath, almost 600 years later, of the so-called Islamists whom the zealous carabinieri had arrested in the noble basilica, sincerely believing they were thwarting an attack of the most odious kind, against Art and civilization—once again the Italian alarm was false, the terrorists were simple tourists they had to release a few days later, the church hadn't blown up, the impious fresco was still in place and the torn-apart Prophet still prey to demons, until the end of time in the Christians' hell, and now the train is starting off again from Bologna, little by little the train advances along the platform headed for Florence, the longest part is over, the longest part was crossing the long plain of the Po just as in the war you had to cross the open space between two hills, chased by the shelter you've just left, hurried on by the one you're going to reach, running all the while expecting the bullet that's going to stop you or the shell that's going to hurl you head over heels launch your limbs your things your guts into the skies split you in half like the Prophet in the shifted earth that dirt of reddened clay where here an eye stuck out, a stray, gelatinous ball, useless in its skull, bound to the mud to nothingness by an absurd filament a trace of brain, there a hand the chance of the explosion left it three whole fingers but not its arm not its shoulder not the head and this extremity with its vanished ring finger lay near a gurgling torso and still as you ran you wondered stupidly what use could a hand be without an arm to jerk off with and without a face to shave, in those leaps of unexpected male humor that make you survive, and yet you ran hard enough to shit in your pants the shells the tanks on your heels just as now the train runs in the dark barely a thousand kilometers away from the slopes that I hurtled down with the Serbs and then the Bosnians hard on my tail: soon the civil gentleness of Tuscany, soon Florence then the *direttissima* line straight to Rome, the suburbs of Bologna stretch out, long grey intestines pierced by the tracks and the train as if by a spear, Dante understood men, *sacci merdae* forever, just as you see them in hell, cut up, dismembered, opened up by an explosion in war, spread apart, in pieces, scattered like an infantry man by a grenade—like the grenade I exchanged in Trieste in 1993 in a bar for three bottles of vodka, I had a grenade in my bag, I don't remember why I'd taken such a risk at the border, the bar owner had talked to us about the "Yugoslav conflict" and what with one thing leading to another we made a deal, he was very happy to have the little khaki object, a deadly pear of a pretty green color and we, we were delighted to have obtained three transparent bottles, we were going to open ourselves up and spread our souls rather than our entrails, Andi and Vlaho and I drank straight from the unhoped-for bottles, we got completely plastered, the alcohol made me lose my balance in the violent wind, in Trieste they affix ropes in the streets so that children old people and drunkards can hold on to them when the bora blows, and it blows from the very mouth of the devil up to a 120 kmh, no kidding, that night despite the improvised handrail I fell down in the force of the gale, I fell down, down, down and Vlaho and Andrija along with me, we laughed like anything when Andrija threw up in the wind and splattered us, Vlaho, me, and a female passerby who wondered for a fraction of a second what these wet smelly drops could be that were suddenly speckling her jacket, before she saw, understood, retched and began running and stumbling away, Andrija didn't need to wipe himself off the wind was so strong, he was a Triton, a fountain spitting out a huge spray of puke that flew back and lapped all over the walls, all over us as we laughed, all over our friendship well-sealed in all fluids, in the stupidity of fluids, in our souls and bodies torn apart by alcohol and war, in blood the debris of life against death like throwing up against a wall, a wall of rifle bullets and Orthodox knives our enemies at the time and now I'm heading towards Rome the Catholic, Rome that Andrija and Vlaho have never seen, never have you seen the chains of Saint Peter in Monti or Bernini's Four Rivers Fountain, neither you Andrija farmer from Slavonia even though you're an ardent believer, nor you Vlaho from Split, nor the little clean-shaven crazy Muslim I killed with my own hands with a knife, with pleasure the way you have a drink, I recognize him, in a rage after unbearable injustice, between the shaky noises from the train, my bayonet an improvised knife in his young Bosnian throat, the joy of his innocent blood bubbling onto my hands, just as Andrija vomited in Trieste in the wind, so vomited the blood of the Serbs eaters of children, or not, what do the reasons for killing matter they're all good reasons in war, after that over-the-border drinking binge between two fronts we went back to Croatia to go to Bosnia, came back to the Slovenians who had made such trouble for us on the way out, much more than the Italians whom we could soften up with my French identity papers and a few pretty banknotes, German of course, from the standpoint of the Europe to come, sitting on weapons and currency like a grandmother on her savings, I was being paid to fight I forget the salary, there are things you didn't do for money, not for the price of a train ticket or the distance in kilometers, I fidget in my seat it's time to go to the bar time to stretch my legs time to take a break in these travels, maybe the only advantage of first class is that the restaurant car is often quite close, I get up, the countryside is still just as dark you can't see a thing outside that's all the better these landscapes say nothing important to me—the little decapitated Muslim, Andrija killed by the shore of the Lašva, Vlaho the easygoing cripple, all of us lined up in our terrible shirts that might as well have been brown, neck cut but no sun, no Apollinaire's *soleil cou coupé*, my pleasure as I sliced the flesh that palpitated with despair of an innocent madman, that salutary vomit on the coat of the haughty lady in Trieste, last acid trace of a disappearing man, that camouflage outfit that brings together soldiers and chaplains, I'll drink them all in one gulp between Bologna and Rome, on the tracks that are so straight, guided, constrained by the rails to another fate, or my own, like the locomotive engineer the only kind of driver who can't decide the route of his machine, forced by metal like one's hand in war towards the victim's throat, he can't deviate, he knows his job, he knows where he has to go, I stumble in the train, with the blade you ignore the slight resistance on the cartilaginous rings of the trachea, asphyxia in blood, the pink and red bubbles of air in his bubbling spray and that reflex of the condemned man, that movement of hands to neck, followed by that contortion of the whole body, it overjoys the one cutting that artery and that vena cava, that pleasure of the executioner, content, he observes the immense puddle grow even bigger beneath the inert head I'm passing through another first-class car, the train seems to have emptied out in Bologna, the restaurant car looks like a provincial brothel, the same red velvet, in Muslim villages I saw handsome male virgins have a sudden rapist's rage in their dark eyes, after coming they would have massacred anyone approaching their prey like hyenas, they wanted to keep for themselves the woman they'd just tortured, giving love in pain a Biblical gesture of an infinite childlike solitary beauty, some cried as they finished off their own victims, who knows where their mothers', lovers' remains were hidden to whom they sent telegrams just as ardent as my own, they wrote letters that no one can ever read since they contain the disappeared gazes of those farm girls torn apart in the mud, sometimes it was funny, Andrija was a champion at making us laugh he had no equal to put a daisy in an ass dripping with cum, shouting *Za dom spremni!* as with an inspired look he penetrated a resistant vagina, sometimes bloody, sometimes scabby, but usually neat, as he said socialism has done a lot for intimate hygiene, thanks be to the devil, still he managed to catch crabs, but it's hard to say if they came from a body, from the straw or from generalized filth, impossible to determine, the louse comes with the soldier and the prisoner, precocious parasites, organisms foretelling the putrescence to come, the real creatures that will truly eat you and that can't be treated with any ointment: bacteria, fungi, larvae, or dogs foxes and crows if you have the bad luck to fall in an out-of-the-way place where no one comes to bury you, to limit to something slow and minuscule the eraser-effect of carrion feeders, which make up the majority of the living organism, just like soldiers, the traveling bartender has a uniform too, he's alone behind the shaking bar that's crossing Italy at full tilt, what'll I get drunk on, how many mini-bottles will I have to gulp down, whiskey would smack too much of a depressed tattletale, of the barracks, I'll choose something more bucolic, some gin, closer to herbal infusion and hence to nature, hedges, thickets, the shores of the Lašva, of Vitez, the plum or grape brandies they make there, like Xoriguer of Minorca terrible juniper concoction of British ancestry, I'll have a gin, dry and warm with a halberdier on the label, in a transparent plastic glass, to the health of Great Britain, to the health of its Queen and of the black horses of Minorca, to Saint John patron of the city of Ciutadella in Minorca, patron of eagles and lost islands, Saint John the Evangelist the Eagle of Patmos first novelist of the end of the world, the bartender is sizing me up, what kind of madman can swallow gin neat with no ice, in a train what's more and I'd be the last one to argue, it's disgusting, it burns and leaves a taste of potion in the mouth, a remedy prescribed by Bardamu himself to cure who knows what somber disease of poverty, we're entering a tunnel, my eardrums are blocked, I feel as if I'm in a cage, I need air, if I could I'd open a window, I'd stick my head out to have my hair tousled by the icy December wind—Stéphanie the brunette her Céline under her arm would lecture me if she were here, she'd say you're not going to drink now, you're not going to get inebriated again, she used the term *inebriated* funny term God knows what book she took it from, I'd choose not to reply, to say nothing, to order my drink or pour myself one calmly without arguing, Stéphanie Muller comes from a family of teachers in Strasbourg, the kind who bleed themselves dry so their children can succeed, they had been so proud of her getting into Sciences-Po, that's where we met before I saw her again a few years later in one of the dark hallways on the Boulevard Mortier, where I was working under the authority of Lebihan lover of oysters—Stéphanie's parents knew she was working as an analyst for the Ministry of Defense, but didn't know where exactly, we all had our secrets, curiously she hated violence so much, weapons and war (odd, given her employer) that I had never really told her about my activities as a Balkan conscript, out of cowardice: for her that whole period of my life was very vague, hazy, a few photos, nothing more, she had never gone to Croatia, she was very surprised to learn that I had spent some months in Venice, in between things, floating like a corpse in the fetid-smelling lagoon, Stéphanie beautiful and brunette wanted to go there, more than once she mounted a fresh attack: why not Venice, she had found a beautiful hotel not too expensive, a vacation would do us good, I had to explain to her that I didn't want to go back there, that I didn't want to see Venice La Serenissima again queen of fog and tourism, not yet, it was too soon, she found that strange, why, why, but ended up agreeing to a change of destination, Barcelona was just as Mediterranean and attractive, in Venice I had been very sick and very miserable I was always cold even rolled up in my rug, I hadn't been able to go back to France, not enough strength, not enough courage and I hid myself right in the middle of the lagoon as I read all night and went out at daybreak one night I gathered together my outfits my uniforms I made a big ball of them that I burned in the shower after soaking it in cooking rum, everything, including the badges: I kept only the dagger, its sheath, and a few plastic crucifixes, knickknacks that they handed out to us by the handful like the keys to paradise that were given to the Iranian volunteers under Khomeini, a reality had to be given to the barbarity that was the beginning of a new life the cloth burned with a thick smoke smelling of crêpes, you don't escape your homeland, I was flambéing my homeland with rum along with my soldier's gear and I was leaving my mother in silence she who had given me this knife and these crucifixes without realizing it it was probably her I wanted to preserve with the war trinkets, the flames of my bathroom holocaust destroyed the illusion of having once had a country with the same ease you down a glass of strong alcohol it's disagreeable at the time you feel its journey down your esophagus and all alone in this bar tearing through the countryside I'll have another, a gin to the health of my zealous Croatian mother, a gin *za dom*, the bartender has guessed my intentions, he smiles at me and gets out another mini-bottle, *spremni*, a gin to the health of the firemen of Venice alerted by the neighbors who took me for a madman, a patriotic gin, my second lukewarm gin, I'd do better to go sit down and go to sleep, not much longer before Florence and not much longer before Rome, if I had gotten out in Bologna I could have gone back to Venice, to the Paradise Lost or the Flying Dutchman to drink spritzes with Ghassan, his crucifix tattooed on his Lebanese biceps, or take a boat to Burano and look at the little fishing houses slant their blues and ochers over the canals, observe the incongruous angle of the bell-tower and spin round in circles the way I'm spinning round in this train that's suddenly going very slowly, we're crossing the black night, even with my eyes glued to the window I can't see a thing, aside from the regular poles of the power lines, aside from a dark shape in the landscape, a mountainous undulation that might be imaginary, might be due to the gin, I have my dose of alcohol I'm slowly calming down, a cigarette and everything will be much better, I'll get to Rome—as if I had a choice, even dead on my seat this train would lead me to my destination, there is an obstinacy in railroads that's close to that of life, now I'm getting idiotic and philosophical, the gin probably, I'll go smoke illegally between two cars, or in the toilet, at least in trains they don't threaten you with a thousand deaths if you smoke in the toilets, it's one of the rare advantages for offenders like me, you can smoke sitting down, which has become a luxury these days, they worry about our health, regardless of who we are, innocent, sinners, victims, executioners, chaste, fornicators we all have a right to the consideration of public health, they're interested in our lungs our liver our genitals with a real solicitude, and it's nice to feel loved desired protected by the State the way those women used to, who said don't drink so much, don't smoke so much, don't look at pretty girls so much, probably the men, my father, my grandfather had to hide for a drop of the stuff in the same way I'm going to take cover to smoke, my grandfather locksmith son of a locksmith made keys and repaired agricultural implements and tools, and that's impossible to imagine today when no one has ever seen a forge, except maybe the bartender, he looks rural, almost like a miner, thickset, rugged forehead, short dense curly very dark hair over fifty I imagine he was born in early 1946 after his father had been busy with his Mussolini adventure his arm raised in salute from Rome to Athens passing through Tirana, a farmer from Campania or Calabria rough but with the big heart of those who make the best soldiers and the best fascists, used to the order of the seasons God family and nature, I picture him freezing in Epirus, pushing a howitzer with no ammunition dragged by two scrawny donkeys, fascinated by the glory of the *bersaglieri* and the genius of Il Duce, confident in victory before taking to his heels facing starving barefooted Greeks who were going to cut off his ears, did he know pleasure with a tall negress in Ethiopia or a coarse Albanian woman with a square face, did he swallow sand in Libya, did he suffer in a Fiat tank where the temperature often exceeds 150 degrees in the full sun, when thirst killed more than the English claymores strewn throughout the desert, pebbles among pebbles, I wonder where the news of Mussolini's fall surprised him, the end of one adventure, the beginning of another, did he know that his village had been liberated a long time ago and that his wife had eyes only for the handsome Yanks, who were young farmers too, from Oregon or North Dakota, his wife forced by her family and her religion to wait for a man about whom she'd heard nothing for almost three years—maybe it was a great love, one of those almost ancient passions that are played out in absence, in illusion, he traveled the war from Greece to Egypt and Russia his ass in the snow his feet frozen while she embroidered her jacket for their wedding day, I'm close to asking the bartender his father's first name, Antonio maybe, he's watching me observe him as I sip the last of my gin, the train suddenly slows down, brakes to approach a curve, probably the train that brought him home in June 1945 had paused here too, a red light between the world that had just been erased and the one that still remained to be destroyed, a woman was waiting for him at the end of the journey, in man's estate when everything is harder, more underhanded, more violent he desired her so without knowing her, Antonio deep down his heart was heavy sad to leave the war he desired this memory with a fervor that sickened him, and I hope he got out of the train I hope that he ran across the mountains until he ran out of breath, sneezing in the blossoming wheat fields, that he let the coolness of the moon caress his shoulder the better to enjoy his unsettling solitude slumped beneath an olive tree I hope he dared to run away during this unhoped-for stop, the train immobilized in the middle of the tracks sometimes you sense you have a chance, there are doors to escape through—Antonio back from the Eastern Front runs through the countryside to escape the fate of Ulysses, the village, his sewing wife, the good hunting dog who will sniff between his legs, he flees the future that he guesses at, sweating blood to support a large family in poverty, emigrate, settle into the suburban raw-cement buildings that emergency services have strewn around cities in the North, where the dog will die first without ever running down a single hare: Antonio back from the war lying near a Tuscan fig tree at night listens to the train start up again, he did well to get out, he thinks, he did well, it's such a beautiful spring night, the first one that smells of hay after years of grease and cordite and stretched out thus between two lives, between two worlds, I imagine it's the perfume of his peasant girl that comes back to him first, if he has already smelled it, leaving Mass, or during the harvest, around Easter time, as she struck the olive trees with a long pole, that mixture of sweat and flowers, that wafting hair under the sun, he speaks to the stars I doubt it, he's not a shepherd out of Pirandello, he's a man coming home from the war, lying there in a field because the train has just stopped, an incident on the tracks, maybe there are many of these soldiers wondering if they want to go back home, trembling still from the German defeat under the caress of green wheat, a little afraid, disarmed, in ragged outfits or in civilian clothes, in a coarse shirt, heavy boots on their feet, he has never seen Tuscany before, has always gone through it in a train or in a truck he's never really taken advantage of these landscapes so civil, so tame, so noble, so human that already the Etruscans and Romans had planted there, barbarians with golden bears romped about in its vines like children, on these hills where Napoleon's soldiers ran laughing after girls, I picture Antonio between two shadowy mountains trying to rid himself of war as he rolls in the grass, with those Italian soldiers forced by Salò's RSI to fight for the Germans, at the end of 1943 all those who refused to go to Russia were deported, they ended up on other trains, headed for Mauthausen after a stay in the Bolzano camp, Bozen the Austrian that is no longer Italy, where they speak German—others escaped the SS and joined the partisans, *i banditi* as Radio Milan called them, many got arrested and deported in turn, Antonio marches in the debacle of the Eastern Front the Red steamroller at his heels while my grandfather, leaving the keys, the forge, the village also becomes a bandit, drawn by weapons and the power they give he learns how to blow up railroad tracks around Marseille, before being arrested by a squad of French Gestapo at the end of 1943, tortured with water and deported to Thuringia to a camp that's part of Buchenwald, how did he escape summary execution in the yard, by the firing squad at dawn, I can guess, I think he denounced all his comrades to escape the pain, he is ashamed, he cracked under torture and handed over his friends, he'll go expiate his treason in Germany as a slave in a REIMAHG underground weapons factory, he'll make ME-262 jet fighters until April 1945—he'll never go back to Marseille, he'll settle down in a Parisian suburb, send for his family, work in a little mechanic's workshop until his death in 1963, he died young, of guilt or the sufferings he endured in the underground camp, where thousands of Italian civilians arrived, deportees from the province of Bologna, rounded up during "anti-partisan" operations—in the mountains we're crossing blindly tunnel after tunnel made by the Germans, mid-1944, killing two birds with one stone, they evacuated the civilian population that supported the partisans and provided a contingent of slaves for the weapons factories, almost 20,000 people were deported from all over Emilia, men and women, only a third saw Italy again, completely forgotten today the Italians died of exhaustion, hunger, beatings or they were poured alive into the cement, which made their mischievous guards laugh so hard they cried, Spaniards Frenchmen Italians Yugoslavs Greeks the whole Mediterranean shore took the path North to go die beneath Teutonic soil soil seeded with all those bones from the South, constrained and forced at first then more or less voluntarily for economic reasons, Spaniards

Italians North Africans Turks all those people will go populate the sprawling outskirts of Paris or Munich, like Antonio the father of my phlegmatic bartender who's cleaning his espresso machine, all these men crossed each other's paths in Buchenwald, Mauthausen, Dachau, in the return convoys, in regiments on the march, some victorious others vanquished, in 1945 there landed in Marseille the French colonial troops demobilized after the victory, goumiers from the mountains and troops from Morocco, Algerian corps, and ten years later it will be the French contingent's turn to set off from there to fight the fellaghas in Algeria, a to-and-fro of war that takes the place of the tide, Marseille the well-guarded port, magical and secret, where, a little before 4:00 in the afternoon, on October 9, 1934, a motorboat from the cruiser *Dubrovnik* berths with Alexander I on board, the long warship dropped anchor offshore, everything is ready to welcome the King of Yugoslavia, the city is decked with bunting, the officials are waiting, the parade horses paw the ground around the touring car that will take the sovereign to the prefecture, it is nice out, my grandfather is twenty-two, he has come out with his very young wife along with a good part of the population of Marseille to watch the monarch pass by on the Avenue Canebière, Alexander Karageorgevitch the elegant is alone, Queen Maria will join him by train straight from Paris, for she is prone to seasickness, the Minister of Foreign Affairs Louis Barthou has come to meet him, distinguished, bearded, wearing glasses, they both take their places in the car that goes up the Canebière, my grandmother has told this story more than once, the two guards on horseback flank the vehicle, the squadron in front, the policemen behind, and suddenly, at the corner of the Square Puget just past the Stock Exchange building a man rushes towards the royal automobile, he climbs onto the left running board, he's carrying a heavy Mauser, he shoots at the surprised Karageorgevitch who faints, a strange little smile on his mouth, the horse guard makes an about-face and slashes the attacker, the policemen on the sidewalk shoot in turn, passersby fall, mown down by the bullets of the constabulary, the assassin cut up by the saber, riddled with lead trampled by the panicking crowd and the escort horses is transported to the nearby police station, the king to the city hall, and the minister to the hospital: all three die almost instantly, Alexander from the cartridges from the giant Mauser, Barthou from a policeman's bullet, and Velichko Kerin the man with a thousand pseudonyms and dozens of different wounds—Kerin or Chernozemski alias Georguiev or Kelemen called Vlado "the Chauffeur" is a Macedonian, that's about all we know about him, he assassinated the King on the joint orders of a revolutionary movement in Macedonia and Ustashi Croatian activists based in Hungary and Italy, three agents of which are arrested in France a few days after the attack and confess to having taken part in it, Mijo Kralj, Ivo Rajić, and Zvonimir Pospisil, on orders of Ustashi leaders including the future Poglavnik Ante Pavelić himself, whom Mussolini would incarcerate a few days later, in order to keep him safe—Kralj and Rajić die of tuberculosis in the Toulon prison in 1939, like Gavrilo Princip their Bosnian colleague some twenty years before, just before seeing the cause of Croatian insurgents triumph in 1941 and the establishment of the NDH under the authority of

Pavelić: Kralj and Rajić died without seeing the triumph, but Pospisil, condemned to life in prison, will be handed over to the new Nazi Croatia by Vichy, irony of fate, as they say, my paternal grandfather was a witness, on the Canebière in Marseille, to the assassination of King Alexander I the worst enemy of my maternal grandfather Franjo Mirković, a functionary in the NDH and one of the first Ustashis, who owed his salvation only to a prompt exile in France via Austria in 1945, my family was formed around this royal death on the Canebière, and my grandmother since then has espoused the cause of her daughter-in-law so well that she tells this adventure to anyone who will listen, *I was there, I was there,* with the benefit of old age she could assure us that she herself shot the bullet at the Montenegrin in the cocked hat, or that she'd run the scarfaced assassin through with her saber, she hesitates, in any case the kind old Marseillaise with the singsong accent is positive, the King was very handsome, very young, he smiled to the assembled crowd as he passed by on that October 9, 1934, which is in a way my birthdate, I killed for the homeland sixty years later, would I have assassinated the hieratic sovereign in cold blood in his motorized coach, maybe, convinced of the necessity of killing the head of the hydra of oppression, I would have found my accomplices in Lausanne, they would have let me in on the plan, the instructions, Mijo Kralj the coarse brute and Ivo Rajić the cunning, if I fail they'll make an attempt on Karageorgevitch with a bomb in Paris everything's ready the dictator just has to behave himself, a toast of gin to the health of Vlado the bloodthirsty "Chauffeur," his face slashed by a knife during a brawl in Skopje the somber, would I have had his cool, his courage, confronted the horses and the dragoons' swords without wavering, in a hotel on the Côte d'Azur, the day before, a young blond Croatian woman would have given me the weapons, a handsome brand-new Mauser C96 she got in Trieste, kindly provided by Mussolini's agents, with two boxes of cartridges and a backup revolver, in the improbable case that the Mauser jams, she is beautiful and dangerous, she knows there's not much chance I'll come back alive, that there's even every chance I'll croak, killed or arrested by the French police, for the Cause, for Croatia, Franjo Mirković Mama's father has been in exile since 1931, in Hungary at first, then Italy, with Pavelić and the other big-name "insurgents," those Ustashis for whom the assassination of the monarch constitutes the first coup and it will earn Pavelić his first condemnation to death in absentia, in France, it's strange that my grandfather chose this country for his exile, a coincidence, he was never bothered outside of Yugoslavia, nor was he even, so far as I know, pursued by Tito's agents who will end up wounding Ante Pavelić with three gunshots in his Argentine refuge, my grandfather was a simple intellectual without any great political responsibilities in the final analysis, unlike his friend Mile Budak, the rural writer great killer of Serbs, a bogus ideologue and Minister of Foreign Affairs in the NDH—Budak won't escape the partisans, he'll end up with twelve bullets in his flesh after a lightning-fast trial, his family massacred near Maribor, the mustachioed pen-pusher didn't have the luck of my grandfather, who had left a little earlier with Mama and her brother for Austria through the Croatian and German lines, in that end-of-April 1945 month of dust, lies, and panic, at the

Slovenian border you have to choose between two routes, the one to Italy and the one to Carinthia held by the British, Franjo Mirković with wife and children is arrested by the English then released immediately, he has money, cousins in France he arrives in Paris at the same time that my paternal grandfather comes back from deportation, in a train, all the trains are leaving in the other direction, southwards now, the soldiers the deported the conquered the conquerors are taking the same route in the opposite direction, just as Antonio the father of my busy bartender goes back to Calabria or Campania and pauses by the train tracks in the middle of a field, will I go back home, what's waiting for me in peace Ulysses is afraid of his wife his dog his son he doesn't want to go back to Ithaca he doesn't want me to down my gin set the cup on the counter I want a cigarette the bartender smiles at me he asks "*un altro?*" I hesitate but I'll get blind-drunk if I have a third, inebriated as the beautiful Stéphanie the sorrowful said, a couple enters the bar they ask for a mineral water and a beer before going back to second class, I hesitate I hesitate I'd like to go out get some air like Antonio back from the war, go on, two's a crowd but three's company I say *va bene, un altro*, what weakness, what weakness, to guzzle lukewarm gin at six euros apiece in a train car, *è la ultima*, that's the last mini-bottle whatever happens I'll have to change drinks, move on to Campari and soda, the last time I got drunk in a train was in the night express that took me to Croatia with Vlaho and Andi, we had taken the bus from Trieste to a tiny no-account village on the Slovenian border to catch the Venice-Budapest stopping in Zagreb around 4:00 in the morning, the steward in our car was a Hungarian he had astronomical supplies of firewater in his cabin, sweet-smelling stuff real eau de Cologne alcohol made from cloves or God knows what Magyar horror, but he was funny and generous, he complained to us about having to go back to war, he spoke a funny Latino-Germanic-Hungarian gobbledygook embellished with a few Slavic words, a tubby guy who smoked like a steam-engine in his cubbyhole, I remember his face clearly as I will remember the tanned face of the bartender of the Pendolino Milan-Rome, *three drummer boys on the way back from war, three drummer boys on the way back from war, rat and tat, ratatatat, on the way back from waaar*, I taught Vlaho and Andrija that song in Trieste, they sang it over and over, in the Budapest train, in the mountains of Bosnia, I'm singing it softly now, *three drummer boys*, not so young anymore, the last able-bodied drummer boy, the king's daughter forsaken on the road, in my country there are prettier girls said the song, Stéphanie posted abroad, I'd like to meet her by chance, or not, so she'd come back, but no, I'm heading for a new life, I'm separating from myself, I'm no longer Francis Servain the spy I am Yvan Deroy promised a new fate a brilliant future paid for with the dead the disappeared the secrets in this suitcase that's getting heavier and heavier, this guilt that doesn't let me go, poor Stéphanie whom I crushed despite myself, I drink a gulp of gin, she didn't suspect anything, she liked plays, cinema, books, she liked to stay in bed for hours caressing me gently, whereas I was sinking into the Zone, I was disappearing not beneath the sheets but into the briefcase and my memories, between missions, contacts, reports, I brought Stéphanie along during my private investigations, "my hobby," as she said, without really understanding either the nature or the interest of the work, she thought I wanted to turn into Simon Wiesenthal or an amateur Serge Klarsfeld, I didn't tell her otherwise—out of laziness, out of an obsession for secrecy, the less she knew the better, after Barcelona she accompanied me to Valencia with the smell of gunpowder and flowering orange trees, she had insisted on coming, always this obsession with vacations, in Carcaixent forty kilometers away Maks Luburić had lived until his assassination in 1969, Luburić the butcher from the Jasenovac camp was also one of the first Ustashis, a companion in arms of my grandfather, so to speak, who especially appreciated murder with a club, enucleation, and dismemberment, which he practiced on an indeterminate number of Serbs, Jews, gypsies, and Croatian opponents—80,000 victims have been identified, how many are still waiting to be discovered, probably four times that many, killed in every possible way, shot hanged drowned starved decapitated with an axe or knocked out with a hammer, Luburić who escaped via Rome found refuge in Spain whence he coordinated post-war Ustashi "activities," I have a letter from him, he is asking my grandfather if he would agree to be the head of the French cell, which the latter probably hurried to refuse, above all not wanting to draw Tito's secret services onto his trail, Luburić's corpse will be found in April 1969 at his home in Carcaixent his skull bashed in and his torso pierced with knife wounds, revenge, revenge, in that village in the outskirts of Valencia where he had decided to settle, on the road to Xàtiva, in the middle of orange trees and ceramics factories, a few kilometers away from the rice fields of Albufera where we stopped to wolf down a delicious paella and stewed eel, Stéphanie was driving the rented Citroën, the landscapes of early October didn't look anything like what I had imagined, the fertile plain along the banks of the Júcar, the mountains began a little further south, the place names often Moorish, Algemesi, Benimuslem, Guadasuar, so many hamlets emptied of their inhabitants by Philip III and the Inquisition in 1609 during the deportation of the Mudejars, the poor Moors transported in galleys from all the ports of the kingdom to African coasts, peasants who had converted to Christianity several generations ago but who persisted in speaking and writing Arabic in secret, the first mass deportation in the Mediterranean, to please the Church and the strict Spanish bishops: many of the 500,000 expelled died on forced marches to the sea, some were thrown into the water by ship's captains who thus spared themselves the journey to the barbarian coasts and others ended up massacred by the unwelcoming Berbers upon their arrival—the kingdom of Valencia thus lost a quarter of its population, leaving certain rural zones completely deserted, only the village names of these descendants of Andalusian Arabs remain, gone are the Moors, as in Alzira that I traveled through with Stéphanie on our way to Carcaixent, Alzira the beautiful homeland of the Arabic poet Ibn Khafaja is now nothing but a block of hideous buildings encircling the remains of an old city once surrounded by ramparts, we stopped to drink an *orxata* on a pleasant square planted with palm trees, one fine early fall afternoon, a little further on a section of the Arab wall survived and some more palm trees, all this bore the ironic name "Square of Saudi Arabia," we started off again for Carcaixent where a surprise was waiting for us: the village was in the middle of a fiesta, decked with bunting thronged with a jubilant crowd that Saturday, we had reserved a room in the only hotel around without knowing it, the receptionist was surprised, *you didn't know it was fiesta?* as if her native town didn't deserve to be visited outside of these crucial dates, the patron's festivals, on the main square a "medieval" market was set up, where nice Valencians impersonated the vanished Arabs in colorful outfits and the knights of El Cid Campeador in armor beneath our windows, we were still in the room when a series of explosions paralyzed me shaving kit in hand, a terrible volley that resonated in your heart and made the open windows shake, a bombardment, I had a second of total panic, my muscles tense, my ears whistling, ready to dive onto the bedroom floor, I didn't recognize that weapon, my brain didn't identify that danger it wasn't a machine gun not mortar shells not grenades it was brutal muffled echoing rapid interminable Stéphanie was petrified facing me I understood firecrackers enormous firecrackers linked to each other under our windows they made the rounds of the whole square an explosion every half-second the little room filled up with enough blue smoke to suffocate us Stéphanie began laughing the pounding didn't stop boom boom boom regularly the stench was infernal and to cap it all off a giant cannonball went off a huge explosion made us double over in fright leaving a strained acute silence followed immediately by joyful shouts applause and bravos, I was so tense that my neck and shoulders hurt, Stéphanie had tears in her eyes, maybe the smoke, my mouth was dry from the taste of gunpowder, in the street more cheerful shouts rose up, what could this extraordinarily savage ceremony be, to what god of thunder were they sacrificing these kilos of firecrackers, Stéphanie and I began laughing at our fear as we sought a little air at the window, the receptionist told us that this ritual was called *mascletà*, and that it was very frequent in Valencia, homeland of fireworks, noise, and fury, Zeus himself must preside over these young pagans, we went out to take a little walk, who knows maybe Maks Luburić the butcher had chosen this corner of Spain because of this martial tradition, which reminded him of the children, old men, and sick people he lined up in a ditch before blowing them up with dynamite or a grenade in Jasenovac on the Sava, peaceful Croatian village where the Ustashis, always concerned with doing things well, had established their contribution to the death camps, in order to kill the Serbs, gypsies, and Jews in the midst of the storks, by the water's edge, in an old brickworks whose ovens turned out to be very practical for getting rid of bodies, Luburić had been the commander of the network of camps around Jasenovac, witnesses described him as a sadist and a coarse brute, in Carcaixent he went by the name of Vicente Pérez owner of a little printing press on Santa Ana Street where he printed anti-Tito propaganda, a fervent Catholic he was well-liked by the people in the village, Stéphanie listened to me, in a crowded bar, glass of red wine in hand, eating salt cod fishcakes, she opened her eyes wide, how is that possible, she found it hard to believe that this little festive hamlet had hidden such a criminal for over twenty years, in the midst of the orange trees, Luburić had even married a Spanish woman and had three children in the 1950s, did they go like me to fight to free Croatia from the Yugoslav yoke that's possible, the little shady streets of Carcaixent smelled of sulfur, around eight o'clock a large part of the crowd headed for the church where Maks Luburić had done so much praying, a Mass was celebrated there in honor of Saint Boniface the martyr, I went in with Stéphanie who even blessed herself with holy water, Boniface according to the martyrology we were given was the steward of a noble matron named Aglaida, they lived in sin together but when each was touched by the grace of God they decided that Boniface would go look for martyrs' relics in the hope of earning, through their intercession, the happiness of salvation—after walking a few days, Boniface arrived in the city of Tarsus and, addressing those who were accompanying him, he said to them *go look for a place for us to stay: meantime I'll go see the martyrs struggling, that's what I wish to do first of all*, he went in all haste to the place of executions and he saw the fortunate martyrs, one suspended by his feet over a bonfire, another stretched on four pieces of wood and subjected to slow torture, a third lacerated with iron nails, a fourth whose hands had been cut off, and the last raised into the air and choked by logs fastened to his neck, as he viewed these different tortures the executioner was carrying out pitilessly, Boniface felt his courage and his love for Jesus Christ grow and he cried out *how great is the God of holy martyrs!* then he ran and threw himself at their feet and kissed their chains, *courage*, he said to them, *martyrs of Jesus Christ* and the judge Simplician, who saw Boniface, had him approach his court and asked him who he was, *I am a Christian*, he replied, *and Boniface is my name* then the angry judge had him strung up and ordered his body to be flayed, until his bare bones could be seen then he had sharpened reeds pushed under his fingernails, the holy martyr, his eyes lifted to heaven, bore his sufferings with joy, then the fierce judge ordered molten led to be poured into his mouth, but the saint said *thanks be to you, Lord Jesus, Son of the living God*, after which Simplician called for a cauldron filled with boiling pitch and Boniface was thrown into it head-first, the saint still didn't suffer, then the judge ordered his head to be cut off: immediately there came a terrible earthquake and many infidels, who had been able to appreciate Boniface's courage, converted, his comrades bought his body and they embalmed it and wrapped it in costly linens and then, having put it on a litter, they returned to Rome where an angel of the Lord appeared to Aglaida and revealed to her what had happened to Boniface, she went over to the holy body and had a tomb worthy of it built in its honor—as for Aglaida, she renounced the world and its pomp, after having distributed all her worldly goods to the poor and the monasteries she freed her slaves and spent the rest of her life in fasting and prayer, before being buried next to Saint Boniface tortured and beheaded, during the homily I thought about Maks Luburić the Croatian butcher, about those whom he had decapitated, flayed, impaled, burned because they were infidels, how many times had he heard the Mass of Saint Boniface martyr patron saint of Carcaixent, under the name Vicente Pérez was he still thinking about Jasenovac or Ante Pavelić great collector of human eyes when his assassin smashed his skull with a log before stabbing him twenty times with a kitchen knife, one warm April night, in the heady perfume of the flowering orange tree, I down my gin to the health of Boniface the little martyr from Tarsus in Cilicia, Tarsus city of Saint Paul and of the Armenians massacred in turn by the infidel Turks under the eyes of Doughty-Wylie the consul fallen in the Dardanelles, my head is spinning, my head is spinning I feel suddenly nauseous I cling to the window jamb, I need some air, the bartender is looking at me, the gin didn't do me any good I'll go splash some water on my face, I stagger in the train's movements over to the nearby john, I close the door behind me sprinkle myself with water as if for a baptism I sit down in the comfort of the brushed steel alcohol was a mistake I haven't eaten anything all day, what the hell am I doing here in the train toilets I'm beat I'll go back and sit down try to sleep a little but first I'll light a cigarette, too bad for the anti-cancer laws, soon Florence, soon Florence and then Rome, what slowness despite the speed, the dryness of the tobacco relaxes me, the tiny toilet is immediately filled with smoke, like the square in Carcaixent after the *mascletà*, as we left the Mass of the martyr Boniface a band was playing local tunes on short wind instruments that sounded shrill and piercing, a horrible sound that bored into our eardrums as mercilessly as the firecrackers, the faithful followed the fanfare while out on the square they were setting off fireworks that exploded in a fountain over the night sky, it was like Naples on New Year's Eve, Naples or Palermo, a tie in pyrotechnical excess, along with Barcelona in the summer on Saint John's Day, a trinity of cities in love with noise, Carcaixent put all its good will into it, the festival was in full swing, after three or four more drinks and a quick dinner Stéphanie wanted to go to bed, I let her go back alone to the hotel I had business to attend to at 25 Avinguda Blasco-Ibáñez the author of *The Four Horsemen of the Apocalypse* and *Mare Nostrum*, what an address, with his advanced age I was pretty sure the man I was looking for would be home, maybe even asleep, if he could find sleep, a little outside of the center of town I spotted a telephone booth, I dialed his number, after four rings a man's voice replied *sí?* I hung up immediately, according to my map the avenue was a scant hundred meters to the south, Ljubo Runjas isn't expecting me, what's more his name is Barnabas Köditz now, he has lived in Spain since 1947, in Madrid at first and then, when Ante Pavelić died ten years later, he settled in Carcaixent, for years he informed Yugoslav intelligence about the activities of Luburić the butcher and other Ustashis protected by Franco, he gave them everything, in exchange for his own immunity—from whom could he be hiding, Ljubo Runjas the sergeant from Jasenovac, at twenty years of age he was a man of base deeds, murdering women and children, by poison by gas by club or knife, he had the hot blood of youth, Ljubo, born in 1922 he will die in his bed, unlike his mentor Maks Luburić whom he betrayed, he helped his assassin flee to France and I suspect him too of having planted one or two knife wounds in his friend's body, out of pleasure, prudently he then left Carcaixent for Valencia, before returning and settling there over twenty years after the fact, for reasons I know nothing of, sentimental ones maybe, maybe financial ones, he's still there at almost eighty years of age when I head for Avenue Blasco-Ibáñez the duel-loving writer, the whole village is at the festival the streets are deserted, dark, the avenue is lined with buildings on one side on the other a few villas looking out onto the orchards by the banks of the Júcar, the night is very dark, no moon, not one star, the stars must not have shone often in Jasenovac on the Sava which the inmates crossed in a ferry to go to Gradina where most of the executions took place, they say that Ljubo Runjas killed almost a hundred people with his own hands in a field in one evening, with a knife, impossible to believe that the condemned ones stayed quietly in their field, he must have had to run after them like chickens, women children old men, Ljubo Runjas had invented a method so as not to have cramps in his fingers he attached the weapon with a piece of leather directly to his palm like a glove, his hand just had a few jobs to do, just direct the blade, the whole movement was in the arm like a tennis player, forehand stroke, backhand, how many humans did he sacrifice in three years in Jasenovac, many more than the animals in his father's slaughterhouse, more than all the lambs of Bosnia on the day of Kurban Bajram, even the Nazis were horrified by the Ustashi methods, the Nazis who sought to protect their soldiers from proximity to the victims, who used technology for massacres ever since Himmler himself, by a ditch near Riga, had been splattered by Jewish blood: in Jasenovac there were no rules no technology no order in death, it came according to the murderers' own sweet whims, firearms, knives, clubs especially, one by one the inmates went through the double door, behind which they got a big hammer blow on the back of the head, next, next, the executioners relieved each other every thirty or forty victims, an amateur business, amateur or at most an eighteenth-century technique—I ring the bell at number 25, the villa is white, with a covered porch, a tiny garden where a short palm tree holds court, no lights, I try again, it's 10:30, a festival day, the porch lights up, the intercom crackles, the same *sí?* as on the telephone, I say very loudly *Dobar večer, gospon Runjas, kako ste?* there is a long silence, has he changed his mind, I picture my old man hesitating in his bathrobe, a buzz suddenly comes through the gate, I push it, there is a man with his back to the light on the porch on top of the steps, I go up to him, I have in front of me Ljubo Runjas the little, 5'4" and shrunk by age, white hair, wrinkled face, prominent nose, large ears, his suspicious and even menacing gaze contrasts with the reedy voice that says to me *I was expecting you much earlier, I'd gone to bed you know*, I don't reply, he signs to me to come in, I talk for a few minutes with Ljubomir Runjas the brutal whom the years have bent, Ljubo the underling, the little murderer will die in his bed, in Carcaixent, without anyone taking the trouble to find him, he asks me how my grandfather is doing, I tell him that Franjo Mirković died in 1982 in Paris, he says *ah, we're all leaving, the patriots are all dying one after the other*, farewell first independent State of Croatia, the black NDH, savage great killer of Serbs, farewell, bon voyage, the false *señor* Köditz looks a little sad, the living room he receives me in is typically Spanish, full of knickknacks, colors, a Virgin with Child on a wall, a silver icon on the 1960s sideboard, here you'd think Barnabas Köditz was a retired German, I ask him why he came back to live in Carcaixent, he answers with a shrug, he looks nervous, in a hurry to get it over with—he slowly gets up, goes over to the sideboard, opens a drawer, takes out a square package wrapped in brown paper, hands it to me, my name is on the outside, written in a fine hand in blue ink, old-style, *Mirković Francis*, I take the package, thank him, Ljubo remains standing to convey to me that the interview is over, farewell, farewell, *bog, bog* he does not hold out his hand, nor do I, there is nothing in his eyes, he leads me to the steps, waits till I've gone through the gate to close the door, and voilà, I'm in the street with a package under my arm, the fireworks are lighting up the night again, sprays of sparkles followed by a muffled explosion, whistling rockets flying over the rooftops, in the package there are a hundred or so annotated photographs from Jasenovac, letters, a long list of numbers, the inventory of the dead, with no names or origin, just the daily tally of deaths, from 1941 to 1945, 1,500 days, 1,500 lines of calculation, all the shot the poisoned the gassed the clubbed the disemboweled the drowned the ones with their throats cut the burned alive all grouped into a number and a date, for each of the sub-camps around the Sava, teeming with storks and carp—in Carcaixent near Valencia the festival is in full swing, an orchestra has taken possession of the square, from time to time a rocket is set off, a firecracker, it is early still it's the old people and the children who are dancing, to the paso doble from long ago, two by two they dance, I pause to watch them for a bit, the couples are elegant, the men stick out their chests and lightly swing their shoulders, the women let themselves be led from one end to the other, the ones who are too old or too young to dance are leaning on the bar or sitting on folding chairs, Ljubo Runjas alias Barnabas Köditz is perhaps already asleep, I think of Jasenovac, I think of Maks Luburić, of Dinko Sakić whom the new Croatia has just sentenced to twenty years in prison at seventy-eight years of age, extradited from Argentina Dinko had been the chief of Jasenovac along with Maks Luburić his brother-in-law: they danced on the shores of the Sava, they danced in this forgotten village in Spain, I clutch the package I'll go to bed now, the paso doble is over more rockets light up the sky, blue and red flowers celebratory explosions for the dead of Jasenovac, I climb the stairs and curl up against Stéphanie, listening to the murmur of the music, in the dark, mixed with the racket of the fireworks and with the breathing of the woman lying there, despite everything she's asleep, she's asleep and I find it very difficult, who knows why, to convince myself that she's not dead, despite the regular breath that lifts her chest as the orchestra strikes up "A Mi Manera," the gentle Iberian version of "My Way"—the next morning, after a sleep full of storks flying over swampy mass graves, after a quick breakfast in the midst of the festival debris, after recovering the Citroën from the parking lot we went to the Carcaixent cemetery to see the grave of Luburić-Pérez, beautiful and well-kept, Stéphanie couldn't believe her eyes, the people around here liked him she said I replied that's right, his children even went to the local school without the tiniest stone being thrown at them, farewell Maks the butcher, we continued on towards Xàtiva not knowing that a few days later Barnabas Köditz would die from a heart attack, farewell Ljubo the bloodthirsty sergeant, your documents have joined the others in the suitcase, the meticulous photographs, the numbers, the administrative letters from Zagreb, farewell—about twenty kilometers away the little town of Xàtiva hovered between the plain and the mountain, the palm trees and the orange trees, the little streets in the center of town were pleasant and the Renaissance palaces were reminiscent of the great families of the area especially the Borgias, who knew power and glory in Rome: the palace where Pope Alexander VI Borgia was born was dark and sumptuous, like the pontificate of its owner, his many children and his passions for coitus, scandal, and politics make him eminently likeable, Stéphanie the Alsatian was offended by the pontiff's lack of respect for the papal institution, *o tempora, o mores*, the popes today want to be prudish mystical vapid and well-washed, the ones from before smelled of depravity and conspiracy, the Borgias spoke Valencian among themselves even in the heart of Rome which makes them historical heroes for the local cause, despite the pleasantly unorthodox whiff of their saga: so Xàtiva was pleasant and we ate well there, a kind of paella cooked in the oven, usually washed down with a mean wine produced in the region of Alicante, this beverage had something medieval and unorthodox about it too, the Jasenovac package was still wrapped in its brown paper and what with the good food and the fornication I forgot the dead and the butchers—four days of vacation, Valencia Carcaixent Xàtiva Dènia Valencia, Stéphanie was happy, she had the enviable ability to be able to forget Paris and the Boulevard Mortier as soon as the plane doors had shut, she erased her reports her analyses as a young secret agent in the wink of an eye, I felt as if she were even more beautiful because of it, with her sunglasses that she used as a headband to hold back her dark hair, she was calm, completely present to the world, armed with Proust and Céline and her convictions supported by high culture, I have the feeling that I miss her all of a sudden sitting on my train throne cigarette in hand, I miss her sometimes, better not think about her, better not think about the catastrophe of the end of our relationship, where is she now, posted to Moscow which she dreamed about, if I met her in the street I wouldn't speak, neither would she, we would ignore each other just as we ignored each other at the end in the hallways on the Boulevard, we weren't supposed to meet each other I was promised another fate I was living on borrowed time Stéphanie was just an illusion, *three drummer boys on the way back from war, three drummer boys, and rat and tat ratatatat, on the way back from waaar*, I have that tune in my head now, the suitcase is very heavy, and the gin does nothing for it—I splash more water on my face, the window in the toilet is opaque, I can only feel the pressure of endless tunnels on my eardrums, between Bologna and Florence, which must not be far now, are we already in Tuscany, what time is it, 7:15, another half-hour before Florence then 300 kilometers till Rome and the new life, if I don't get out on the way, if I don't take advantage of an unexpected stop to try to escape Fate, but the choices were already made a long time ago, I'll hand over the suitcase, I'll follow it through to the end, in the fall of 1990 I began the journey in a train from the Gare de Lyon, I was crossing Italy for the first time, determined, a little anxious still, strong from my military knowledge ready to place my sword at the service of my country, now it will go back in its sheath, farewell Francis Mirković the butcher from Bosnia, farewell, farewell Andrija the fierce, rest in peace, in the train to Zagreb we sang *three drummer boys* as we drank, now I've drunk alone *and rat and tat, ratatatat*, now I'm alone in the night locked up in this cubbyhole, I'll have to find the courage to leave it, the strength, just as sometimes in war you're afraid to go out, one night on the front in Bosnia two guys had to go reconnoiter the enemy lines, as close as possible to see where the Chetniks had set themselves up, Andi immediately volunteered and he chose me to go with him, in theory I had a higher rank than he but who cares, I agreed, we armed ourselves, weapons and ammunition, I remember I broke a shoelace as I tied my boots too forcefully which made Andrija laugh out loud but which seemed a bad omen to me, maybe Athena wouldn't accompany us this time, the daughter of Zeus was looking elsewhere, we left in the darkest part of night around 2:00 a.m., we began to go down the hill between the trees, slipping on the wet earth, I was scared stiff, because of the darkness or the shoelace, I don't know, my rifle clanked against the buttons on my jacket I was obsessed by this sound I was sure it was going to get us spotted Andrija skidded sideways sprawled onto his back swore like a trucker in a low voice, we should go back, I thought, we should go back right away before the real catastrophe, it seemed imminent, *shit it's like looking through an African's asshole* Andrija whispered that didn't make me laugh but he was right we could be passing an entire regiment without realizing it, the lower down we got the steeper the slope became, we'd have to cling to the tree trunks to get back up, the Serbs must have been right below us—we stopped to listen we heard nothing, aside from an owl in the distance, maybe the goddess didn't abandon us in the end, the night smelled of earth of grass and of the cold damp the calm was far from the racket of war Andrija looked at me as if to say should we climb back up? the valley was plunged in darkness there was no enemy around here that's for sure just an irregular rustle of leaves like hesitant footsteps down below I grasped Andi's shoulder put a finger to my mouth someone was approaching, the owl suddenly falls silent, someone was trying to climb the hill and panting, on our right—Andrija smiled, happy finally not to have schlepped all this way for nothing, my fear came back, what rotten luck, kilometers of hills and we come almost nose to nose with the Chetniks, how many of them were there, I strained my ears in vain I could hear just one of them, one single guy wheezing and breaking branches, this must be what deer and bucks feel when the hunter approaches, pieces of branches and a tightening of the chest Andrija signs to us to move to the right to intercept this noisy oaf, maybe a civilian, but what the hell would a civilian be doing in the middle of the night in the middle of the front, maybe one of our own, lost, was climbing back to our lines, Andi the brave moved away as quietly as possible veered off to the right the unknown man would find himself between the two of us in a few seconds I could hear him distinctly now the fat quarry was advancing slowly towards Andrija I hid behind a tree my mouth was dry I held my breath the Chetnik passed me I caught him by the legs he fell into the mud Andi jumped onto his back gagged him with his hand to stifle his cry of fear, I took his weapon, held him by the ear, aside from the panicked breathing of the Serb the hill was silent, Andi put his dagger under the petrified soldier's neck and made him sit down opposite me he was in his forties with bulging eyes I whispered *if you shout we slit your throat, ok?* he nodded Andrija removed his hand but not his blade, *what are you doing here?* I asked, he stammered *they sent me on reconnaissance* he was so afraid he had difficulty speaking, his breath stank of onions, I asked *where are the others?* he replied *I'm all alone,* with an air of despair, *liar are you jerking us around or what?* the knife pressed a little harder on his Adam's apple he blanched *I swear to you, I swear, I'm all alone, I was supposed to go look at your lines, I got lost*, I believed him, the front had shifted the previous day after their offensive, they wanted to know where we had withdrawn to, just as we wanted to know where they had stopped, I asked him the question, *down below, on the other side of the river*, that was logical, probably true, we'd be able to take our catch with us, this fish with the bulging eyes gone to spy on us alone in the night, Andi asked me in a low voice *should we go?* as I got up I noticed that our Serb had a game bag at his side, a canvas bag, I felt the weight of it the soldier rolled his frightened eyes, I opened it, it was full of bloody billfolds, gold chains, bracelets and wedding rings, a highwayman of corpses, he came back at night to strip the dead that we hadn't had time to bury during the day, scattered around in no man's land, maybe a spy but definitely a vulture with a panicked look, I heard the owl hoot in the distance, the Serb suddenly tried to free himself, to run away, Andrija the furious fell down swearing I pulled the trigger on my rifle by instinct two explosions ripped through the night followed by groans of pain I went over to the soldier he was writhing in the freezing mud I took his haversack his rifle Andi slit his throat in one enraged motion wiped his knife on the dead man's jacket *come on we're going back up*, we went back up, with difficulty, Andrija griping cursing the Chetniks I listened to the owl singing carrying the dead man's soul to Hades, *three drummer boys on the way back from war*, the third was sleeping up above like a baby, he didn't even wake up when we went to bed, after handing our somber booty over to an officer, the mortal remains, papers and jewelry of the abandoned dead—a few months before Andrija himself joined the underworld, Andrija shot down shitting behind a bush by a Muslim squadron that came out of nowhere died as he lived, ironically, fallen in his own shit like Robert Walser in the snow, three bullets in the chest thrown backwards into the smoking shit, pants around his knees, immobilized by the runs weapon in hand, no doubt he was laughing all alone and saying *Za dom spremni* as he heaved, Andi I miss you, in the early morning the fog the taste of the bronze of combat I said to you in a low voice "you're not going to go shit now, *nećeš valjda sad da kenjaš* do it here if you want," that gave you a good laugh, poor stubborn proud Croatian fool, you had already thrown up on me one winter night I could have put up with your shit, I would have preferred it to your death, fallen in irony Andrija I press the black plastic button and the water that flows down the steel sides of the ultra-modern train toilet is a torrent, a thin river that carries everything away flushes my urine onto the tracks and crossties going by at 150 kmh to soil eternal Tuscany with an immense pleasure

back to my seat, my moving cage, eyelids closed: there's nothing to be done, it doesn't matter that I'm exhausted pathetic half-drunk bladder emptied I still can't manage to persuade Morpheus to carry me far away from this train for a while, to find Andrija in a heroic dream, Stéphanie in an erotic dream, or even a nightmare inspired by the thousands of dead in my suitcase with the horror photos, I open my eyes, the little crossword-puzzle couple is quiet, calm, she's sleeping with her head on her companion's shoulder, he's reading, that's what I should do, go back to my book, find Intissar and the heavenly Palestinians, I remember as a child with my sister in order to pass the time during long car trips we'd play at guessing the starting point and final destination of the cars we passed, where does the little crossword-loving couple on the other side of the aisle come from, where are they going, it's too simple in a train I know they got on in Milan and are going to Florence or Rome, but to do what, I have the feeling he's a professor, a teacher of something, of the violin why not—yes, that's it, he's a violin teacher, he looks like a fiddler he reminds me of a friend of my mother's she played chamber music with, his companion had been his student, that's for sure, although she looks more like a harpist or a flautist: corduroy slacks, flowered blouse, long hair not too clean, or at least not as clean as it would be if this woman had been, let's say, a pianist or a violist, being a spy makes you observant—plunged into the Boulevard Mortier in the headquarters of darkness and secrecy, of strategic or trivial information, often you forget where you are, the job becomes routine, the investigations, the cross-checking, the files, the summaries, the reports, the correspondents, the secret agents, the middlemen, the friends, the enemies, the propaganda, the sources, the manipulation, the human or technological information, all that blends in with normality, with the everyday, the way a civil servant makes entries in the big register of births, marriages and deaths, without them affecting him in the slightest, their births, deaths, marriages, divorces, adoptions, marginalia: the passion that was there in the beginning evaporated quickly, Lebihan the man of oysters and pelada was right, he said to me scratching himself *you'll see, it'll pass*, like an itch, I guess, the curiosity the joy of learning evaporate in time—the first two years I was convinced my recruitment had been an error, that the administration would realize very quickly it had made a mistake, that my past and my family's past disqualified me as a spy in the service of the Republic, surely the director of the preliminary security clearance had done his job poorly, despite the three months or so of various investigations after the result of the recruitment exam, I wondered how the Agency could have decided to include such a politically and militarily dubious element, susceptible to slightly pro-fascist and foreign sympathies, it was one more mystery among the mysteries of that Temple of Isis that is our quarters where only the initiates meet, priests, demiurges, and oracles of the shadows, how naïve I was—of course the gods of the Boulevard had planned a fate for me, they hadn't overlooked a thing about me, quite the contrary, when the time came they would make use of these defects or these qualities, with time and numbed by habit and state-employment preoccupied with myself I had forgotten that I was a pawn like any other in the quarrels of Zeus, Hera, Apollo and Pallas Athena, a pawn used for carrying out an aim as obscure as the clouds amassed over inaccessible Olympus, that's one way to console yourself, I could also say OK I was fooled deceived manipulated used, nothing else, and even this suitcase of hidden documents, of my endless investigations hadn't escaped them, they probably wanted it, facilitated my task, just in case, all that might be useful one day, one day all this will have its usefulness, you don't escape, probably despite my precautions they'll learn the identity of Yvan Deroy soon enough and will add it to my file, you never know, they might have need of the good Francis some time or other, they might need his information, his knife, his naïvety, maybe someday Stéphanie having reached the top of the information hierarchy will try to get her revenge, beloved of the gods she'll only have to ask them for my head and the Kraken will appear on a private Italian beach, at Porto Ercole, Hercules Port, on the Argentario for example they'll put an unknown substance in my *spaghetti alle vongole* and I'll die of drowning an hour later when I dive into the Mediterranean, the blue cemetery, at the very spot where Caravaggio, another lord of decapitation, dropped dead: an impeccable and very Italian death, *a French tourist passed away from a heart attack after drinking copiously at a meal. Rapidly approaching his fiftieth year, the Frenchman Yvan Deroy, on vacation on Mount Argentario, joined the sad list of the imprudent who don't wait for three hours after lunch before swimming*, the local paper will say, between two society gossip columns, and my death will not shake the cosmos, far from it, at most they'll find a little place to put my body on the White Island at the mouth of the Danube where they buried Achilles, if I haven't been eaten by the morays and congers, next to Andrija great tamer of mares, and basta—I want to open the suitcase, to reassure myself, my life insurance, they'd say in spy movies, life insurance that I'll sell to feverish cardinals and Franciscans, agents of the Great Archivist, I get up, the little suitcase is still discreetly handcuffed to the steel bar of the luggage rack, I can't be bothered to get the key out, I could pick up Rafael Kahla's book again, find Intissar and her Lebanese adventures again, in Cairo during the informal meeting of honest traffickers half the participants came from Lebanon, and I myself was coming from Beirut where I had met the secretary of the richest of them, Rafiq Hariri the good-natured, fond of grilled quail and lamb tartare who had assured us of his participation, both personal and financial, by no means negligible, in our work, an offering to the gods of the Zone, so they would be merciful to him: of the Lebanese present in Cairo at the time the great majority died prematurely, Elie Hobeika the butcher of Shatila blown up in his car on January 24, 2002, Mike Nassar a major gun-runner on March 7 of that same year, and so on, Ghazi Kanaan the vigorous ogre welcomed all these future corpses to his home for dinner, on January 22 Elie Hobeika is invited over to the home of the Syrian with the prominent features, what does he say to him, they certainly don't talk about the Palestinians massacred in the camps in 1982 in front of the eyes of the Israeli army, nor of the Islamists reduced to ashes by the government of Damascus that same year, maybe they talk about the proceedings that Belgium is instituting against Ariel Sharon for crimes against humanity, in which Hobeika is summoned to testify, they smile, maybe they even laugh at the good joke the Belgians have just played on Sharon, it's highly unlikely but you never know—the Syrians wanted above all not to lose in the post-9/11 storm, the invasion of Iraq, the Oriental New Deal of Bush the simple, the ardent, Damascus was afraid, poor Hobeika, everyone had wanted his death, the Palestinians, the Israelis, the Lebanese, that's maybe why Ghazi Kanaan invited him to dinner, he caresses him one last time like a sick old dog before it's euthanized, he knows he's going to sacrifice Hobeika before he talks too much, urged on by the necessity of the noose that's tightening, and basta, in novels they call it sacrificing a pawn, or in trade jargon "clarifying the situation," *we're going to clarify the situation* meant that in all probability someone was going to disappear, in the great clarity of a car bomb, Hobeika the dashing commander of special forces of the Phalangists during the civil war had in his trunk two bottles of compressed air, a mask, and a pair of flippers, he liked scuba diving, he had bad luck, he liked scuba diving and one morning he was going down Hazmieh to Beirut when an insignificant car exploded as he went by the two diving bottles also blew up, ripping open the back seat he was sitting in, piercing Elie Hobeika's body with shards of steel and chair springs, farewell nice diplomatic butcher, he had no time to think about anything before the dark veil covered his eyes, farewell, he didn't see the flares of the Israeli army guiding its soldiers through the little streets of Shatila, those nights in September 1982, three nights and three days of knives of submachine guns for how many Palestinians massacred, no one knows, between 700 and 3,000, according to sources, they buried the corpses with bulldozers, in secret, the Israeli army had asked Hobeika's militia to rid the camp of the terrorists that were still there, rid the camp of terrorists yet to be born, of terrorists in the making, of retired terrorists and of possible engenderers of terrorists, that's what the Lebanese with the long blades must have understood, those conscripts of the Phalangist Party founded by Pierre Gemayel the athlete, admirer of that fascistic Hitlerian order he discovered at the Olympic Games of Berlin in 1936, he would take the name of his movement from Spain, Mediterranean symmetry once again, Beirut and Barcelona touch by folding over on the Rome/Berlin axis, surely Pierre Gemayel with the Brylcreem in his hair pictured a Spanish fate for his country, a victory of the nationals after a sad but necessary civil war, I want to go back to Intissar and the Palestinian fighters but I'm too sleepy to go on reading, I make myself more comfortable, my legs stretched out onto the opposite seat, I'd almost take off my shoes after all why wouldn't Yvan Deroy take them off, in a first-class car, for me though my upbringing is such a heavy burden that I wonder if my socks are clean, if they're free of holes and in my doubt I refrain, the humiliation would be too great if upon waking the flautist or harpist on the other side of the aisle saw my big toe sticking out of a misshapen knee-sock, the hypocrisy of the well-polished shoe hiding the foot's wretchedness, just as my pants are hiding faded underwear with a sagging waist-band—the world of appearances is like that, who can claim to know his neighbor, I had been very surprised to find a photo of a child in Andi's bag, carefully put away between the pages of the little Bible that he never opened because, he said, he knew it by heart, the photograph of a young girl of about eleven or twelve, with pigtails, Vlaho and I had immediately started in on him, it's your fiancée, she's not bad, we passed the photo back and forth like a ball without him being able to get it back, *come on guys, that's enough, give it back*, we had begun teasing him about the obvious advantages of such youth, virginity assured, the absence of cellulite, all the macho lewd remarks that came into our heads and Andrija exploded he looked at us as he shouted with all the rage he was capable of, one hand on his knife, if he had been armed he would have gunned us down on the spot, Vlaho the magnanimous immediately handed him the snapshot as if he had received a divine order and then we had seen two tears stream down the cheeks of Andi the furious, he caressed the young girl's face before pressing it to his heart and putting it carefully away, in his pocket this time and when he raised his head he smiled, he smiled and said *that's my sister you pair of assholes*, we had been stunned and ashamed, ashamed of having forced Andrija's tears and of having discovered his weakness, as ashamed as if we had brought to light a terrible infirmity, as ashamed as if we had discovered, despite ourselves, that he had a tiny penis or a single ball, the warrior had feelings, tears, Andi's tenderness was all the more inconceivable to us because he never spoke about this little sister, out of shyness, because he himself was ashamed of his affection as I am of my holey sock or my tramp's underwear or my informer past my cop's life as I'm ashamed of having been afraid of having been cowardly of having dumped Stéphanie, Marianne, my mother, all the weight of the endless shame of Francis the coward, who is trying today to redeem himself with a suitcase and a borrowed name, in Rome the city of great forgiveness and of indulgences, or rather in the outskirts of Prato, we're almost in Florence, Prato birthplace of Curzio Malaparte the restless—the ex-fascist disillusioned journalist owner of one of the most beautiful houses in the world in Capri is buried in his birthplace a stone's throw from here, like a good Tuscan, nowhere near his villa on the Neapolitan island, that immense stone staircase between the sea and the rocks, sublime parallelepiped where God knows how Godard managed to film *Contempt*—Brigitte Bardot skinny-dipping in the inlet at the base of the steps, Fritz Lang spinning around, Michel Piccoli smoking and I imagine Georges Delerue on the rooftop terrace with the magnificent view, playing the cello: in that dark house, the Piccoli-Bardot couple comes apart in the midst of filming

Ulysses, a film by Fritz Lang, and when the shrewd warrior sees faraway Ithaca from his hollow vessel it's the villa of Curzio Malaparte in Capri, lost in the midst of the waves like a boat, Curzio Malaparte's real name was Kurt Suckert, his father was German, at the age of sixteen the young Kurt signs up and takes part in the First World War, back home he develops a passion for the "social revolution" promised by the *squadre d'azione*, those eccentric militiamen who tortured leftist men by making them drink castor oil until their intestines were completely liquid: Malaparte became one of the first theoreticians of fascism before being disappointed by Mussolini in 1928, Malaparte the disillusioned was a prolific journalist, he was the special correspondent for the *Corriere della Sera* with the Axis forces, in Croatia, in Poland, and then on the Russian front, in 1943 he interviews Ante Pavelić the Croatian Poglavnik, in *Kaputt* he tells how the Slavic Führer with the big eyes was a friendly man, somewhat reserved, a fervent Catholic, in his office he had a basket full of shellfish without shells that Malaparte thought were Dalmatian oysters, to hell with oysters, Pavelić said to him, it's a gift from my Ustashis, a hundred Serbian eyes offered to the head of the triumphant homeland, Curzio Malaparte tells this story in a novel, is it true, what do I know, in any case it's true for a number of Serbs and no less a consequential number of Westerners, apparently Malaparte denied this on his deathbed, which seems to me even more unlikely, why would he care, on the verge of the great plunge, about the dictator's reputation, it was just one more stain on his name, didn't matter, what did a hundred victims matter a few enucleations it could just have well have been fingers ears noses balls or birth certificates it didn't matter Malaparte's portrayal is no doubt quite realistic, Pavelić the discreet smiling friendly cultivated man was at the head of a band of assassins, like it or not, he ordered the detention and violent death of enemies of the Croatian people, he was neither fundamentally anti-Semitic nor profoundly anti-Serb, he was just pragmatic, in that great Céline-ian pragmatism of the 1930s–1940s according to which every problem calls for a solution, every question an answer, to each his own devil, the Jews the Serbs the communists the fascists the Freemasons the saboteurs and everyone sought to resolve his problem in a definitive way with the help of some group or other—the subordinates sought above all to get richer, Globocnik the man of Trieste, Ljubo Runjas the Valencian exile, they sought above all to fill their pockets with goods taken from the dead, they were no ideologues, just nice little corpse robbers on a large scale, on the scale of millions of men and women gassed or shot, and Malaparte's eyes are only the sticky gaze of all those dead men their bodies humiliated and robbed, Curzio Malaparte the equivocal the fickle who goes from fascism to cynicism to resistance to communism before joining the lukewarm bosom of the Holy Roman and Apostolic Catholic Church in a grave in Prato pretty town in Tuscany that the train is thundering through, I had given his novel *Kaputt* to Stéphanie, her pout said a lot about what she thought about that sort of author, I the uncultivated neo-fascist dared to give her books, I didn't have the good fortune to be admitted into the circle of culture, Stéphanie who however loved me passionately couldn't bear what I was, someone who had begun to read late in life, out of boredom, out of despair, out of passion, and perhaps it was out of jealousy that she looked down on my reading, she wanted to convert me to her, I had to study, to pass a test to advance in rank, she kept reassuring me *you graduated from Sciences-Po you can pass, in-house it's just a formality*, I secretly thought that I would then have to combine Proust with Céline, that all of a sudden I'd have an orgasm as I dipped my croissant into my coffee and I'd become a doctor, I prefer Lebihan his bike and his oysters, indeed my job was subordinate from the salary point of view but I was fine, I was able to devote myself to drinking, to mourning, to my notes, to my shadows, of course I didn't play in the adults' playground as she did, I didn't have the no doubt pleasant sensation of controlling the planet, or at least a piece of it, drawing maps of prospects and possibilities for change in other words all the prestige that comes with the future and with anticipation in a world of pen-pushers, that illusion of decision, I had enough experience to know that there's always someone higher up, a lieutenant general above the major general, or vice-versa, I don't know anymore but maybe since Stéphanie was a woman of responsibilities in an extraordinarily macho world she couldn't understand why I threw in the towel before even reaching the rungs of the Agency ladder, she who, ever since the age of twenty-seven, dealt with the Defense Minister's cabinet, the directors, the heads of God knows what party in the Elysée or the Ministry of the Interior—Stéphanie felt poor, the more she glimpsed the world higher up the more her own means and income seemed laughable to her, whereas what with the many and various bonuses I myself always had the impression of being rich, the tenant of a not too tiny top-floor two-room apartment, owner of three shirts a package of photographs and a Zastava 1970-model pistol with no firing pin so I wouldn't be tempted to use it, I never deprived myself of anything, she spent all her time asking me but how do you do it? how do you manage to get by financially? I had no idea, for Stéphanie money was above all there to be hoarded, accumulated, amassed, deposited, for later on, for God knows when, for God knows what, she already owned her own apartment, every month she deposited a fortune in the bank and still found a way to economize—we were in love, inseparable as the blind man and the cripple of Jerusalem: she saw for me, she guided me in the dark and I carried her, or vice-versa, we loved the missing part of the other, the part that wasn't there and this attraction to absence was as strong as anti-matter doomed to destruction to explosion and to great silence, a real romantic novel, apparently love is one of the constants of universal literature—as strange as that may seem I remember that phrase of Lebihan's the lover of mollusks and bicycles, the man able to expedite a contingent of suspects to Guantánamo and to wolf down two dozen oysters, once he talked to me about love, but it wasn't about him or me or the secretary, it was *Les Misérables*, in his semi-detached house in the suburbs (I picture a semi-detached house in the suburbs, but maybe after all he lived in a sumptuous apartment on the Quai Voltaire) he regularly watched a serial adaptation of the novel on television, with delight, and every morning commented on the actions and gestures of the characters as if, for him, there was a real *suspense* there: Lebihan actually didn't know the end of the *Les Misérables*, he'd say Francis, Francis, yesterday Marius kissed Cosette, or something like that, and I'd reply *ah, love, Monsieur Lebihan,* and then he'd say *love is one of the constants of universal literature, Francis*, which made me speechless, I must say, I had never thought about it, Lebihan no doubt was right, Rafael Kahla speaks well about love, between Beirut and Tangiers, in his elegant little book, a Palestinian passion of heavy-booted fighters, what will happen to the noble Intissar, where was I, I earmarked a page, here:

Now Marwan is dead, his body turning black in the Beirut sun near the airport, barely a hundred kilometers away from where he was born.

Ahmad. Ahmad's presence beside Marwan disturbs Intissar. Ahmad the cruel. Ahmad the coward. What were they doing together? Ever since the incident they were linked solely because of a shared cause and a cold hatred. The first time she saw Ahmad, though, something in her trembled. It was on the front line, a year earlier, when some fighters were returning from the South. Ahmad was almost carried high in triumph. He was handsome, with an aura of victory. A group of Fedayeen had gotten into the security zone, confronted a unit of the Israeli army, and destroyed a vehicle. Even Marwan admired their courage. Intissar had shaken Ahmad's hand and congratulated him. Men change. Weapons transform them. Weapons and the illusion they create. The false power they give. What you think you can get because you have them.

What use could the weapon lying on her lap like a newborn possibly be? What is she going to get because of it, three olive trees and four stones? A kilo of Jaffa oranges? Revenge. She is going to win peace of soul. Avenge the man she loves. Then defeat will be consummate, the city will collapse into the sea, and everything will disappear.

•

"Hello, boys."

"*Ahleeeeeen ya Ahmad*," the card-players reply.

Ahmad has one arm in a sling, he is smiling. He hasn't seen Intissar. Habib congratulates him on his discharge from the hospital and, with a move of his head, draws his attention to the young woman sitting on the floor.

She feels her throat go tight.

Ahmad goes over to her. She gets up. He looks her sadly in the eyes.

"Intissar . . ."

He puts on an appropriate look, a look of mourning. He lays down his weapon to express his condolences to the widow.

"Intissar, there was nothing to be done . . ."

She feels a flood of tears rising but she tries to control them. She's a fighter. Fighters do not cry in public.

"We were on reconnaissance, just before. One of their tanks was hidden behind a wall, with its engine switched off, dawn was just breaking, they got us in their sights with the machine gun, Marwan fell, I was hit by a ricochet. A scratch, thank God. Him, he was . . . he was in the line of fire, you understand? Impossible to pull him away."

She remains impassive.

"And now? And now? You think it's possible to go look for him?"

"I don't know. I don't know, they probably moved the tank right after, but . . ."

"Tonight?"

"You . . . You want to see him?"

"How?"

"Maybe we can get a glimpse of him, from up there. Habib, you think I can let her climb up onto the roof? It's quiet, isn't it?"

Habib gives a slight, strained smile, and says: "Yes, if you want, but be careful, if they spot you they'll think you're snipers and bomb us for sure. Watch out for reflections off weapons and binoculars, OK?"

She feels her stomach churn. Hunger. Or the prospect of seeing the body in the afternoon sun. She wonders if Habib knew that Marwan might be visible from the roof of the building. Probably. That's defeat. You don't go looking for the dead anymore. You don't want to see them anymore. Ahmad has hung a pair of binoculars around his neck. She lets him go first, because she knows he has a tendency to stare at her buttocks in her canvas pants at the slightest opportunity. He tries to see through them. That made Marwan furious, that Ahmad can't peel his eyes away from her ass. The climb is complicated. To reach the second floor, you have to go out of the building and go in again through a rocket hole by the staircase, a staircase that no longer exists, replaced by a pile of rubble and debris where a rickety ladder has been set up. Ahmad climbs, she grabs the ladder in her turn, he holds out his hand to help her, she pretends she hasn't seen him and, athletic, jumps up onto the landing. The first five or six steps are missing from the stairway to the third floor; you have to hoist yourself up with your arms. Once again, Ahmad offers his help. She doesn't want to touch him. She jumps, then drags her hip up onto the step. She is in good shape. She begins sweating in her canvas but doesn't want to wear just a T-shirt, even though underneath it she's wearing, chaste carapace, a thick bra, almost a bustier. She confines herself to unbuttoning two buttons of her jacket. The floors in between are easier to reach, but the top two are mostly destroyed, most of the roof has collapsed, you have to climb onto tilted slabs of concrete, keeping clear of the iron bars sticking out. The sun is relentless. The dust, effort, and heat make her terribly thirsty. Her throat is totally dry; she can't manage to utter a word. They crawl through a passage on the terrace cluttered with rubble and cartridge cases. The sun pins them to the cement. Around her, Beirut lies in haze. To the right the mercury of the sea and the immense wasteland of the airport; to the left, the sports arena and the Shatila camp. In front, the grid of ruined little streets, cut into four by two large streets strewn with burnt cars, trash, and the dark spots, like puddles of oil, of asphalt melted by phosphorus. So that's what's left of the city. Ramshackle remains, rubble, stardust. And in the middle Marwan's body.

Ahmad has gotten as close as possible to the corner of the roof and gotten out the binoculars from their case. He is scrutinizing the battlefield to the south. Intissar has gone over to him, almost touching him, despite her disgust. Ahmad has frozen. He whispers: "Look, over there, the Israeli positions. Their tanks are hidden in those streets over there. At the corner of the big street you can see Marwan."

She feels herself trembling. She needs to urinate, all of a sudden. She doesn't know if she should take the binoculars Ahmad is handing her. The sun is a little behind them, they're backlit, the Israelis can't notice their presence. She looks. With her eyes blurred by tears or sweat, she sees nothing. She wipes them off with her sleeve. An indistinct, vague, rapid image, a concrete wall, a twisted streetlight. She gets her bearings. She is afraid of the instant the corpse will appear in close-up on a sidewalk. With her eyes, she follows the street Ahmad pointed out. She sees it. She goes past it. She comes back to it. She has a taste of bile in her mouth. A feeling of nausea. It's Marwan. You can only see his arms outstretched, his head turned to the other side, his hair, his blackened back. His blackened back. The big dark stain on his jacket. The flies buzzing around him. She removes the binoculars to cry. It is really him, and he is really dead. She doesn't cry. She picks up the binoculars again. She looks one more time, then, mentally, makes note of landmarks, to be able to reach him. That street, there, then right, then left and straight ahead, she should end up right at the corner where he's outstretched. She checks the route with her naked eyes, almost 300 meters. The twisted streetlight like a tree to orient herself.

It's nothing, 300 meters. Ahmad is carefully wiping the lenses with a sketchy rag. She turns back and returns to the shelter of the roof at a crawl. Ahmad follows her. He watches her legs and buttocks sway. One thigh moves away from the other, her pants are stained with sweat. Intissar has only Marwan in mind. It is four o'clock. He was killed more or less twelve hours ago. She rifles through her horrible memories, imagines what a corpse that has been abandoned in the sun for twelve hours looks like. Flies on coagulated blood, in the mouth if it's open, on the eyes if they're open. Rigor mortis that might not yet have begun to pass off. And it must be sheltered a little by the shadow of the wall. She weeps hot tears. She suddenly wants to shout Marwan, Marwan, Marwan, she goes back down as fast as she can, she scratches her wrist on a rod in the concrete, almost sprains her ankle leaping onto the debris. Ahmad follows her with difficulty, in silence. After reaching the ground floor she goes back to the card-players and collapses in a corner. She is hot. She is thirsty. She is shivering with pain. Marwan the last dead man of the defeat. Marwan the corpse of the falling city.

•

A few days before, in the bedroom of the requisitioned apartment they were occupying in Hamra, Marwan was still saying: In 1975, all hopes were possible. The Movement was strong and unified, the Lebanese on the left were staunchly on our side, even Syria, we thought, the only traitors were the Jordanians, and maybe the Egyptians; the occupation of the West Bank and Jerusalem was recent, not irreversible, the October war had shown that Israel was not invincible, the world was beginning to hear about the Palestinians, Beirut was beautiful, full of Marxist intellectuals and poets, and leftist Europeans who wore the keffiyeh and got drunk in the bars in Hamra, there were glorious actions in the South, money, Soviet weapons and Fedayeen who were training in armed combat. Can you believe we thought we could liberate the country? From our point of view, our thousands of soldiers seemed colossal. They were. They were for the Palestinians in the camps and for the Lebanese on our side. Our internal struggles, our disputes were shelved. We were stronger than ever. Look at us today, surrounded, betrayed, our last city reduced to nothing. The Lebanese are conking out on us. The Arabic world is going to root us out like a cyst, throw us back into the sea to who knows where. If we leave now we'll never come back, Intissar, believe me. If Beirut falls, Palestine will be an Israeli garden, and we, if we're lucky, will be their farmyard animals. We have to fight. Here you can see Galilee, smell it. It is there. Our people are there. I'd rather die for Beirut than rot slowly on a rock in the Mediterranean.

Marwan is rotting now at a crossroads. Marwan did not marry her. Intissar didn't need to ask him why. He said to her: You want me to make children who will live in wretched camps getting shelled by the Phalangists? She saw hope in children. For him hope was in fighting. The struggle. Defeat has welded Marwan to the ground of Beirut. He has fallen. She loves Marwan's generous nobility. They fought alongside for two years. Thanks to him she became a combatant. Everyone knows her, respects her. She holds her head in her hands. She is crying. Habib brings her a bottle of water, in silence. She drinks. Her canvas pants are soaked with sweat and tears. She'll never see Marwan again. She must see him again. Yesterday he left in the afternoon for the outpost. The bombardments had fallen silent. No planes. He kissed her gently on the lips. She had wanted him. To hold him. To have him inside her. She caressed him. He laughed, he kissed her a second time and left.

Intissar gets up. Ahmad is watching Habib and the others play cards, discussing the negotiations. Rumors. Possible destinations. Where will they go to play cards, and for how long? Intissar suddenly wonders if she'll go with them. Without Marwan. For an unknown destination. To fight for what? There will always be time to think about it. Now, courage. She has to convince them to go look for the body.

She goes over to the group of cardplayers.

Ahmad is staring at her. She doesn't know if she should see compassion in his gaze or lust. Or both at once, maybe.

"I . . . I want to go look for him," she says.

Habib sighs. Ahmad opens his eyes wide. The others drop their cards.

"Intissar, wait. You can't go there alone. We'll go tonight."

Habib looks as if he has resigned himself to accompanying her. He didn't even try to refuse or mention the danger of the expedition.

Suddenly, a low-flying plane rips through the sky. Then another. The players get up.

"It's started up again," says Ahmad.

At over 400 meters a second you can cross Palestine and Lebanon in so little time. The Israeli aircraft need only a few minutes to reach their bases in the Negev or in Tel Aviv. A bomb explodes, far behind them. The phosphorus burns on contact with the air for hours. The wounds it causes are terrible, they don't stop burning.

They are too close to the Israeli lines to risk anything. Without a doubt it's civilians who are burning. She remembers the first bombings at the beginning of the invasion. Dozens of victims in the hospital in Gaza, so many children. Horribly burned. The doctors couldn't believe their eyes—for phosphorus, they consulted the manuals to learn how to treat the wounds, you needed copper sulfate; they didn't have any, so they watched the hands or feet melt until they disappeared. Then the hospital itself was bombed. Then the neighborhood was reduced to ashes. Then there was the battle for Khalde, then the battle for the airport, then a ceasefire, then the siege, then sporadic battles, and now Marwan is dead.

Which doesn't stop the Israelis from continuing to drop a few bombs on the crumbling city now and then. A candle wavering. From Mazraa to Hamra passing through Raouche, West Beirut is an immense refugee camp, a giant field hospital. Those who fled from the South have joined the displaced from Fakhani, from Shatila, from Burj al Barajinah, from Ouzay where the houses are in ruins. No more water, no more electricity, no more gas for the generators, no more medicine, no more food. The only respite is at night, when the relative coolness of the sea air coincides with the pause in the bombings. Until the early morning. In the bedroom in that apartment in Hamra, in the last days, that was when they made love, in silence so as not to disturb anyone, with the window open to take advantage of the breeze. Four days? Four quiet days during the negotiations between Arafat and the Americans. A respite, an idle period before the inevitable fall.

"It's begun again," Ahmad says.

The second bomb sounds closer, they can hear the shrill cry of the plane moving away from the anti-aircraft fire. She wonders what the pilots can see, from so high up. They must see as far as Damascus, beyond the mountain. Apparently, when Leila Khaled hijacked the TWA plane, she forced the pilot to fly over Haifa, to see Galilee from above. Marwan told her that. He will never see Palestine. Does it still exist, even? She does not believe that there is a city in Palestine as beautiful as Beirut, in winter, when you can see snow on Mount Sannine from the Corniche. A city plunging into the sea like Beirut in Raouche or in Ramlet el Bayda. A city with a lighthouse, hills, luxury hotels, shops, cafés, restaurants, fishermen, lovers by the water's edge, more nightclubs, brothels, universities, politicians, and journalists than you know what to do with. Dead people, too, so many you don't know where to put them. What will she do with Marwan's body? She'll undress it. She'll wash it herself. She'll bury it. If it weren't forbidden by religion, she'd build a big bonfire and burn it. On the beach. Like a beacon. She'd watch Marwan go up in smoke into the summer sky and rejoin Palestine through the air, with the Israeli planes. No, she'll bury him in Lebanese soil. In an improvised, temporary cemetery full of Palestinian graves. To whom does the land belong, anyway? To farmers and to the dead.

"Another one," says Ahmad.

This time the explosion is huge. The building trembles and they are covered with dust. The cataclysmic noise and the vibrations threw Intissar to the ground. Her ears are whistling. She gets back up, dusting herself off. Carefully, two fighters go out the back to see where the bomb fell.

Why go on bombing if they know they've won? What isn't already shattered? She feels an impotent rage building up inside her, a white-hot fury, as happens every time. What can you do against planes? The few SAM-7 and -8 missiles they have are unusable; not enough people know how to use them properly. Marwan. Tonight they'll go look for Marwan's body, she'll bury it, she'll cry, and she'll wait for everything to collapse.

•

The war had displaced her many times since 1975. From her parents' house to this room in Hamra. Seven years. The first autumn of the conflict, around the time of her twentieth birthday, it was butchery. Armed posses, axe massacres, shootings, pillages, bombings. Then habit set in. She remembers demonstrations, strikes, universities closed, the massacres of the Quarantaine, the siege of Tell Zaatar, it became a kind of macabre routine. Until that morning in August 1978, almost four years ago to the day, when her parents died. Both of them. The attack completely destroyed the PLO headquarters, 150 dead. Mourning struck her down. For the months that followed, she was wiped out. Wandered ghostlike with no weight on the ground. The apartment empty, the windows taped to keep them from shattering when the bombs fell. Permanent twilight. Endless menstruation, a body that kept bleeding. No willpower, nothing. She was floating, like Beirut, according to international agreements. Losing Marwan today isn't any harder. Or less hard. Start everything over again, always. Lose the city, each time, the city that began to liquefy beneath the bombs, to empty itself out slowly into the sea, the enemy at its ramparts, everywhere. Thinking is useless. Let come what may. She'll go recover Marwan's body, wash it and bury it, and then, then, according to what the Americans, the Israelis, the Russians, and other distant gods decide, they'll do with her what they like.

Nightfall comes slowly. She remembers waiting for the end of the Ramadan fast, in spring or summer, endless. When she was little she cheated—she was too thirsty in the late afternoon, she went to drink in the bathroom, and then, ashamed, asked God for forgiveness. Helping prepare the *iftar* dishes and the countless pastries was a real torture. Her mother suspected that she cheated, of course, but she didn't say anything. She smiled all the time. How did she manage to resist, her mother, with her hands in the food, preparing the soups, the dumplings, the cakes, the drinks—her father arrived a few minutes before the *adhan* and the breaking of the fast, the sky of Beirut was already tinged with pink and saffron, Intissar was seated at the dinner table, the dishes were served, she felt like a runner at the starting line. Her parents were not religious. They belonged to the Marxist left of the Fatah. Ramadan had nothing to do with religion. It was a victory over self, and a tradition. A victory for Palestine, almost. A tradition that linked you to a world, to the world of childhood and the orange *qamar eddin* imported from Syria, to lentil soup, to tamarind juice from India, to cinnamon, to cardamom, to the night falling gently over an entire people who were stuffing themselves, before singing, laughing, or watching Egyptian movies, old celebratory movies where Samya Gamal always bewitched Farid el Atrash. Intissar tried to dance like her, swaying her bony hips, moving the chest that she didn't have yet, and late at night they slept a little, until the shouts of dawn and the beginning of the new day of fasting.

Now she is waiting to go recover Marwan's corpse. Habib and the others have started up their card game again while they smoke. From time to time one of the fighters will take a look outside, a quick patrol. You'd think the Israelis won't try anything as long as negotiations are in progress, but you never know. They won the battle of Beirut. No one can prevent the city from falling. Intissar admires the morale of the soldiers. For them, this defeat is only a stage. They survived the Catastrophe, the war of 1967, Black September; they will survive the fall. The Cause will survive. They will start over from zero somewhere, wherever it may be. Until they recover a piece of land to settle on. A homeland that is not just a name in the clouds. Not her. If the city falls she will fall with it. She will fall with Beirut and Marwan. She pictures her own body beneath the sun in a narrow street, pierced by Maronite knives or Israeli bayonets, in the midst of a pile of corpses.

However long the dusk may seem, night always ends up arriving.

Habib and his soldiers eat some halva with a little bread. Ahmad offers her some, but she shakes her head. Yesterday it was Marwan who would have handed it to her. Fighters are the same, they do exactly the same things they did yesterday, smoke, play cards, eat halva or sardines; Marwan died for nothing, nothing has changed in the world, absolutely nothing, someone plays in his place, someone eats in his place, someone offers Intissar halva in his place, the city will fall, the fighters will leave and Marwan will stay there. Intissar drowses for a bit, her arms crossed, her chin resting on her chest.

Habib awakens her, touching her gently on her shoulder.

"Get ready, we're about to go."

She gets up, stretches her legs, empties her bottle of water, isolates herself in the out-of-order bathroom piled with excrement, which she leaves almost immediately, on the verge of nausea.

It's still just as hot. She takes off her jacket for a bit; her khaki T-shirt is soaked. She withdraws a little into the half-light and takes off her bra. So much for modesty, decency, or the comfort of running. She throws the sweat-drenched bra into a dark corner.

As always before an operation, her heart is beating faster, her mouth is dry. She has strange cramps in her jaw. She concentrates, checks her weapon, the ammunition, the grenades. She makes sure her laces are tied and her belt notched securely. She is ready. Habib and the others pass around a last joint and a bottle of water. Ahmad, Habib and Intissar will go out. The other three stay here in case. One of them has settled into the seat behind the machine gun to be able to cover their retreat if something goes wrong. The second gets the rocket-propelled grenades ready, and the third finishes the hashish as he looks at the ceiling.

Habib doesn't need to explain the tactics or spell out the marching orders. They are trained and hardened, they understand each other in silence. The summer night is clear, there is some moonlight, they'll have to cling to the walls. All three of them know that the Israelis will only attack if they feel threatened, if they think a commando is trying to infiltrate their lines. In theory, even though Marwan was shot down, a ceasefire is in effect. They go around the building to reach the main street by the other side and follow the sidewalk south. They pass a few meters away from the improvised gunhole where the muzzle of their machine gun sticks out, and turn right into a little street that penetrates the Israeli lines. Intissar feels a strange pressure in her ears. She can hear herself breathe. They have already covered a hundred meters. Just 200 left. They progress quickly, as quietly as possible, then freeze to scrutinize the night. A few noises, in the distance, cars, from time to time. They will have to carry Marwan. 300 meters. Ahmad guides them into a passageway between two buildings and freezes. By gestures he conveys that the crossroads with the twisted streetlight where Marwan fell is just in front. She should not have come. She realizes that now. She should not have come—Habib and Ahmad knew it. They also knew that it would have been impossible to make her change her mind. She feels herself trembling. The body is there, on the other side of the street, behind that collapsed building. She glances over, sees the charred metal pole twisted like a tree, its shape stretched out. Ahmad and Habib busy themselves around Marwan. She watches the end of the street where the shots came from. The bullets that tore through Marwan's back. Over there. Total darkness. Silence. Habib and Ahmad cross the street quickly, they are carrying Marwan, Marwan's head lolls back, his eyes are aimed upwards, to look at the sky, they hurry to get back to her, Habib stumbles, he falls forward, lets go of the body that falls heavily onto the ground, Intissar feels tears flowing down her cheeks, they are in the open in the middle of the street, she is afraid, on the left they hear an abrupt detonation, a tiny pop like a cork, followed by a high-pitched whistle, and suddenly the night is lit up in red, she sees as if in full daylight the terrified faces of Habib and Ahmad, the twisted neck of Marwan on the ground, his mouth open, his hands rigid, Ahmad lets go of Marwan's legs and runs to take cover, Habib huddles down, gathers Marwan and begins to pull him all alone over to the street, she hears shouts in Hebrew, Ahmad reaches her out of breath and turns around, shouting: "What is that idiot doing? Run, Habib, run, let him go and run," Habib does not let Marwan go, he drags him as fast as possible, just twenty meters to go, then ten, Intissar hurries to help him the instant a timid Israeli volley scatters the wall on their right with bullets, a big caliber plop plop plop plop chips the cement in the night that's come back now, the flare fell on a building, she gets hold of Marwan's hands without thinking, they are hard and cold, they are no longer hands, she lifts him from the ground carries him with Habib, he is heavy the street is again plunged into darkness, that's it they're under cover, her heart about to explode, Intissar's eyes are drenched in tears and sweat, she collapses against the wall to catch her breath. Forty centimeters away from her, Marwan's face. In the half-light she can make out his fixed stare, his open mouth, the trail of blood on his chin and cheeks, his shirt has ridden up to his neck from the traction, also black with blood. Habib murmurs: "Come on, quick."

Ahmad picks up the corpse by the arms, Habib by the feet. One is missing a boot, which fell off in the middle of the street. The milky-white foot seems to gleam in the night.

She follows them as she surveys the rear, no more noise, no more anything, the Israelis have spared them, that's for sure, they didn't aim their fire. They were impossible to miss, in the line of sight, almost motionless, the machine gun could have cut them in half. They let them carry the body away. Little by little, as they walk, Intissar calms down. Ahmad and Habib are struggling. They stop regularly to catch their breath. She feels empty. Her tears have disappeared. The return trip is always shorter. They reach the post safely. The three fighters cheer them. They saw the light of the flare, heard the gunfire.

Habib and Ahmad set the body down in a corner and wrap it in a dirty blanket that had been lying there. Ahmad avoids Habib's gaze. Contacted probably by radio, Abu Nasser and two other guys whose names Intissar has forgotten arrive. Abu Nasser lifts the blanket to look at the corpse. He gathers himself in silence, replaces the shroud, his eyes clouded with tears.

"Marwan was the best of us all. The bravest."

She feels tears rising again. Marwan is so far away.

Ahmad's wound has re-opened. A bloodstain is growing on his T-shirt.

Abu Nasser takes Intissar tenderly by the arm.

"What do you want to do, Intissar? We have a car. I'll take you wherever you like."

Habib and the other three have lit up another joint and have begun playing cards again. Habib the impenetrable fighter. Courageous and loyal. He waits. He hasn't even mentioned the incident of the machine gun and Ahmad's cowardliness. Noble. She walks over to the little group and holds out her hand to Habib.

"Thank you. See you soon."

"It's nothing. Marwan was my friend. Take care of yourself."

It's almost 1:00 in the morning. Intissar feels exhausted. She can't even manage to think. Marwan is dead. His body is there. Abu Nasser has exchanged the dirty blanket for a dark-green plastic tarp found in the car. Intissar wants to be alone. Alone with Marwan. She asks Abu Nasser if he can drop her off at her place in Hamra.

"And Marwan? You want . . . You want us to leave him at the hospital?"

"No. At my place. At our place. Tomorrow morning I'll bury him."

"You . . . you're sure?"

"Yes, Abu Nasser."

"OK, it's up to you. Tomorrow morning I'll come back with a car. The day should be calm. Or, if you like, we can take care of it now."

"No. Tomorrow morning. Thank you, Abu Nasser."

"Let's go, then."

The soldiers who are escorting Abu Nasser carefully place Marwan in the back of the Jeep. Ahmad gets in too. Abu Nasser has Intissar get in in front. He likes to drive. Despite being a higher-ranking officer, he always drives his own vehicle. He sets off noisily. Drive fast, without stopping. Even at night, you have to be careful. Abu Nasser is an important link in the military command of the PLO. You never know. Behind, his two bodyguards are holding their weapons at the ready.

They pass the checkpoints without any problems; everyone knows Abu Nasser, even the Lebanese militia in the Murabitun, the PNSP, or the People's Party. At night, when the danger of Israeli attacks is a little more remote, Beirut seems to have a tiny burst of energy. The flickering butane lights in the rare open shops, the fighters at the streetcorners—all the last spasms of a dying animal.

Having reached Hamra, the Jeep stops in front of the dark apartment building where Intissar lives. Abu Nasser cuts the engine.

"In back of the car there's a crate of bottled water. Take it. Tomorrow morning I'll be there."

Her voice trembles a little.

"Thank you, Abu Nasser. Thank you very much."

The soldiers get out of the Jeep, except for Ahmad. He nods to her, one hand clutched over his wound. She takes the carton of water. The bodyguards follow her with the heavy green tarp.

She climbs up to her floor, opens the door. The little apartment is plunged into darkness.

The soldiers set down the corpse; she lights the first candle she sees. She thanks them. She sits down next to the yellowish flame and immediately starts crying. She is exhausted. The strange smell of the body invades the room little by little. She thinks. She goes into the bedroom to get the gas lamp.

Marwan is a hero. A martyr for the cause. A great soldier. Respected of course by Abu Nasser, but also by Abu Jihad and the others. He refused to surrender. He wanted to fight until his last breath. He died shot in the back by a machine gun during a reconnaissance mission to plan an operation. To continue the resistance. Fortify the city. Not let it fall into the enemy's hands. Now, in the middle of the night, in the silence, all that seems laughable. Even to her, the fights she has fought, the expeditions into the South, the battles against the Phalangists, the men she's killed, all that is very far away. Useless, pointless. She realizes that she forgot her weapon at the post on the front. It's a sign. That never could have happened during the last two years. Marwan has no more weapons, she will not have any either. The city is suspended in air. After seven years of battle. Tears of rage and sadness fill her eyes. She takes off her jacket. In her closet, everything is khaki, dark green, camouflage. She finds a grey nightgown. She'll take care of the corpse. She sets the lamp up in the little bathroom. There is no shower stall, just a plug in the middle of the tiled, slightly sloping floor. She carries in the crate of bottled water. Abu Nasser is thoughtful. Without this gift she could never have washed the body. She will put it on the bed, in a white sheet, and she will watch over it until the car arrives tomorrow morning. Then they'll come pick it up and bury it. Somewhere. If the Israelis leave us alone. She gathers her courage and drags the tarp into the bathroom. She pulls off the plastic, uncovers the stained outfit. The deformed face. The dark beard. She trembles, she has tears in her eyes. Kneeling next to Marwan, it really is him, all of a sudden. She sees him there despite the distance of death. He has returned into his body. She has trouble taking off the jacket and T-shirt, the arms are stiff, she cuts the clothes off with scissors. His torso. There are four black wounds on his torso. Where the bullets came out. Big, well-defined, fatal. Made to go through armored tanks and walls. They surely continued their trajectory without even slowing down. The smell of meat, of death. She cuts off the pants, takes off the single boot. She takes all the bloody clothes, on the verge of nausea, throws them into the kitchen sink, pours a little lamp alcohol on them and sets them on fire. Who will worry about smoke in besieged Beirut? She has a brief bout of nausea. She makes sure nothing can catch fire around the sink and closes the door.

Marwan, naked in front of her on the bathroom tile. His eyes closed, his faced hardened by the contraction of the jaw. The surprise of death, the surprise of the 12.7 caliber projectiles that went through his chest, perforated his heart, his lungs, broke his ribs. She takes a sponge and pours a bottle of water onto Marwan. Intissar is no longer trembling. She is no longer crying. She caresses him gently. Little by little she erases the traces of coagulated blood on the torso, around the mouth, the nose, on the stomach, delicately. Marwan the warrior. The first time they fought together, along the boundary line, her training was scarcely over. She wasn't afraid, she had confidence in herself, and confidence in Marwan to guide her. Marwan was one of the most respected officers. A brave man. The Palestinians had nothing to do with the amateurism and anarchy of the Lebanese militia. Once the artillery had fallen silent, they had prepared a perfect trap for the fascists, a pincer that had crushed them. She remembers the final assault perfectly: the taste of brass in her mouth, the noise, the running between buildings, she sees again the first volley she shot at a moving human target, and her surprise when she saw it killed, she remembers the excitement of combat, powerful, sexual, fierce, which was appeased, late at night, in Marwan's arms. The pleasure of victory. Intissar is the only woman to have destroyed a vehicle and its occupants with an anti-tank rocket. She watched for a long time as the blackened corpses were consumed in the flames of the overturned car, full of a mixture of satisfaction, fascination and disgust. She knows that her cause is just. She didn't start the war. It was the Zionists. Then the Lebanese allied with the Israelis. Then again the Israelis. And now, defeat, the heavy boots that no longer move forward. Marwan who could no longer run fast enough to avoid the bullets. Martyrs abandoned on a sidewalk corner. Bodies washed in apartment bathrooms. The city that's falling and, on top of it all, exile.

destitute magnificent those Palestinians with the heavy boots what a story I wonder if it's true Intissar washes Marwan's body it's very sad all that so sad, I'd have liked to wash Andrija's body caress it with a sponge one last time, the stories intersect, Marwan's clothes burning in the Beirut sink like my uniforms in my Venetian bathroom, one more coincidence, poor Intissar, despite the victory cries of some people the summer of 1982 must not have been one of the more cheerful ones, I wonder if Rafael Kahla the author of the story was in Beirut then, no doubt, it's likely, how old is he, fifty-four says the back cover, yes it's possible he was just going on thirty at the time, Marwan's age perhaps, September 1982 the shadow is looming heavily over the Palestinians, they'll take refuge in Algiers then in Tunis, all those fighters scattered in the Zone—Rafael Kahla about whom

I know nothing left Lebanon maybe at the same time as Intissar, maybe to go into self-imposed exile in Tangier, Tingis of the Phoenicians where he will meet Jean Genet, with whom he will talk again about the Palestinians: in September 1982 Jean Genet spends a few days in Beirut in the company of Leila Shahid the diplomat for the Cause, the very active representative of the PLO in Paris who had a file with us as long as your arm, I forget how but the two lightheartedly send Genet to Shatila on Sunday, September 21st, the first day of autumn and the day after the massacre, Jean Genet the heavenly gravedigger strokes the bluish corpses swollen from flies in the narrow streets of the death camp, he walks around, his gaze follows the deceased over to the common grave, he discovers silence and stillness, the smell of flesh in the scent of the sea, maybe that's the meaning of Rafael Kahla's story, Marwan's body abandoned at a crossroads, unreachable, Intissar washes Marwan's body just as Genet washed the bodies of the old men and children who were killed in Shatila, in front of the eyes of Israeli soldiers who provided the bulldozers to erase the blunder—Andi old friend I couldn't go look for you, I couldn't, we heard the volley of gunfire we saw you there, lying in your excrement, and we began fighting, the shots whistled around us, the same bullets that had just gone through your chest, I didn't have time to cry, no time to caress you, ten seconds after seeing you and hurrying towards you I was stretched out on the ground weapon in hand forced to crawl to escape, to run away leaving you there because we were almost surrounded, trapped, outnumbered, overwhelmed by the pack of mujahideen around us, the last time I saw you your eyes were wide open to the Bosnian sky a smile on your face a contraction I didn't have Intissar's luck, I fled in a cowardly way maybe because I didn't love you enough maybe my own life mattered more than yours maybe life isn't like it is in books, I was a crawling animal frightened by the sight of blood I had often thought that I could die but not you, we thought you were immortal like Ares himself, I was afraid, all of a sudden, I fled in a cowardly way, an insect trying to escape a boot, we all ran away abandoning you there in the countryside quivering with spring, but don't worry you are avenged, you are doubly avenged for Francis the coward is in the process of disappearing, after his long journey among the shadows of the Zone he is erasing himself, I will become Yvan Deroy, I owe you this new life, Andi, it's over, I'm off, we'll see each other again on the White Island at the mouth of the Danube, when the time comes, farewell Marwan farewell Andrija and shit now I'm crying, this story made me cry I wasn't expecting this, it's unfair I rub my eyes turn my head to the window so no one sees me I'm not in very good shape I'm exhausted probably I can't manage to stop the tears it's ridiculous now all I need is the conductor to show up, how foolish I'd look, crying like Mary Magdalene a few kilometers outside Florence, it must be the effect of the gin, a trick of perfidious Albion, no, that story is taking me back without my realizing it, too many details, too many things in common, better set the book down for now, even in Venice in limbo in the depths of the lagoon I didn't cry much and now almost ten years later I'm weeping like a schoolgirl, the weight of years, the weight of the suitcase, the weight of all those bodies collected right and left preserved embalmed in photography with the endless lists of their lives their deaths I'll bury them now, bury the briefcase and all it contains and farewell, I'll go join Caravaggio in a pretty harbor at the foot of a little mountain, stuff myself with pasta till it's coming out of my nose, learn the *The Divine Comedy* by heart and write my Memoirs and poems like Eduardo *Che* Rózsa the international warrior, just after Iraq I saw him again on TV, by chance, in a British documentary that Stéphanie almost forced me to watch, she wanted to know, Stéphanie wanted to know what I had seen what I had done in the war, for her those two years of my existence were the key, the heart of the mystery, she wanted to cure me of it, she was convinced I had to talk about it, that I had to empty myself of my memories and confess and she'd listen to me and everything would be all better, of course I knew she wasn't ready to hear me, so I said nothing, but she returned to the attack trying by every means possible to make me speak, she invented pretexts, *today I read a very interesting article about Eastern Slavonia returning to Croatia*, I could see her coming a mile off, I'd say Oh? she'd insist *what is it like, over there?* and so on, I'd get irritated without understanding that at bottom her questions were legitimate, and also she was so beautiful I liked being with her so I was patient, at the time out of respect for the Agency we were living in hiding so to speak, obviously everyone must have known, Lebihan the paternal boss winked at me, he who was so discreet, so professional—I dry my tears, that's it I'm not crying any more, thank you Mr. Lebihan, it's over, nothing like your reddened face to soothe my aching heart, on the other side of the aisle the flautist is still sleeping, her husband apparently hasn't noticed anything, he is looking out the window, trying to pierce the darkness of the countryside, soon Florence, then the train won't stop any more, it will go fast now, I hope, in a little over two hours I'll be at the Piazza lost in the crowd of tourists, when I think that I could have been there at ten in the morning if I hadn't missed the plane, a trick of the gods without a doubt, a prank of Fate to punish me with twelve hours on the train, this morning scarcely had the TGV gotten underway than I fell asleep to awaken in the Alps, in the middle of snow and ice peaks around Megève, it's the effect of the amphetamine that woke me up probably, I feel as if it's been a constant night for forty-eight hours for days for years will I see the dawn will I see the dawn will Yvan Deroy the madman see the dawn tomorrow morning as he leaves his hotel room like a good tourist he'll go to the Forum or to Saint Peter's, Rome city of autocrats of assassins and sermonizers, I hope tomorrow it will be broad daylight, I hope daybreak will come too for Intissar, the rosy-fingered dawn will envelop Beirut and Tangier, Alexandria and Salonika, one after the other, will draw them out of the shadow, in our war there weren't many women, a few cold savage ones and others who were tender and friendly, who came as nurses, as cooks, the women were mostly widows mothers sisters, victims, the others were just the exception to the rule, women were mainly images in wallets like the sister of Andi the brave, or Marianne whose photograph I too carried, like all soldiers since there have been painted images—I never looked at it, the photo, I never took it out of my pocket that image of Marianne taken in Turkey by the sea, it was slowly growing moldy along with my credit card, between the folds of leather bleached by sweat, in the beginning I wrote letters, we wrote letters, except Andrija whose parents were right nearby: unlike Marcel Maréchal and the *poilus* of 1914 I never knew what to say, I was ashamed maybe or afraid of frightening my family, I dished out commonplaces about the powerful enemy, about the courage of our troops, about victory and I said I was doing well, that I wasn't taking any needless risks, that I had good comrades who were watching out for me, that's it, then of course the letters became spaced farther apart, they were replaced by a few quick phone calls made for free from some operation HQ, more and more rarely, and quite certainly my parents and Marianne got used to the idea that nothing serious would happen to me, since I didn't give them any news, either good or bad, but I knew afterwards that my mother was still pretty worried, that she went to church every morning at 7:00 to pray for me and that she burned a considerable number of candles, maybe that's what saved me after all, all that smoke all that melted wax in the 15th arrondissement in Paris, I find it hard to picture my sister in my place at the front like Intissar, who knows, she might have made an exceptional fighter, after all she is capable of deploying a wealth of contrariness, she is headstrong and patriotic—Marianne wrote to me often, she related her days as a Parisian student to me in detail, gave me the latest cultural and political news, told me she missed me and urged me to come home as soon as possible, she had assumed the role of the faithful fiancée, she would have made a magnificent widow, even more so than Stéphanie, Stéphanie would not have waited for me, she had too much of a feel for the current situation and for time, a taste for the present, much less Christian, in this sense, than Marianne the bourgeois, Stéphanie wanted to know, though, she was curious about the war she had seen the photo where we were all three of us holding court, Andrija and Vlaho and me in uniform, it had become an obsession, to understand and make me "clear the air" as she said, erase the trauma that she imagined, that's why I saw Commander Eduardo Rózsa again in a documentary on Channel 4, Stéphanie showed up at my place one evening for dinner saying look I recorded this show yesterday, we could watch it, it might interest you, she was surely lying, the film was dated 1994 not very likely that any channel had shown it the day before, she must have moved heaven and earth to find images showing foreign fighters in Croatia, she thought I had fought in an international brigade, which could easily have been the case, I was in a good mood I said why not, if it makes you happy, after all we'd have to go there eventually, I was just back from Trieste I felt happy, it had rained all throughout my stay with Globocnik and Stangl, among the remains of Aktion Reinhardt scattered over the Adriatic, I was happy to see Stéphanie again, we had had dinner, I should never have let myself be persuaded to watch this film, it was in fact an investigation into the death of the British photographer Paul Jenks, dead from a bullet in the neck on the Osijek side, in mysterious circumstances, Paul was a photographer mainly for the *Guardian* his companion Sandra Balsells worked at the time for the London *Times*, she too had covered the war and in 1994 she made the journey to Croatia again with a television crew to try to figure out how

Paul had been killed, the man she loved, that seems easy to say, she returned to the place where he died on the front where they had worked together in 1991, Stéphanie stared wide-eyed at the screen, she discovered flat desolate landscapes covered in snow, the immense Slavonic plain, she discovered the grey and khaki of war, as if she saw them for the first time, because she was in my presence, I should have known it would end badly, I should have understood from the way she clutched my arm, the way I was beginning to feel cold, in front of the television screen, I listened to what the Croatian soldiers were saying behind the English commentary, guys I thought I recognized sinister faces at every checkpoint, a blackened aluminum kettle that could have been Vlaho's, a street in Osijek, mismatched uniforms, straight flat highways, muddy fields, destroyed farms, the smell of frost of gas of burnt rubber and the frozen face of Sandra Balsells in back of the car, her few words, the flowers she puts in the ditch where Paul Jenks fell, near the railroad a kilometer before Tenjski Antunovac a poor village that had been occupied by the Serbs, the journalists suspect that the bullet that hit him in the back of the skull didn't come from that side but from closer by on the right, from the headquarters of the international brigade headed by Eduardo Rózsa the patriot, when I heard his name I started, he appeared on the screen, just the same, a little chubbier maybe, Rózsa the smiling, with his round mug his somber eyes and his humor, of course he denies everything, he says that's impossible, that Paul Jenks was killed by a Serb sniper from Antunovac, that the other journalist found strangled during a patrol happened unfortunately upon a Chetnik scout, what could he say, Sandra Balsells observed all these soldiers who may have killed the man she loved, Stéphanie watched Sandra Balsells and then me, she looked as if she were asking, what about you, what do you think? who killed Paul Jenks? while my eyes were glued to the screen, in January 1994 when the journalists return to Croatia there is a permanent ceasefire on that part of the front, they get those white ice-cream trucks from the UN which help them get into occupied territory, where the Serbs are, they want to go see the four demolished houses of Tenjski Antunovac, the Serbs are friendly and cooperative, they agree to let them climb up to the highest point, a firing post in the ruins of one of the last houses in the village, a soldier even brings them a magnificent sniper's brand-new M76 with a very handsome gunsight so they can see with their own eyes, and here Sandra Balsells takes the weapon, she presses her hand against the angle of the butt and puts her eye against the sight, under the black lens-hood, she looks straight north towards the ditch where Paul fell, what is she thinking at that instant, what is she thinking, she is in the exact same position as the shooter who may have killed Paul, beneath the same roof, an identical rifle against her shoulder, she observes the details of the Croatian post 800 meters away, so precise in the crosshairs it seems you just have to stretch out your arm to touch them, there is no longer a corpse in the ditch, she sees the spray of the frozen yellow flowers she put there, is she picturing Paul's body, is she crying like Intissar the Palestinian I don't think so, she keeps silent, her long golden hair caresses the varnished wood of the weapon, Athena the perverse has given her the possibility of seeing what no one has ever seen, the dark side, the very hand of death her eye pressed against the lens her breath precise, Sandra lets go of the rifle, a Serb soldier takes it, does he know who she is probably not, they go back down the ladder, get into their car again after thanking the Serbs for their hospitality, in the back seat Sandra doesn't know anymore who killed Paul, if it was Rózsa's mercenaries the Chetniks or the goddess herself, she has doubts, Stéphanie is moved to tears, I pour myself a big glass of hard stuff the investigation continues, John Sweeney is now questioning Frenchie, Eduardo *Che* Rózsa's Welsh adjunct in the international brigade, not a bad guy, a soldier, he reminds me of Vlaho with his jagged teeth, I wonder if we would have bumped off a journalist if we had to, no doubt about it, after all a photographer is a kind of spy bought by the highest bidder, a parasite who lives off war without fighting it, all those freelance guys were like us, young and inexperienced at the beginning of the conflict, like us they trembled with fear beneath the shells from the Yugoslav tanks, for most of them it was their first assignment, their first contact with war, like us they saw their first corpses like us they shoved their gear in front of their comrades and exchanged bloated, exaggerated tales, everyone outdoing each other in the number of horrors they'd seen, or how close to death they'd come, I'm not watching the screen I'm plunged into my memories I've understood that they'll never find out who killed Paul Jenks they'll never know I keep drinking leaving Stéphanie to her disgust with mercenaries soldiers Slavonic hail at the end of the tape she stays silent a while she hesitates to ask me questions she doesn't know where to begin suddenly she realizes something she says *so you killed people?* and

I'm flabbergasted, this cultivated mind is incapable of admitting that she too is touched indirectly by violence, splattered by my actions, this civil servant who prepares strategic options for the French army doesn't realize what there is at the other end of her work, *no, I spent a few months gathering mushrooms and singing dirty songs*, I feel a mute rage rising in me, what exactly does she want to know, *but . . . how many?* it reminds me of those teenage trysts, when you ask "so you've slept with how many guys?" *I have no idea*, Stéphanie is stubborn, she looks like a judge, she insists, *a lot?* I answer truthfully, *I have no idea, it's impossible to know,* and she is so ignorant of what I'm talking about that she thinks she can see on my shoulders thousands of corpses, all of a sudden, she imagines I'm Franz Stangl or Odilo Globocnik, she has tears of anger in her eyes, she feels deceived, she is discovering that her lover is a murderer, I down my drink at one go and pour myself another, *you're an alcoholic killer*, she says between sobs and she begins laughing, laughing and crying at the same time, then she calms down, she calms down dries her tears and says *oh my, oh my*, she gathers herself together, things follow their course in her mind, she's pragmatic, she's curious, she wants to know, she wants to understand, she wants to put herself in my place she insists *and what's it like to kill someone?* with a small hesitant voice, almost beseeching, so I explode, I think of Lowry and Margerie in Sicily, I say to her you'll see for yourself, I get up I find the Yugoslav 7.65 in the wardrobe Stéphanie is dumbfounded like a good conjuror I hand her the weapon I show her the cartridges in the clip I shove the breech lift the safety catch I say to her you see there's a bullet in the chamber she is paralyzed with fear I go over to her I say you want to know what it's like to kill someone? so I grab her by the wrist I put the gun in her hand she doesn't react I place my finger next to hers in the trigger she doesn't understand she is paralyzed with fear and surprise I stick the muzzle in my mouth Stéphanie shouts no no no she fights I put pressure on her finger she presses despite herself on the release shouting noooo instinctively she hits me with a terrific left jab worthy of Zeus in the mouth the pistol goes click and that's it, it falls heavily onto the wood floor, Stéphanie collapses too, she's hiccupping as she sobs, she looks as if she's going to throw up, she is curled up on the ground her hair hides her face and I leave, I leave her there like that lying alongside the little black Zastava with no firing pin, to go running down the stairs running down the street running onto the bridge over the Montmartre cemetery and so on until the Place de Clichy without even noticing that it was raining I arrive soaked at a bar a burning pain in my jaw I order a brandy that I down in one gulp, I feel my spirits lifting—my spirits are lifting in the midst of drunks, as the jukebox is playing Claude François's "As Usual," the original version of "My Way," what idiocy, what got hold of me, and it's my turn to have a big sticky cry, standing at the bar, in the midst of a choir of lushes who are repeating in chorus *as uuuusual*, guilt is flooding through me again now, 1,500 kilometers away and months later, it all can't be ascribed to the alcohol, what cunning god breathed that idea into me, that macabre, violent farce, Stéphanie convinced that my skull was going to shatter and stain the ceiling, Sandra Balsells her eye in the gunsight, Intissar washing Marwan's body, Malcolm Lowry with his hands around his wife's neck, what a trip, the train slows down, we're in a suburb of Florence the sublime, capital of beauty and tourism—the museums even the Uffizi gallery always give off a funereal smell, artworks, artworks stuck in time and space hung on a nail or placed on the floor, artworks that are more or less macabre like Caravaggio's decapitations or stuffed human beings, in the Cairo Museum Nasser forbids the crowd of tourists from seeing the mummies of pharaohs, those little men dried by time their inner organs carefully preserved in alabaster vases, ever since his adolescence Nasser has found it disgraceful that colonialist foreigners come to satisfy their curiosity in front of the embalmed remains of the glorious fathers of Egypt, imagine, he said, that a group of Arab archeologists wanted to unearth the kings of France in Saint-Denis to exhibit their coffins and their most intimate bones to the view of all, it seems to me that the French government would oppose that, it's likely, after all the head of Louis XVI was brandished on the Place de la Concorde but we haven't seen it since, so Egyptian mummies are locked up in a big room forbidden to the public, except that of Tut-Ankh-Amun and his wooden sarcophagus—on the other hand the Egyptians don't have that same delicacy with the dozens of animals swaddled 3,000 years ago, ibis, dogs and jackals, cats, swallows, garter snakes and cobras, calves and bulls, falcons, baboons, perch and catfish, a whole zoo preserved in strips of linen and resin fills the Cairo Museum, dignified and dusty like an old Englishwoman, a museum of natural history, before in this kind of establishment they didn't hesitate to exhibit stuffed men, I read somewhere that a little city in Spain by the sea still possessed, not long ago, a 150-year-old bushman warrior, in a glass cage, with spear and tackle, the plaster skin was regularly repainted ebony black which earned him the nickname *El Negro*, he sat in state between two human fetuses that were swimming in formaldehyde, in the company of a two-headed cow and a five-footed sheep, the Bushman had been bought in Paris at the taxidermists Verreaux Fils that provided half the museums in Europe with specimens of various species, *El Negro* disinterred secretly the day after his burial in Botswana was sent to Paris by boat accompanied by a number of skeletons from the same cemetery, after having been eviscerated his skin dried with salt his body smeared with a special preparation, stuffed in France he immediately interested a veterinarian who set him up in 1880 in his collection, I forget where near Barcelona, by the Mediterranean, and the nice black man with his spear and a borrowed loincloth was the delight of generations of Catalan schoolchildren, for he was four and a half feet tall, more or less their height, and I imagine the children playing at hunting lions in the playground after having seen it, for almost a hundred years: dusted, repaired, repainted *El Negro* was forgotten in the back of a provincial museum until one day they decided to give it a proper burial, out of decency, there had to be an international campaign for the museum of natural history in question to agree to part with the jewel of its collection, but the Bushman ended up finding its way back to Africa again, on a plane, the government of Botswana organized a national funeral for this unknown warrior whose remains now rest next to his own people—in Florence the Noble of course there's no stuffed black man in the

Uffizi gallery, no animal or human mummies, pictures statues gods goddesses saints all the nobility of representation, from the perfectly proportioned busts to the golden hair of Botticelli, one of the most popular museums in Italy, where Caravaggio's aegis sits enthroned, the Gorgon's blood-red face on a round shield, a corseless head with crazy eyes, the snakes are still moving in Medusa's mane, did cultured Stéphanie admire Caravaggio so obsessed with decapitated heads and blood, maybe, always that curiosity about death, that desire to see her own death in that of others, to guess, to pierce the secret of the final instant just as Caravaggio depicts himself in the suffering face of the Gorgon with the cut neck, Stéphanie curious about my war exploits, my courage or my cowardliness, Stéphanie lying on the ground, broken with fear and tears, next to my useless 7.65 abandoned on the floor, did she get an answer to her question, was that really what she was asking me, I'm obscure even to myself, rattled by Fate like a convoy in this tunnel where traces of humidity gleam on the blackened concrete underneath Florence city of flowers

airbrakes shrill cries obscure pain in my ears intense light the train stops Santa Maria Novella Saint Mary the New the Florentine train station the sign is blue the letters white I straighten up stretch, travelers bustle about the platform women men, men women it must be cold here too everyone's bundled up in heavy coats some ladies have furs angora blue lynx chinchillas real or fake in Venice there were many furriers for the incredible quantity of stuck-up old cows the city contains the most freezing city in the Mediterranean caressed by Siberian winds coming in from the Pannonian Plain, as frigid as Constantinople and that's cold, stores with their display windows overflowing with mink and golden fox, shops equipped with immense refrigerators to preserve all these pelts through the summer, let's hope for the furriers' sake that global warming is the prelude to an Ice Age, the diversion of the Gulf Stream will make the Rhone freeze in winter we'll all have astrakhan shapkas on our heads we'll be able to skate to Ajaccio long-distance Valencia Majorca in a sled the Moroccans will invade Spain on horseback and the apes on the Rock of Gibraltar will finally die of cold, dirty animals apes, thieving and aggressive, so human they won't hesitate to bite the hand that feeds them noisy lewd exhibitionist masturbators, maybe they'll adapt to the new climate conditions, the simians, orangutans with long white fur will make their appearance on the new ice floes they'll be hunted for their skins it will be a real pleasure, a real end-of-the-world pleasure, the last man chasing the last monkey on an ice shelf floating in the middle of the Atlantic and so long, farewell, end of the hominid primates, on the platform the ladies in furs watch their husbands carry the luggage, the couple next to me hasn't budged, so they're going to Rome, four people enter our car, a woman in her sixties sits down opposite me on the seat vacated in Bologna by the *Pronto* reader, she doesn't have a mink but a black wool coat that she has folded to store above her seat, a rather broad but harmonious face, hair almost white, eyes dark, a pearl necklace above a red cardigan upper-middle-class the statisticians or polling institutes would say, she searches through her handbag to get a book out, she hasn't favored me with a look, the train will start up again soon, soon it will start up again for the great descent nonstop to the Termini, I remember a scene in *Amici Miei*, the film by Monicelli with Tognazzi and Noiret, on this same platform, the five friends with their virile noisy friendship play a hysterical game, they wait for a train to leave and give the passengers leaning out the windows a resounding smack in the face, the men and especially the women, and this sport makes them die laughing, so much that one of the characters says this magnificent phrase, *how happy we are with each other, how happy, it's too bad we're not gay*, with Vlaho and Andi we could have uttered the same phrase with the same conclusion we were happy together in Osijek on our jaunt to Trieste in Mostar in Vitez we were happy strangely happy war is a sport like any other in the end you have to choose a side be a victim or a killer there is no alternative you have to be on one end or the other of the rifle you have no choice ever or at least almost never, we're leaving in the other direction, like Santa Lucia in Venice or Termini in Rome Santa Maria Novella is a dead-end, we start up again, now I'm facing my destination, Rome is in front of me, Florence streams past, noble Florence scattered with cupolas where they blithely tortured Savonarola and Machiavelli, torture for the pleasure of it *strappado* water the thumb-screw and flaying, the politician-monk was too virtuous, Savonarola the austere forbade whores books pleasures drink games which especially annoyed Pope Alexander VI Borgia the fornicator from Xàtiva with his countless descendants, ah those were the days, today the Polish pontiff trembling immortal and infallible has just finished his speech on the Piazza di Spagna, I doubt he has children, I doubt it, my neighbors the crossword-loving musicians are also talking about Florence, I hear *Firenze Firenze* one of the few Italian words I know, in my Venetian solitude I didn't learn much of the language of Dante the hook-nosed eschatologist, Ghassan and I spoke French, Marianne too of course, in my long solitary wanderings as a depressed warrior I didn't talk with anyone, aside from asking for a red or white wine according to my mood at the time, *ombra rossa* or *bianca*, a red or white shadow, the name the Venetians give the little glass of wine you drink from five o'clock onwards, I don't know the explanation for this pretty poetic expression, *go have a shadow*, as opposed to going to take some sun I suppose at the time I abused the shadow and night in solitude, after burning my uniforms and trying to forget Andi Vlaho Croatia Bosnia bodies wounds the smell of death I was in a pointless airlock between two worlds, in a city without a city, without cars, without noise, veined with dark water traveled by tourists eaten away by the history of its greatness, the Republic of the Lion with a thousand bars, in Morea in Cyprus in Rhodes the Mediterranean East was Venetian, the galleys and galleasses of the doges ruled over the seas—when I visited the Arsenale with Ghassan, telling him about the Battle of Lepanto facing the immensity of the harbor basins, in front of the shapes of the docks and piers, I understood the infinite power of La Serenissima, a stone lion stolen from Rhodes good-naturedly guarded the port of the greatest arsenal in the Mediterranean, *pax tibi Marce evangelista meus*, peace be with you, Mark my Evangelist, that's what an angel said to Saint Mark when he was sleeping in a boat on the lagoon, before crossing the Mediterranean and dying near Alexandria, in a place called Bucculi, the house of the bullock driver, where he had built a church, the angry pagans martyred him without delay, the white-bearded saint, they tied him up and dragged him to death behind a cart over broken cobblestones singing *let's bring this steer back to his stable*, in Beirut during the civil war they liked this torture very much, a number of prisoners died attached with barbed wire to a Jeep crossing the city at top speed, torn to bits scraped bare burned by the asphalt asphyxiated their limbs dislocated like the Evangelist in Alexandria and Isadora Duncan the scandalous in Nice, in 828 the Venetians stole Mark's relics from the Egyptians to offer him a final resting-place in their city, in that Byzantine basilica with the five domes, with the gold-encrusted nave the only church in the world where you can reply *et cum spiritu tuo* with your feet in the water, Saint Mark's the floodable—the Zone is rainy, Zeus often drowns cities in terrifying downpours, Beirut Alexandria Venice Florence and Valencia are regularly submerged, and even once in Libya desert of deserts in Cyrene the sparkling I witnessed an apocalyptic storm, divine punishment rained down on the ruins and the few tourists who had dared to come to the land of Qaddafi the sublime madman, they had sent me to negotiate the purchase of highly important information on Arab Islamist activities, the Libyan agencies were unbeatable on this subject and Qaddafi sold his entire store of it in exchange for reintegration into the league of nations, he gave everything he knew about the activists he had more or less supported, closely or remotely, everyone in the shadows rejoiced at the Libyan information, the British, the Italians, the Spaniards, Lebihan the bald lover of mollusks also rubbed his hands, a good operation, he said "go to Libya, you like to travel, it's probably interesting" he didn't believe a word of it obviously, a country where there wasn't even a bicycle race worthy of the name and where you had to eat atrociously spicy horrors, I agreed especially in order to see Cyrene and Ghebel Akhdar the Green Mountain country of

Omar Al Mokhtar who had caused the Italians no end of trouble before dying at the end of a rope in 1931, the white-bearded sheikh fought against the soldiers of the new Rome almost barehanded, in that piece of desert Italy had taken from the Ottomans in 1911—Rodolfo Graziani in charge of organizing the repression copied the methods of the British in South Africa and the Spanish in Cuba, he emptied Cyrenaica of its inhabitants, sending 20,000 or 30,000 Libyans into camps, on foot across the desert without supplies, sure of decimating them, he was *draining the water to catch the fish*, before Mao Zedong had codified revolutionary guerilla warfare, in the same way that the French in Algeria fifty years later would "round up" Muslim civilians inside barbed wire in order the better to control them, always camps, more camps, Spanish camps for the people of the Rif Italian camps for the Libyans Turkish camps for the Armenians French camps for the Algerians British camps for the Greeks Croatian camps for the Serbs German camps for the Italians French camps for the Spanish it's like a nursery rhyme or a marching song, *look, here's some black pudding, here's some black pudding, for the Armenians the Greeks and the Libyans, for the Belgians there's none left, for the Belgians there's none left,*[1] etc., monument to the poetry of war, in Croatia we sang to the tune of "Lili Marleen" words from who knows where, *i znaj da čekam te, know that I'm waiting for you*, Andi had even composed a version of his own, which involved cutting off the balls of the Serbs and defending the homeland, poor Lili, by the barrack gate, she has

1. A reference to "Le Boudin," "Black Pudding," the French Foreign Legion's hymn.—Trans.

to wait some more—it was in Libya that Rommel's soldiers voted in the song written by Hans Leip during the First World War, the Afrikakorps soldiers in the Cyrenaic liked the melody of the woman waiting across from the barracks, in front of the big gate, beneath the lamp post, they wrote hundreds of letters to implore the radio to broadcast it more often, curiously the German station that transmitted to North Africa was in Belgrade, it was from Belgrade that every day at 21:55 precisely there rang out *wie einst Lili Marleen, wie einst Lili Marleen,* and the sweat-covered soldiers wept their last drops of water somewhere between Tobruk and Benghazi in front of their lamplit encampments, Rommel himself wept, Rommel telegraphed to Belgrade to ask for more, more, more Lili, always Lili, the British sang it in German until the propaganda provided them with an English version that the BBC also repeated several times a day, Tito and the partisans whistled it in Bosnia, the Greeks of ELAS in Gorgopotamos, the surviving Italians in El Alamein sighed *con te Lili Marleen* and even we, forty-five years later, sang it by the Drava, *i znaj da čekam te*, it will be impossible to get this tune out of my head now, it's going to accompany me to Rome with Andi's voice and his obscene words, in Cyrene in Libya visiting the Greek ruins a dozen kilometers from the sea I whistled "Lili Marleen" and thought of Rommel's soldiers and of Montgomery, before the storm broke and almost drowned me in the middle of the immense temple of Zeus, I found refuge under the awning of a soda and souvenir stand run by a nice Lebanese a Phoenician lost in Libya who was bored stiff, he told me in flawless French, fortunately there are a few tourists, he added, I drank a local Coke, the racket of the rain on the sheet metal prevented us from continuing the conversation, the air smelled of wet dust and salt, lightning tried to knock down the cypress trees and the Greek columns the water transformed the whole site into a pool of mud that the beating rain struck with the rumbling thunder in a purplish-blue light streaked with thick lines of rain that ricocheted off the earth like bullets so hard that there was no shelter to be found, the Lebanese man laughed, he guffawed with a nervous laugh drowned out by the hammering of the storm, he tried as well as he could to protect his makeshift counter and the interior of his stall, I was sheltered but still soaked to the waist, Zeus finally took pity, he put the lightning back in its box, the sky opened suddenly in a great white light, I said goodbye to the Phoenician from Sidon lost among the cans of Pepsi and the Doric columns, and I resumed my journey to Benghazi—in a rented car, the exchange rate and standard of living let you buy all the seats in a shared taxi and escape suffocation or thrombosis, Lebihan wasn't very happy I was going to sightsee in Cyrenaica, even though he loved the movie *A Taxi for Tobruk*, from which he had taken one of his favorite phrases, *an intellectual sitting down doesn't go as far as a brute who walks*, that's what he said to me when I spoke to him about Cyrene, *you remember Ventura in* "A Taxi for Tobruk"*?* of course, I remembered Lino Ventura and Charles Aznavour, I replied *as for me I prefer Ventura in* "The Army of Shadows," that gave him a good laugh, and set him scratching his scalp with a grin, *The Army of Shadows, oh, that's good*, Libya's main disadvantage was the dryness, a dry dry dry country not a drop of alcohol from Egypt to Tunisia, tea, coffee gallons of fizzy drinks but not a beer not a drop of wine nothing nothing nothing aside from bootleg in Tripoli, if that, Tripoli the sinister Italian capital of the Immense Republic of the Masses and of its leader the sly dictator whose personal bodyguards made all the heads of state in the world pale with envy, a real company of guards made up of sublime and dangerous amazons, muscle-bound women armed to the teeth real fighters for the Guide of the Revolution champion of the cause of African Unity writer poet great protector of his people, builder of the artificial Great River that leads fossil water from the Sahara to the coast for irrigation, blue oil after black gold, the September Conqueror's dream to govern a green country, green like Islam, a green Africa, he gave Libya the permanent river that it lacked to rival Egypt, now they grow lettuce in Tripolitana, lettuce and tomatoes, my storm must have been an unheard-of piece of luck for everyone maintains that it never rains in Libya and that the climate change isn't going to make things any better, far from it, hard to picture the Sahara flowering, barely 3,000 years ago there were gazelles monkeys wild horses eucalyptus baobabs breadfruit trees everything was scorched in a giant heatwave, everything, all that remains are cave paintings by the inhabitants of that era and skeletons buried beneath tons of silica, they say that in 1944 the Bedouins of eastern Libya all became military archeologists, they dismantled burnt tanks and abandoned cannons, recovered empty ammunition crates, objects left behind in fortifications, the merchants of Benghazi sold tons of hole-filled blankets, pierced cans, rolls of barbed wire, and even a music box, the only souvenir I bought in Libya, a little varnished music box with a woman's face painted in lacquer on the lid, the shopkeeper in the old city near the Al-Jarid souk told me its story, the little object, about four centimeters by two, had been made near Vienna and given to a soldier on leave, the looters had found it on his corpse buried by the collapse of a sand trench, along with letters, two photographs a broken watch and other personal effects that the nomads had no use for but which they sold at a good price in town, along with six antitank mines that the sands had vomited up a stone's throw away from the body, nice fat yellow mines all round and new and heavy, the merchant who bought the lot didn't know what use antitank mines could be in peacetime but, aware of the danger, he stashed them away in a corner in the back of his shop where no one could handle them by mistake and forgot them, he forgot them so completely that they didn't explode until November 1977 during the People's Revolution, when the Revolutionary Committee wanted to get hold of the hidden goods of this imperialist collaborator, the chief of the Equality Squad had never seen a German mine, he thought he'd discovered gold or precious metal, so yellow, so heavy, so well-hidden in a suitcase at the very back of a depot, the *Tellerminen 35* were live, no one had realized it, the Bedouins had crossed the desert for three days with this explosive burden, the merchant in Benghazi had carefully stored them away without the 150 kilos of pressure necessary for their exploding being reached, and the socialist ardor might have spared them even longer, if the head of the troop, greedy and curious, hadn't picked up a hammer lying nearby to open these pretty golden containers: the thirty kilos of TNT they contained sent flying not only revolutionary zeal, but also the shop where it was, and once the dust had settled the only thing found intact, in the debris and rubble, was the little music box, open, which was playing "Lili Marleen" in the midst of the ruins as if nothing had happened, the soldier killed thirty years earlier was whistling his revenge, his wife had given him this original portrait so that he'd think of her as he listened to his favorite song, in the middle of the Sahara, she was waiting for him like Lili, in Vienna, he never returned, reported missing among the Libyan sands, she learned nothing more about him, sometimes she imagined he was still alive, sometimes that he was dead, did she think of the painted music box, ordered specially in a shop on the Kärntnerstrasse, did she hear, in one final dream, the explosion of the mines in Benghazi on November 12, 1977, the very day of her death in the Franz-Josef Hospital, at the age of only sixty-two, as there rang out one last time the little metallic tune 3,000 kilometers away, in Libya, *wie einst Lili Marleen, wie einst Lili Marleen*, the last breath of an Austrian grenadier who decomposed a long time ago—I gave the music box to Stéphanie when I returned, I told her this anecdote that I got from the seller, she picked up the little mahogany object with her fingertips as if it were a piece of corpse, before burying it in a cupboard like the *Tellerminen* in the back of the shop near the Al-Jarid souk, is the last trace of one of the 50,000 Germans who died in combat in Africa still in a Parisian armoire, Lili is still waiting somewhere, *wie einst Lili Marleen*, I'll get out at Termini whistling like a GI in 1944, that's always better than humming *look here's some black pudding*, always better, is that the strange martial tune that so fascinated

Millán-Astray the one-eyed during his visit to the French legionnaires of Sidi Bel Abbès, Millán-Astray the crippled symbol of the martial aspects of the Franco regime establishes the Radio Nacional de España and becomes in a way Minister of Propaganda, a soldier-Goebbels passionate about the *Bushido* samurais and warrior honor in all its forms, son of a civil servant a prison director José Millán-Astray spends his childhood in the midst of criminals and delinquents, a cadet at sixteen sent at eighteen as sub-lieutenant into the last Spanish battles overseas, to the Philippines first where he will win fame defending small forts lost in the jungle, until the very end, he displays an uncommon physical courage, a sangfroid worthy of Andrija great shepherd of warriors, he returns decorated and emboldened to establish the military school, then he's sent again into the colonies, this time to Morocco: it's there he loses his arm and his eye in two skirmishes, during the war in the Rif against the little warriors of Abd el-Krim—in the spring of 1951 Millán-Astray is seventy-one, the old general in love with beheading Berbers devotes himself to culture to theater to Zarzuela to poetry, like his sister Pilar, a popular novelist famous in Madrid in the teens, at seventy-one Millán-Astray the wild beast presides over an obscure institute for the Glorious Disabled of War and Homeland, he loves to have his picture taken, one of his main pastimes consists of frequenting photographers' studios, in plain clothes, in uniform, with his grandnephews, with his daughter, with medals, without medals, he photographs his mutilated body, his frightening face where a piece of the left cheekbone is missing, carried off by the projectile that also deprived him of an eye, photos with an eye patch pirate-style or a dark monocle, the right sleeve hanging down, empty, Millán-Astray the immortal has his photo taken in order to slow down the decay of his body, to document it forever, who will remember him dashing and noble, Millán-Astray sees himself with a great moral nobility in these rigid photographs, a knight, a gentleman, upright and courageous servant of the country, a man of honor, he continues to take part in the activities of the Radio Nacional de España, with the aide de camp that Franco's army kindly keeps providing him, he likes concerts very much and that Saturday, April 14, 1951, in Madrid he is in full uniform to go listen to a young twelve-year-old prodigy play Bach and Scarlatti, Millán-Astray prefers operetta, like his sister, but no matter, the concert that spring afternoon is important, organized for the glorious disabled of the patriotic war, Franco will not come, he is busy, Carmen Polo his wife with the wide hips will be there, with her daughter Carmencita and her husband who have just celebrated their first year of marriage, personalities, distinguished guests some come from Argentina to talk with Franco the Iberian Duce last representative of international fascism: by a coincidence that only history knows how to concoct Ante Pavelić is in Madrid, accompanied by his chief of staff, Maks Luburić, he will be in the hall too, Millán-Astray the glorious founder of the Legion does not know them, he just knows the pianist is Croatian, that her name is Marija Mirković and she is accompanied by her father a rather distinguished man a fervent Catholic—they arrived the day before and are full of praise for the beauty of Madrid, the churches, the historic splendor of the capital of Philip II the Prudent, Millán-Astray shook the hand of this child prodigy of the piano, timid but with a determined gaze, who is traveling across ruined Europe with her Bach fugues, the Scarlatti program is an exception, a homage to Madrid, the young girl and her father of course went to see Leganitos Street behind the Gran Vía where the Neapolitan composer had his residence, Domenico Scarlatti the prolific music master of the Queen, virtuoso on the harpsichord, my mother worked for the occasion on two difficult sonatas that she plays super-fast, as they must be played, she often told me about this concert, she still has glass-covered photos in silver frames with the Spanish coat of arms, the invitation card with its red velvet ribbon, my mother, blushing, still remembers having missed a grace note in the seventh bar of a Scarlatti sonata, I wanted to go too fast, those people were there to listen to me play fast, I jumped over a trill and the sonata collapsed beneath my fingers, I slipped from measure to measure like someone who has tripped in a stairway it was horrible—in the first row Carmen de Franco with her hard features, Millán-Astray the one-eyed, Pavelić great collector of Serbian eyes and ears, Luburić the butcher of Jasenovac, what an audience, just six years after the end of the war Pavelić and Luburić were still on good terms, they still harbored a secret hope to reconquer lost Croatia, incognito the Poglavnik had come from Argentina to Madrid to negotiate for Franco's help—the Caudillo hadn't received him, entrusting the affair to a subordinate, he had advised him to stay quietly in Buenos Aires and let himself be forgotten, Perón's government was welcoming—Pavelić was taking a calculated risk by coming to Madrid, he would return there a few years later, protected once again by a very Catholic Spain, my mother aged twelve on April 14, 1951 was giving a concert for the orphans of Carmen de Franco and the disabled veterans of Millán-Astray, I imagine the old one-eyed one-armed general must have seemed frightening to a child that age, the concert was broadcast live on Radio Nacional de España, the press obviously didn't mention the presence of the distinguished Croatian guests, I wonder if my grandfather was happy to see them again, those dressed-up Ustashis, maybe he would rather have forgotten them, still the fact remains that my mother was permitted to have herself photographed with Pavelić the reckless egomaniac, with Millán-Astray the old lion of the Rif with trembling hands, asthmatic and decrepit, with Carmen de Franco the severe bigot, to the cheerful rhythm of Bach fugues, to the sound of the piano that profitably replaced military marches, *soy un novio de la muerte, I am the bridegroom of death, a man marked by the claw of Fate, who links himself by the strongest tie to the loyal company of Death*, what a song, all of it to Spanish oompahs that sound like they come straight out of a running of the bulls, the Grim Reaper's household pets, artistically massacred by matadors dressed in bullfighter's outfits, my mother at the age of twelve played in front of those knights undone by age, knights of the mournful countenance marked by war and death in all its forms, marked in their own flesh like Astray or in the flesh of others like Luburić, I too am engaged to implacable Moira, Hades's niece, in my train rumbling towards nothingness, wearing the death mask of Yvan Deroy the mad, rushing to Rome and the end of the world in the midst of invisible Tuscan hills accompanied by phantom passengers and memories of massacres in my suitcase, son of my mother dubbed, during that Spanish ceremony, by the warriors present, she received the energy from those proud soldiers to transmit to her son an inflexible, fierce history, a share of Fate like a burden on my shoulders, everything connects, everything connects, the silence of the audience, my mother's hands striking up Contrapunctus XI in *The Art of the Fugue*, *re la sol, fa mi re, do re mi*, not too fast, to let the four voices answering each other be heard, to warm up her fingers also, halfway through the piece the audience starts nodding off, it takes a little less than ten minutes for Marija Mirković my progenitor to come to the end of the fugue, with brio, so forthright already, so metronomic that despite her youth she manages to play as if she had four hands, what comes next will wake up the masses, prelude and fugue in D minor from the first book of the *Well-Tempered Clavier*, Millán-Astray stares wide with his one eye to follow the fingers of this gifted child so frail on her red velvet bench, in the spring light when Madrid smells of flowers and green Castilian wheat, frail but determined Marija promenaded her Bach and her Scarlatti sonatas through all of France, to Holland, to England, at twelve in a cream-colored dress she was applauded by all of Europe, she has already received more roses than she did in her entire life, she knows who she's playing for on that April 14, 1951, she wants to do well, Carmen Polo de Franco the austere will present her with a medal of the Virgin to thank her, my sister still wears it today—my sister received holy inspiration from the dictator's wife, I received the tutelary looks of Millán-Astray and Luburić my professors of military nobility and my patriotic conscience in the cold cruelty of the neatly combed Pavelić, those are the fairies who leaned over my cradle, the first snapshots of my history, on one hand my grandparents witnesses to the assassination of King Alexander on the Canebière, on the other my mother plays Bach and Scarlatti for Pavelić the man who had ordered the attack, the games of destiny, *wie einst Lili Marleen, wie einst Lili Marleen*, what solitude in this train now that there's nothing left to do but let yourself be carried to Rome, to do what, to do what else in Rome to take revenge on barbaric Fate or find a welcoming grave, I'm beginning to glimpse my share of fate, did my mother know what god she would be the instrument of and in what battle, when she made a brief curtsey to the Croatian dictator and to Millán-Astray in Madrid—maybe she envisioned a great career for herself as a soloist, before the miracle of age diminished and before, despite the efforts of her Conservatory professor, Yvonne Lefébure, herself a virtuoso at the age of ten, she discovered herself to be when all was said and done an entirely ordinary pianist, whose passion for the instrument, perhaps blunted by adolescence, the terrible weight of tradition, and then of family, weakened and became a small flame maintained by pedagogy: dozens of relatively gifted girls from good families came to her place to prepare for the entrance exam to the upper Conservatory, why did she marry a man who had little appreciation for music I have no idea, why have I myself never been able to bear my mother's repertory, allergic to Bach, Scarlatti, and all the rest, I know these works by heart though, I am resistant to art, insensitive to beauty, as Stéphanie the brunette said who liked my mother enormously, she said it's a stroke of luck to be the son of such an artist, how was it that you never learned how to play the piano, damned if I know, maybe I didn't have the gift, quite simply, I was much better at sport, programmed to be a warrior probably, which doesn't mean anything really, swift-footed Achilles plays the lyre and recites poems in his tent—my sister Leda learned all the piano she wanted to, for years, clinging to my mother like a crab on Andrija's balls, I was the audience, I had to endure private family concerts on Sunday afternoons, after lunch my mother called out, *come on everyone, come here, Leda's going to play something for us*, my sister strutted like a pigeon in heat, put her fat buttocks on the stool everyone present sat down on chairs in a row facing the instrument she sits in front of, sonatina by Clementi number God knows what, etc., my stoic father applauded loud enough to bring the house down, bravo sweetie-pie bravo that was perfect, my mother a teacher to the tips of her toes said yes, it was good, *but*, but the tempo, but the crescendo, but this, but that, every Sunday we waited for my mother's *but* after the applause, I was ashamed for my sister, when I think about it, I was ashamed that she made such a spectacle of herself, a shame mingled with jealousy perhaps, what did I have to show, me, what can earn me my family's applause, Leda slipped into the mold prepared for her, a perfect young lady, sweet and diligent, then a deadly boring woman who unearthed a magnificently insipid husband to whom she has given perfectly inane children who will end up in a bank or in insurance, and voilà, the pianist Marija Mirković surprised Millán-Astray in Madrid on April 14, 1951, without knowing who this rigid general with the frightening appearance was, and now, hundreds of kilometers farther away, Francis the coward is thinking of his mother and that famous invalid in a train hurtling towards nothingness in an Italian night, alone like a star on a cloudy evening, into what obscure mold did I slip, what professor emerging from the shadows will say to me *it was very good, but . . .* Lebihan maybe, between oysters and bicycle races, or Maurice Bardèche himself the old fascist will say to me *you did well, but . . .* maybe Ezra Pound the radio commentator of Mussolini's Italy will walk out of the shadows to murmur *it was perfect, but . . .* or Tihomir Blaškić the colonel of Vitez will leave his Bosnian retreat to shout to me *vrlo zanimljivo, ali se . . .* Marianne will take her five children by the hand they'll all wait for me on a train station platform to give me a kick in my privates saying *you can do better*, and Stéphanie the tall sorrowful one will look at me like an angel announcing the end of the world I'll understand that I could have been better, I know I didn't measure up, men fall in esteem, ghosts please be understanding it's the end of days Francis is tired, he is laboring beneath his burden, understand, you who are all very Christian and believe in the bearded man with the heavy cross, take into consideration the pain of Francis the suitcase-carrier huddled in his first-class seat, crushed by alcohol fatigue amphetamines the dead and the living as if he could no longer stop his brain his thoughts the dark landscape rushing by and the specters who nibble at his feet, look there's the moon, we've pierced the clouds the planet is in the middle of the window, it's shedding light on central Italy somewhere around San Giovanni Valdarno, Saint John on the Arno city of the beheaded Baptist, halfway between Florence and Arezzo, in two hours I'll be in Rome, the hardest part is over, I pick up the book on the tray, Rafael Kahla was born in Lebanon in 1940, says the back cover, and lives today between Tangier and Beirut, strange phrase, between Tangier and Beirut there is Ceuta Oran Algiers Tunis Tripoli Benghazi Alexandria Port Said Jaffa Acre Tyre and Sidon, or else Valencia Barcelona Marseille Genoa Venice Dubrovnik Durres Athens Salonika Constantinople Antalya and Lattakiyah, or else Palma Cagliari Syracuse Heraklion and Larnaka if you count the islands, Tangier guardian of the lower lip of the Zone, so Rafael Kahla the Lebanese writer resides partially in the westernmost branch of his Phoenician ancestors, Carthaginian Tingis today an ocher and white city capital of illegal emigration of tourism and contraband, with the port full of Africans hoping for an unlikely departure for nearby Spain, I picture Rafael Kahla living in the Medina, in one of those traditional houses with a central courtyard whose rooftop terraces have a magnificent view over the bay, one of those houses where William Burroughs settled at the end of 1953, he was coming from Rome, he was coming from South America where he had sought out the *yage* of the seers and telepaths, he was coming from Mexico where he had killed his wife Joan with a bullet in the head, he was coming from New York where he had fallen in love with Allen Ginsberg who had sent him packing, Rome bored him to death, too many statues, not enough beautiful boys, not enough drugs or freedom, *Rome that died crawling of an eye disease* he would write, Burroughs prophet of psychotropic drugs would survive Kerouac Cassady Ginsberg and his own son Billy Burroughs the drunkard, he would survive morphine heroine

LSD mushrooms and would die at the venerable age of eighty-three—in Tangier he settled into a *pension* that served as a brothel for homosexual Europeans, he liked this rat-filled hole, the hashish is cheap the Riffian catamites very young whom poverty propels into Western arms, William Burroughs writes *Interzone* and *Naked Lunch* in four years of marijuana opiates alcohol and male prostitutes, he loves the countryless city of international trade, nest of spies arms traffickers and drugs, the gate to the Zone inspires him, William became a writer because he killed his wife, drunk, in a bar in Mexico playing at William Tell with a glass, one bullet right in the middle of the forehead this vision haunts him the red stain the head tilting back the blood trickling from the open skull the life escaping, Lowry the drunkard almost strangled his wife many times—why did Rafael Kahla the Lebanese author become a writer, maybe for the same violent reason, I picture him fighting during the war in Beirut, who knows, he killed a comrade by mistake or savagely massacred some civilians, just as Eduardo Rózsa the Hungarian volunteer in Croatia great killer of Serbs might have had the two journalists he took for spies killed before he embarked on writing autobiography, Burroughs the visionary sees his dead wife again, in Tangier, he talks to her at night, he even thinks of her when the little Arabs are licking the wounds of his soul, he thinks of Joan dead and especially in the city that doesn't exist exotic drifting somewhere between the Atlantic and the Black Sea, at the Café de France, at the Café Tangis where the service is fast and fresh says the handwritten sign Burroughs soars between two worlds like a vulture over the Sonoran desert, in Tangier the

White sullied by time, among the *dings* of his typewriter carriage and the sighs of all the paying coituses in the neighboring rooms—in Venice between two worlds in a city adrift lost in history I didn't write, I drank I walked I read dragging my dead behind me just as Burroughs did his, I read histories of ghosts that suited me nicely, I had chosen Venice because I hadn't been able to go there with Vlaho and Andi, too far, too expensive, our Adriatic expedition had stopped in Trieste the Habsburgian, I left Zagreb in a bus for Venice with my khaki canvas gear I checked into a hotel in Cannaregio I remember it had been so long since I'd taken out my credit card that it was stuck to the billfold and had little greenish spots on the back the receptionist took it with an air of disgust I felt as if I stank of war I must have stunk of war grease guns humidity tobacco green knapsacks my hair so short my eyes wide-open and red I was thinking of staying for two days in Venice and taking the nighttime Marco Polo to Paris finding Marianne again with the white breasts and something fell on me I didn't have the strength, stuck between two worlds I paced up and down the city at night the city of great silence fog and plague, I found the apartment in the Ghetto by chance passing by a real estate agency in San Polo I left the hotel bought a telephone card called Marianne one freezing-cold evening from a nearby booth I spoke to Marianne but I wasn't speaking to her I was looking at the boats and dinghies moored in the tiny canal two meters from the public telephone, I said to myself I'm going to stay here for a little while I think, she answered I'll come if you like why not I wanted her to come and warmed by her voice I went back to wrap myself up in my Oriental rug and stare at the ceiling—what saved me from drowning in Venice, I don't know, Marianne maybe, or Ghassan, or myself, the ghost of Andrija who lived inside me, his fury, if I had had an ounce of willpower or culture I could maybe have written like Burroughs in Tangier but I was quite incapable of it, I was incapable of anything it was Marianne who called my parents to tell them I was doing well that I was resting in Venice, I was resting, I drank my meager accumulated reserves and my Parisian savings and took my last amphetamines, I didn't have any creative drugs, drugs were for being able to walk for hours, at night, to sleep little, like on the front, to be on the alert but this time for nothing, to tremble when a stranger appeared out of the fog, to mount nocturnal ambushes against specters, drunk and drugged I hugged the walls of buildings walked like a hunted man an imaginary rifle in my hand, I glanced every which way at corners before crossing at a run, bent low as if an elite sniper had me in his sights from a window in the Guardi palazzo, I caught my breath with my back to the wall before throwing a fictive grenade into the blind spot, my heart was pounding 180 beats a minute I am in the heat of battle in the noisy silence of the lagoon, I set a deadly trap for the Vaporetto No. 1 the only one to go up the Grand Canal at night, I wait for it with an anti-tank grenade launcher at the end of an alley near the Academy drunk crazed I aim at the small lights dancing over the dark water I shoot I imagine the line of fire whistling reaching the craft exploding illuminating the façades of the palaces and churches I picture the explosion the heatwave makes me close my eyes I got it I got it I sank an enemy vessel the American tourists are sinking into the darkness to join the rats what joy I light a cigarette and go back to haunt the streets always playing at soldier and doing this for hours for entire nights obsessed with my memories, and it's easy, in the Venetian half-light, to live out your nightmares in solitude, for there's nothing living around, aside from the dead shadows of the fog and the cries of the foghorn, when she arrived Marianne said to me I feel as if you're returning from very far away, yes I'm returning from afar, I was incapable of sleeping with her I still had the contact of prostitutes on my skin of raped Muslims of corpses I was no longer inside myself I was in the Bardo the waiting room of wandering souls and little by little the more I drank with Ghassan the more I found a physical position in the nighttime world a new being I felt as if I were finding my footing again as if I were walking a little on the water of the lagoon that sort of illusion and the more I thought I was recovering a new body the more I wanted to try it out on Marianne's who was sinking into depression as she prepared for her teacher's exam getting up early working all day running for half an hour every afternoon at six o'clock sharp at the Zattere she never felt like making love, while I was returning to life, my specter's sex stood straight up like a cypress in a cemetery, I was emptying Marianne of her desire her vitality and her money too, I was pumping her dry, I was exhausting her as I drew her to the bottom along with me, when I went out at night for my nocturnal insomniac walks until I found Ghassan she would ask me to keep her company in the humid silence of the Ghetto, I stayed whispering maybe, yes, why not, playfully, and sometimes she was so desperate with solitude that she gave in, her legs spread, all dry, I hurt her and panted coarsely on her shoulder and she didn't move an inch, resigned, her eyes closed, the ejaculation plunged us immediately into sadness I was ashamed of having forced her and she, she understood that I was going to leave her alone anyway once desire was satisfied in order to escape the shame and avoid her gaze I sneaked away as she pretended to be asleep, in the stairway my balls empty I tugged the black hat on my head, overcome with cold I ran to warm myself up always in the same direction, towards the Quay of Oblivion the bars of Aldo, Muaffaq the Syrian or the Paradise Lost, I crossed the deserted main square of the Ghetto, in Venice everything closed early, an anti-noise rule of the phantom city—dying cities begin by regulating their agony by advancing the closing hours of establishments in distress incrementally, until they're converted into tearooms with a special permission to stay open until midnight, the dream of mayors justly elected by old cows in furs who've already gone to bed by happy hour, ridding the most silent city in the world of the last sounds of life: the tourists go to bed early, the tourists' feet are killing them and they go back to the hotel quickly to throw their last strength into lovemaking, before sleeping the sleep of the just, rocked by the soft lapping of the Grand Canal on the pilings and docks, for it will not be said that they never fornicated in the capital of gondolas and romanticism, they forget that romanticism was an illness of death, a kind of black plague of sentiment and madness, they forget that *it's so romantic* actually means *it's terribly morbid*, Marianne felt it, even though she wasn't consumptive like the Lady of the Camellias, but subject to the assaults of a more or less violent, more or less drunk ex-warrior, who roughly resembled all the clichés of complete male chauvinism, and still today in this train that's three-quarters empty I have the sensation of a failure an unforgivable violence like with Stéphanie almost ten years later—close your eyes Francis I squeeze out a tear of rage impossible to forget impossible even in sleep maybe Burroughs in Tangier was in a similar state, beside himself, fighting the black beast of memory and shame the owl with the spider's feet stuck in a corner of memory, like Marianne Stéphanie the brunette with the long hair the expert in the geopolitics of the Zone is stuck to my personal ceiling like an insect, too many things there are too many things everything is too heavy even a train won't manage to carry these memories to Rome they weigh so much, they weigh more than all the executioners and victims in the briefcase over my seat, that collection of ghosts begun with Harmen Gerbens the old Cairo-dweller, Harmen Gerbens with the sad mustache imprisoned in Qanater in Cairo, strange fate, escaping the Dutch police to end up locked up in Egypt, you'd have to be Saint Christopher to bear all that, the forty-three photos of Gerbens and his pages of commentaries in his journal, Gerbens the rapist documentary-maker great director of concentration-camp pornography, in the beginning I didn't know why I was recovering this information these names and photos right and left, in the immense files at the Agency, at first, then farther and farther away, why does one do things not out of the wish to know, not out of a need to understand, to conquer a place in the world that's becoming undone, Burroughs in Tangier was fighting against his own violence with opiates alcohol and kif, like

Malcolm Lowry with firewater, Tangier a drifting city a city of grand illusions and contraband, lost alone on the thick lower lip of the Zone, William Burroughs is American, he misses the banks of the Mississippi, the well-ordered avenues of New York, the palm trees of Palm Beach, he is elsewhere, that night in October 1955, he isn't sleeping, he isn't writing he isn't reading he's sitting on a wooden chair his eyes lost in the darkness, outside or inside, he's smoking a joint of hashish paste, the window is open it's still nice out despite the fall, William is forty-one, the age of man's estate, behind him beyond the badly whitewashed wall he hears groaning, someone groans, two seconds, three, stops and starts again, a rather slow, calm rhythm, a man is groaning with his mouth closed Burroughs breathes in his smoke, his hearing so strained that he feels as if he's a bat flitting around in the next room, his ears so wide open that he hears the groaning man's clenched teeth grating, Burroughs feels very clearly the base of his scrotum contract, the more he listens the more his sex swells, what happiness, he unbuckles his pants to let his tool loose, in the open air in the grey smoke-rings, he breathes on his penis, he watches the member's single eye snatch up the marijuana, the tiny lip of that carp-mouth open to smoke in turn and become bigger and bigger, he observes his penis hardening to the rhythm of the man's moans in the next room, curious, interested then fascinated by the blue veins running through his own flesh, William puts the joint down for a minute to take hold of the plastic bag on the table, he is in darkness, he can concentrate on the groans that continue, faster, stronger, in the neighboring room, beyond the noise of the plastic which is stuck to his mouth, his nostrils, he has trouble breathing, the more he breathes in the less air reaches his lungs, his head completely covered by the bag, his hand contracts over the burning flesh between his legs, he begins to groan too and the more he moans the more air he lacks the more air he lacks the more he jerks his huge organ his ears are buzzing he's very hot he sees red soft strong bodies pressing against him Burroughs is completely inside himself and outside himself the bat has become a flying beetle he rubs harder breathes violently his saliva slips onto the bag he is with Joan the androgynous he is with Joan the dead androgyne it's she who takes him she buries two fingers into his throat and two others into his anus he feels sick his glottis contracts he is asphyxiated he crushes his prick like a fish it spurts empties out explodes, Burroughs explodes almost fainting his semen flies into the night the viscosity floats for an instant like the orgasm he cannot cry out he cannot cry out he's going to die his eardrums are ringing he flails his arms and legs he is drowning the sperm falls onto his thighs the instant he rips the bag off breathes in breathes in breathes in he comes a second time as he opens his eyes the misshapen room sways around him in the sonorous silence of Tangier, completely collapsed in his chair Burroughs gulps in air, gulps in air, gulps in air, far away, his heart flown away, in complete, soft, relaxed wellbeing, smiling he observes a globular drop a white filament hanging from his finger, he looks at it for a long time before licking his finger curiously and lighting up the joint again, the smoke burns his irritated mucus membranes, completely relaxed, the grocery bag on the floor now, Burroughs feels the reed fibers of the chair bruising his ass, he is thirsty, he downs his beer in one draught, does a poem come to him, does a fragment from *Interzone* come to him, does something else come to him besides sleep, the heat will wake him the heat the broad daylight his arms folded on the table collapsed dirty the extinguished hashish still in his hand conquered by pleasure and death in the blue-tinged reflections of the Bay of Tangier guardian of the Mediterranean—the next morning William Burroughs is still trembling, aching, he pours water on himself in the communal bathroom and goes down to lose himself in the bustle, where will he have his coffee, I picture him at the Baba bar, I don't know if it existed yet at that time, the Baba Café in Tangier seems as if it's always been there, since the unscrupulous merchant Phoenicians ancestors of Ghassan and Rafael Kahla the writer, tables chairs old posters on the wall friendly waiters the legends of Tangier have all sat there, I imagine Burroughs there too, Bowles the blue man, Jean Genet, Tennessee Williams, Mohamed Choukri the half-starved wretch, at the Baba Café today there is a poster of the Barça the FC Barcelona a soccer club the Moroccans love I don't know why they feel united to this Catalan team that doesn't have half as many titles as its Madrid rival, maybe the colors of its blue-and-red jersey remind them instinctively of some glorious episode, did Jean Genet like soccer I have no idea, he certainly liked to watch those handsome athletes running around scantily dressed on green grass, Genet reaches Barcelona thirty years before coming to Tangier the murky, Barcelona is a dark city a port that smells of fried food and thieves, where there's dried blood on the pocket knives with their worn-out handles, in the alleyways crammed between the port and the Avenue

Parallel Genet falls in love with a Serb stinking of brilliantine and filth, Genet gets a hard-on for crime, Genet gets a hard-on for crime the way others do for the army, Genet gets a hard-on for a Serb deserter of the Foreign Legion, a one-armed Serb, a thief and pimp, who humiliates him and whom he humiliates, a Serb who served during the First World War, who survived the defeat, the debacle and lost on the highways enlisted with Millán-Astray Death's betrothed, to end up also disabled like the general in love with decapitation, then a beggar a thief an opium dealer and a lover of Jean Genet the sodomite visionary, Stéphanie in Barcelona looked in vain for the traces of that glorious time when the writer coupled with sailors for a few pesetas, without thinking that it was of course impossible, that her own condition as a tourist was the very proof of the disappearances of the city that Genet had glimpsed just before the civil war, money and foreign visitors implied the end of shady neighborhoods, and it seemed to me very cowardly to look today nostalgically for traces of the humiliation of the poor the whores the thieves while staying at a ritzy hotel for the European bourgeoisie, whereas she couldn't bear the contemporary version of those pre-war plebeians, all day North Africans stood leaning against a wall waiting for something that wasn't going to happen, the fat black whores had shouting matches with the emaciated underage whores from Eastern Europe, all of them packed in, forced by cops with fast-acting nightsticks to a few tiny streets, to a crossroads where they kept returning between strongarmed arrests, required not to scatter into more peopled places, ordered to act discreet or disappear as if by magic, usually expelled without ceremony, Barcelona wanted to eradicate prostitution in the street and reserve it for the flashy modern brothels where there was a shower in every room and a certificate of hygiene—Stéphanie the curious played at frightening herself suggesting I take her to a pleasant cat-house, where we could have slept with a very clean pretty woman, the idea was very exciting to her, I remember at the hotel one night when she had drunk a little she whispered her fantasies into my ear, of course I played along, I explained the customs of bordellos to her feeling her desire mount, obviously I knew that Stéphanie was a well-brought-up girl, limited by her social class and her education and that she'd never go to such a place, but no matter we were on vacation far from the Boulevard Mortier far from international conspiracy dossiers and serious things, aside from Zone business I didn't go out, the house of Francesc Boix the photographer of Mauthausen the Bota camp the police building on Vía Laietana where the Francoists tortured anything that fell into their hands the model prison on Entença Street that the father of Millán-Astray had run I had to think about all that when I went to bed with Stéphanie, Stéphanie Proustian in the morning Célinian at night, I'm thirsty all of a sudden, I could go back to the bar drink something maybe just a glass of fizzy water to wet the inside of my mouth dried out by gin and tobacco, outside it's dark despite the moon, hills undulate at high speed, this express doesn't pass through any more towns, there's nothing but countryside between us and Rome, I observe the curves of the flautist sleeping on her companion's shoulder, her lingerie shows through her sweater, Stéphanie was very partial to grey V-neck cashmere sweaters, she wore them with nothing underneath except a black bra, women left Genet indifferent, I think, not Burroughs, he had a child with Joan before he killed her in play—of all the heroes of Tangier, Paul Bowles Jean Genet or Tennessee Williams Burroughs is probably the only one who slept with women too, that October morning in 1955 after his first experience of hypoxyphilia delicious suffocation William Burroughs has a coffee calmly at the Baba or at the Tangis, Tangier is living through its last year of independence under the aegis of the international community, as we say, in 1956 the sultan of Morocco with his hooded coat and his little donkey entered the city, nothing was left to the Spanish except Ceuta and Melilla, and to the French only eyes to cry with, even though Morocco wasn't exactly part of my Zone I still went there once on a mission, for purposes of international anti-terrorist cooperation of course, the Moroccans were very advanced on that issue they had already begun to hide the Islamists the leftists and the democrats in the desert ever since the 1960s, in very dry open-air prisons, in Kenitra, in Tazmamart then in Outita, a very recent prison that had no reason to be envious of its more famous elders: Moroccan methods were simple if not efficient, it was a matter of imprisoning the largest possible number of the poor, the unemployed, of tramps of all kinds, religious or not, for having gone to the same street, the same school or the same neighborhood as an opponent, which didn't increase the popularity of the government in place but duly filled the kingdom's prisons—the Moroccan intelligence agencies always had a grudge against us, or rather our relations were always under the shadow of Ben Barka, and every time a French judge got out some letters rogatory or a former cop came out with revelations about the affair they took offence, made obstacles for us while still vaguely understanding that we couldn't do much about it, after all they didn't just kidnap him, their Ben Barka, and dissolve him in acid or bury him in the furthest reaches of the desert, that was taking a big risk, the proof is that we're still talking about it, once again I took advantage of my mission to go see a little of the country, Casablanca and Tangier in a fast train, an entirely agreeable train what's more, without of course the Pininfarina design of today's Italian rapid-transit trains, in Tangier I had looked for the pension-brothel where Burroughs stayed the visionary telepath and I had tried to read *Naked Lunch*, without success, aside from a few pages at random, nor did Tennessee Williams inspire me, or Bowles the tea-drinker, Genet's grave was in Larache quite far from there, I sat at the Baba Café with a newspaper to make myself look busy, I had put up at the Fuentes pension, on a tiny square in the old city, a tourist for tourist's sake might as well go all the way, I was playing for time, I was playing for time before going back to Paris to see Stéphanie again and that obscure boulevard where I buried myself in papers and the commentaries of Lebihan the bicycle king, he was quite close to retirement, in limbo between active life and the house in Normandy, and he realized that himself: ah, Francis, I'm not into what I do anymore, my heart isn't in my work, you understand? he'd spend hours looking off into space, until he was overcome with guilt and began running every which way looking desperately for something to do, something that would give him the feeling of being one of us again, indispensable, thereby wasting a huge amount of energy like La Fontaine's fly around the coach horses, Lebihan who was usually so long-suffering no longer knew how to approach a mountain pass, that bike fanatic was pedaling in the void, trying to pass everyone on the false flats, Francis *you have* to go to Morocco, I knew my Lebihan so well the man with the incurable alopecia, I'd pretend not to hear, go where, why, I have a lot of work right now, then I'd see him stand up on the pedals immediately, Francis I'm getting a mission together right away, it's vital, you can try to find out the name we're missing in file Z., try to get them to agree to an exchange for file Y., pay attention, read the prospectus, Francis, the A. file is going to gain a lot of importance, the economic situation is pressuring us every day, Francis, the job is floundering, the drainpipe's leaking go over there at least they'll get the impression that we're interested in them, Francis show them we can do more than those computer geeks, there Lebihan was unfair, in fact by complete chance we were responsible for a magnificent memo on *The Methods of Communication of Q. on the Internet*, Lebihan didn't know a thing about computer science and he was very proud of it, of that memo, the quantity of information to deal with made Internet specialists almost inoperative, unless some madman sent an e-mail in Braille to ask for news about Bin Laden's health: in the era of the Web human ways of getting information were finding their hour of glory and Lebihan, about to go into retirement, was going slightly off his rocker, the man trained during the Cold War was regaining some strength for a fresh onslaught, from time to time he'd shout as he scratched himself *Francis, Francis, you haven't made any progress on the K. affair*, and Francis huffed, Francis spent hours checking vague memos from incongruous posts to make progress on K., as he dreamt about Croatia, Bosnia, action and the sounds of bombs, Francis thought about his dead comrades, about Stéphanie's ass, about thousands of buttocks swaying in provocative panties, all hidden by the grey flannel slacks that are the daily lot of civil servants, but our specialty, information, made us capable of deciphering, of seeing the thong of this one or that one and so feeding our desire, day after day, for those administrative secret underthings—in Tangier there was no question of underwear, quite the contrary, I was stunned by the absence of women, replaced by African men, Saharan men, Sub-saharan men, all hoping for a quick passage to Europe and its glories, the city seemed full of hunted, waiting men, their eyes lowered, the whole Kasbah harbored timorous illegal immigrants and obese smugglers, a whole country waiting, Tangier stopover city where human trafficking replaced the contraband of drugs weapons and influences, all those poor guys in limbo had to survive waiting for their passage to Spain, the Fuentes pension looked like dozens of others, the more or less friendly staff appreciated Western tourists, as for me I was tempted to set off for Algeciras with a load of illegal immigrants, to become illegal myself, to disappear, to forget Francis the ex-warrior low-level spy Stéphanie the great strategist Lebihan the bicyclist and the whole works, I should have, I should have, if I think about it I was on the point of changing my life three times, once in Venice in the black water of a canal, once in Tangier in a sleazy hotel, once more today, done, that's it, my name is Yvan Deroy the mad, every time an angel appeared, every time there was a divine intervention a miracle like they say to put me back on the rails that are guiding me now to Rome, in Tangier I was wandering through the alleyways of the Medina or by the sea, between the Atlantic and the Mediterranean, haunted by Burroughs drugs and death, pursued by Stéphanie and our relationship that was becoming more difficult by the day, by the suitcase that was getting heavier and that I imagined would sink me in a boat in the middle of the Strait of Gibraltar: in Tingis the Phoenician the saint turned out to be an old Riffian with thick grey curly hair, his mustache almost white, who was drinking beer in a crowded noisy café, as I was killing time leafing through *Naked Lunch* without understanding a word at the next table over, he spoke to me first, he asked me *you are French?* and after I absentmindedly agreed he went on *I don't like the French*, with a big smile, I immediately took to him, I said *me neither*, me neither I don't specially like the French, or anyone else for that matter, the old man's name was Mohamed Choukri he was a writer, known as the White Wolf in Tangier which he had been crisscrossing for forty years, he knew all the taverns all the whores with the suppurating wombs all the foreigners drawn by exoticism by the troubling delicacy of those morbid lands he had known Bowles and Genet he was a little pitiful with his hobo's soft plastic bag in which he lugged around his complete works to sell to tourists, aware of being a living legend, a piece of the city, gnawed like it by the Crab, Choukri said to me *I have three distinct and independent cancers, believe it or not*, they could have been named like the nails that crucified Christ, poverty, violence, and corruption, he had the three cancers of Tangier old Mohamed with the first name of the Prophet, he was dying, I bought his novels from him *For Bread Alone* and *Time of Errors*, whose titles seemed to me wonderfully appropriate, Choukri asked me if I had come for the kif, the boys, or the nostalgia and I was hard put to reply, what could I have said, I came because Burroughs killed his wife, or something like that, that didn't hold up, I came because Burroughs almost died asphyxiated jacking off with a plastic bag over his head, I came because I was trying to cure myself of my own cancer, I ended up muttering *I came to take a* patera *to Andalusia*, he smiled, *ah you're a journalist, there are a lot who make the trip, it's the latest fashionable subject*, I wanted to say no, I wasn't a journalist but a spy, Choukri the dying asked me to buy him a beer, I ordered two, *don't worry, your paper will pay*, he was always smiling with caustic irony, every five minutes someone came over to him to shake his hand, he who had eaten his own mother's heart during the famines of the 1940s in the Rif, he was so hungry, he who had gotten lost in the big city just before independence, who had followed Jean Genet and sought his friendship out of self-interest, as Genet himself would have done with others twenty years earlier, Choukri his youth spoiled by poverty and the ignorant stupidity of his family redeemed himself, he became a writer by sucking the talent of Genet, Williams, and Bowles, who didn't ask for anything better, Choukri hoisted himself up to the light by walking on those famous old men for whom he didn't really hide his scorn, or at least his reservations, Saint Genet got angry at him when he learned about the publication of *Jean Genet in Tangier*, and now Mohamed Choukri the man of resentment eaten away by cancer was drinking his final beers and telling me about the riots of 1952, the international authorities harshly repressed the demonstrations for independence, Mohamed was seventeen, at the Grand Souk Square the army set up a machine gun battery and began firing at the crowd, Choukri said that he had seen his first corpse killed by a bullet there, he had seen people dead before from hunger disease or stabbing but never anyone killed by firearms, a large-caliber one at that, and he had been strongly impressed by the power of the projectile, the way men were killed *in mid-flight* he said, bullet-riddled dead even before they hit the ground, leaving bodies that were seemingly free of violence, face to the ground, the blood that was slowly spreading over the clothes contrasted with the panic of the crowd running in all directions to the rhythm of the machine gun, I thought about Burroughs shooting a bullet point-blank into his wife's head, of Lowry strangling Margerie, of Cervantes three times bested, in Barcelona, in Lepanto, in Algiers, maybe Choukri too became a writer at that exact instant, when his father beat his submissive mother more out of habit than for pleasure, when he was forced to steal to eat and finally when he ran to take refuge in the Kasbah to escape the gunfire, humiliated by the three powers, familial, economic, and political, I looked at Mohamed the grey in that cheap bar in Tangier next to the smoke-yellowed poster for the Barcelona soccer club, Choukri with his air of a celestial tramp, pretentious and humble at the same time, close to the end, maybe already blind to the world around him, turned towards himself his story his tragedies his masks without ever emerging from them, he will always be the haggard emaciated abused child of the Rif, he will always be the teenager running to escape the French and Spanish bullets, and I tell myself that even if I took a boat headed for Europe as an illegal immigrant I'd still be myself, Francis son of his parents, son of the Croatian woman and the Frenchman, of the pianist and the engineer, the way they say Achilles son of Peleus, Ajax son of Telamon, Antilochus son of Nestor, we're all going to rest on Leuke the White Island in the mouth of the Danube, all the sons of their fathers' fate, whether they're called Hunger, Courage, or Pain, we will not become immortal like Diomedes son of Tydeus changed into a peacock, we're all going to conk out, kick the bucket, and find a pretty resting-place, Mohamed Choukri the greedy generous down-and-out is already in the ground, Burroughs the elite marksman and Lowry the drunkard too, even the Pope is going to drop the crozier any minute now, me too, maybe I should give up the fight and give in to death and defeat, admit I'm beaten and go back to irony and to the black galleys like Cervantes, but to where, it's too late, I could have gotten out in Florence now it's too late, no more stops before the final destination, I'll have to follow it through to the end, I'll have to let myself be carried to Rome and continue the battle, the fight against the Trojans great tamers of mares, against myself my memories and my dead who are watching me, making faces

a tunnel is blocking my eardrums, I'll go back to the café car, that's the best thing to do, I leave Rafael Kahla's book on my tray-table and head for Antonio the bartender, the swaying makes me stagger in the middle of the car I almost sprawl onto an offended nun, she must have gotten on in Florence I hadn't noticed her before, there always has to be a nun in an Italian train, a nun some Boy Scouts some bohemian musicians a *Pronto* reader a spy a pretty blonde and an illegal immigrant, all the characters needed for a play or a genre film, or even a canvas by Caravaggio, there are more people in the bar now, the passengers are beginning to get hungry and thirsty, it must be close to eight o'clock: Antonio recognizes me, he says ironically *a gin?* no, not a gin, a beer, the bubbles will do me good, the Holy Spirit of fermentation, the large bay windows of the restaurant car are bathed in moonlight, between Arezzo and Montepulciano, everywhere hills and vines, the beer is cold, the label is pretty, blue and white, with a picture of a big sailboat with the nice name *Sans Souci*, Carefree, that's a good omen—in Thessalonica the Byzantine there was a similar boat moored outside the harbor, by Aristotle Square, a magnificent three-master with a black-and-white striped hull, elegant, low on the water, it wasn't the *Sans Souci* but the *Amerigo Vespucci* a boat-school belonging to the Italian navy, in 1997 Salonika was the cultural capital of Europe, this exceptional event had to be celebrated with dignity, I passed through there by chance back from my first Greek vacation as a new spy, farewell Algerian cutthroats, make room for sun ouzo and shish kebab, I had brought *Drifting Cities* by Tsirkas, which talked about everything except Greece, Jerusalem Alexandria Cairo instead I had bought this novel as a good tourist to read native literature, as Marianne would have done who devoured Yasar Kemal by the shores of well-guarded Troy, I was wasting my time there, the Greek islands were disappointing, what was I looking for there, I have no idea, the Dodecanese were just a traffic jam of cars disembarking from rusty ferries, windswept treeless islands, the sea was turbulent and terribly blue, the clusters of vacationers come from all over Europe went round and round in circles from inlet to inlet from beach to beach from tavern to tavern, and of course solitude was just a pure illusion, given the size of the citadel and the number of French tourists who frequented the area—in Patmos, at the foot of the grotto of Saint John the Evangelist, all the traditional houses were repainted white so often that the white didn't have time to dry, pilgrims and devotees were added to the tourists come for the scuba diving and the windsurfing, on an island of a disturbing beauty, mountainous, rocky, dry, perfect if it had been deserted, which was not the case, far from it, people were climbing over each other, by day the ferries discharged day-trippers like a cargo of wheat, thousands of round grains invaded the little streets headed for St. John's monastery, in a giant humming noise, a murmur of muffled voices and flashes snapping despite the blinding summer light, for an hour or two at the very most, then the flood surged back to the boat immediately followed by another load, and so on from 9:00 in the morning to 7:00 at night, impossible to imagine that there were so many cruise boats in the Aegean Sea, an incalculable number, and only when darkness came, when the stars replaced the people and scattered the sea with equally countless glimmers could one, by an effort of the imagination, in the noise of the waves lapping against the rocks, in the shadow of the dark mountain, imagine the visionary presence of the herald of the Apocalypse and the end of the world, the Eagle of Patmos deported by the Romans to this inhospitable rock, coming from Ephesus the golden, I picture him at night, haunted by the cold and visions of the end of days, his eyes wide open onto the nothingness of the sea plain, certain that this cave would be his last home, peopled with animal cries with the neighing of horses with the sighs of the dying with body-less heads with sick people with terrifying abscesses with fallen angels with fornicating demons, in the pale rays from the kingdom of heaven that the friendly moon casts on the sea, John the Evangelist will survive the ordeal of the island, a magnanimous

Caesar would send him back to Ephesus, he would die his fine death, after himself digging a ditch to lie down in, in the circular choir of his primitive chapel—in Patmos in my very rustic inn I had nightmares in which a stranger gave me cylindrical boxes like hatboxes and recommended I carry them with me to Paris as contraband, they were heavy, I ended up opening one, it contained a desiccated muddy human head with its eyes hanging out of its sockets, the head of one of the Tibhirine monks and I woke up with a start, impossible to rid myself of the images from glutinous Algeria, so I went to submerge myself in the icy water at the base of the rocks, I stayed until dawn rolled up in my towel on a flat rock, until daybreak transformed Poseidon's realm with the azure plume into phosphorus, then I climbed back up to the village to have a coffee and eat a dense heavy roll stuffed with olives or an almond cake watching the landing of the first invaders of the day, and then I got tired of nightmares the evangelist had no miracle for me, I set off in turn on a ferry for Rhodes, island of the colossus, of knights and forgotten mosques, which was Ottoman from the beginning of the sixteenth century until 1912, when the Italians decided they wanted the crumbs of the dying Empire, they had conquered a piece of desert in North Africa and a string of stones in the Aegean, of which Rhodes was the mountainous steep-sloped pearl, the landscapes looked like Troy, pine groves rising high above the sea, twenty or so villages were dotted all around the tear-shaped island, whose shore was eaten away by hotels and seaside resorts—I soon abandoned my car to take refuge in the old city of the main town, in little streets behind the thick walls of the knights of Jerusalem, in the shade, in the Juderia, the old Jewish neighborhood, in a medieval building called the Hotel Cava-d'Oro: the Juderia smelled of absence, there was just a handful of Jews left in Rhodes, a dozen miles from the Turkish coast, there was nothing left of a community of 2,000, the only believers in the synagogue of Kahal Shalom were Israeli tourists, and in the pretty inner courtyard of the hotel, at breakfast-time, I heard them speaking Hebrew while the Jews of Rhodes spoke Ladino, Judeo-Spanish memory of the kingdom of Spain that had expelled them, the island had been a refuge for them, for a few centuries, before European punishment caught up with them and sent them to live in the clouds in the sky over Auschwitz, of all the Jews deported mid-1944 only a hundred or so would return, they'd settle elsewhere, Rome, France, the United States, deserting their native island touched by absence and nothingness, in the Jewish Museum in Rhodes I watched Nazi persistence charter three old rusty barges to transport the *Juden* from the Dodecanese to the transit camp of Haydari near Athens, then make them cross the Balkans by train, through Salonika Skopje Belgrade and Budapest, to hook the cars up to the endless freight cars that sent the Hungarian Jews to their death, the Teutonic functionaries knew their job, despite the allied bombings, the partisan attacks, the movements of troops that had to be brought back from the East, the reinforcements and supplies to be conveyed to the front they found a way, when the Red Army was already in Poland, to set up convoys going from Asia Minor to Galicia, to send a few thousand Jews to their deaths all the more docile since they knew nothing about the anti-Semitism, the ghettos, the extermination in progress, far, very far away, on an island with such imposing ramparts that it seems impregnable, protected, they thought, by the memory of the Knights Hospitaller of Jerusalem and of Suleiman the Magnificent, Rhodes looked more like the Middle East or Cyprus than like Patmos, there were mosques, fountains, Latin churches dating back to the Crusades, and the imposing palace of the Grand Master that looked vaguely like the Crusaders' citadels in Syria and Palestine—so many dead things plunged me irremediably into nostalgia, my nightmares had ceased, replaced by insomnia, which I treated with huge swigs of undiluted ouzo until I was sunk in a dreamless blackness, at the price of deafening snores that earned me the unsympathetic reproofs of my Israeli neighbors, despite the medieval walls separating us, the Jews of Rhodes so far as I know were the ones who came from furthest away to be caught in the spiderweb of Auschwitz, the only ones along with the Jews from Corfu to begin their final journey on a boat, the solitude so pleasant at first was weighing on me, the Juderia of Rhodes stank of absence of deportation and sunscreen, I put the car back on a ferry headed for the Piraeus, I said to myself that vacations were extremely annoying things, and even though I thought the knights of Jerusalem were more or less agreeable, future masters of Arab Malta and employers of Caravaggio, I wanted to find a big city again, a capital, activity and not just idle tourists like me moving around in the midst of the ghosts of Crusaders and dead Jews: the bar on the train is full of Americans, they're going to Rome, a group of tourists, a bunch of friends in their early sixties, blonde women, tall men, their teeth redone, nice people, Sans Souci beer in hand I listen to them commenting on their hotel in Florence, it wasn't bad, they say, *by European standards*, I don't know if this remark is supposed to be positive or negative, maybe we'll see each other again at the Plaza, the most American, most decadent of the luxury hotels in Rome, why didn't Yvan Deroy choose the Minerva Hotel in front of the Bernini elephant, the elephant with the long trunk, or the Grand Hotel on the Piazza Repubblica, the one belonging to Alfonso XIII of Spain the collector of slippers, so close to the train station, or another of the 100,000 luxury hotels in Rome, each one haunted by its famous visitors its corpses its ghosts, Yvan Deroy will be a phantom among others, the last beer of Francis Servain the secret agent, the last beer of Francis Servain offshoot of Hades, it had to be called Sans Souci and be a boat—after two days sweating in Athens in a dusty deserted city, after gathering my thoughts in the Temple of Zeus, after having revered the green-eyed goddess and her peerless beauty I had sweated so much and was so covered in dust that I dreamt of the Great North and the glacial cold, I thought of Lebihan and his scorn for anything south of Clermont-Ferrand, the old man was right, Athens was disemboweled, they were building a subway line the gods were not very happy to have their cellar drilled into like that and took revenge by sinking newspaper kiosks underground parking lots and inattentive foreigners into the abyss, Hephaestus the lame and Poseidon the earth-shaker caused quite a bit of trouble for the harried engineers, not counting the pompous archeologists from the Antiquities department who wanted to analyze each pebble taken out of the excavations, which made

Athenians say that their subway wouldn't be ready till the end of days, the Hellenes were a proud people but not without irony, in August obviously they were all on vacation, and around Omonia Square only somber Albanians and broke travelers walked, in the dust and the apocalyptic noise of pneumatic drills, under the maternal gaze of the goddess on top of her Acropolis, I thought of Albert Speer the Führer's architect inventor of the theory of rubble, conceiver of buildings destined to become beautiful ruins a thousand years in the future, ruins like the Greeks and Romans had, which Germany was sadly lacking, Adolf the Determined didn't back away from anything for the good of his people, so Speer sketched Doric temples with unheard-of proportions that once eaten away by time would have constituted a magnificent Forum, a sublime Parthenon in the middle of Nuremberg and Berlin, Speer was a strange architect, the planner of vestiges of the future, great builder of arms factories—at the Nuremberg trial Francesc Boix formally recognized him, he pointed him out, he saw him in photographs during his visit to Mauthausen, accompanied by Kaltenbrunner, head of security for the Reich, in the stairways of the death quarry, what is Speer the artist thinking at that instant, in the dock with the accused, singled out by a Spanish communist photographer, Speer who denied ever knowing anything, ever seeing anything, ever hearing anything, the Führer's friend sitting in the midst of the rubble, where the American bombs had accelerated the work of time: in Athens slaves built the Acropolis, slaves would build the monuments of the Reich, many would die, true, but many had died building the pyramids and no one today thought of demolishing them or of damning their architect, that's what Speer must have been thinking the little rich man in the dock between an SS officer and a Wehrmacht officer, he got out of Spandau Prison in 1966 and I imagine him a few months later, at the age of sixty-one, traveling through Greece in the company of his son Albert Jr., who at that time was planning the urban development of Tripoli in Libya, and who would go on to build in Iran and Saudi Arabia, does Albert Speer Sr. remember the stairway in Mauthausen as he climbs the steps to the Acropolis, or the young Spaniard who pointed him out in Nuremberg, not very likely—in 1947 Boix also goes to Greece, at the beginning of the civil war, on assignment for *L'Humanité* and *Regards*, he photographs Zachariadis the general secretary of the communist party and spends some time in the mountains with the DSE partisans, before returning to Paris and dying there, in the meantime he had also gone to Algeria, where the same Speer Jr. would much later design a suburb that would, without him knowing it, house my GIA cutthroats, and Boix would follow the Tour de France, which delighted him, I haven't seen his photos of Greece but I suppose he knew how to talk with the communist fighters, after all he had been one too: I left for the north, instead of taking the ferry to Igoumenitsa I still had time to kill so I went back up to Thessaly, maybe it was cooler there, I was pouring with sweat in the car with all the windows open, in Bosnia in 1993 there was a brigade of Greek volunteers who fought alongside the Serbs, a handful of fanatics who distinguished themselves around Sarajevo especially, I hadn't met any of them, fortunately, the Arab mujahideen and the Russian auxiliaries were quite enough, even if they'd been in skirts and clogs with pompoms like Thomson and Thompson, great Orthodox solidarity on one side, Muslim fraternity and Catholic harmony on the other, in the train's bar the Americans are talking loudly, they're laughing, they're happy, they seem to have been playing golf all their lives around Seattle, so pale are they, they're drinking mineral water and Chianti, maybe their parents were soldiers in this region, in the company of Moroccan goumiers and Algerian infantry of the French Expeditionary Corps, in June 1944, around Lake Trasimeno, between Montepulciano and Perugia, after the victory of Monte Cassino, that famous victory that the Moroccans and Algerians had celebrated by robbing killing pillaging and raping anything that fell into their hands, including livestock according to the complaints lodged at the allied police station, great soldiers were also excellent bandits, they had gotten a fine reputation for themselves ever since they'd landed, their officers closed their eyes or preferred to take the law into their own hands, after all it was wartime, in Sicily things hadn't been so easy, the civilians hid in the mountains and they say that more than one soldier "who had behaved badly" had been found cut into pieces by an offended father or husband, around Naples the French soldiers of the colonial troops had set off an avalanche of complaints about theft, theft and murder, not counting the various perversions related by the Neapolitan prostitutes, no matter the Moroccan mountain troops and the Algerian infantry corps were great soldiers, they had proven it many times, and they would prove it once again in Monte Cassino, their heroism was equaled only by their perfect savagery, they climbed the rocky slopes under fire of the Germans entrenched at the top, they died bravely, sent to the front with their mules, their donkeys, and when they were victorious had bled freely were quite dead chopped up cut up crushed by bombs and stones the survivors scattered into the countryside to take their share of honor, beautiful dark-haired virgin girls tanned from laboring in the fields, sheep, goats from which they made smoking hecatombs, the gods licked their lips, the soldiers in the colonial troops carried everything off on their mules, even mattresses, and when the farmer tried to resist, refused to hand over his wife his daughter his mother his sister his sheep and his wall clock they slit his neck with pleasure, weren't they conquerors, they were applying the law of war, they could take everything down to the last stone if they wanted, magnanimous they usually consumed the women on site and only rarely carried them away, they weren't any worse than the bombs that had razed the abbey of Saint Benedict at Monte Cassino, when there wasn't a single German inside, tons of explosives dropped in vain from beautiful B-17s those angels of destruction, the same angels that wiped German cities off the map, the original Benedictine abbey lay in fragments, Pope Pius XII in Rome was furious and silent, he knew how things stood, humped peasants and a few atrociously violated goats were nothing compared to a building of that value, Italian civilians and the walls of Saint Benedict the ascetic gardener were chalked up to profit and loss, Rome fell, Pius XII rushed into the arms of his liberators *mit brennender Sorge*, with a keen anxiety, the Pope spoke German better than English, after ten years spent in Bavaria, Pius XII the clever had managed to keep the Vatican intact in the tempest, facing Mussolini then the Reich, with immense cowardliness and great courage, according to which version you heard, it is to be feared that Pius XII was neither exceptionally spineless nor particularly brave, that he feared the Reds more than all the others, he negotiated the Lateran Accords with Mussolini, congratulated General Franco for having delivered Spain so nicely to the Church, dared to chide the Führer for his attacks against Catholicism, asked the martyred Polish faithful to be patient for a while, hid a few Jews in his gardens, the Pope preferred to lower his Papal tiara over his eyes for a while so as not to be blinded by what he could have seen, there would always be time to forgive the killers and beatify the martyrs, and the list was long, the list was terribly long, like the Americans who were burying bodies with backhoes during the liberation of the camps, Dachau, Bergen-Belsen, Mauthausen, hundreds of women and men went into the ground, millions had already gone there, in flames and into the air, like the 60,000 Jews who were missing from Salonika when I went there, certainly in 1945 no one recognized the city anymore, almost half the inhabitants had disappeared, I found a hotel very close to the sea a stone's throw away from Aristotle Square and the White Tower, in the new city that is so reminiscent of Alexandria in Egypt, the elegant whitewashed buildings burned in the evening sun setting from Mount Hortiatis to bring a little coolness to the avenues crushed by summer, people strolled along the seafront, their mouths open like asphyxiated fish, cooler air rose little by little from the sparkling gulf, the rigging of the *Amerigo Vespucci* began clinking in the warm breeze, the light faded and projected bluish shadows onto the glasses on the café terraces in the square, it was logical for Salonika to remind me of Alexandria founded by Alexander the conqueror of Asia, the one who had profited from the lessons of Aristotle quite close to this place, before spreading the fury of his armies to the ends of the earth, I felt immediately rested in Salonika, the last chapter in *Drifting Cities*, a story about survivors of the communist saga took place there, by a strange chance the book had caught up with me on my trip, the heroes drank Macedonian wine in a tavern on top of the ramparts, remembering their dead, a libation, the handsome Manos killed by a grenade his corpse attached to a mule's tail and dragged over the rocks, Pandelis and Thanassis shot, the bony rheumatic women would take care of their memorials, was it the wind coming from the north, from the nearby Balkans, from Serbia possibly, was it the novel by Tsirkas or the Macedonian wine but once the last page was finished I was trembling as if I were about to collapse, where were they, Andrija the Slavonic, Vlaho the Dalmatian, lost in death or in their mountains, *sing, goddess, their memorable names*, the names of the ones who left me, whom I left, for the first time I felt as if I were locked up in the Zone, in a hazy shifting blue interspace where a long threnody rose up chanted by an ancient choir, and everything was spinning around me because I was a ghost locked up in the realm of the Dead, condemned to wander without ever making an image on photographic film or being reflected in a mirror until I shattered my fate, but how, how could I extricate myself from this empty shell that was my body, I paced Salonika top to bottom and bottom to top, the icons the saints the churches the ramparts over to the prison of Heptapyrghion on top of the Acropolis, Constantine the Philosopher, Cyril the apostle of the Slavs who left from Salonika for a long journey ended his life in Rome, you can see his tomb, beneath the narthex of the San Clemente Basilica, on the Lateran slopes, maybe when I get to Rome I'll go lie down too in a humid basement, in a cave, a catacomb, and I'll let Yvan Deroy the fortunate take his leave, let him walk to his fate and abandon me to decay, I've almost finished my beer, my Sans Souci with the proud ship, the tourists from the New World don't seem in a hurry to go back to their car, me neither, above my seat is the little suitcase chained to the luggage rack, what does it really contain, why did I want to document the Zone from Harmen Gerbens the Cairo drunk, all those images, those names, down to my own, down to the terrible photos of Bosnia, including the souvenirs of Jasenovac, the throngs of massacred in Mauthausen, the documents from Globocnik and Stangl in Trieste, my father's torture photos, the Ottoman telegrams in code addressed to Talaat Pasha, the Spanish lists of the mass graves in Valencia, the massacred of Shatila, the laughter of Alois Brunner the senile in Damascus, may they rest in peace, may I rest in peace, since everything's going to be over soon, may the apocalypse come and the warming or the freezing the desert or the deluge I'll entrust my personal ark to the eternity specialists and farewell, the madman on the platform in the Milan train station was right, one last handshake before the end of the world, one last contact one last exchange of information and goodbye

shut up in this car my ears blocked by the tunnels and the weird compression of air they cause, the Florence-Rome *direttissima* line is nothing but a long corridor dotted with open passages, you forget that air is a substance except when there's not enough of it or when it stiffens against your eardrums, no matter how accustomed to them you are explosions always shake you like an old tree, you tremble, you tense up despite yourself your arms hug your body your chin jerks up and makes you bite your tongue your fingers quiver and become flesh tuning-forks, you crouch down when you hear the shrapnel whistling, then the air comes back along with silence, silence which is even more terrifying since you're always wondering when the next shell will arrive, where it will fall, if it will hit its target and scatter you into the azure like the clod of earth and leaves you've just seen flying up during the last impact, you wait, and the explosion surprises you again, the same bright yellow flash, the same compression of the atmosphere, the indescribable striated racket of metallic throbbing, that one didn't fall far away, you had to be drunk or drugged or both to endure this tension for long, this powerlessness that made you feel like a blade of grass or a mole beneath the hoe of some divine gardener: the only one who didn't seem affected was Andrija, we never saw him tremble, he only crouched down when it was strictly necessary, he remained perfectly calm in the storm, waiting for the lull to go back on the attack, his helmet resting high on his forehead with an air of defiance, it was as if he knew he was protected by Zeus master of lightning, immune beneath the thundering aegis, Andi the brave was not a braggart, his courage was linked to a perfect innocence, for him the bombs were nothing but noise and pieces of metal, not much more than artillery practice, that's all, he wasn't picturing the effect these explosives could have on his body, not even unconsciously, and yet he had seen what it was like, guys pierced with smoking shrapnel, amputated disemboweled or just grazed, but he had such faith in his destiny that nothing could touch him, and nothing did—the shelling over, he carefully prepared his gun, his ammunition, ready to confront the tanks, ready to defend our blockhouse or our trench like a lion, whereas for Vlaho, Sergeant Mile, or me the end of the bombing signified the beginning of another, different fear, but at least equally intense: that of the assault, the assault you sustain or the one you launch, and in our position, with no men or equipment, it was hard to decide which was more terrifying, waiting for the tanks or going to meet them, we launched a counter-offensive to liberate Vukovar we were going to have to fight like lions to retake first the village of Marinci on the road to Vinkovci, my first large-scale battle, and it was the same for Andrija—he compensated for his own inexperience with exceptional courage and waited bravely under the rain of shells while I thought I was going mad, my mouth dry, deaf, thinking soon we'd have to go, go oust the Yugoslav army from its positions and leap onto their tanks in little groups armed with a few RPGs, confront their machine guns their mortars their rifles, we were ready, our boots well-laced like Intissar the courageous, ready to drive back the Serbs great tamers of mares to the ramparts of Belgrade, I trembled under the cannon fire, the 3rd regiment of the Yugoslav artillery was bombarding us at the rate of one salvo every twenty or thirty seconds, the dawn was rising over the extraordinarily flat fields opposite us, mud and corn rotting underfoot, lying flat, a brownish plain in the grey of the sky still warm that early fall, not at all the dreamed-of day for dying, not at all, in the distance straight in front on the other side of the road the battle had already begun and the surprised JNA were falling back, we had to advance to cut off their retreat and allow our flank to take Marinci before continuing on to Vukovar, I looked at the checkerboard patch sewn in haste onto Andi's shoulder to give me courage, at least we knew what we were fighting for, for a country for a surrounded city for liberty and it's very strange to think today that I contributed to the liberation of a country that is starting to matter less and less to me, distant, hazy, where I almost never go hey that's it I could settle on the coast or on an island, rent a little house and wait quietly for the end of the world, in Hvar or Trogir, my dead would come to nibble at my feet at night, I'd sleep poorly there too many ghosts in that neighborhood, what I need is a new place with no memories no ruins underfoot, a virgin sky crossed by an airplane a fragment of azure where everything remains in suspense, higher up, higher up than the trajectories of shells that exploded around us in that trench we never wanted to leave, except Andrija who champed at the bit like a good wild horse, weapons in hand, all prepared, all ready, the devil himself was going to dash forward, the devil or the army of angels, depending, at the order of the boorish Sergeant Mile we left, forward, forward, and my brain suddenly turned white like the flag of someone surrendering, naked, empty, giving way to the body thrust out of its shelter by sheer courage and the noncom's kick in the pants, go on, Andrija the courageous sparkled in the grey-fingered dawn, his rocket launcher on his shoulder, we wanted to shout roar cry out but we had to keep silent, run like lightning to sprawl down into the mud at the place where we thought we could intercept the trajectory of the T55 silhouetted on the horizon like a toad in the corn, at full tilt, one, two, three, four, five tanks are approaching the ground vibrates slightly this one is mine, this one is mine and they're not expecting to find us here, hope makes us feverish, they've fallen into the trap, I help Andi arm his rocket, I rise up quickly to observe the movement of the tanks, ten seconds more, Andrija the brave straightens up aims calmly and lets loose his line of fire, *above all do not stay standing up waiting for the result of fire*, back to the ground to the insects your nose against the earth a 12.7 volley cuts through the corn around us, we crawl to the right as fast as possible, as fast as possible, everything becomes a game everything becomes a game we hear the impact of the RPGs the shouts the engines the disordered fire of the tanks we reload we reload quick we glance over three tanks are burning the one we got is immobilized Andi got it, a caterpillar tread in the air its turret is damaged the trap is open Serbs are trying to extricate themselves from the doomed vehicle, a wounded horse, I'll finish it off, I raise the viewfinder, I have the joint of the turret in the middle of the target it's off, this time we watch the trajectory of the shot, straight line of fire, one of the occupants half-outside sees the trajectory heading straight for him, paralyzed, go on, *move* I think get out two seconds the missile skids onto the bottom of the tank and explodes, tatters of flesh and uniform streak the pure yellow of the flame and project a long red and blackened spray, the tail of a rooster in a summer light, Andi looks at me, stunned, and mumbles *shit, bullseye*, I don't have time to reply, a bomb explodes a few meters away from us, we have to move again, under cover through the corn, towards the trench to move to the left, the tanks have changed their course to come around from in front, more are on the way, more and more, dozens of tanks trapped in the fields, trying to escape, a band of mules or a herd of buffalo, they blunder into invisible barriers, mines and anti-tank batteries, they know they can't make a U-turn, they have to go through, so they advance despite everything among the carcasses of their predecessors, that's the only victory I remember, the only real victory in the middle of an endless series of defeats, we had retaken Marinci, the road to Vukovar was open, who knows what would have happened if Tuđman hadn't immediately stopped the offensive, we didn't understand a thing, not a single thing, not one, our first victory and it was useless, our fear and our dead were all to no purpose, the gods were protecting the Serbs, Troy would take a very long time to fall, Zeus had decided thus, and we were shaking our weapons beneath the Scaean Gates in vain, like someone brandishing a broom against a wall, we had won a battle and the next day or the day after that Hector son of Priam kicked us in the nuts again, into the very bottom of our ditch near our vessels, the agony of Vukovar would last one more month, hard, brutal, a city turned into a cellar, a rat-hole, a cage that would give way as soon as General Panić took the trouble to strike it effectively, on October 14th Marinci was retaken, the road cut off again, the city surrounded for a month of hell and a few thousand corpses, today the strategists and historians state that the sacrifice of Vukovar saved a lot of time, time needed to train and prepare the Croatian army, that's possible, we however saw in it mostly the command of Zeus, Andrija groused like a child, kicked empty cans, he would have preferred to be inside the besieged city rather than fifteen kilometers away in the middle of wiped-out farms and hamlets, hunting for pigs, I was having my first nightmares, I heard bombs all night long, I saw over and over again the Serb soldier exploding on top of the T55 turret, so precisely that I could have drawn his frozen face, paralyzed with terror before the rocket rushing towards him to propel him into death, all those faces are superimposed on each other now, the terrified the decapitated the burned the bullet-pierced eaten by dogs or foxes the amputated the broken the calm the tortured the hanged the gassed, mine and others' the photographs and memories the heads without bodies the arms without bodies the dead eyes they all have the same features, it's all of humanity one icon the same face the same sensation of pressure in your eardrums the same long tunnel where you can't breathe, an infinite train a long march of the guilty of victims of terror and revenge, an immense fresco in the Church of No One, and the divine Andrija in the middle, furious beneath the ramparts of Ilion the well-guarded, shot by a bearded man surprised at discovering a soldier crouching around the edge of the woods, one more dawn, a dawn of saffron rose or tar it's all the same, the day before we had drunk a lot, we had drunk too much, I got up in a bad mood, him too, Andi couldn't find his knife, his bayonet, he had a headache, he blundered round in circles looking for them, he moved all his things, so I handed him my own, just so he'd stop griping, that doesn't matter so much today, that dawn, those movements in the mist, I would have killed the whole earth to avenge Andi and recover his vanished corpse, pillaged and mutilated no doubt, bury it burn it or return it to his people, the world was beginning to crack, the fissure got wider in Venice, it got even bigger in the years of shadow on the Boulevard, a tunnel today a tunnel to Rome, think of something else Francis, think of Yvan the mad, think of the New World, of those nice sexagenarians on vacation knocking back Chianti and laughing, think of the endless landscapes, the lakes, the bears and infinite forests there are in their lands, lose yourself in the immense night of Tuscany pierced by the railroad like a shield by a spear, by a gaze, the way you calmly scrutinize a canvas, the head of Medusa on the wall in the Uffizi

in Rome in 1598 Michelangelo Merisi called Caravaggio organizes his first decapitation: he has the head of an old horse cut off by an athletic brigand recruited in front of one of the many houses of ill repute around the mausoleum of Augustus, in his studio he attentively observes the naked killer's muscles bulge under the weight of the sword, the curve of shoulder when he brings the blade down onto the animal's throat, the nostrils smoking from fever, prostrate with illness the animal is condemned Caravaggio has no time to draw it of course, he studies the reflection on the metal when it penetrates the neck the spurt of black blood that soaks the warrior's thigh and turns purple, the horse's legs convulse, the metal returns to the charge, the savage mercenary again lifts the weapon and strikes higher up opening a new wound the horse has stopped moving the man has reached the vertebrae, the executioner is red and soaked to his waist, he bends forward to finish his work, Michelangelo Merisi watches him grasp the mane cut off the last pieces of flesh and with his left hand brandish the heavy head, effortlessly, it is dripping and its eyes are staring, Caravaggio feels nauseous, his two domestics throw buckets of water over the shuddering executioner, one can almost see his heart beating in his hairless chest, Caravaggio starts drawing, muscles, swords, gushes of blood, while the hired killer washes himself, before Merisi the invert pays him for something entirely different, a ritual that was much more reprehensible at the time than the death of a sick horse, Rome is a somber dangerous city full of daggers disfigured prostitutes cutthroats dark alleyways, Caravaggio loves this city, after his flight he won't rest until he returns to it, even though Naples has its charm, its distress, even though you can find lovers and heads to cut off as far as Malta the prim, it's always Rome the plebes of Rome the pomp of Rome that will attract Caravaggio the sacrificer, the man in love with bodies night and decapitation, Rome that's coming quickly closer in the Tuscan night, tomorrow the Americans to whom Antonio the bartender is serving another Chianti might stop at Saint Louis of the French, San Luigi dei Francesi, on their way to the Piazza Navona, to see the three canvases in the Contarelli Chapel, the calling, the inspiration, and the martyrdom of St. Matthew, among the most famous works by Caravaggio, the sword of the naked man standing over the saint lying on the ground, the beauty of the angel, a few meters away in the first chapel to the left are the commemorative plaques for the French soldiers who died in Italy, the officers of free France who commanded Moroccans Tunisians Algerians Senegalese West Indians, no one looks at them, poor forgotten guys, the Moroccan troops and the Algerian goumiers, sacrificed so easily by the allied generals—withdrawn from the Italian front in July 1944 after having left 10,000 dead and missing there, they take part in the landing in Provence, will travel across all of France before crossing the Rhine in April 1945, it seems to me I've seen their mule trains from the window, in Italy the fear of "Moroccaning" becomes a real panic, blown out of all proportion given the facts, a few hundred violent acts by the colonial troops, they had to eat, to cheer themselves up, to earn something from war that otherwise gave nothing but pain, the French officers had the authority to send their soldiers to the firing squad at the slightest misdemeanor, without any further ado than a note sent to headquarters, there were about a hundred of these, a hundred guys shot for one reason or another, among the thousands of members of the French Expeditionary Corps that would not see the Atlas again, the Rif, Constantine, Kabylia, many of the survivors would put their military experience to the service of the FLN a few years later, some would be tortured, killed without warning or caught in ambushes facing the colonial officers who had led them to victory or to a plaque, a little marble plaque a few feet away from Caravaggio's *Saint Matthew*, a plaque to summarize the thousands of names in French cemeteries scattered throughout Italian soil between Naples and Lake Trasimeno: in Salonika, once *Drifting Cities* was shut, between taverns and bottles of Macedonian wine, thanks to a travel guide bought by chance in a newspaper kiosk I went to see the Zeitenlick necropolis, the cemetery for the Balkan campaign, where there are 9,000 French graves and the bones of 8,000 Serbs from the years 1915–1917, forgotten next to a large avenue, in the middle of town, the survivors of the Dardanelles, landed in 1915 to support the retreating Serbs, in the necropolis there is a well-kept British plot, a Russian section, an Italian monument, a giant Serb ossuary, a corner for the Algerian Muslims, for the Jewish French, for the Buddhists from Indochina, the Madagascans and Senegalese the whole world had come to get murdered by the savage Bulgarians the Germans and their Austrian allies, and the whole world was resting now between the cypresses on the Avenue Langada two kilometers away from the sea, in the August sun, I thought back to my visit to the Dardanelles with Marianne six years earlier, hundreds of pages earlier, now by chance on my own I saw the next episode, the names of those who were still alive when we were discovering the tormented landscapes along the peninsula, the forts of Kilitbahir, Cape Helles, now I could follow their journey, 9,000 more had keeled over a little further away, in the meantime I had waged war myself, I had stopped over in Venice, Marianne had left, I had become a civil servant of the shadows and I found myself alone by chance in Thessalonica before all these graves that so to speak belonged to me, the way Atatürk's native house belonged to me climbing the little streets of the high city, a restored Ottoman residence, ocher-pink, Mustafa Kemal whose museum I had visited in the Dardanelles, his path was opposite, eastwards, to glorious Anatolia, when he was born in 1881 Salonika was the second-largest city in the Ottoman

Empire, peopled half with Sephardic Jews and half with Turks, Greeks, Slavs, and Europeans, Pabst's *Spies from Salonika*, that film fascinated me when I was little, why in 1912 after the Balkan Wars did Mustafa Kemal continue his military career, until he sent the British and the French back to the sea in Gallipoli, then sent the Greeks from Asia Minor in 1923, as for the Jews they pursued their studies, until the Germans caught them in 1941, so that by mid-1943 only a handful remained, scattered among the mountains with the Resistance—the transit camp in Salonika was next to the train station, the trains began leaving in March 1943, for Treblinka, Sobibór, and Birkenau, by August 50,000 people had been deported, and almost 40,000 gassed, I learned all that in the Jewish Museum, before the communities of Athens and Rhodes the community of Thessalonica was destroyed by Alois Brunner the furious specialist, who had arrived in Greece in February 1943, until then anti-Jewish measures had been limited to prohibiting bicycles and radios, Brunner took things in hand, the bull by the horns, he organized a Jewish police of hoodlums to help him in his task, and six months later not a single Jew was officially left in Salonika, the last *Prominenten* including Grand Rabbi Zevi Koretz were put onto a train headed for one of the camps of Bergen-Belsen, not a question of extermination for him, the Germans feel they owe him something, as well as the 300 Jews of Spanish nationality whom Franco's consul is calling for, the surprising Spaniards insist on recovering their Jews, so a convoy leaves for Bergen-Belsen, whence a transport is organized for the south, and the Sephardim take the return route to the lands of Isabella of Castille that they left 400 years earlier, through Vichy France, do they meet one another in the stations of Narbonne or Bordeaux, the ones heading for destruction and the ones escaping it, I have no idea, after arriving in Spain they were confined in military buildings in Barcelona: in January 1944 those inhabitants of the Aegean coasts found themselves on the other side of the Mediterranean, after weeks of trains, transit camps, negotiations, privations, and illness, from Macedonia to Saxony from Saxony to France from France to Catalonia before finally being sent to Spanish Morocco, undesirable on the homeland's soil, and undertaking, for themselves this time, a new exile that would lead some as far as Palestine, luckier in the end than Grand Rabbi Zevi Koretz: he died of typhus just after the liberation of the camps, Zevi Koretz the German-speaking Ashkenazi had understood Alois Brunner's orders very well and had scrupulously carried them out, he thought he was acting for the best, maybe he was afraid of German violence, maybe he didn't know what was awaiting his fellow-citizens around Krakow, we'll never know—leaving the Museum of Jewish Presence my solitude is beginning to feel more and more weighty, I'm hot, I'm thirsty, the long summer afternoon still has time ahead of it so I'll go eat and drink in an air-conditioned place, thinking about the journeys of the children of Israel, and trying to imagine Salonika speaking Judeo-Spanish, French, and Turkish, between a hammam, a mosque, and two Byzantine churches, that year the city is the cultural capital of Europe, sad recompense for the few survivors of the former Jerusalem of the Balkans, like Leon Saltiel, whose Memoirs I bought in the museum, Leon Saltiel is Jewish and a communist and after the first measures of the SS in the beginning of 1943, roundups, branding, he joins ELAS, the Greek partisans, in the mountains, where he takes part in some heroic actions, until civil war broke out between the Resistant factions in the beginning of 1944, then Leon Saltiel left the Resistance to return secretly to Salonika accompanied by a comrade from Ioannina, Agatha, with whom he is hopelessly in love, he realizes that his entire family has been deported and that the collaborators are selling off Jewish property, he conceals himself with his fellow fighter and lover at the house of a friend, Stavros, but he is denounced, arrested, tortured and sent to Mauthausen, he arrives after an atrocious journey, in the company of Yugoslav partisans and another Greek Resistant, Manos Hadjivassilis from Macedonia, he too crossed the Balkans on foot rifle in hand before being arrested in Slovenia, Manos kills himself as soon as they arrive in the camp, he throws himself onto the barbed wire, the SS guards finish him off, Leon Saltiel speaks many languages, he makes friends with the Spanish communists who organize resistance in the camp, did he meet Francesc Boix the photographer, it's likely, Leon Saltiel is sick during the liberation, he stays for two months in an American infirmary, between life and death, he is up and about in June 1945, 3,000 kilometers away from his country, he learns that there has been a civil war, that there has been fighting in Athens, that the communists are opposing the British and the royalists, Leon wants to see Agatha and Salonika again, he gets a passport from the Red Cross and starts out on the long journey, on foot through Austria and Hungary, he reaches Belgrade where he is arrested for reasons he doesn't understand, ends up being released and sent back to Italy by way of Zagreb with a contingent of prisoners of war, in Venice after two weeks of medical quarantine in a humid transit camp they put him on a train for Ancona, in Ancona he meets some Greeks, they find him a spot on a freighter that finally berths in Patras on December 1st, 1945: on his thirtieth birthday Leon Saltiel is in Greece, he reaches Athens easily and from there gets to Salonika, he's afraid of what's waiting for him, in the meantime his hair has grown back, his poor civilian clothes provided by the Red Cross are in ruins, his clogs too, he has a wild beard, hollow eyes, he goes to the center of town, back up Egnatia Avenue, he'll go back to where he started from, to Stavros's café the place where he was arrested, he'll drink a coffee with no sugar, calmly, watching the few post-war cars jolt by, he veers off to the left, to Santa Sophia Street, to the border of the upper town, it's almost 6:00 p.m., he has a few drachmas in his pocket given to him by his coreligionists in Athens, they also suggested they let someone know of his arrival by phone, he refused, now he's just a hundred meters away from Stavros's place, Leon Saltiel hesitates, he could go back down and see the building where his mother lived, his brother-in-law's shop, even though he knows there's nothing left there, that they're all dead, he knows it better than anyone for he has seen the piles of corpses, the summary executions, he has smelled the stench of burnt flesh, when the icy wind made the Danube ripple, he could go to the synagogue, the community has surely planned something for the returning ones, he must not be the only one to come back, he could also go to party headquarters, he doesn't know if he wants to all that much, to talk, tell stories, explain, there were a few Greeks with him in Mauthausen, a dozen, no Jews, they all died, one of them hanged himself with the cord that was holding his pants up, *Adonai, Adonai,* Leon has never been religious, the last of his comrades died of pneumonia after the liberation, others had arrived after the evacuation of Auschwitz, some even from Salonika, but they had already left again when Leon got out of the infirmary, the Americans didn't know how to repatriate him to Greece, he walked along the Danube as far as Vienna, the soldiers looked at him as if he were one of the walking dead and now at the corner of the street a hundred meters away from the café he hesitates, he is ashamed, Stavros is a good friend, was he captured by the Germans too, Leon Saltiel goes up to the café terrace, he glances inside, waits an instant, enters, walks up to the bar, Stavros is there, he hasn't changed, he stands in front of him, without saying anything, Stavros glances at him absent-mindedly without recognizing him, annoyed Leon sits down at a table, he waits, he doesn't know what to say, he says Stavros a coffee with no sugar please, busy behind the counter the man repeats the order to the kitchen, one no sugar, Leon is at a loss he hesitates to shout Stavros it's me he remains silent a woman emerges from the kitchen holding a little aluminum tray it's Agatha, Leon lowers his head, she puts the coffee and the glass of cold water abruptly down on the table, Leon stares at the brown froth in the little cup, he has seen the wedding ring on her right hand, he suddenly thinks of Aris Andreanou who hanged himself in the showers with his belt, of his overlong twisted neck, his eyes looking up, his mouth open, he waits patiently for the coffee grounds to settle, he knows now that neither Agatha nor Stavros is going to recognize him, because he is a ghost, because for them he is dead, he suddenly understands why and how he was arrested, Leon Saltiel drinks his bitter coffee, then a little water, he throws down a coin that rattles on the metal tray, and goes out—I do the same, halfway through Saltiel's Memoirs I pay for my drinks and I go out, I've been reading for a good two hours in English, something I haven't done since the worthy Institute of Political Science in Paris, the afternoon is far advanced, I climb up to the old city sweating, I need air, I need to see the sea from high up, tomorrow I'll leave I'm not really sure why but suddenly I want to take my car and go north, to go back to Paris by road, to go through Bulgaria and Serbia, after all I have a French passport, it's August, there are tourists, I'll go through the Iron Gates and follow the Danube to Budapest, to see the other side, what does the river look like in Voivodina, on the other shore, in 1997 the war had been over for two years, the region was catching its breath again, what a funny idea when I think about it, to go throw myself into the jaws of the mustachioed Chetnik wolf, without permission, I wasn't supposed to go to that sort of country, in theory I was supposed to ask for special authorization for all movements abroad, which beats everything for a spy, but really, I didn't think much could happen to me, aside from my car breaking down, I'd never seen either Belgrade the white, or Novi Sad the Austrian, maybe the Serb souls buried in the military cemetery in Salonika had put this idea in my head, they were trying to take revenge on my Austro-Hungarian ancestors who sent them to their graves, they wanted to lure me into a trap and drown me in the Danube, in October 1915 Kaiser William II backs up the Austrians in battle, on October 9th Belgrade is taken, the Serbs withdraw on all fronts, all the more so since Ferdinand of Bulgaria, to whom Macedonia and Kosovo have been promised, has just stabbed proud Serbia in the back, retreat is necessary, the army is destroyed and its scattered remains will be added to the Allied Front of Salonika, where they will fight until 1917, in all almost 300,000 Serbian soldiers would meet their death during the First World War, they say, while the Austrians would put their occupied country to fire and sword—the report by Rudolph Archibald Reiss in 1915, used for years as propaganda, came back to me, those nice men disemboweled, civilians enucleated, vaginas opened up by bayonet to let the semen of dozens of troops ooze in, noses cut off, ears torn off, all described with the coldness of the forensic police specialist: whether it was used by one side or the other didn't take away any of the veracity from the testimony, attested by the force of the revenge, the hatred of whoever espouses that revenge, hatred he will purge, dozens of years later, using it against his enemies, out of fear, fear stemming from tradition, from the legend that impels him too to go towards the other with his blade leading the way, the way the stories of Serbian atrocities drove us, in fear, to cut their corpses up into pieces, terrified no doubt that such warriors had the power to come back to life, the series of Serbo-Croatian massacres always proved the previous story right, without any one ever being wrong, since everyone, like the Austrians in Serbia, could cite an atrocity committed by the other camp, the Other per se, you had to erase his humanity by tearing off his face, prevent him from procreating by cutting off his balls, contaminate him by raping his women, annihilate his descendants by slicing off breasts and pubic hair, return to zero, annul fear and suffering, history is a tale of fierce animals, a book with wolves on every page, *Chedo*[1] is going to cut your throat my child, and he will surely do it, just as surely as you yourself, he thinks, have already burned his brawling offspring in the burning ditch, for us the collective stems from the story of individual suffering, the place of the dead, of corpses, it's not Croatia that's bleeding it's the Croats, our country is where its graves are, our murderers, the murderers on the other side of the mirror are biding their time, and they will come, they will come because they have already come, because we have already gone to cut their ears to a point, put our stakes in their wives' stomachs and tear out their eyes, a great wave of screaming blind men will cry for revenge, will come defend their graves and the bones of their dead, as surely as the tide, having gone out, comes back in to the rhythm of the moon's movements, I want to take my car and travel across the land of my enemies, I want to drink some pear brandy in Zemun watching the Sava swell the Danube, to see if the girls are pretty, to listen to turbo-folk sung by the buxom wife of Arkan the Tiger, to buy myself a T-shirt with the head of Milošević or Mladić on it and laugh a little, I want to laugh

1. A nickname for "Chetnik," Serb. —Trans.

thinking that a few years ago this waiter might have killed me without batting an eye around Osijek and that it's over now, it's the Kosovars' turn, then the Albanians will take revenge in turn and eat Orthodox Christians for breakfast, we're all attached to each other by indissoluble ties of heroic blood, by the intrigues of our jealous gods, all that is over, after a few years of purgatory in an office in the midst of files I'm in the last train before the end of the world, before the great light and the revival, when there will be zebras gazelles and lions that will from time to time eat a stray tourist, when we'll drink a superb Norwegian wine, when Yvan Deroy, at seventy years of age, will watch the monkeys playing on the slopes of the Argentario planted with eucalyptus and breadfruit trees, the Americans are impatient to get to Rome, me too, I've been in the train far too long, one of the American women looks vaguely like the woman at La Pomponette last night, she must think I'm a poor guy, I feel all sticky as if I were leaving her place, her dark concierge loge on Rue Marcadet, men are spineless, they want to fight hunt fuck drink sing from time to time and play soccer, they're cowardly faced with their passions, I'd like it all to be over like in *Modern Times*, when Chaplin links arms with his beloved and sets out on the road, I couldn't take Stéphanie by the arm, when I went back to my place two hours later passably drunk and soaking wet after the incident with the pistol she wasn't there anymore, the gun was still on the floor in the same place Stéphanie was gone I took a pencil and paper and wrote her a letter of excuse, explaining to her that I knew of course that the weapon couldn't work, that it was a very bad joke, and then I ended up crying over my fate as a former fighter to attract her pity, how the war was still too present for me and idiocies of that sort, a sentimental cowardly drooling letter so she'd forgive me, love makes you do stupid things, I thought, I was drunk but not blind, I put the letter into an envelope which I deposited in her letterbox as I went to work, it had its effect, my missive, I made sure I didn't come across Stéphanie on the Boulevard Mortier before she read it, and the next day I added another bit, flowers, delivered to her place around eight o'clock, when I was sure she was home, and I don't know if it was the calming effect of the roses or the balm of my excuses, but at 8:30 precisely the phone rang, it was her, she asked me if I wanted to go out to dinner, as if nothing were wrong, I said OK, we can meet halfway, around République for instance, she chose a chic restaurant on the Canal Saint-Martin, when I saw her by the water I hugged her close in my arms, apologizing in her ear, she said never do that to me again, OK? and promise me you'll throw that gun away, I said of course, of course, not meaning a word of it, I kept it for a lot longer, the little Zastava, in the end I gave it a few months ago to Lebihan for his retirement, with a brand new firing pin bought on the Internet, he liked it very much—neither Stéphanie nor I saw that this incident had opened up a breach, a place for violence, I didn't understand that the tide was rising, that it was going to catch us, that the more I filled the suitcase with names and pictures, the more I sought to avoid the memories of Croatia, Bosnia by diving into the Zone, the wider the crack grew, and Stéphanie the great strategist who spent her days with generals and Cabinet ministers was blind, or maybe not, like Marianne she let herself be seduced by the dark side, the taste for danger, warriors gleam with a dark light like Ares himself, Andi the wild was attractive too, a handsome brute despite his ugliness, one of those angelic devils who so pleased Jean Genet the introvert in love with Palestinian fighters, Andi would have done anything to possess a girl like Intissar the Palestinian, I'm sure of it, I wonder if Rafael Kahla the writer was a fighter himself, if he had dealings with those Palestinians, we all tell the same story, at bottom, a tale of violence and desire like Leon Saltiel the Greek Jew in his Memoirs, the betrayed Leon who wanders through deserted Salonika, his family, his friends have disappeared in the camps, his comrades are hiding in the mountains of Macedonia and Epirus, with armed groups that will soon resume fighting the fascist monarchy, Agatha married Stavros, they're the ones who denounced him to the Germans, every day in Mauthausen he thought of Agatha before falling asleep, he constructed an idyllic love for himself in order to survive, clung to her memory as if to a tree so as not to fly up the crematorium chimney, Agatha's eyes, Agatha's hands and today in half-dead Thessalonica that solid wood is now nothing but an old keel eaten away by the sea, Saltiel wanders around for many days before deciding to go back to the family apartment, now occupied by a surviving cousin whom he makes promise not to reveal his presence to anyone, Leon locks himself up for eight days, for eight days he drinks and smokes in the dark, pursued by the brief agony of Manos Hadjivassilis the electrocuted, by the twisted neck and open mouth of Aris Andreanou, by the wedding ring on Agatha's finger, nothing and no one is left to him so Saltiel decides to make an end of it, exhausted by suffering and alcohol he coarsely ties together a short rope with a sheet, knots one end around his neck and looks for a high spot, a pipe, a beam, to tie the other end to, no success, he finds nothing high up that could support his weight, so despairing, the sheet still around him, he climbs onto a window ledge to throw himself into the void, it's late, the night is fine, a cool wind caresses his bare legs, the sea is quite close, the sheet with which he was going to hang himself is a pleasant scarf, the sea breeze draws Leon Saltiel out of the mist, Zeus the assembler of clouds has seen his distress and comes to his aid, the black pain fades away is mixed with the sea spray with the moondust and stardust on the gulf of Salonika, Leon clings to the windowsill, he is standing five floors above ground, he has almost hanged himself and thrown himself into the void, what for, who for, there is no one left, he goes back into the apartment collapses on his bed and falls into a sleep of the dead, the rope still around his neck—the next day Leon trims his beard but doesn't shave it off, he has had a dream, he saw his fate clearly, he puts on a nice shirt, a handsome jacket, too bad if all these clothes are too big for him now, too bad, he is very busy all day, he is active until late at night, he doesn't tremble even during the most difficult moments, when Agatha cries out, pleads with him, when her skirt bares one of her legs, Leon Saltiel methodically carries out his duty, like a bailiff or an accountant, before rejoining the communists in the mountains, in 1948 he is arrested and deported to Makronisos the prison island, for political reasons, which have nothing to do with the torture of Agatha under the staring eyes of Stavros gagged tied to his chair, or with the leather belt around the young woman's thin throat, or with the bullet that a little later goes through the neck of Stavros the traitor to cut short his agony: Saltiel returns from his second deportation in 1953, and, still according to his Memoirs, leaves Greece once again in 1967, during the dictatorship of the colonels, he won't return until 1978, to die, in Salonika, and it wasn't to die among his people, since his people, Jews, communists, Agatha, Stavros, had all disappeared a long time ago—I wonder why Agatha denounced Saltiel, out of love no doubt, love in troubled times, I imagine they had thought out a plan to rid themselves of the nuisance, she and Stavros the snitch, maybe, or maybe she had nothing to do with all that, Saltiel doesn't say if he tortured her out of pure vengeance or to find out, to find out if she had really given him away to the Germans, a Communist Jew, a real treat for the Gestapo, Saltiel doesn't explain either how he escaped the firing squad in the prison yard of the Heptapyrghion, at the very top of the town, did he talk, did he trade information to get sent to a concentration camp instead, already putting one foot in the grey Zone, our own, the Zone of shadows and manipulators, Salonika pearl of the Aegean reminded me of Alexandria, in the lower town the noble façades of banks, insurance companies, shipping lines from the beginning of the century sat in state, like the cotton market and the Bank of Egypt in the Egyptian metropolis, Aristotle Square looked a little like Saad-Zaghloul Square in front of the Cecil, where all the British tourists went on pilgrimage, the nostalgic crowded around the bar at the Hotel Cecil with a book by Lawrence Durrell in their hands, looking for Justine or Melissa and pretending not to notice the renovations and improvements of modernity, the *business center*, the plastic plants, the obvious kitsch of an international luxury hotel, whereas they were looking for the red leather from before the war, the smoke of cigars, the Greeks the Italians and the Jews of Alexandria, the war and Nasser little by little sent them into exile, to the North, today Alexandria is an immense Egyptian city more populous than Paris, sanctimonious and poor, but it takes pride in a beautiful library, built by a government in love with pharaonic projects, one of the emptiest libraries on the planet, symbol of the regime of Mubarak the opinionated, a beautiful grey shell in Aswan marble—nothing returns from what has been destroyed, nothing is reborn, neither dead men, nor burned libraries, nor submerged lighthouses, nor extinct species, despite the museums commemorations statues books speeches good will, of things that have gone only a vague memory remains, a shadow gliding over sorrowful Alexandria a phantom shivering, and that's all the better no doubt, all the better, you have to know how to forget, let men animals things leave, with Marianne I had met a well-born British couple who were exploring the city in a horse-drawn carriage, they didn't want to take a taxi, they were willing to pay hundreds of maravedis to sit enthroned behind a team of scrawny horses driven by a turbaned Egyptian, the Englishwoman was wearing cream-colored jodhpurs and a close-fitting jacket, the man was in a safari jacket with a wide-brimmed hat model ANZAC 1915, and the only touch of color in this riot of earth-tones was their faces roasted by the Egyptian sun, two ripe tomatoes under old-fashioned hats, he was reading the guide to Alexandria written by E.M. Forster in 1920 and she *Death on the Nile*, they were a little over twenty and very much in love, of course they were staying at the Cecil, we had discovered these specimens in a historic patisserie near the Grand Place, and it was like finding two pteranodons at the traffic circle on the Champs-Elysées or two dolphins from the Yangtze in the Seine, Marianne was delighted to talk with them, although she was a tiny bit jealous of leather luggage and luxury hotels, their English was very refined, very elegant, accompanied by the bobbing of a prominent Adam's apple, they were at their ease sunk into armchairs in the immense patisserie, sipping teabag tea, they were well-informed cultivated knew Cavafy by heart and ancient Greek, real characters, I wasn't especially jealous, the ruddy British girl was bony her breasts flat nothing to compare to Marianne's white blouse whose buttons looked as if they were about to pop from the pressure, Marianne whole and spontaneous was leagues apart from the affected Englishwoman, the Egyptians seemed not to notice anything abnormal, they were happy with the tips and other bakshish the young couple showered them with, in the greatest colonial tradition—his name was James and he was Scottish, a fan of rugby and Greek statuary, they offered to take us on an excursion in their carriage, to Montazah, to visit the palace and gardens, I wanted to say we'll see if ridicule does any harm, but I abstained, after all it was amusing and the next morning we were ready, Marianne was wearing her "country" outfit, a red gingham blouse and a little matching scarf, we piled into the coupé despite the cries of the turbaned postilion, who wanted us to take two vehicles, James ended up convincing him to accept the overload for our weight in pounds sterling, and we were off, in the midst of taxis and crowded buses and exhaust in traffic jams car horns tram bells the mare's feet struck hard on the asphalt at a jogging pace, we were shaken by the tired springs our eardrums pierced by the constant scrape of the badly greased axles and the carriage-driver's shouts who whipped his palfrey like a madman, it was a wonder to watch dung escape from the animal's ass and pile up on the pavement at every stop, we weren't about to win the gold sulky, despite the coachman's aggressiveness toward his courser, to reach Montazah we had to travel six or seven miles, the horse had trouble trotting, which got her a double ration of the whip, our British friends sat enthroned, straight as I's in the jolts, taking in the landscape of the sea plain, proud and happy, to the point where I wondered if we were seeing the same thing, the distress of the old nag sweating under the charioteer's meanness the poverty of Egypt the hell of the traffic the discomfort of the jiggling cart the whiffs of diesel oil from the buses the begging children black with filth who ran after us and whom the driver chased away like flies lashing them with his knout, maybe our hosts had visions of Cleopatra, of Durrell, of Forster, of Cavafy, blinded by the lighthouse of Alexandria, Marianne wasn't much at ease either, the cars passed us in a fury honking their horns, forty-five minutes later we were in Montazah, why did the British have to love their barouche, I was exhausted my buttocks beaten to a pulp almost as much as the heroic nag's, the palace in question was in the midst of magnificent gardens planted with mangos pepper plants bougainvillea oleanders, a castle that looked as if it had been built from red-and-white Legos an exceeding strange building, Austro-Ottoman-kitsch for Farouk forced to abdicate by the Free Officers, by General Naguib and Nasser the Alexandrian with the thick eyebrows, finished with princes and princesses of sumptuous palaces, make way for martial themes and shouted speeches of the revolution underway in the tremolos and sighs of Umm Kulthum the chubby-cheeked, since there wasn't much to see aside from the gardens we went to drink mango juice at the terrace of a hotel that the tourist board had had the good taste to place by the water like a black chancre with twenty floors, our phlegmatic friends had another visit to suggest, this one more original, it involved going to see the childhood home of Rudolf Hess the aviator friend of Hitler and vice-Führer of the Reich, Alexandria had produced everything, poets warriors spies singers high-ranking Nazis, for James it was an almost familial visit, *Hess fell into my uncle's garden*, he said, in May 1941 Rudolf Hess at the controls of a Messerschmitt modified for the purpose flies to Scotland under the nose of the English coastal defenses, and, short of gas, parachutes down to land on the property of a Scottish nobleman dumbfounded by the unexpected appearance of Hitler's dauphin in his hydrangea, we still don't know why, probably to try to negotiate peace with Great Britain before the invasion of the USSR, without the Führer's orders perhaps, Churchill immediately had him locked up in the Tower of London, then sentenced to life in prison in 1946 at Nuremberg the deranged aviator went to keep company with Speer the builder of Teutonic temples in Spandau Prison, mad amnesic hypochondriac depressive his agony would last until 1987, in sadness and solitude, the last inmate of a jail demolished after his death, in his last years Rudolf was haunted by the memory of the bay of Alexandria, all day long he sketched Greek porticos and views of the vanished lighthouse, obsessed with the city he had left eighty years earlier, the Mediterranean light last flame of his empty eyes, unable to remember his trial in Germany but speaking of his Italian governess with tenderness, of his garden, his school, the girls in white dresses, the receptions at the Place des Consuls, his swimming lessons at the Chatby baths, his father's splendid villa in the Santo Stefano neighborhood, a stone's throw from the sea, fourteen years of childhood in Alexandria and over forty years of prison, what to think about, what to remember, did he think of Antony and Cleopatra when he took his life at the venerable age of ninety-three, one hot August day Hess managed to isolate himself in a garden shed in the Spandau bastion with five feet of stolen electric cable that he twists around his neck, he squeezes hard with the help of a window bolt, more ingenious than Leon Saltiel, more determined too, Hess asphyxiates himself to escape overlong life, the interminable fate of the recluse, Hess warrior with no battles, with no glory aside from an air raid and an exceptional longevity, having left Alexandria in 1910 the man of no interest the war criminal with no war dies in the ambulance where they try hard to revive him, last great living Nazi last representative of an extinct species, James the eccentric Scot had reason to be disappointed, at the spot of the Hess family villa by the sea there was a grey building similar to hundreds of others in front of the Corniche, might as well say in front of the highway, no more luxuriant garden, no more sumptuous residence, the trace of Hess's fate had been erased without a qualm by modern Egypt, so we got back into the jolting carriage in the midst of the yellow taxis and warning signals to get back to the center of town, the horse had begun to limp and stubbornly refused to trot, it kept to a walking pace and unleashed the fury of the coachman who shouted, standing up to whip the obstinate horse with all his strength, furiously, the leather lash struck hard and scattered flies and drops of sweat, the old nag shook its neck, neighed, it looked ready for the knacker's yard, its driver was in the process of finishing it off, the animal stumbled from time to time on the asphalt, in the carriage the ambiance was nothing to write home about, the Brits no longer looked at the gleaming sea but at the horse on its last legs receiving the turbaned charioteer's fury, Marianne ground her teeth and let out a little yelp every time the whip came violently down on the animal, four young proper Europeans were responsible for the torture of a nag covered with foam, its nostrils dilating, but no one got out, the carriage ended up bringing us back to the front of the Cecil, James resettled his hat straight on his head and paid the agreed-on price to the coachman who demanded extra for his poor Rosinante, and the Scotsman told him literally to fuck off, if I understood right, with great pleasure—he was close to taking the whip himself and administering a neocolonial thrashing to the Egyptian, the British are sensitive when it comes to horses, he however was responsible for the suffering of the little mare, we separated as good friends promising to see each other again, every time I returned to Alexandria I thought of the anachronistic couple, of Rudolf Hess and the carriage, lunching with my Egyptian generals lovers of whisky great hunters of terrorists, they proudly showed me the construction site for the new library, let's hope it experiences a fate different from its burned-down ancestor, a respite in time before ending up drowned by the rising water of the Mediterranean, after the polar ice melts, its beautiful ash-colored granite jetty transformed into a smooth pleasant beach for the laughing seals, who will play there sliding on their bellies trumpeting with delight

everything is harder once you reach man's estate the sensation of being a poor guy the approach of old age the accumulation of sins the body lets go of us white traces at your temples veins more prominent your sex shrinks ears stretch illness lies in wait, alopecia Lebihan's fungi or the cancer of my father laid low by Apollo and Machaon's knife can do nothing for it, the arrow was too well embedded, too deep, despite many operations the sickness returned, spread, my father began to dissolve, dissolve then dry out, he seemed increasingly taller, drawn out, his immense pale face was furrowed with bony crevices, his arms were emaciated, the man who had always been so low-key was almost completely silent, my mother spoke for him, she said *your father this, your father that*, in his presence, she was his Pythia, she interpreted his signs, *your father is happy to see you*, she said when I visited, *he misses you*, and the paternal body in its armchair said nothing, when I went over to him to ask him how he was my mother replied *today he's very well*, and little by little everyone lost the habit of addressing him directly, we consulted his oracle, my father remained sitting for hours on end reading Saint Augustine or the Gospels and it was strange that a scientist, an engineer, a specialist in the most invisible kind of matter found a place for God at the heart of his waves, he was settling his account with the beyond no doubt, preparing his passport for Hades great eater of warriors, we were all convinced he was going to get better, get better or drag his illness out for years, but the Moirae had decided otherwise, and Zeus himself could do nothing, so after a visit to my parents I went back to my place stopping by the bistro below to drink a few shots before climbing up to pick up a book too, any book, to pass the time, the Zone documents or whatever the bookstore on the Place des Abbesses palmed off on me, trashy novels literature essays everything came through there, ever since Stéphanie left in place of her skin I had to caress thousands of pages in solitude, enough to make you mad, like Rudolf Hess in his interminable prison, my father was fading away my mother was holding up and playing ever more difficult pieces four hours a day furiously, Chopin Liszt Scriabin Shostakovich nothing resisted her, the Boulevard was grey and more somber than ever, the sword of Maréchal Mortier was rusting now under the directorship of Jean-Claude Cousseran, diplomat specialist in the Zone, from Jerusalem to Ankara not excluding Damascus, pleasant cultivated and intelligent, not much liked among the experts of intrigue and shadow plays, all that was too high up for me, from my office I saw nothing but Lebihan who wheezed from meeting to meeting waiting for his discharge, the reforms and transformations of flow charts, the budget given to such-or-such agency to the detriment of some other, in other words everything that makes up an excessively opaque administration, about which no one really knows exactly how it functions, not even us: by magic the reports files missions weekly or special bulletins still reached their destinations, the propaganda and various manipulations ended up getting the better of Cousseran and his team, overthrown by staunch Chirac supporters, Cousseran left for Cairo as ambassador, he must still be there, by the shores of the Nile, a stone's throw from the zoo, watching the monkeys gamboling from his big varnished desk while he absentmindedly initials his insignificant documents on a magnificent green leather blotter—I down my Sans Souci to his health, it's very pretty this beer bottle with the white boat on a blue background, we must be nearing Orvieto, the landscape is undulating gently in the moonlight, the Chianti has made the Americans very jolly, they keep chuckling, Sans Souci is bottled for Moretti Inc. in Udine says the label, Udine capital of Friuli beautiful Venetian city where Franz Stangl was billeted at the end of the war, in charge of the fight against the partisans once the camps of Bełżec, Sobibór and Treblinka were destroyed, closed for lack of customers, mission accomplished: Globocnik, Wirth, Stangl and the happy band of the Aktion Reinhardt had eliminated two million Jews from the General Gouvernement of Poland, with carbon monoxide gas, according to the method tested by Wirth the savage in Bełżec, and all these sinister technicians of destruction were sent in early 1944 to the *Operationszone Adriatisches Küstenland* the capital of which was Trieste the Hapsburgian, the place was dangerous, uncontrollable, groups of Resistants held entire regions and mounted deadly operations against the Germans, like the one that cost Christian Wirth his life in May 1944, maybe they had sent them there for that very reason after all, so they'd die, so that the only real witnesses of the camps in Poland would disappear, witnesses of the mass graves where the badly burned bodies of hundreds of thousands of asphyxiated men women and children rested, Globocnik nicknamed Globus by Himmler was born in Trieste when it was still Austrian, the swine was detested by anyone with an ounce of sense, he was a liar, a thief, willing to do anything to increase his personal wealth which he had built by appropriating a share of the Jewish possessions intended for Berlin, because massacres brought in millions and millions of reichsmarks, might as well combine business with pleasure, thought Globus the ironic, just like Wirth the pretentious, only Stangl wasn't cunning enough to fill his pockets, he was a little spineless Austrian cop who ended up mechanically carrying out unpleasant tasks, he drank a lot after Treblinka, he drank a lot, for him the Jews were wood, freight that had to be "dealt with," he hated having to go by himself to see the bodies taken out of the gas chambers, he secretly detested Wirth the mustachioed brute, Stangl liked beautiful things, in Treblinka he had organized a Kommando of gardeners to strew the camp with ornamental plants, and had even installed a little zoo, with turtles a monkey and a yellow-and-white parrot, where he liked to spend hours on end in the tropical heat while 500 meters away, in the death camp, corpses were being roasted all the blessed day, in Treblinka Stangl wore a handsome immaculate white jacket, his virginal carapace, those were the days, in Udine he was afraid, especially after the attack on Wirth on the road to Fiume, he spent most of his time closeted in his office and only went out when he absolutely had to, mainly to go to Trieste, he was solitary, even though he sometimes drank and played cards with Arthur Walter and Franz Wagner, with whom he had traveled through the whole extermination chain, from euthanasia of the mentally ill in Germany to the shores of the Adriatic, where everything was going badly: the Slovenian, Croatian, and Italian partisans were at least as numerous as the few troops left to them after the collapse in the East and the Allied advance into Italy, the end was near, at what moment does he realize that the war is lost, maybe in June 1944, maybe before, when he arrives Stangl is at first posted to Trieste itself, as the head of a police transit camp called La Risiera di San Sabba, set up in a former factory for the processing of rice, where arrested partisans come through with Jews who were about to leave for Auschwitz, Mauthausen, Dachau, or Buchenwald depending on the transports, Globocnik's diligence soon fills the place out, in the beginning of 1944 Wirth asks Erwin Lambert a gas and cremation technician to build an oven there to get rid of the bodies of the 5,000 people killed on site, usually with a club, their ashes are thrown, at night, into the nearby sea by the Ukrainian executioners whom the specialists in destruction have brought with them, in Trieste the White, port of Austria Italy Slovenia and Croatia, in 1992 with Vlaho and Andi on a binge we didn't see anything of the city, bars bars icy wind rain fried fish a long seafront a whitecapped bay lined with hills a lighthouse a few rare girls in grey coats running to take refuge in empty taverns, we were staying near the train station in a *pension* run by Slovenians, Vlaho was sulking, he didn't understand what the hell we were doing there, when we could easily have gone to his place in Split and party and raise hell, tourism didn't justify everything, what's more Italy was ruinously expensive, but it was a change from Zagreb with its deserted nightclubs and whores' bars full of soldiers and mafiosi the sad ambiance of the capital of our country at war, in Trieste I forgot the fighting the dead comrades for a while, for Andi it was all the same, so long as there was something to drink, we stuffed ourselves on spaghetti with seafood washed down with white wine before going to nightclubs that were no doubt also very sad but which seemed to us the height of gaiety, because we were the only soldiers there in the midst of the students of Trieste, they had no idea where we could be coming from, despite our smell and our short hair, *three drummer boys on the way back from war, three drummer boys*, I remember dancing for a few minutes with a young Italian in her early twenties, she kept smiling at me, we danced shoulder to shoulder without exchanging a word, she had long hair pulled back, pleasant features, I thought if she wants me I won't go back to Herzegovina, to Bosnia, I'll stay in Trieste, if she wants me,

Aphrodite was coming to save me, she danced with her wrists up to her forehead, her head bent forward, she wore a black cotton long-sleeved dress that contrasted with her fair skin and her blond bangs, at her neckline a brooch gleamed, a little ceramic red rose, at times she raised her eyes and looked at me smiling, the music was a Pearl Jam or Nirvana hit I forget, she was murmuring the words, her feet made her hips sway right and left rhythmically, once the song was over she smiled at me one last time before moving slowly away, with measured steps, Andi took me by the arm to pull me over to the bar, I hesitated, I watched the girl being swallowed up in the crowd and I went to drink vodka with Andrija and Vlaho, they were smiling too, we thumped each other on the shoulder, then I went to look for her, she had disappeared, in the muffled din of the nightclub that would soon be closing, I hadn't understood, I couldn't understand the shape Fate sometimes takes, I went to Bosnia, I signed up for a few more months of war, maybe she would have saved me, that unknown girl, who knows, when we went out we went to find some whores, to console me said Vlaho, maybe that girl would have saved all three of us, in Italy there were no brothels but shady bars where a few sad dumpy Albanian women were hanging around, I declined, Vlaho our champion nothing could diminish his libido since his cold got better disappeared into a back room with one of them, we kept drinking, drinking still and always as if the world were turning liquid, the whole world, and we went back to Herzegovina—forty years earlier the members of the Einsatz R. drank everything they could in Trieste, the Wirths, the Stangls, the Wagners got drunk unremittingly while waiting for death or defeat, the tired Ukrainians forgot themselves in the rage of torture and the whip, scattered between Udine, Fiume, and Trieste the old companions in massacre saw little of each other, and when they did meet they didn't talk about Poland, about Treblinka or Sobibór, in the meantime Stangl had gone back to his place in Austria, to see his wife and children, he missed them, he was anxious for the war to be over, to go back to the comfort of his hearth, I wonder if he intuited that the dead of Treblinka and Sobibór would prevent him from ever returning to his home, probably not, all those guys lost on the shores of the Adriatic must have been dreaming of an improbable victory of the Reich, or clinging to the illusion that they had hidden their crimes well enough, which weren't even crimes, in any case, for Stangl it wasn't a crime since the Reich had excluded these bodies from humankind, wood, they were wood that was suitable for burning, a mistake of nature to be rectified, a prolific species to be eradicated and even if the stench was extremely unpleasant it was impossible to recognize oneself in these imploring victims dripping from the filthy cattlecars, euthanasia with carbon monoxide was painless after all *they were well treated*, Globocnik had dealt with Poland the way you attack a field of potatoes that had been invaded by beetles or blight, Wirth and Stangl had carried out their duty, with varying degrees of pleasure and enthusiasm, and it was very hard to bear, this responsibility, especially when they had to reopen the mass graves that the gases of decomposition and putrid fluids made ripple like the sea, what a weight all that was, take out all those compressed liquefied bodies pierced with worms burn them on big grates built from railroad tracks, Wirth the ingenious had even recycled a stone-crushing machine to get rid of the bones that didn't burn, *the most fertile land in Poland* said Wirth the humorist, *we're leaving here the most fertile land in Poland*: upon leaving, once the camp was destroyed, to mislead the curious they had set up a little farm for a couple of Ukrainians, where the land was in fact so fertile that the beets and cabbages grew huge, the wheat sprang up before their eyes, the bread the woman kneaded for her husband required almost no leavening, the ash and fir trees grew in record time, carrying in their nascent trunks their leaves and needles the sap of dead Jews, their substance and memory up to the sky, there is nothing to see in Treblinka, nothing to see in Sobibór, aside from immense trees sagging beneath the snow in silence, they rustle, that's all you hear there, a movement of branches and the crackle of footsteps on the ground, nothing more, a doe, a fox, a bird, the great cold of the plains, the flowing River Bug, the terminus of absence, nothing—in Trieste the Einsatz R. so well-trained went on with its labors, its war effort, against the Slav partisans and dissembling Jews, Globus began by transforming the great synagogue devastated in 1942 into a warehouse for despoiled possessions and he got down to work, roundup after roundup the little community of Trieste was sent to Auschwitz or Dachau passing through the San Sabba camp, farewell Trieste gate to Jerusalem departure-point for ships from Lloyd's that were taking the first emigrants to Palestine, Trieste meeting-place of the Ashkenazi of the North and the Sephardim of the South, farewell, it didn't matter that the agents of Aktion Reinhardt were tired or that they were heavy drinkers, they all knew their job, counting rounding up misleading expediting exterminating, in the beginning of 1944 the method was perfected and who better than Wirth or Stangl knew what was waiting for the Jews at the end of the journey, there is a little bit of Trieste, of Corfu, of Athens, of Salonika, of Rhodes in the land of Poland, bluish ashes, Rolf the Gentle told me all this in Trieste, Rolf the Austrio-Italian is neither Jewish nor Slavic, Rolf Cavriani von Eppan is a cousin of the Hapsburg-Lorraines and the Princes of Thurn und Taxis inventors of the postal services, born in Trieste during the war, a little mustachioed gentleman last descendant of a ducal family that used to own half of Bohemia and Galicia, Rolf knew why I had come to see him and he showed me around the city, Trieste had changed quite a bit since 1992, as I remembered it there hadn't been so many pedestrian malls the buildings weren't so white the people not so elegant, I wondered if I was going to see the girl from the nightclub, the one who had let me go to Bosnia, just as Stéphanie had let me go to Trieste, let me fill my suitcase and without realizing it set me off to Rome and the end of the world, Rolf Cavriani had agreed to meet me in a beautiful café decorated with mosaics and wood moldings a stone's throw away from the synagogue, Rolf is the owner of an international banking compensation company that launders the money of thousands of more or less legal enterprises by making it pass through tax havens as opaque as they are exotic, he owns a castle outside of Salzburg a manor house in Carinthia and a magnificent villa perched above Trieste, where he rarely goes, nostalgic for a time when the Empire held the region, when Joyce the drunk Berlitz professor haunted the brothels and taverns of the old city, destroying his liver: in July 1914, a few days after the shots fired by Gavrilo Princip the tubercular from Sarajevo Joyce is on the main quay of Trieste in the middle of the crowd, a vessel belonging to the Austrian navy has just berthed, the bells are sounding the alarm, the whole city is there to see the remains of Franz Ferdinand and the beautiful Sophie solemnly brought to land in a catafalque covered with the flag with the two crowns then conveyed to the train station, where a special railway car will carry them to their tomb in the Artstetten Castle, do Joyce and his very young wife understand that these imperial corpses and the Serbian bullets signify the end of the city they know, and that soon the First World War will send them to the North, to boring Switzerland, and will bring an end to a stay of almost ten years in the Hapsburg port: when he returns the man with the little hat and the veiled eyes will not find the city he knew, Italianized, cut off from the Slavs, the Austrians, its immense port empty of all activity, in competition with Venice La Serenissima hidden in the shadows, farewell Trieste, Joyce will go to Paris—on July 3, 1914 on the main quay his companion Nora takes him by the arm, impressed by the royal coffins, she says to him *how sad, they say she was beautiful*, James does not reply, Sophie's beauty doesn't matter much to him, not many things matter to him, in any case, that very night he'll have forgotten everything, in one of the bars of Trieste the tolerant where he will get drunk, to the lugubrious sound of the foghorns of the mortuary boat that is sounding its departure, without his realizing it, one of the unsuspected consequences of the pistol shot of Gavrilo Princip the TB victim, an assassination in Sarajevo sends Joyce to Paris, Joyce said when *Finnegans Wake* was published that at night nothing was clear, Joyce such a wise professor during the day became a lustful drunkard by night, obscure to himself, obsessed with money, with a God he didn't want, with shameful urges, for very young girls that looked like his own daughter, fragile and alienated like Yvan Deroy the mad, Joyce wanted to write a piece of shadow, 600 pages of a dream of all dreams, all languages all shifts all texts all ghosts all desires and the book had become living dying sparkling like a star whose light arrives long after death and this matter was decomposing in the reader's hands, unintelligible dust because Joyce did not dare to confess his secret desires, the violence that inhabited him and his guilty love for his own daughter, he was forced to hide it in writing, poor little man with the perforated ulcers and sick eyes, Joyce had been happy in Trieste, in the brothels of the old city, the brothels and hangouts that have disappeared, today the Irishman from the continent is a tourist attraction there like any other, like Italo Svevo or Umberto Saba, statues are erected to them in the streets they frequented, statues so alive that you want to take your hat off to them, Rolf Cavriani took off his hat to Joyce to Svevo to Saba whenever he passed them thus petrified by Medusa the decapitated Gorgon, at a bend in the street, between two stores, in front of the municipal library, and I don't know if these bronzes are life-size but they all come up to your shoulder, headgear included, which made Rolf say laughing that to be famous in Trieste you had to be little, that today's inhabitants couldn't bear grandeur, their past and foreign grandeur, and so they belittled great men in the secret aim of surpassing them by a few centimeters, the way a guy with an inferiority complex uses inserts, Cavriani von Eppan had his complexes too, much more tragic ones, he had never used his title of duke, and that ate away at him, for not only was this duchy about to disappear with him but even while he was alive he didn't dare make use of it, which earned him both the ire of his ancestors from beyond and a great shame in this laughable life, Rolf Cavriani was born in his great villa in Opicina, on top of Trieste, a stone's throw from the old road to Vienna, in 1941, his father died of illness not long after his birth, during the defeat his mother had carried the very young Rolf to holy Austria, just before the debacle, before Tito's supporters occupied the region for a while and took savage reprisals on the few soldiers and civilians they could find here and there, then the family had returned a few years later, my mother was a very capable woman, said Rolf, she was wealthy, and this wealth allowed her to turn her nose up at the new European borders, as she had done in 1918, she continued, like my grandparents before her, to spend six months every year in Trieste, spring and fall, summer in cool Carinthia and winter at the theaters and operas in Vienna, for my mother the nation or party in power was absolutely immaterial, he said, she had excellent relations with everyone, the Italian royalty, the fascists and even the Nazis, God knows though that they hated nobility, which didn't mean she wasn't afraid, that great lady, especially at the fall of Mussolini in the chaos of autumn 1943 when the communists had begun to massacre the fascists right and left and throw them into bottomless *foibe*, until the Reich intervened she had taken refuge in impregnable Austria, and similarly when the defeat was there, in April 1945, she had hurriedly cut short her spring stay to return to the hoarfrost of Carinthia—her relations with the German occupation authorities were cordial, she watched them burying their dead in the military cemetery close to her residence, with all the same a profound disgust for stiff-arm salutes and the Nazi flag, out of pure aesthetic concern, understand, there was never a woman who had less ideology than my mother said Rolf, she had high-ranking Wehrmacht officers over for dinner, Colonel Kalterweg with the strange name, dashing Hohnstetter commander of the panzers, and even a few SS officers, especially Rösener and Globocnik the Trieste native, after all he had been *Gauleiter* of Vienna, and Rösener was the commander in chief of military operations in Slovenia, he sometimes visited Ljubljana, my mother didn't much like them, it was almost a social obligation, during the few times she spent in Trieste during the year she entertained little, that was normal, she knew nothing of the horrors committed in Slovenia or Poland, you know? still when Globocnik offered my mother a brigade of laborers to rebuild the wall around her property she accepted, could she have refused, I suppose so, but could she know that Globus the perverse was going to send her a commando of partisans who were about to be executed, with an escort armed to the teeth, guys fished out of the special jails of La Risiera di San Sabba to go play at being masons, their lacerated torsos still bore the marks of the tortures they'd undergone, she housed them in the beautiful vaulted cellar, because a solid metal grille closed it off, the escort stayed in the outbuildings with the servants, this was in February 1945, imagine, everything was lost for the Reich, it was just a question of weeks, my mother was in Trieste since the Red Army was approaching Vienna, the wall did need to be repaired, an entire section had collapsed, the poor Slovenians or Croatians set to work, closely supervised by their warders, the work went quickly, I remember I was almost four and I think I saw those convicts in our garden, I was fascinated by the guards' weapons and uniforms, you understand, the repairs were almost finished by early March, the news was bad, the Allies had just crossed the Rhine in Germany and were approaching Italy, it was agony, my mother much altered by events decided to organize one last dinner, a farewell dinner, with Rösener, Globus, Kalterweg and others whose names I don't know, a few women too of good Austrian and Trieste society, they all knew the game was up, that soon they'd have to go take refuge near Klagenfurt to avoid the Yugoslav partisans who were massacring everything as they went, nevertheless the evening was very gay, everyone wanted to forget the war, to forget the imminent end of the Reich and the enraged messages from Berlin that were giving orders to burn the land, the last crates of champagne were opened in euphoria, the gramophone kept spinning, the women had put on their most beautiful dresses, all that must have had a whiff of the apocalypse about it, the end of a world, after midnight the guests were drunk, they sang "Lili Marleen" at the top of their lungs, without caring either about the proprieties or the women present, my mother must have been shocked I suppose, maybe not, maybe she was tipsy too, after all my father had been dead for almost three years, she could have a little fun, the times were dark, a little joy was welcome—I imagine Rolf's noble mother drunk, her eyes glittering her dress riding up a little revealing her black stockings felt up from afar by the lustful gaze of the fat Globus, I imagine the fear, the fear of defeat and punishment in the Nazis' eyes, the thousand year Reich was indeed going to provide beautiful ruins but much sooner than Speer had foreseen, we left the elegant café for a little stroll, Rolf von Eppan was in a nostalgic mood, he took me to the wooded neighborhood above the station where Globocnik had his villa, requisitioned from a certain Angelo Ara, at Number 34 on the Via Romagna, a beautiful Art Deco residence that Globus the ingenious connected by underground passageways to the courthouse buildings where he had his offices, it reminded me of his house in Lublin in Poland, just as strategically situated, next to the SS quarters, the occupation administration and the HQ of Aktion Reinhardt, a villa with two floors and a garden, just like the one in Trieste, Lublin the red was prettily paved, a commercial artery led to the monumental gate to the old city cut in half by the Nazis to install the ghetto there, the dark little streets were not reassuring at night, a little lower down was the castle, a big rather austere barracks, I was there in winter, an icy snowy winter that had no reason to envy the winter of 1943 where temperature is concerned, in the center of Lublin not many things had changed, I was staying at the Grand Hotel, transformed during the war into a *Deutsches Haus*, with an officers' mess, Stangl had slept there with his wife when she had come from Austria to visit him, it had become a giant hotel with Communist rooms, grey wall-to-wall carpeting and formica cabinets, there were two splendid bars, one looked out onto the square, with a piano and high ceilings, the other was cozier, more intimate, the former library of the *Deutsches Haus*, in the morning I had taken Stangl's road, to Sobibór, near the Ukrainian border, miles and miles of magnificent forests, under snow, flat forests, without a hill in sight, so smooth you could have slid to Moscow without realizing it, not a mountain this side of the Urals, birch trees, birch trees to the heart's content, birch trees and a few firs, there were not many cars, mostly pedestrians who walked by the side of the road to get to the nearest bus stop at the outskirts of villages, and then nothing else, the forest, I had passed the railroad which told me I was headed in the right direction, the heat turned up high in the car, the silence and the noise of the engine, the noise of the engine of the Russian tank that Stangl and Bauer had brought from Lvov, the malfunctioning diesel engine propelled black gases into the little brick room at the end of the open-air corridor bordered with thick hedges made of branches stuck in the barbed wire, the naked Jews ran with their feet in the snow in the winter it wasn't necessary to whip them much the cold whipped them well enough the cold and the snow are effective the shouts the door the silence and the sound of the engine, in the interminable straight line I suddenly see a young woman in a black coat standing by the road, alone at the edge of the trees, I must have been dreaming, no, she is really there in the rearview mirror, what is she doing motionless by the side of the road in her coat a little black shoulder bag a thousand miles away from any inhabited land I hesitate to make a U-turn, she must be waiting for the bus, next to trees collapsing beneath the snow, there is nothing here, no village no farm no house just a woman in the middle of the cold the snow and the dead Jews is she waiting for me, a reincarnation, a ghost, strange omen, I don't do anything, silence and fear, like many others I do nothing, I don't turn my car around, a sign indicates the train station of Sobibór on the right, a snowy path in a dense wood, my wheels spin at times, there are blankets of fog I am approaching the terminus then the narrow-gauge line, Stangl's house where he drank vodka with comrades whom he detested, the train station, the important little camp where thanks to German meticulousness hundreds of thousands of bodies were processed, tons of flesh among the birch trees, there it is, the terminus is approaching, the end of the line, there is nothing, a green cabin the museum closed in winter I park the car against a heap of snow, behind me railroad workers are sending off a train loaded with logs, nothing changes, they're laughing because I got covered in snow, next to a memorial that no one visits, before they laughed because strangers came to die in these lands made for hunting deer for wood for snow but not for running naked towards a tank engine started by a red-faced German, the Poles have a good laugh when faced with disaster, they're used to it they've been working here for generations, I've come to see so I get out of the car but I know that the trees aren't going to speak, I sink into the whiteness up to my ankles I go forward into the forest, a wide lane leads to a clearing where there is a great dome of silence, the Eastern terminus, here end the railways that leave from Salonika Westerbork Ternopol Theresienstadt Paris from so many cities and villages, the only traces are those left by the does and birds in the snow, there is nothing but the unimaginable and the tallness of the trunks, the wind blows gently the sky is opaque I wander around for a while in the clearing without trying to determine exactly where the buildings were the ditches the bodies my brain is white as linen white as virgin skin I pushed the car managed to make a U-turn and started off again for Lublin, the young woman wasn't waiting anymore in the middle of the deserted forest, back at the Grand Hotel I'm stone-cold, frozen stiff I sat down in a club chair in the immense bar wondering what Stangl the gardener drank when he was here with his wife, the night was pitch-black, outside vehicles were skidding on the melted snow turned muddy, I was very far away, very far, I ordered a tea in an immense and glacial solitude, a blind man came in accompanied by an old lady, she sat him down at the piano, a black ancient-looking baby grand, he said a few words and started up a ballad by Chopin, the instrument was out of tune and sounded off-key, I quietly finished my tea, determined to brave the cold and the snow to buy myself a bottle of vodka in the closest supermarket and confront the long Polish night, the blind man attacked "My Way" in a particularly mawkish tempo, a sign said *for the blind and crippled* next to a wicker basket, I left him all my change—in Trieste there's no pianist in the luxurious restaurant where Rolf the banker took me, he's talking to me about Globocnik the snake, I don't dare ask him if Himmler's man was his mother's lover, probably not, Globus the boor must not have been tempting to Austrian nobility, or vice-versa, Rolf Cavriani von Eppan the nostalgic has been keeping us informed about the covert accounts of his clients for years, companies, various mafias, façades for suspicious activities, out of philanthropy, or almost, and I suspect him of acting in the same way with a number of European agencies, which explains why his business is prospering and out of the law's reach, Rolf the son of the duchess who was slumming it with champagne with the heads of the *Adriatisches Küstenland* early in 1945, who had the idea first, back then, Kalterweg, Rösener, or Globocnik the swine, we'll never know, Mme la Duchesse maybe, maybe the mother of Rolf the cynic asked the same question as Stéphanie, the great question with no answer, as the soldiers in black uniforms told them about their feats of arms, *what is it like to kill a man?* Globus hooted outright with laughter, he answered you're about to see, Madame, after you, and all the guests blind drunk thought it was an excellent idea, a demonstration, a demonstration, the women hitched up the bras on their breasts, rearranged their creased dresses to head for the cellar where the ten Slovenians were piled up behind respectable iron bars, the prisoners saw the charming company coming down towards them without understanding, pausing at the bottom of the steps, a meter away from the grille, they got up, Rösener took out his P38, Kalterweg too, the panic-stricken Resistants huddled against the walls like insects Rösener said who wants to begin? and a very drunk lady answered me! me! Rösener took her by the waist put the weapon in her hand feeling her up a little they went over to the bars Rösener guided her arm she saw a shadow in the right corner she pulled the trigger the shot resounded under the beautiful vault the wounded Slovenian shouted and collapsed the audience cried bravo! bravo!

encore! And the four pieces that belonged to the SS present were emptied onto the poor guys like the bottles of champagne before everyone wanted to try their hand at death the explosions vibrated in the powder-heavy air the blood spattered the whitewashed walls the women quivered with fear and pleasure, sobered up fast by the adrenaline, the dying men twisted onto the corpses of their companions, the guests' ears whistled in the great silence that always follows massacres: everyone went back upstairs without saying a word, Globus the rational gave orders for the bodies to be collected and burned at La Risiera which they should never have left, the women were pale, Hohnstetter too, Globocnik himself felt a little melancholy, he shouted *cognac! cognac!* and the trembling majordomo immediately brought him a bottle of grappa, Rolf's mother asked to be excused, she wasn't feeling very well, and she went back to her apartments to take refuge in her son's room, next to the heavy sleep and tender perfume of unattainable childhood—the young Eppan had of course no memory of this, he was sleeping piously in his bed, but his mother's diary is very clear, he says, that's what happened, even though the duchess certainly minimizes her own role, unable to confess, even alone in the intimacy of her journal, what might really have happened that night, as an epitaph she notes that she walled up the part of the cellar where "the events" as she calls them took place, so as never to see the place again, Rolf recently added a brass plaque to it engraved, *here died ten Slovenian heroes killed by the Nazis*, a commemorative plaque in his own house, a memorial that he alone can see, when he goes downstairs to look for a good bottle for his guests: when we leave the restaurant the day is beginning to come to a close, the sea has very soft, very smooth grey tones, Rolf is in a nostalgic mood, he would readily order a cognac or a grappa like Globus but he is in a hurry to come to an end, the documents are in the trunk of my car he says, we walk over to the parking lot, Rolf strides a little hunched over, I feel as if he's hesitating about whether to tell me something, he pulls up the neck of his tweed jacket to protect himself from the breeze, his noble Daimler is bottle-green, with a Liechtenstein license plate, even the trunk gives off a scent of leather and luxury, Rolf grabs an elegant bag, he hands it to me saying it has no value, you know, I nod, it has no more value than a corpse or a name on a grave, poor Rolf the noble from whom the Nazis took away his title, from whom history took away his title, he is getting revenge by giving me these documents, the reports from Globocnik to Himmler between 1942 and 1945, all the activities of the Aktion Reinhardt in Poland and Italy, he is getting rid of a weight, Rolf, he looks relieved at contributing to the filling of the suitcase, he shakes my hand, I thank him for lunch, he sketches a smile and gets into his car, Rolf doesn't know that I know his dilemma, I know that vengeful Fate wanted him to be born Duke of Auschwitz, Duke of Auschwitz and Zator, Rolf von Auschwitz und Zator, an ancient princely title going back to the eleventh century, that is his name, the name of his ancestors which the Nazis tarnished, forcing his coat of arms to remain in shadow forever, Rolf whose fief is today linked to the largest death factory ever built bears the weight of history more than others, I wonder if one should laugh or cry at his heraldic scruples and his mother with the troubled friendships, the sun has set, I walk slowly up the seafront, two million dead aren't so heavy, in fact, words and numbers on paper, men are great technicians at taking notes, at keeping things brief, ever since well-guarded Troy the bearded bard and Schliemann the archeologist great spotter of warriors, I'm going to arrive in Rome very soon, very quickly, render unto Caesar, render unto eternity, get hold of the ransom for my cowardliness and then what, then what, find Sashka again the only female painter of icons, in her closed world, Sashka the blind with the big light-colored eyes and her apartment in Trastevere, I don't know if I want to see her again, she doesn't have the power to reach me, to cure me, or the will to either, I feel I'm going to destroy her like Marianne, torment her like Stéphanie, who will take me out of myself, who like Intissar will come to look for the corpse of Francis fallen between the lines, who will look into the eyes of my murderer, observe my ghost in the distance through the gunman's sights, Sashka is a dream of ice, one of those mirrors that do no good since they always enclose us in our own image, in our future grave, what will I do when this train arrives in the station, when its brakes wheeze against the Termini platform, I met Sashka by chance she doesn't know me I don't know her any better than her brother the volunteer for the savage Serbs, front against front waiting for the angel to inspire us, despite the signs that the unpredictable gods have placed on our pathway, Jersualem lost in history, Nathan the busy survivor promptly cutting off Palestinian lives, the bullets the shells exchanged in Slavonia, and Rome, Rome where all roads lead before being lost in the night what will I do you're always tempted to retrace your steps to go back to where you lived, the way Caravaggio painter of decapitation wanted to see Rome again, despite the luxury of Malta the rotting beauty of Naples, constantly and ceaselessly Caravaggio desired the Eternal City the shady neighborhoods the cutthroats around the mausoleum of Augustus the casual lovers games brawls laughable life where will I go back to, me, to Mostar crushed by the shells to Venice with the handsome Ghassan and Ezra Pound the mad, to Trieste to the cursed villa of the *Herzog* von Auschwitz, to Beirut with the fierce Palestinians to Algiers the white to lick the blood of martyrs or the burnt wounds of the innocent men tortured by my father, to Tangier with Burroughs the wild-eyed murderer Genet the luminous invert and Choukri the eternally starving, to Taormina to get drunk with Lowry, to Barcelona, to Valencia, to Marseille with my grandmother in love with crowned heads, to Split with Vlaho the disabled, to Alexandria the sleeping, to Salonika city of ghosts or to the White Island graveyard of heroes, what would Yvan Deroy the mad do where would he go I watch the Americans having fun talking loudly in the restaurant car, outside the countryside is still just as dark Antonio the bartender is preparing to close his mobile bar we're going to be there soon, we're going to be there soon, and then what, what are you going to do Yvan where are you going with your thirty pieces of silver in your pocket find a welcoming tree a rope not too rough for your delicate neck, rejoin Sashka the unreachable and her turpentine smell, the turpentine of Chios or Cyprus thick blood of the pistachio tree, throw yourself once again into a river look for a weapon to put in your mouth or one bottle too many, nothing very original my old pal Yvan you who were destined for great things in the kingdom of shadow, now you want to find the light again, and it's a dark night, it's a dark night on December 8th on the verge of winter the rain is going to pour down in Rome the furious Tiber will carry thousands of plastic bags tons of the various species of junk that will decorate the trees at Christmas when the water level drops, Joyce the unusual detested Rome and the Romans, I picture him with Nora eating a soft lukewarm pizza behind the Piazza Navona, swearing, Joyce has a beautiful grave in Zurich next to Elias Canetti's, that's an idea, Yvan, a handsome tomb in Zurich, a stone's throw from the zoo, an isolated place to enjoy the ballet of the monkeys and the lions' roars, lying down quietly with your hands behind your head—just an hour now till Rome say the Americans good news or bad, I don't know the train is moving at top speed now we're rocked from right to left depending on the tunnels I sit back down, it's long, an hour, it's long and it's short opposite me the lady who got on in Florence doesn't even glance at me absorbed in her book, I'll pick mine up again, I want to know what will happen to Intissar, maybe she can save me, she was washing Marwan's body in the hot Beirut night, and now:

And now, defeat, the heavy boots no longer move forward. Marwan who didn't run fast enough to avoid the bullets. Martyrs abandoned on a sidewalk corner. Bodies washed in apartment bathrooms. The city falling and, at the end, exile.

Intissar caresses Marwan with her sponge, one last time. She has never felt so close to him as in this final touch. Half-light and solitude, though. The lives that the Israelis have destroyed, Beirut that the Israelis have destroyed. Sometimes weapons turn against you. You always end up washing corpses. Marwan had promised to be by her side forever. He lied. Rubbing his torso, Intissar guesses why he went on a dangerous sortie with Ahmad the coward. He wanted to know. He was eaten away by doubt. He might have died because of her. He wanted to know. Ahmad the hero of their cause desired her. A year ago, when Ahmad had come home victorious from his ambush in the South, and when

Marwan had left to go over to Tyre, she had been a little dazzled by Ahmad's attentions. He courted her discreetly, always waiting on her hand and foot. He was watching over her in Marwan's absence, he said. Marwan is dead, his body gleams from the reflections of water on his chest. She never betrayed him. Know that, Marwan, I never betrayed you. She couldn't tell him, it was impossible to talk about. If he had known Marwan would have taken a gun and killed Ahmad. Now he's the one who's dead, dead along with his suspicions.

Intissar's hand shakes, her eyelids quiver, the memory of shame, so powerful, draws tears from her. She tries to remember a prayer for Marwan. *Bismillah ar-rahman ar-rahim*, and what else? She sees Ahmad that night. Ahmad the coward who gets her to drink beer on the Corniche, in the early summer, when Beirut is so beautiful. They talk of this and that, the war little by little grows more remote. Marwan little by little grows more remote, why not acknowledge that, with the effect of the alcohol and the calm night. Let's go get a bite to eat, says Ahmad. He takes her supposedly to find comrades who won't come. Leaving the restaurant, Intissar is a little drunk. She drinks very rarely. Ahmad accompanies her back to her place, did she sense the trap, did she know unconsciously what was going to happen that's making her cry from rage today, why, why, do we know what's hidden inside us, what we're capable of, Ahmad pressed her against the wall in the entryway to her apartment building, he kissed her for a long time, she was so surprised, so surprised that she let him do it, or maybe it was desire, she was no longer Intissar the determined combatant, she had disappeared, her will destroyed by alcohol and the confidence she had in Ahmad, it was the image of Marwan that woke her, the difference in the sensation of the kiss, the lips less soft, less pleasant, more violent, she shook herself, she shook herself violently pushed away the man in front of her before climbing the stairs four at a time and locking herself up in her apartment, ashamed, ashamed of her desire for Ahmad the coward, her physical desire, impossible to hide, especially from herself in the intimacy of a deserted bedroom.

•

Defeat has beginnings. The fissures presage collapse, fine cracks predict catastrophe. The will begins to give out, hope wavers. Intissar watches her tears falling onto the dead man's chest. Her desire had soon changed into hatred. She hated Ahmad. When Marwan returned he guessed something. Her hatred was too visible. The silence. She hadn't said anything, he had promised to be by her side forever. The war, the front, and disaster. Intissar takes Marwan's stiff hand as if it were alive. Now you know. She strokes the dead fingers. Her sorrow is so great that it covers everything. Marwan spoke to her often about his mother, his mother's tenderness, her generosity. So pure. So perfect. She who had loved her husband passionately, always near him, she took care of him when he was wounded, fed him when he was hungry. She cuddled her children, embroidered and sewed for them. She tried not to think about Palestine, not to think about going back. Her country was her family, nothing more. Marwan was like Abu Nasser. He would fight to the end, he said. Die standing up. Like a tree. Not let himself be demeaned by the Israelis. Now he was lying there, beneath Intissar's last caresses, before joining the roots of trees felled by the bombs.

Urgent knocking on her door snaps her out of her funereal daydream. Probably someone alerted by the smoke in the kitchen. She puts the sponge down and tears herself away from Marwan's body. She picks up the lamp. The neighbors have to be reassured that the building isn't on fire. There are so many corpses in the city that no one would be surprised to find one here. But flames make them anxious. She opens the door halfway. A violent shove of a shoulder on the door sends her sprawling onto the floor, half unconscious. She glimpsed Ahmad in the opening. She tries to gather her wits, she has tears of pain in her eyes, her nose aches. Ahmad has closed the door behind him.

"I came to bring you this."

He throws a piece of white cloth in her face, which she doesn't immediately recognize.

"You left it on purpose, didn't you?"

The bra she abandoned in a corner of the post. Ahmad is looking at her legs and her underwear beneath the raised night-dress.

"You're mine now. Marwan isn't here anymore."

Everything has its price. Everything has a cost. If only he could get up. God, make Marwan get up, make Ahmad disappear. She feels exhausted, overwhelmed, aching, powerless. She won't have the strength to fight. She won't resist. Ahmad's real face dances in the orange light.

He bends over her, catches her by the hair and pulls her violently into the apartment, she slides over the tile, half raises herself, shouts with surprise and pain, falls silent, he throws her onto the unmade bed, she buries her head into the pillow. Her gun is still at the front. Her strength, her willpower are there too. She wants to disappear. She hears Ahmad's belt and pants fall onto the floor next the bed. She doesn't want to look. She doesn't want to see him. She stiffens when a feverish hand searches between her legs to undress her. She struggles instinctively, Ahmad takes her by the hair and crushes a knee into her kidneys, Ahmad is talking but she doesn't hear him. She doesn't want to hear him, she feels a moist contact, Ahmad spat on her closed thighs, she doesn't want to hear him she doesn't want to feel him she doesn't want to feel those two clumsy fingers penetrating her sex she doesn't even want to groan. Marwan, please. Marwan help me. Ahmad crushes her he is lying on top of her his breath against her neck she doesn't hear him he doesn't succeed he pushes her roughly shakes her he tries to turn her over she clings to the edge of the bed she doesn't want to see him she doesn't want to see him he hits her pulls at one of her legs she resists he spits again hits her again Ahmad presses with all his weight on her he doesn't succeed he gets annoyed she feels sick she feels sick and suddenly there's a terrible noise in her ears, a huge detonation, very close, deafening, followed by a warm liquid pouring onto her left shoulder, into her hair, against her cheek, a smell of powder, a smell of blood, Ahmad collapsed on top of her, she pushes him away and rolls to the bottom of the bed, she is on the ground, she crawls in the dark to the bathroom, she touches Marwan's cold body, she stretches out, she faints next to him.

•

Abu Nasser wakes her gently in the Beirut dawn. The pale light dazzles her. Abu Nasser supports her, helps her get up, pours water over her face, she drinks, sees herself in the mirror, covered with blackened blood. Marwan is lying on a white sheet. Abu Nasser almost carries her to the bedroom. On the bed, Ahmad is stretched out, half his head gone. The wall is splattered with flesh and blood. Abu Nasser has tears in his eyes. His handsome uniform is stained now. He was dressed for the burial of his son, she thinks. Abu Nasser helps her put on a bathrobe. Two soldiers carry Marwan's body on a stretcher.

"I'm taking you home, Intissar, it's over."

He gently takes her arm. She hears him shout orders to the fighters accompanying him, throw this bastard into the first ditch you see. Abu Nasser will have Intissar move to his house in Raouche. He will go alone to bury his son. Marwan will disappear into the ground.

Intissar will not be there to hear the din of the city falling behind her, exile will open up like a precipice in the middle of the empty sea, an immense shadow into which useless rifles and abandoned tanks will sink, caresses of the dead and the living, far from the enemy and from the fight that gave its fragile and vertiginous meaning to the existence that defeat has just annihilated to send her into anxious wandering, a roaming where her feet, which felt the disaster first, listlessly strike the earth and, as if they were afraid now of wounding it, will never leave their mark on it again.

By dint of tenderness, Abu Nasser managed to make her let go of Marwan's heavy 9-millimeter that she was still hugging with all her strength, like a part of herself.

what a story poor Intissar Marwan puts his gun in her hand, his ghost saves her, there are loves, promises that withstand death, especially in books, books and plays, the Palestinians will be scattered throughout the Mediterranean, some to Tunis, some to Algiers, some to Syria, Arafat the grey will try to return to Lebanon to Tripoli in 1984 with his fighters before the Syrians send him back to the sea with a nice kick in the rear, the way you'd kick a dog, poor Intissar, Ahmad poor guy victim of his desire and his violence, victim who makes victims, like us in Bosnia, like the fair-greaved Achaeans, the ones that will sack Troy kill children and carry off women into slavery, me I haven't saved anyone, either by letting my gun lie by the bedside or by being resurrected from the dead, no one, neither Andi nor Vlaho, and no one has saved me, not Marianne not Stéphanie not Sashka the blonde, I wonder if Rafael Kahla is like me, why does he write these terrifying stories, did he try to strangle his wife like Lowry, or did he kill her like Burroughs, did he incite people to hatred and murder like Brasillach or Pound, maybe he's a victim like Choukri the wretched, or a man three times vanquished like Cervantes—who will wash my body once I'm dead, it's very sad this story, very sad, a city falling, collapsing, a city breaking like glass in the hands of those who think they're defending it, Barcelona in 1939 Beirut in 1982 Algiers in 1992 Sarajevo in 1993 and so many others, so many others with the masses of fighters doomed to death or exile, like Intissar, alone with Abu Nasser, Intissar the innocent who thinks she's paying for a sin she did not commit, I still have two stories left to read by this Rafael Kahla, other war stories, sometimes you come across books that resemble you, they open up your chest from chin to navel, stun you, I'd like to have Marwan's nobility, is that still possible, let's think about it Yvan what are we going to do in Rome aside from getting properly plastered taking a bath and treating ourselves to a new suit, dark and luxurious, how to become Marwan, tomorrow morning, once the money is acquired and the dead in the suitcase are buried in the Vatican archives, what am I going to do with the piece of gold of Charon the ferryman, how to set death's obol on each eye of all my corpses, Cocteau said about Ezra Pound the old madman that he was "the rower on the river of dead," now I'm in the same situation or very nearly, Ezra Pound has a beautiful grave in San Michele the cemetery by the sea in Venice, the foggy little island off the Fondamente Nuove where the celebrities are crammed in, a green plot with a tiny plaque in the shade of the cypress trees for the fascist preacher of Radio Roma, obsessed with money and Jews, to the point of madness, of course in Venice I had no inkling of the magical *Cantos*, of Apollo's oracle in 110 chapters, closed, esoteric, strange, which cover the past century in ten languages 800 pages and end in Rome, poem with these lines, *Le chapeau melon de saint Pierre / you in the dinghy (piccioletta) astern there*, if I had the volume of the *Cantos* I'd use it now to read my cards, open it haphazardly and see where it sends me, to Gethsemani Kyoto Pisa New Orleans to the City of London to Paris no definitely not to Paris, Ezra Pound the godless prophet shouted anti-Semitic diatribes and insults at the United States his homeland over the waves of the fascist radio, I wonder what the Americans in the café car would think of him, maybe they've visited San Michele, Venice the surprising is probably the only city in the world where lovers and couples on their honeymoon go to the cemetery, Venice eats away at your soul as surely as nitre on a cave wall, it was Stéphanie who gave me an anthology of Ezra Pound, with a tender little inscription, *to my favorite fascist* and the date, I had told her about my youthful passions for raised-arm salutes and shaved skulls, bad acquaintances, the weight of heredity who knows, my devotion to Brasillach the martyr by whom I hadn't read a single line aside from his prison poems and a few texts on cinema, in our very Parisian high school Yvan was the real fascist, the violent ideologue, in combat boots bomber jackets the whole end-of-century bad-boy uniform, he came from a real family of historic Nazis firm believers who scorned the rank populism of the Front National, Yvan detested the Catholic

Church which had to be brought to heel, he hated with a fine fury anything that wasn't him, Jews communists Arabs British fairies the swarming Orientals the perverted capitalists corrupt politicians an endless list of hatreds and disgusts motivated by the reading of paranoid screwball pamphlets decorated with swastikas, crosses paty, rosy crosses, every possible kind of cross imaginable except the Gaullist Cross of Lorraine, fasces battle-axes sheaves of wheat crossed spears brandished swords glaives dark helmets, photocopied on bad paper or venerable newspapers from the good old days that he had to cover in plastic to keep them from crumbling to pieces so much had they been handled, Yvan had a real passion, ardent and contagious, I let myself be convinced by his admirable rage, probably I was predisposed to it, despite my grandfather's escapades in the Resistance: my father was worried about my new acquaintances, my politicization and my black shirts, my mother of course said to him youth will have its fling, it was Yvan who had me meet Bardèche the historic, it was a pilgrimage, a little journey of initiation to the land of the master, who what's more was charming, he offered us tea and a lecture just a tiny bit confused about collaboration Jewish manipulations and the importance of *The Charterhouse of Parma*, I remember the old man had an upper lip that trembled, an uncontrollable tic, physical expression of resentment, from time to time a drop of shining mucus beaded on his nostril to end up falling on his dressing gown without seeming to bother him in the least, the great Maurice liked me, he asked me what I wanted to study, I replied "political science" and he smiled, I couldn't really tell if this smile was ironic scorn for that noble subject or an encouragement, then the worthy Mussolinian writer gave us little gifts, a brochure denouncing "the farce" of the Nuremberg trial for Yvan and *The History of the Spanish War* which had just been reprinted for me, with a dedication, *to Francis, wishing you the best for the future*, with a slightly hesitant pen, the brother-in-law of Brasillach the Catalan added a commentary, it's something, he said, this book is constantly being reprinted in Spain, we had immediately seen and understood the whole interest of this war, Bardèche and Brasillach inseparable Laurel and Hardy went many times to the Iberian peninsula between 1936 and 1939, to witness the democratic anarchy and the importance of Franco the savior, they saw Europe on the march in it, thanks to Mussolini's troops, Hitler's planes, the Reds destroyed by law and order, they demonstrated that the massacres attributed to the nationalists were inventions of Republican propaganda, that the real bloodthirsty ones were the *rojos* the Reds the great eaters of clergymen, they defended the greatness of General Yagüe the fine strategist, from Millán-Astray's Legion, the Italians with the handsome black feathers, and thus began a long battle of numbers that Bardèche would continue alone after Brasillach's execution, all the corpses are communist or Jewish propaganda, all the dead served the USSR or Israel, so they didn't exist, or hardly mattered, Bardèche is the champion of the avenging scrawls on gravestones, you're not so dead as all that in Badajoz, there aren't as many dead as they say in Auschwitz, that's all lies to hide the crimes of the Republicans or the Resistance, those are the real criminals, the ones who raped nuns with pleasure before sending them to the firing squad, the ones who tortured the middle class in the prisons of Madrid and Barcelona, today his blindness seems so obvious to me that he could only be guided by hatred, a fierce secret hatred for those who had taken away from him the man he loved, Brasillach the martyr, a hatred of the Jews so strong so powerful that he couldn't even manage to convince himself of their extermination, pursued by Jewish ghosts into his grave, the old Bardèche, senile, convinced of the universal conspiracy against the Good and the Right, Yvan my friend also firmly believed in these theories as old as the world that declared international Jewry the enemy to be killed, despite all my efforts I had difficulty convincing myself of the danger a few philosophers journalists or psychoanalysts could represent for the nation, I was a feeble anti-Semite, a bad racist, Yvan said to me it's because you don't deal with Jews or Arabs, if you knew them you'd hate them immediately, I trusted him, even though my beloved history books on the twentieth century proved precisely the contrary, according to Yvan that was because all of history had been written by the Jews, which no doubt explained his deplorable grades and his lack of interest in the subject, Mr. Moussempès our teacher in senior year was a nice man from the Landes a native of Dax with a strong southwestern accent difficult to suspect of crypto-Semitism however, his Gascon fluency made him an extraordinary orator when it came to telling about battles diplomacy political intrigues it's probably thanks to him that I miraculously passed the prestigious entrance exam for the Sciences-Po later, Yvan respected me mostly because of my Ustashi background and my family photos full of dark uniforms, adolescence is in love with images, images and strong friendships for life and beyond the grave secret oaths arms raised above a patriotic altar, Yvan's madness showed through at times but only rarely as I remember it, sometimes he became fixated on a subject and spun in circles like a record on a gramophone, for days and days locked up in his room reading the same minuscule paragraph over and over without saying anything but *that's it, that's it, that's it* ad infinitum, a fragment of a speech on the economy by Hitler involving currency and inflation, for example, could set off one of his attacks, he'd stop going out, couldn't even manage to drag himself to the bathroom and urinated into plastic bottles reading the text in question over and over, that's it, that's it, that's it, as if he had discovered the Holy Grail, he was writing a biography of the Brothers of Christ, a treatise on their importance in the occult struggle against communism, where he traced the origins of all the secret societies defending the West to the forgotten children of Joseph and the Virgin Mary, the ones who remained in the shadow even though they're mentioned in the Gospels, also baptized by John the Baptist the Beheaded and I forget what else, his anxious parents wanted him to go to the doctor but that was obviously impossible, because psychiatry and all of psychology were in the hands of the Jews who were trying to corrupt him, to rot his brain, and so on until the dawn of a day like any other, in the springtime, a little while before graduation, on the way to high school Yvan came nose to nose with people putting up posters from I don't know what party for I forget which election, peaceful-seeming guys in their forties who were decking out a municipal billboard for the purpose, I don't know why but Yvan saw red, he savagely attacked them, furiously, with the bike chain he always carried in the pocket of his orange-and-black jacket, he lashed one man's face threw himself onto the second like a baboon tore off one of his ears with his teeth showering him with kicks in the groin, possessed, enraged, relentless, the third man didn't think twice faced with the surprise of the attack with its extraordinary violence with his companions' screams of pain with Yvan's roars he brought the glue-brush down on his skull, a good straight strong blow that split his occiput and got him a huge number of stitches, even today no one can say if that fracture of his skull played a determining role or if his madness was already well advanced but Yvan went to the emergency room at the psychiatric hospital and then to a rest home for uncontrollable lunatics, Yvan schizophrenic paranoic catatonic and violent, incurable despite the tons of medications, electroshocks and various therapies his doctors have tried, Yvan plunged into the dark, when he speaks it's to recite a paragraph from *Mein Kampf* or anti-Semitic insults, *the yids the yids are trying to assassinate me*, during his few minutes of consciousness a week Yvan is terrified, terrified or utterly violent, depending on the treatment that never managed to "stabilize" him, lost in the limbo of resentment and fright—for me the shock was terrible, Yvan had fallen in combat, brought down by a blow of that campaign bludgeon on his skull, I immediately went to see him at the hospital, I talked for a long time with his parents, and soon faced facts, he had a real fracture, a fine furious madness worthy of Ares, which brought tears of sadness to my eyes, I thought I'll avenge you, I'll avenge you, I'll avenge Yvan with the staring eyes and the lolling tongue, Yvan the pale chained to a chair and shouting to the death: I saw his mother quietly crying afraid to approach him, afraid to approach her own son whose failing brain was oozing violence hatred and pain, now I'll avenge you old pal I'll give you a new life, you've gotten a little bit out of the asylum, your name at least, even if it's with my face on your passport, Francis has slipped into the useless body of Yvan the Terrible for his reincarnation—after Yvan was committed I passed my baccalauréat to go get bored in a private preparatory class where I was supposed to be taught the subtleties of scholarly essays and general knowledge, I was bored stiff, I wanted violence and revenge so much that I went slogging in the army for sixteen months, Yvan would have liked that a lot, the virile songs and the nocturnal sagas, the maneuvers, the training in weapons, tactics, and orientation, until that trip to Egypt on my own to celebrate my discharge and meet Marianne the prudish—my Nazi stories made Stéphanie laugh a lot, especially the episode of Yvan the poor guy felled by a glue brush, still she was a little sorry for me, for having lost all that time, she said, all that ideological time she meant, before yielding to democratic reason, I replied *halfway*, I only yielded halfway, I've never voted in my life, neither did Ezra Pound, I suppose, I have no idea, he too the deranged poet wrote epic-political poems to the glory of the fascist economic model, against usury and usurers, from his house on the outskirts of Genoa the American said terrible things about the leaders of his country with keen hearing who condemned him for high treason in 1943, Pound replied that he didn't see how the simple fact of talking into a microphone even loudly could constitute treason, he was going to pay for it dearly, locked up in 1945 in a cage in the middle of a military detention camp in Pisa, a cage three meters by three with a canvas roof two meters from the ground, Pound slept on the concrete a surveillance spotlight constantly on, in the humid heat of the Tuscan summer, secluded in this hutch that prefigured the ones in Guantánamo, never leaving it, watched day and night, humiliated, gaunt, Pound ended up cracking and was rushed to the infirmary—he barely escaped the death sentence, probably because the authorities decided that he was in fact crazy and that his case required not the firing squad but psychiatry, Pound the friend of Joyce of Eliot of all the artists poets musicians in Paris and elsewhere was declared an officially deranged enemy of the people and sent back a little while later to civilian life, he hurried to return to Italy scarcely had he stepped off the liner than he greeted the journalists come to meet him with the fascist salute, so that the reporters had the impression, for the space of a second, that they were the ones coming back from afar and Pound, Pound the scrawny bearded man, who had never budged, who had already remained in a phantom country, his arm raised high to the rhythm of the clicking of martial heels and iron boots, the inner country, where there is only oneself, no enemies no treacherous Jews no money no perversions pain or lies, poor Pound it didn't matter that he knew thousands of obscure Chinese ideograms he lived enclosed, in the company of statues and busts of himself, he outlived Eliot Yeats Joyce Hemingway William Carlos Williams Cocteau to end up croaking in Venice at the age of eighty-seven, in Venice the humidity is deadly, me too I very nearly succumbed to the mildewy beauty of the City of the

Doges, what am I going to do now, you leave a lot of things by the wayside convictions comrades women objects you cherished you thought you'd keep all your life wedding rings gold chains tattoos you get tired of scars that fade away, as for Vlaho he got used to his new condition he doesn't moan about Fate he accepts, despite the phantom pain, it seizes him from time to time he told me, in Bosnia we were running in front of the great Serbian winter offensive of 1993 we were running as we had rarely ever run before, turning back from time to time to fire a shot or shoot a rocket nothing very effective we were running watching the villages burning behind us we told ourselves we were going to cover the distance all the way to the sea or the Neretva if it went on like that there was nothing to be done, then the front stabilized by a miracle we found ourselves in the trenches hurriedly digging fortifications burying mines trying to defend a ridgeline the United Nations helicopters roamed around us it was a real temptation to down one but of course that was forbidden, we could only at most take a potshot at the white paint on their tanks, just so they'd hear ding ding ding inside and feel they weren't welcome, then those guys would go back to Split saying "they shot at me, they shot at me" which earned them glory and prestige over a beer while we were freezing our balls off in the mud, Yvan Deroy the mad might have enlisted with me if they hadn't committed him, there wasn't more than one Frenchman in the ranks of the HOS until its dissolution after the attack on Zagreb and the assassination of Kraljevic in Bosnia, Yvan would probably have detested the filth the cold and the ideological confusion, despite everything I felt I had found my cause, Croatia and the Croats, God and country, liberty, beautiful Liberty guiding the people in the painting by Delacroix, she who never appeared before the Serbian tanks with her breasts bare: what we saw arriving in front of the Yugoslav tanks were scruffy, panic-stricken refugees, wounded and crying but never with flag and rifle in hand or face turned to the right, torso so luscious you wanted to bite it, all that is fine for painters and filmmakers, for us it took on a different quality, that of poor shivering guys fighting for a scrap of land a farm a valley a village on fire their families and comrades dead in a great storm a blizzard of flames and fright worthy of Hephaestus the lame, the Scamander afloat with decaying carcasses, mutilated bodies, debris of houses and ruined hamlets, what we had seen in Slavonia stretched out, augmented, resounded endlessly, in a duel of violent acts and savageries on this one or that one, Serb or Croat or Muslim, according to all possible combinations of horror, the Russians and Greeks next to the Serbs Arabs and Turks next to the Muslims Catholic Europeans next to Croats bastions of the West all these lovely people hated each other, Andi had said to me you'll see, you'll hate the Serbs and Muslims sooner or later, I was surprised, the Serbs maybe, but the Muslims, and Andi had been right, I had a burning hatred in my chest, instilled there by Eris the indefatigable goddess of Strife, which took a long time to calm down—I never went to Serbia, in the end, despite my hesitations in Thessalonica city of the absent, I headed west, as always, towards the luminous west, in Igoumenitsa I put the car on a ferry headed for Corfu the British, Corfu last stop before Ithaca, without realizing that I would find thousands of Serbs there of course, I didn't know the twists and turns of Atropos the implacable who had made many fates meet on this little island, fates driven by hatred and war, it's hard to understand hatred when you haven't experienced it or when you've forgotten the burning violence the rage that lifts your arm against an enemy his wife his child wanting revenge wanting pain for them make them suffer too, destroy their houses disinter their dead with mortar shells plant our semen in their females and our bayonets in their eyes shower them with insults and kicks because I myself had cried when I saw the solitary body of a beheaded kid clutching a toy in a ditch, a grandmother disemboweled with a crucifix, a comrade tortured enucleated grilled in gas like a shriveled-up grasshopper, his eyesockets empty and white, almost gleaming in the carbonized mass of the corpse, images that still today set my heart beating faster, make my fists clench, ten years later, like Andi's corpse seen lying in his steaming droppings in the middle of the idyllic landscape of a Bosnian valley, there's nothing to be done these images lose none of their force, how to rid myself of them, how, where to leave them, to whom can I confide them, Vlaho the disabled doesn't have to carry this weight, he's happy in peace funny and serene, he left his burden in Bosnia, during an absurd counter-attack to get out of our muddy trenches, we hurtled down the hillside like devils and the shells began to rain down, my helmet fell half over my eyes, Vlaho is just on my right, Andi the furious is in front of course right in front, fleet-footed Andi, I shout to give myself courage, we have to reach the edge of the trees and try to stay there shells are flinging up waves of soft earth grass and metal my ears are whistling I have no way to breathe I run without having time to breathe my lungs blocked I am running solely on adrenaline like a robot on its battery Andrija has reached the first trees he has disappeared under cover I'm almost there, I'm almost there and a huge explosion knocks me down, I've collided with a wall of hot air, the breath of a dragon, I've gotten a huge hit in my helmet, it rang like a bell, I'm on the ground, stunned, I don't hurt anywhere, it's the silence, I can hear only my breathing, my face is splattered with mud, I sit up cross-legged, in the great buzzing, I see Vlaho a few feet away lying on his stomach a second explosion wakes me up, I can hear again I hear the rumble of the shells volleys of shots machine guns I get up and run bent over to Vlaho, I accidentally kick a smoking forearm, a hand sliced off I mechanically pick it up still shocked I go over to the Dalmatian lying on the ground his elbow neatly severed by a huge piece of shrapnel, I call out to him *Vlaho Vlaho kako si kako si Vlaho* no answer, his eyes are closed, his heart is beating very quickly, very quickly and weakly, I grab the wound to check it blood flows through my fingers two other comrades come to the rescue, they put a makeshift tourniquet on it and drag him to cover, he's bleeding from his side too, the shrapnel burned the canvas jacket and opened a blackish wound below his ribs, I realize I'm still holding Vlaho's severed arm, I let it go, I feel nauseous all of a sudden, Andi arrives with a nurse, I look at the pale contorted hand on the ground, the friendly hand with the pink bone, the right hand, right or left I have no idea I sit down on the ground no I collapse rather I collapse onto the ground and pass out, with probably Vlaho's dead palm on my forehead, to sponge away my sweat one last time: when I come to Andi is next to me, pale too, I say to him his hand his hand give him back his hand, as if it were still on me, Andrija looks at me without understanding, the hand isn't there anymore, I hear the noise of gunfire straight ahead, we have to go there, all the rest of the day we fight thinking that Vlaho is dead, dazed and too caught up in the battle to think, Andi explains to me that the nurses covered Vlaho with a blanket his hand with a plastic bag and carried all of it to a first-aid post, might as well say to Hades, here Machaon lacks supplies and above all it is almost impossible to evacuate the wounded, I feel empty, empty weary and sad, no shouts of revenge, no cries, no tears for now, just the rifle that feels a little heavier than usual, Vlaho so loved to feel girls up with both hands, one on each buttock, I have the secret hope that they'll be able to sew it back on, so cleanly cut off by the metal, that should be easy, a good cast a few stitches and we'll see him tomorrow or the day after alive and bawdy as ever, Vlaho is just twenty years old, twenty he needs his life his two arms to drive badly at breakneck speed and trim his vines, fortunately our counter-attack comes to an abrupt end, the Serbs give us a good kick in the butt and we climb back up the hill with many losses and a lot of trouble to position ourselves in a destroyed village, our unit is lagging a little behind as soon as we're settled in we send our guys to go find out about Vlaho, relieved we learn that he's out of danger, a haughty medic tells us he's been evacuated, so with a naïve childlike voice impressed by expertise Andi asks the question I had on my lips, and . . . and his arm, did they put it back on? the doctor makes him repeat it before bursting out laughing, he replies *Moraće se naučiti tući lijevom,* he'll have to learn to jack off with his left hand, we stayed there with our mouths open, hung out to dry by all-powerful medical science that has just thrown our hopes into the trash where Vlaho's limb is slumbering, his fingers of a driver, a shooter, a handler of bayonets and burrower in females, his fingers will decompose before he does, it's strange to think that, like his baby teeth somewhere in a box with his grandmother's jewelry, his forearm is planted in Bosnia, a tree with no fruit, should we set up a plaque to it, here lies the right forelimb of Vlaho Lozović, whose remaining body rests elsewhere, the way those traffickers of medieval relics scattered corpses from Byzantium to Barcelona, bones by the ton, a tibia here a femur there, ossicles for the poor skulls for the rich, a fragment of Saint Somebody for the devotions of peasants frightened of hell, a chunk of the deceased to take out on feast days, the bone will be on display in its gilded reliquary, to ward off plagues poxes wars curses nothing like parading a piece of a stiff, the all-powerful head of Saint Matthew Saint Luke or Saint John the Baptist, we should have preserved the arm of Vlaho Lozović the Unknown, Vlaho the Smiling, Vlaho who accepted, who left the violent acts of his right arm by the wayside, sins war and revenge, he didn't close himself up in the circle of reprisals, Vlaho, he was still in the hospital in Mostar when I told him about Andi's death, his round face was suddenly covered in tears, I almost said don't worry, I avenged him, but he wouldn't have understood, that wouldn't have consoled him, Vlaho the magnanimous, he was just sad, immensely sad at the departure of his friend, without hatred, without rage, I hugged him, we'll see each other soon, I lied, the day before I had gone to the headquarters of the HVO in Vitez to announce that I was pulling out, that I'd had it, and there in front of Vlaho facing his eyes shining with tears I didn't have the courage to repeat it to him, two or three days later though he went back to his home in Split, I could have waited for him, but I didn't have the strength, I had spent all my energy in revenge, in the fury and dangerous crossing of the Muslim lines, by the only road (a path, rather) that we still controlled, I was exhausted by that absurd war where the allies against the Serbs were killing each other fifty kilometers to the east, our positions paralyzed, Andi with no grave his corpse taken away to be probably exchanged later in a truck of dead bodies I couldn't bear any more, I couldn't bear any more militia highwaymen disguised as soldiers, I was emptied out, no more friends no more anything no more desire, I had the image of Andi in my head lying with his pants down to his knees and the vision of the living-dead arm in the grass, I thought I saw it digging into the earth like a crab trying to hide itself, I said goodbye Vlaho, out of habit I held out my hand to his stump, Vlaho the debonair caught my fingers in his left mitt, he gave me one last smile, and I left for the North—maybe I too should have cut off my criminal hand, I might not be in this train ten years later, on my way to Rome the Catholic great reservoir of remains, I wasn't able to accept the hand held out by Marianne, or Stéphanie, Sashka doesn't offer anything, lost in her colors and the faces of illuminated saints that she paints all day long, what I am is of no interest to her my past is of no interest to her my life is of no interest to her she lives in her pictures, Christ

Pantocrators, praying Virgins, Saint Georges, Saint Michael the Archangels, Saint Innocents, Saints Cosmas and Damian, which she sells at a very high price to sincere believers who do not know that women can't paint icons, the prudish angel doesn't whisper into their ears, we have in common neither language nor passion nor history, she is so far away, I'm not going to rush over to her place after all I'll wait, wait and see, maybe I'll manage to detach myself, detach myself from the suitcase from Vlaho's arm from Andrija's corpse from Sashka and the whole works, in Venice I thought I'd succeeded, in Venice queen of fog everything almost ended in a canal, the way Leon Saltiel the Jew from Salonika is about to hang himself or throw himself out the window before finding peace in revenge, the way Globocnik the killer brings an end to his days by biting a pen full of arsenic when the Allies capture him, the way Hess the inexhaustible manages to strangle himself with a cable, the way Manos Hadjivassilis throws himself onto the electrified barbed wire in Mauthausen, the way my Islamists blow themselves up in Jerusalem and see the city from high up their eyelids blinking in the middle of the sky, but they fished me out, they gave me a second life which I lost in the Zone everything comes in threes what's waiting for me before the end of the world, what's waiting for me, the friendly hand was sliced off in Bosnia, Yvan Deroy the mad has been far away for years, Sashka the unreachable lives in the gilt world of images, my father never emerged from his silence—I picture him alone with the cries of his own ghosts, he the son of a Resistant and he tortured Algerians as ardently as the Gestapo did his old man, they had perfectly remembered the lesson of water-boarding and the bike wheel, for the good of the community, if those rats didn't talk bombs would go off, Frenchmen would die, it was mostly Algerians who died, how many, 500,000, a million, we'll never know, the ones who died in combat, died from torture, died in prison, died from a bullet in the head, died inside the barbed wire of the detention camps, the suitcase is full of them, names testimonies secret reports memos from generals repentant or proud of their work and pictures, hundreds of photos, what could possibly have motivated all those soldiers to document the horror, why did the armed forces take the trouble to photograph electrocuted Algerians, half-drowned Algerians, beaten up Algerians, maybe to refine their techniques or give an account of their activities to anxious Parisian authorities, you see we're not idle, here we're grinding away, we're slaving away, we're keeping busy, did they get a glimpse of the catastrophe, the exile of a million people repatriated in 1962, a million French Spanish Italian Jewish gypsy Maltese German refugees crossing the Mediterranean to scatter from Alicante to Bastia, the greatest maritime displacement since the expulsion of the Mudejars 400 years before, Bône and Oran emptied of half of their inhabitants, Algiers of a third, desertion desolation victimization the memory of the dead, plunge a country into hell, their executives in the FLN will turn into skillful executioners and torturers too, lost in the Zone where I counted the blows the throat-slittings the decapitations the massacres and the bombs, lulled by the exotic sound of the patronymics of the emirs of the GIA and the AIS, the rising generation confronted the old ones from the war of independence, some of whom had fought in regiments of mountain goumiers on the Italian slopes, the world turns, the great-great-great-grandchildren of immigrants from Minorca sent to colonize Algiers in 1830 would return to Ciutadella city of horses and of Saint John the Baptist 130 years later driven out by the valorous fighters of the FLN and the French torturers, murderers letting fall dark cloudbursts of victims, all those circles drawn on a golden shield, it's the mothers who provide the weapons, Thetis the loving consoles Achilles her child by giving him the means to take revenge, a breastplate a sword a blinding shield in which the whole world is reflected, just as Marija Mirković my mother provided me with homeland history heredity Maks Luburić and Millán-Astray the one-eyed hawk, don't cry Achilles, dry your tears and go avenge yourself, be reconciled with the remorseful son of Atreus and kill Hector with your fury, revenge, revenge, I feel revenge rumbling through this train hurtling through the hills, my innocent neighbor still has her eyes glued to her book, she doesn't know who's sitting opposite her, she can't imagine that her fate has crossed mine, that soon the white pearls of her necklace will be in my possession, her bag, her wool sweater, I'll dance on her body in the light of the Tuscan moon the bronze gleaming in my hand, ready to sack Rome with the wide walls, Rome conquered by the victorious Allies, Rome pillaged and burned by the swordsmen of the Hapsburg son of Joanna the Mad, Rome split open by the intrepid Normans, by the fierce Visigoths, by the Gauls with the short blades, Rome daughter of Aeneas with the swift spear, Rome descendant of Ilion in ruins, revenge, revenge for Patroclus son of Menoetius, for Antilochus son of Nestor, revenge, one more ransacking, more hecatombs, libations, smoking pyres for Andrija the Slavonic who begged me in a dream to find his body, to burn it, revenge, for the lost arm of Vlaho the magnanimous, seeding the land, vengeance, for everyone, the glaive heated by warm blood, the time is coming, I feel it the train is vibrating I'm almost there I've almost reached the end of the journey, in the black landscape my eyes closed skeletons spinning and rattling they're the sparks of color of the inner world calm your breathing, Francis, try to breathe regularly and let the thoughts flow that are leading you towards revenge, let Dream, the messenger, incubate his oracles in you, in the Middle Ages they were afraid of sleeping for fear of being assailed by the terrible succubae that gave pleasure, a hidden and confused pleasure, squat men frightened by the universe woke up in a sweat with a cursed erection that they concealed poorly from their panic-stricken wives, I venture Queen Mab hath been with you, Mab the messenger, with her team of magic fireflies, no bigger than an agate-stone, what would she say to me, to me, the tiny fairy of the kingdoms of the night, nothing, last night all steeped in alcohol in cold caresses in a concierge's lodge drowned in shadow, against the body marked by old age of the ugly woman with the bitter tongue, after the pleasureless ejaculation and the shame, once home ashamed and sad I collapsed on my sheetless bed in the empty apartment, my last night in Paris, Queen Mab has brought me to Sashka, to her tiny studio in Trastevere I see her pale hands stained with gold paint she is painting a pious picture of four crowned saints, four Dalmatian martyrs Severus, Severianus, Victorinus, and Carpophorus, handsome and brown-haired, she explains that they were skillful stone-carvers whom the Emperor Diocletian wanted to employ in his palace in Split to erect a pagan statue, of Jupiter the unyielding or Venus the temptress, the four artists had sworn their faith to Christ and refused to carve the idol, which enraged Caesar, he sentenced them to be whipped to death, the executioner belabored their bodies for days on end, with no noticeable effect, the four men resisted both the leather and the metal balls, the stripes on their skin disappeared as the torture went on, Diocletian the inflexible was scarcely moved by the miracle, he had them enclosed in four iron coffins that were thrown into the Adriatic where they sleep to this day, among pale blue jellyfish and wrecks of Venetian galleys, the four pious sculptors are reborn under the brushes of Sashka the iconographer, she has in front of her an illuminated book from which she draws her inspiration, a linden board hollowed out with a chisel and covered with *levkas*, the haloes of the four saints applied with gold leaf, the little sable brush with which she fills in the background with brown ocher, then the clothes with silver-white vermilion-red cobalt-blue, slowly and meticulously the magic image takes shape, it's wonderful to watch Sashka work, among the Theotokions, the Saint John the Golden-Moutheds, the dizzying Stylites, the red dragons, Demetrius of Salonika pierced by spears, Theodore emperor of Byzantium, John Climacus on top of his ladder, James cut into pieces, a crowd of martyrs, of colors, of almost identical faces, the four little Dalmatian sculptors find a golden life in the magnificent shadow of martyrdom, before joining the seabed, Sashka the serene is not moved by all these massacres, she is protected by Luke the Evangelist, patron saint of painters and doctors, there is great gentleness in her drawing, infinite patience, when I met her I thought she was the angel herself appearing to me in her golden halo, at night, the troubled night of Rome, at a café terrace, back from an endless visit to the papal chancellery, Campo de' Fiori, right next to me Sashka lit the square up the whole bar had eyes only for her, in that place they offer you peanuts with your aperitif, whole, in their stringy shells, and the customers looked like monkeys in the zoo, compulsively throwing the useless husks on the ground: the terrace littered with goober shells crunched underfoot, opposite the statue of Giordano Bruno the tortured, I imagine the spectacle, in February 1600 the filthy ribalds from the vicinity came to check if the impious one given over to the flames would cry out despite the gag, everyone ran up to hear the flesh crackle and fill their nostrils with the aroma of human meat, at the very place where today tourists are gulping down peanuts, Bruno the swordsman magician cosmologist occultist and poet was a great traveler, he visited half of Europe before being betrayed by the Venetians and brought before papal authority: that same authority recently expressed its regrets about burning him, sorry, they say today, for having tortured a naked philosopher chained to a metal stake on a pyre of logs, Giordano Bruno dead by pontifical stupidity opposite the bar where I shelled peanuts without being able to drag my eyes away from the young woman so beautiful, so present at the table next to mine, in the company of a man who was devouring her with his eyes, she didn't seem to be paying attention to his concupiscence, even less to my own or to the carbonized body of Bruno, her eyes were too light for the demon to be reflected in them, too light, I heard her rolling pretty *r*s, she spoke Italian slowly, calmly, with a slight accent, I was sure she was Slavic and I prayed secretly for her to be Croatian, or Slovenian, or even Serbian, I would have had a hold over her through language—of course she had to be Russian, from Russia mother of Orthodoxy tanks and assault rifles, that's all I knew, I could have itemized to her at leisure all the models, the variations, the calibers or secret activities of Great Russia in the Zone, at great length, spoken about Russia's equivocal relations with certain Arab countries, about the curve of the cartridge clip, the Kalashnikov's stroke of genius, but no, we talked about Jerusalem the gentle, about my entomological field trips in the Libyan desert or in the north of Morocco, quickly, without insisting, she is not curious, Sashka, she lives in a world of images, she expects nothing from anyone, especially not from words—I asked her why she had left St. Petersburg and she told me that she hadn't left St. Petersburg, she'd left Leningrad, precisely because Leningrad was disappearing, that she had arrived in Jerusalem by chance, with a contingent of fake Jews looking for a host country, and there wasn't a single ideological ulterior motive in her, no nostalgia, she was just uttering facts, when I asked her if she wanted to go back to Russia she replied simply that the Russia she knew no longer existed, that the city of her childhood had disappeared, that the people, the streets had changed, but she added immediately it's just as well like that, and what for another would have been an utter I-don't-give-a-fuck attitude in her signaled a detachment, an elsewhere, her life is in her gestures, in the movements of her brush, of her wrist, in her eyes riveted on a saint to be reproduced, a face to be modeled, the drape of a garment, she doesn't have any pretensions that she's creating, inventing new representations, no, she repeats ad infinitum what tradition has left to her, content to be able to make a living from this singular activity and towards me she acts in the same way, Sashka the distant, if I'm there so much the better, if not, too bad, she doesn't try to convert me to anything, does she see me, even, she sees what I show her, which is nothing, or so little, disarmed by her simplicity and her statue-like forms, how could she know, if I don't tell her anything, she has neither the universal maternity of Marianne the generous nor the devouring curiosity of Stéphanie the headstrong, Sashka is a mirror from which I keep myself hidden, my face veiled so as not to be reflected in the tormented faces of the executioners scalding the saints, whipping them to death before drowning them in the Adriatic like the four crowned ones from Split—in 1915 it was hundreds of bodies with no coffins they sent to the bottom, valiant Serbs, a little south of Corfu last stop before Ithaca, the British have a taste for islands even in the Mediterranean, Minorca Malta Corfu Cyprus belonged to them, and their ships with the bulging sides were masters of *Akdeniz*, the Turks' name for the Mediterranean, the White Sea, when I landed in Corfu coming from Igoumenitsa after having crossed the steep-sloped Epirus the British were knocking down huge beers in the shade of ad-covered umbrellas on the coasts of Phaeacia, forget about Nausicaa washing her laundry on the bank, what was awaiting me was a Greek cop with a big mustache he ordered me to move my car as fast as possible, hitting the tired automobile's roof hard with his club, *quickly car quickly*, as if he were addressing a horse, despite the pink Brits the pretentious French the mistrustful Germans and the rowdy Italians the island was beautiful, the narrow old city looked more like Venice than Athens, thank God, and even tired of vacation pursued by the heads of decapitated monks and apocalyptic evangelists in my sleep Corfu wedged between the imposing Venetian fortresses was a repose, it was a pleasure to get lost there, to drink for a long time watching the sea lick the wounds on the walls, the Ottomans had tried to take the island many times, without success, Phaeacia last rampart of the West had held strong, the inscriptions on the walls recalled the siege of 1716, when the Turk had made his appearance for the last time off of Palaio Frourio, as in Malta the heroic before the defenders with their shining cuirasses had resisted the cannons, the sapping the continuous assaults of the fierce Easterners, there were masses of Croats and Dalmatians among the mercenaries defending the city, I imagine one of my ancestors flung into the sea by a cannonball, after having recommended himself to God having been brave and having sent many Janissaries to Hades: there almost was a mosque in Corfu, as there was in Rhodes, as in Belgrade, as in Mostar, Ares decided otherwise, it's the only building missing in the old city, no Trojans at the bronze doors of the palace of Alcinous the grey, or almost none, strolling by chance through the colorful streets I chanced upon a building that announced *Srpska Kuća*, Serbian House, a museum devoted to the retreat of Peter I's army in 1915, the soldiers in the ossuary in Salonika had passed through Corfu, before being sent back by sea to the Balkan front, just as the French and the English had survived the Dardanelles to end up in a grave in Thessaly, the valorous survivors of the most terrible military retreat since Berezina had fallen later on facing the Bulgarians, the museum was moving, dozens of period photos related the fierce rout of the Serbian army defeated by the Kaiser and his Austrian ally, through the mountains of Montenegro to the Albanian coast where the French took them on board, a retreat with women and children, on foot in the snow, long columns almost without food traveled for 400 kilometers in the intense winter cold, carrying their king on a straw chair, an entire country was leaving for the sea, 150,000 died along the way in the mountains of Kosovo and the outskirts of Podgorica, victims of the cold, of hunger, of German bullets, they kept dying after they arrived, malnourished, exhausted, installed in makeshift camps on the little wooded island of Vibo before the entrance to the harbor, with no tents, almost with no medical care, nothing could be done to keep them from dying, they fell like flies at the rate of 300 a day, the French and the British couldn't get over it, they had survived the most terrible of all journeys to keel over by the thousands once they'd reached their destination, they were no longer supported by their homeland's soil, they were in a foreign land, in the rain, on a rock in the Ionian Sea, there was no room to bury all these people, these thousands of people so the French hospital-ship *Francis of Assisi* the charitable took on board truckloads of corpses to go bury them at sea a few miles away, these Serbs from Belgrade who had never seen any sea but the Danube, they rest today dissolved in the waves, in the stomachs of thousands of fish and marine algae, the immense blue cemetery where Thetis descends to adorn their memorials with flowers, their children's too, who died with them—the survivors prepared again for war, reorganized by the allies returned by boat to the other side of the Balkans, where they bravely started up the fight again, and Peter I the brave, over seventy, who had survived humiliation, illness, defeat, and exile to Corfu, could be crowned King of Serbs, Croats, and Slovenians, my king, I looked at him, old and sick, carried on the shoulders of his soldiers in the snow, flanked by an Orthodox priest and a doctor just in case, and I was proud that he was in a way my king, the only one what's more, his son Alexander would be assassinated in Marseille in front of my grandfather's eyes by the hired assassins of Pavelić the patriot, at the end of the war Corfu was strewn with Serbian cemeteries, the whole island was a tomb, the generous Greeks had lent their land for the dead and their theater for the Parliament, those same Greeks would in turn go to fight around Sarajevo the well-guarded, an exchange of graves, Serbian ossuaries here, Hellenic burial grounds there, the great circle round the rim of Achilles' shield, the macabre humor of the relentless gods—as I left the *Srpska Kuća* I felt a little melancholy, I felt cold despite the August heat, I went and sat down at a café terrace my eyes on the blue necropolis thinking about Peter I Karageorgevich, who had fought against so many enemies, against the coarse Prussians in the French army in 1870, against the savage Turks in Bosnia in 1875, against the well-helmeted Austrians in 1914, exhausted, the old Montenegrin monarch forced to leave his country on foot, without however abandoning the homeland and the liberation of the Slavs of the South, sure that in Slavonia and in Bosnia he would have given us a real kick in the rear, the old Saint-Cyr military school alum with the white panache who swam across the Loire to escape Bismarck's soldiers, Peter I found himself in exile on the island where Kaiser Wilhelm spent his vacations, in the shadow of a splendid palace called the Achilleion, with luxuriant gardens, planted with cypress, laurel, and palm trees, where the statue of dying Achilles contemplates the blinding blue of the Mediterranean, he prays to Thetis his mother, the place is completely devoted to the furious son of Peleus, to the eternal cycle of revenge: the palace was built by Sissi, Empress of Austria Queen of Hungary, who liked to come live a few months a year by the wounded warrior's side, before she in turn was assassinated on the banks of Lake Geneva by Luigi Lucheni an Italian anarchist with a stiletto right through her heart, was Kaiser Wilhelm II thinking of her when he rested his feet in the water, or rather of the son of Peleus conquered by Fate, or even of the Italian assassin, whose head he had seen preserved in formaldehyde at the Hotel Métropole in Geneva, the only hotel in the world to pride itself on human remains, Lucheni decapitated post mortem by a Swiss fetishist after he had hanged himself with his belt in his cell, Corfu was overflowing with dead people famous or unknown, ever since Poseidon had his revenge on the sailors who had brought Ulysses back to Ithaca by turning them to stone, I was spinning in circles among corpses, from bar to bar, museum to museum, the plague victims of Lazaretto Island gave way to Greek resistants and communists shot during the civil war, the 2,000 Jews imprisoned in the old Venetian fortress before being deported to Auschwitz, the sea seemed to have no bottom, it contained too many bodies, even the body of Isadora Duncan, who spent six months in Corfu in 1913 to get over the death of her two children drowned in the Seine, the American dancer with the bare feet was pursued by Athena jealous of her beauty, the tall silhouette of her ghost danced naked in the summer night, I imagined the movements of her torso, her hips draped in a transparent cloth among the shadows of the gardens of Achilles, among Sissi the empress, Kaiser Wilhelm II and Peter I of Serbia, now I see the handsome Sergei Yesenin at her side, in the darkness of the train window, Yesenin hanged at the age of thirty in his room at the Hotel d'Angleterre in St. Petersburg, after having written a farewell poem in his own blood, Sashka looks like him, she has the same round face, the very light eyes, an eternally childlike face accentuated by blond hair, Isadora Duncan knew only three words of Russian and Yesenin no foreign language, they didn't speak, they danced, they drank, Sergei especially, Isadora says in her autobiography that the poet was passionate, so passionate that he could spend a week without sobering up, so passionate that he married the dancer eighteen years his senior, so passionate that he left her to go back to Russia and plunge into depression, in Corfu in the heart of summer it was hard to imagine the long night in Petrograd in December, the cord and the pipe in the room of the respectable hotel or else the last thoughts of Yesenin the hanged man, we still don't know if he really committed suicide, maybe two or three somber Chekists helped hang him from the heating pipe, aided by the passivity of his permanent drunkenness, Sergei Yesenin dies in the absent sun and the first sheets of ice clinging to the shores of the

Neva, his hotel room looks out onto the front of Saint Isaac's Cathedral, could he glimpse through the window the catafalque of General Kutuzov Napoleon's destroyer, between two gilt icons, probably not, the Revolution had closed the doors of churches to transform them into warehouses, forbidden to people, for the obstinate Bolsheviks were so superstitious that they feared the harmful influence of the very form of the building on Marxist zeal, if they were changed into theaters or meeting houses, as had been suggested in the beginning by suspicious pragmatists, who were perhaps liquidated as cleanly as Yesenin, Yesenin in love with his mother Russia cemetery of the Grande Armée where the 300,000 soldiers of Napoleon's Old Guard lie mowed down by the frost or the cannons in 1812, the cavalrymen ate their horses that died of hunger, the Belorussian peasants ate the cavalrymen that died of hunger, Napoleon lord of Corfu for ten years dreamed of the sun of Austerlitz and of the victory of Lodi as he crossed the bridge over the Berezina erected in haste by the genius of the pontoon builders ancestors of the French sailors who transported the survivors of the Serbian army through the Ionian Sea, among them the Serbian soldier Jean Genet fell in love with in Barcelona, Stilitano the coward with the missing hand—in Corfu near the palace of Achilles Venetians Ottomans Frenchmen Austrians Serbs met and even an American dancer in love with the Russian poet, Isadora Duncan would die not long after Yesenin the alcoholic saint, in the same way, her neck choked cervical vertebrae crushed along the shores of the Mediterranean, dragged behind a car like the snipers in Beirut, the goddess jealous of her beauty and her multicolored shawl snags it in the rear wheel of the convertible driving at top speed on the Corniche, in Nice, it's evening, a light September breeze is blowing in from the sea, to protect her fragile throat and her soft breasts the dancer wrapped herself up in her immense scarf that snaps in the wind like a deadly pennant, when the driver accelerates the silk scarf gets caught in the axle immediately tightens and drags Isadora out of the vehicle, onto the pavement, her head against the tire's rough rubber, in the time it takes for the driver to stop she's already dead, sitting with her back against the spokes of the blue Amilcar, her eyes wide open onto the Mediterranean, her head stuck to the car, her tongue sticking out, like Saint Mark the Evangelist hauled on the paving stones by a cart near Alexandria, Saint Mark accompanied by the lion on the icons painted by Sashka the angel as blond as Yesenin: she paints martyrs and I collect corpses, bodies scattered in the snow, arms fallen on the ground, bones sleeping at the bottom of sea graves, Corfu last stop before Ithaca seemed like one of Fate's points of inflection, the home of the implacable Moirae, I drank a final ouzo in the garden of the palace of Sissi the stabbed empress, watching Achilles massacre the Trojans, I thought one last time about the Serbs chilled to the bone, about Stilitano the one-armed coward, about Isadora caught again by divine vengeance after her children and her husband, and I started off again for the North—the North, that is the shadow of Maréchal Mortier where I was going back to officiate a few days later, Mortier great killer of Spaniards, Teutons, and Slavs, his boulevard a proud address for our arcana, barely had I arrived than I found Lebihan who welcomed me with a So Francis, ready to get back in the saddle? he was surprised I wasn't more tanned, after a stay on the islands, I told him nothing about my vacation other than the names of exotic places, what was there to say, dead Greeks dead Jews dead Evangelists and dead Serbs, I returned one more time to the battle of Algiers, dead Muslims, the GIA had a new emir and was changing their strategy, or rather abandoning all strategy for the tactics of cutting throats, at night Queen Mab the tiny fairy incubated my azure-colored dreams, arid mountains plunging into the sea and television Nausicaas, to console me probably for the darkness of the day, the ritual, the offering to Maréchal Mortier, the Porte-des-Lilas metro line, the change at Belleville, the smell of peanuts and sweat of the Parisian metro, getting out at Pigalle, Blanche, or Place-de-Clichy, depending on my mood, to stop by and have some drinks in the midst of the crowd of drunkards at the bar in the 18th arrondissement, commenting on another sort of news, usually connected to sports, to teams that aren't doing so well, to results that are always disappointing, losing or winning at dice, with the surprising sensation, for someone returning from vacation, of discovering your family, your friends, and your house still in the same place, a place where there's somewhere to drink, what's more, and where you can crush your butts out on the ground without risking a reprimand, you find yourself patting the owner's dogs as if they were distant cousins, endless demonstrations of affection, everyone's happy to see you again, everyone celebrates with relief that this haven of manhood hasn't yet been conquered by females the police or public health, and once you're nice and tipsy you go back up to your place, you leave the zinc under your elbow for the zinc over your head, with all the windows open in order to get rid of the heat of Paris in early September, an armchair, a detective novel, and the warm smell of asphalt that invades the room as night falls—Stéphanie didn't like my rituals, neither the bar nor the trashy novels, when the passion from the early days fades away, these nice character traits turn into unbearable defects, little by little the crack becomes an abyss of reproaches and annoyances that has to be filled with the plaster of lies and dissimulation, month after month, summer after summer, burying myself in the Zone, filling my briefcase with corpses right and left, as I traveled to Damascus Jerusalem Cairo Trieste Valencia, I was detaching myself from her as surely as from Marianne in Venice: my guilt after the incident of the fake suicide changed into constant aggressiveness, everything went downhill, into the bottom of the sea, the way a shroud becomes unraveled thread by thread, this is going to end badly, we thought sometimes, each at one end of Paris in our respective apartments, it will all end badly, and one day as I got out of the Intercity coming from Frankfurt at the Gare de l'Est, exhausted after a sleepless night in the Prague train in the company of a talkative railway fanatic, having gone back to my place with new documents for my suitcase of catastrophes, my devil's cauldron, a little jetlagged, confused, hazy, having reached my place in the early afternoon I didn't go to the office right away, to check some minor details and put in an appearance, I should have, it's very cowardly but I should have gone instead of taking a shower and sitting quietly in my armchair gazing off into space, she rang the doorbell at around five o'clock, I heard her voice on the intercom and I was surprised, she hardly ever came to my place, almost never and especially not without warning, she knew I was supposed to get back from Prague in the afternoon she had left the Boulevard a little early to run here, I heard her climbing the stairs, a little anxious, why was she coming, maybe one of those proofs of love that you plug the cracks with, a surprise, she came in smiling and kissed me tenderly saying just *surprise!* she asked me if I'd had a good trip, she observed the disorder, the clothes scattered on the floor, the photographs, the books, the papers cluttering the ground and she laughed, *at least you're faithful to your mess*, she was in good form, very beautiful, her hair falling loose absorbed the light, she went into the kitchen to put something in the fridge, I should have guessed, I should have but I didn't want to, I was tired, happy to see her, but surprised and tired, I hazarded *I forgot your birthday, is that it?* she gave a slightly false laugh, *how stupid you can be*, she simpered, almost inane all of a sudden, she was at a loss, looked for a place to sit down, decided to remain standing, I had a foreboding of something despite myself, I didn't say anything, she chatted, I handed her the little transparent crystal star from Bohemia that I had bought for her, the object carved by the slaves in Theresienstadt wrapped up in red tissue paper, I said look, this is for you, she said oh, that's nice, thanks, thanks and she was so nervous as she tore open the wrapping that the trinket fell down, that got on my nerves, for no reason, I picked up the gleaming star saying hey, watch out, and I was holding it when Stéphanie whispered *I'm expecting a baby* and let herself slide into the armchair, looking at me intensely, I didn't say anything, I wasn't sure I'd understood, the usual phrase was I'm pregnant, I'm pregnant and not I'm expecting a baby, I handed her the little glass star, *you almost broke it*, her eyes misted over a little, she murmured that's all you have to say? we were on opposite sides of a river, making incomprehensible signs to each other, I replied and you? I felt absolutely nothing at this announcement, nothing, four unreal words, I turned my head away, she said *I'm such an idiot*, we never keep our mouths shut at the right time, I stammered no, no, she got up, muttered *I knew I shouldn't have come*, I repeated no no, she got annoyed, she shouted *am I staying or leaving?* we never keep our mouths shut at the right time I sighed *whatever you like*, she trembled and went out almost running leaving me alone with the Prague star still between my fingers—I didn't rush over to the stairway I didn't shout come back I sat down in the chair to look my share of fate in the face, impossible to imagine what Stéphanie's words represented impossible to see what there was in her belly I remembered the last time we had slept together four days before but it wasn't that coitus it was another one lost in the number of coituses of the previous weeks, during the weekend in Istanbul maybe, you can't know did Stéphanie know, what, what was there to know, it was there in front of me have a child don't make the choice of Achilles the sterile but that of Hector, Hector talks with Andromache his wife of the beautiful *peplos*, on the ramparts of Troy, Hector protector of his city, his wife begs him tenderly not to go to war, not to go, not to leave great-walled Ilion, despite the cowardice of his brother Paris the wretched fop, he sweeps her complaints away with a gesture, he says "leave the toils of war to men," for you the children, for me the keen sword, I know that I'm going to die and that Troy will fall, that's how it is, I will have a child, there'll be a sparkling mobile in a colorful nursery, a male or a female, and Troy will fall, there will be an Astyanax somewhere who will look like me, who will carry his father on his shoulders the way I carry mine, outside of the city on fire, I saw myself with my father on my back, and him with his, a pyramid of fathers as high as the ladder of St. John Climacus, all of them overlapping each other laughing like demons at seeing their sons bending beneath them, so I got up and went into the kitchen, I rushed over to the bottle of champagne in the fridge, that's what Stéphanie had put there, a bottle of champagne, and joy came over me, a powerful joy that resisted the Veuve Clicquot, that lasted despite all the drinking, in my chair, trying to understand what had just happened, I drank alone, I had forgotten Prague the trains the Czech railway fanatic the suitcase foreign criminal investigation departments I thought about rattles women contracting sweating bloody thighs, with the help of alcohol I saw myself wiping a bead of sweat off Stéphanie's forehead in the middle of labor, changing the diapers of a hairy monkey, brown as night, a little scrap of a man, discovering the relationship between primate and its progeny, soon I was drunk, it was time to go to bed let Dream bring me the news and I accidentally crushed the crystal star, next to the armchair, I crushed it with my shoe, by mistake, I heard it crack, the glass broke into a million glittering pieces, I was drunk, I was drunk I sat down on the ground to watch my tears of sorrow set off slivers of light as they fell on the debris of the dead object—the gods are fighting, the gods are fighting among themselves they are taking back what they have given, a child, that was a very small hand to pull me out of the water, a tiny paw to drag me out of the darkness, the next day Stéphanie the proud went to the gynecology clinic on the Rue des Lilas a stone's throw away from our boulevard, she insisted, she trotted out all her persuasion her professional cards procured straightaway a meeting with the psychologist and the anesthetist, Stéphanie decided it, in the late afternoon they put a sort of vacuum between her legs, I didn't know, I called her without success for twenty-four hours, I was shaken, anxious and happy, I kept calling her, I was afraid I'd wounded her, frightened her like a wild animal, the wild animal was me my father was right, old Priam was right, she couldn't have a child with a barbarian, the choice of Achilles is no choice, the Moirae decided for him, Stéphanie decided for me, so much the better, so much the worse, who knows what would have come of this offshoot, son or daughter of workers in the shadows, I didn't understand, I didn't understand why, the day after that I managed to speak with her for five minutes, in a café on the Place de la République, she was very pale, defeated, she said to me *you are a monster, I know everything about you you are a monster, I never want to see you again*, how could she have changed so quickly, two days before she arrived at my place holding a bottle of champagne and now I was a monster, maybe she'd hoped for a transformation, a change, until the very end, maybe she had imagined she could live with the monster, I said nothing, I looked at her with a great sadness, she left, I had been a father for forty-eight hours, a monstrous father who eats his children, it was 7:30 I ordered a plum brandy, a little brandy of mourning for the tiny fists of the one I would not have, then another, for the monstrous barbarian, then a third, for my own dad, a fourth, for mortals, the poor fate of mortals, a fifth, for the gods who were fighting on top of Olympus, a sixth, for revenge, for the revenge that would come one day, sweet and bloody and when the joint closed I was so drunk that the waiter had to support me by my jacket collar so I wouldn't collapse before reaching the cold, grey, wet sidewalk

Sashka, painter of the soul like Saint Luke, Sashka the distant, Sashka blond angel of Jerusalem is not of this world, Nathan Strasberg gloomy secret agent told me that in Jersualem you always find a mystical energy, a spiritual breath, whether you're Jewish, Christian, or Muslim, in the gold leaf the incense and the memories of that heart pierced by intransigent monotheism, Intissar the Palestinian fighter if she exists might be in Palestine today, now, by the tomb of Arafat the pale, the father of the Palestinian nation, who was forgiven everything, even his millions of dollars, even his wife, even his countless political and military mistakes, because he was the Father, who died mysteriously in almost Soviet circumstances of secrecy and lies, pushed down the stairs by his children, for the times change, the sons wanted power in turn, power and money, money especially, Arafat Abu Ammar the brave sent to Hades by the zeal of his lieutenants, by fierce history, Nathan was happy and sad at the same time to lose such an enemy, happy that time had managed what the Mossad had so often fumbled, but sad too, sad, for Arafat, he said, we knew him, after all, we had locked him up like a monkey in the zoo, today everything's going to be more difficult, more violent, Gaza's piles of trash catch fire, the tires, the rockets, Gaza the lowest depths of the Zone the only place in the Mediterranean where you won't find a single tourist on the immense beaches cluttered with rusty barbed wire plastic bottles sadness misery Gaza the insane continues on its way to the end of the world in hatred and cries for vengeance, abandoned, and the only comforts that reach it are the few missiles that absent-minded pilots launch from time to time from the sky always blue onto a car the courtyard of a mosque a house a street in Rafah in Khan Younis in Gaza everything is so close together it's impossible to aim said Nathan sighing, civilian victims were the Israeli army's cross to bear, pursued by the ghosts of dead children, despite its handsome olive tanks its airplanes its elite troops, what can you do, you have to defend yourself avenge yourself fight against your enemies it's like that, Gaza immense Indian reservation with no alcohol where a million and a half Palestinians are waiting, waiting for a job a government a country in that capital of sadness adrift, Waste Land with no ruler, the only fallow land in the Mediterranean, rubble with no owner where the population is fed through a judas hole gouged open in a wall—in Paris I saw in an exhibition Stéphanie had dragged me to an installation by an artist named Hugo Orlandini, the replica of one of the detention cages in Guantánamo, life-sized, a parallelepiped of wire fencing with a cot a Turkish-style toilet in gleaming steel a fluorescent orange pajama carefully folded on the mattress slippers an elegant black cloth bag for the head, so this is where the guys we had given to the CIA ended up, the United States of America was getting its revenge by slowly and scientifically torturing everyone who fell into its clutches, charter flights of suspects took off from Egypt from Greece from Israel from Spain from Pakistan from France from England to populate these metal aquariums in a law-free zone in eastern Cuba the island of Communist hope of rum and salsa, prisoners of war with no war no lawyers and no names, Muslim suspects made to confess anything at all by water-boarding them left to rot in the sun depriving them of sleep of food beaten by guards who were having a great time with these orange half-starved insects, Hugo Orlandini's cage spat out music, the music that the humiliated ones of Guantánamo endured all night long in their hutch, music therapy, an eternal pop tune came out of the shiny hole of the john, a voice from beyond the grave intoned "My Way" to them in a loop, Sinatra was supposed to interfere with their guts through their tortured anus and convert them *from within* to good taste and Western culture, Hugo Orlandini's replica fascinated the visitors who tested the solidity of the walls, and they all, all, including Stéphanie, fiddled with the narrow door to see if it was open or locked and played with the lock, one particularly interested onlooker couldn't resist the temptation and stole the pajama and the slippers, I picture him dominated by his wife, all the night long, dressed in orange with a black cloth over his head, Sinatra in the background on the record player, his turned-on housewife burying all sorts of incongruous objects inside him—*men men men*, Joyce would have said, Ezra Pound the mad in the Pisa concentration camp was subjected day and night to a bombardment of light and noise, the furious loudspeakers didn't leave him in peace for a single second, from sunset to dawn the Andrews Sisters penetrated the poet's brain, *drinkin' rum and Coca-Cola / Go down Point Koomanah / Both mother and daughter / Workin' for the Yankee dollar*, and his mental health reeled, he tried to take refuge in his imagination in Rapallo the Genoese, in his pretty house facing the sea, facing the calm reassuring Mediterranean, at the place where a Dionysian Nietzsche had had the idea for his *Zarathustra*, imagining eagles and lions in the clouds above the fallow sea, Pound a few days before his death walks one last time in Burano and Torcello, he strolls in his death throes round the Venetian lagoon, near the leaning belltowers and the fishing boats, he thinks of the violin of Olga Rudge the faithful, of concertos by Vivaldi carefully copied out for years, Pound the silent has forgotten fascist Italy, he is looking for forgiveness and rest, farewell revenge, he has seen the light, the little light of Canto CXVI, *to confess wrong without losing rightness: Charity have I had sometimes, I cannot make it flow thru* being right for having been wrong, Pound goes toward the great void, *a little light, like a rushlight*, he sees a sliver of light, the swift glimmer of a match, *to lead back to splendour*, it guides him towards splendor, in the stagnant water of the lagoon, into which he would have plunged if Olga hadn't so insisted on holding his hand at the moment of death—who will hold my hand, Sashka has her fingers full of martyrs, Stéphanie was right, I am a monster, a monster of selfishness and solitude, they should have locked me up in the cage of Hugo Orlandini the artist, condemned to hearing "My Way" for eternity, or "Lili Marleen," or "Three Drummer Boys" sung by an infantry company, so much music in my life—in Syria Alois Brunner the butcher of the Jews of Austria Greece France and Slovakia had been sentenced to a similar punishment, forced to bear for forty years the quarter tones of Arabic melodies he hated, locked up in his little house on the road to Bloudan near Damascus, guarded like a deluxe hostage by different Syrian regimes, Nathan Strasberg had kindly given me his address, if you get a chance give him a bullet in the back of the neck for me, I didn't get the opportunity, Brunner driven mad by the threnodies of Fairuz by the muezzin and the stridencies of eastern pop was devoured by hatred, prisoner of those who had saved him from the death sentence: like Franz Stangl before him Brunner went to Syria with a fake passport in 1954, he felt safe in Damascus, protected by the enemies of his enemies, pure transitivity, and time passed, time passed, Alois the hyperactive feels reclusion weighing on him, he doesn't like Syria but there's nothing to be done, emigrating to South America is already too dangerous and the Syrian governments have realized the potential interest of their captive, here's someone who could play a part in a future negotiation with Israel, in 1970 the coup d'état of Hafez al-Assad makes the conditions of his stay a little rougher, placed under house arrest, forced to change his address constantly to avoid the revenge of the Mossad which sends him letter bombs several times, depriving him of a few fingers and an eye, Brunner takes refuge in hatred, hatred of the Jews whom he would love to kill again, hatred of the Arabs who are sheltering him and above all of their unbearable music and their vile food, Alois Brunner glued day and night to German TV along with his dog is bored, he gives a few interviews to the Austrian press, in which he asks to be thanked for having rid Vienna of the cumbersome Jews, he would like to speak more often, Brunner the mad, but the Syrians prevent him, they officially deny his presence on their soil, Nathan Strasberg was wrong, when I arrived in Damascus to see Alois the man responsible for the deportation of Leon Saltiel the Jew from Salonika he was already in his grave, dead in 1996 at the age of eighty-four, a little senile perhaps, at his home in the arid hills west of the Syrian capital, Brunner died no one knows how, with the television on, his corpse was discovered fifteen days later half eaten by the Doberman who had stayed too long without food, then buried secretly in an unmarked grave—the Syrian from Homs who sold me copies of police photographs thought it absolutely unfair that one could end up half decomposed and eaten by your own mutt, in a bathrobe, alone, in a foreign country what's more, deplorable, I asked him what had become of the dog, he made a face of complete disgust, I have no idea, I suppose they killed it on the spot, the last victim of Alois Brunner, a black canine with sharp teeth, forced to eat the thin calves of his master to survive a few more days, Brunner one-eyed hate-filled amputee had clung to existence until the end, with rage in his body, Nathan was very happy with the photos and the information, he bought me a bottle of champagne at the King David Hotel, while a beautiful Russian pianist with long blond hair played "My Way" on a gleaming Steinway—there was no one to hold Brunner's hand at the instant of death, no one aside from a female Teutonic announcer live from Munich via satellite, the gods had abandoned him, the Syrians didn't know anymore what to do with this awkward guest, time passes, Rome is approaching, I'd almost ask the violinist who looks like Hemingway to play a little tune for me, the way Olga played for Pound from time to time, *erbarme Dich, mein Gott* from the *St. Matthew Passion*, *have pity, Lord*, or some other tearful thing, and his companion would sing the evangelist's words, Matthew dead of a sword in the back in Ethiopia, as he was praying, his arms raised to heaven, facing the altar, Matthew whom Sashka paints leaning over his writing desk or in front of his tax gatherer's scales, Matthew whom Caravaggio in love with decapitation represents in the process of counting his money, I am nearing Rome, I am nearing Rome the eternal light, what am I going to do, Yvan old pal what are we going to do in Rome visit the churches look for an unlikely redemption in the images of the martyrs, get drunk, chase the whores on Via Salaria, a stone's throw from the catacombs, the little suitcase discreetly handcuffed is still above my seat, what does it contain really, what did I put in it, all those dead, all those intersecting fates, the whole world, a fetus in a jar of formaldehyde, the essence of tragedy, the energy of revenge, *erbarme Dich, mein Gott*, mother, cry for your missing son, mother, cry for your son who is gone, my parents, my grandparents, my countries, my victims, the sordid photos of Harmen Gerbens concentration-camp pornographer, the terrified faces of Dutch resistants whom he made pose in Westerbork, the black dust of Cairo, the light of Alexandria the unforgettable, everything is closing, everything is closing as the train emerges from the tunnel to rush into the suburbs, slowly, now, slowly step by step I'm almost there, the railroad is rolling corpses like the impetuous Scamander, the elegant woman in front of me has taken out the *Corriere della Sera* from her bag, the young Italian businessman grandson of Agnelli apparently spent the night in the company of several transsexuals and took a mixture of cocaine and opium, brave little man, he's out of danger according to the evening paper, Turin must be radiating joy, Agnelli the grandfather historic head of Fiat had driven a tank of the same brand in North Africa in 1942, what irony, he could test the quality of his materiel himself, did he sing "Lili Marleen" as he drove like Vlaho, *i znaj da čekam te*, I'm tired, I'm so tired, if I close my eyes now I'll wake up in Rome that's for sure once there I'll take the briefcase and my bag not forgetting the book by Rafael Kahla Marwan's body and Intissar's sorrow, I'll wait for a taxi at Termini or I'll go on foot by the deserted Via Nazionale the countless tie stores closed like my eyelids, *three drummer boys on the way back from war, three drummer boys*, I sang this song to my sister to put her to sleep, I loved singing her songs when she was little I wasn't much bigger myself but I felt as if I were a giant in comparison, Leda sucked her thumb in her crib I stroked her cheek through the bars, *king's daughter, give me your heart, king's daughter, and rat and tat, ratatatat*, that's very far away all that's very far, Leda is in the fog, unreachable, incomprehensible, Catholic housewife with whom I share only genes and silent reproaches, my family is very far away now, my mother the weeping widow, my father in the flesh-eating coffin, in Ivry, from him I've kept memories of electric trains and photographs of torture, in silence, a great figure a Napoleon at Saint Helena poisoned by his own memory, pursued by the hundreds of thousands of souls of his Old Guard he sent to Hades, *if you aren't good Old Boney will carry you away* they said to English toddlers to frighten them, my mother used the same tactics, *watch out, I'll tell your father everything*, and the threat of informing was enough to make us swallow anything even lamb brain, why, my old man was neither violent nor tyrannical, just silent, I don't remember him ever lifting a finger against me, ever, he never even threatened me, never one word louder than another: mothers attach us to them as much as they can, we think we look like them, we think we have their perfection their art their beauty their goodness then we see that's a lie, we're men, a portrait of the silent father, a copy, a moving statue, so we don't know where we're sent to, where we're going, on invisible tracks, why we're moving away so surely from mother and sister, a magnet is drawing us toward an abominable world of shouts in the night, Ghassan the Lebanese told me his father locked him up in a very narrow closet, complete darkness, he didn't have room to sit down he stayed standing up paralyzed with fear without even daring to knock on the door, he cried in silence until someone came to free him an hour or two later: he feared this punishment so much that he was extraordinarily docile and obedient but despite everything they sent him from time to time to this storeroom to teach him how to live, to teach him injustice and the desire for revenge, so he'd be inhabited by a silent hatred, an energy in this world of suffering, Ghassan laughed as he told this story, as soon as he was of age to carry a rifle he enlisted in the nearest militia, he wanted his father to be proud of him, proud of him and a little frightened by the power of the gun, so he'd understand that it was his turn to be able to send him into the closet with a movement of the muzzle, revenge turns only rarely against fathers, it is expressed elsewhere, against strangers enemies traitors prisoners leftists Muslims Ghassan remembered mostly the smell of the cubbyhole, smell of Lysol cleaning fluids and rags, smell of a pharmacy an embalmer actually, or a taxidermist, he remembered it immediately when he was in the dark, he said, in complete darkness he instantly rediscovered the smell of the closet, Ghassan the warrior—Venice was once and for all plunged into the beyond, we were floating there in a long coma, an endless darkness, before the salutary kick in the balls I almost passed into it, one dark moonless night a broomcloset night or a night of the tomb drunk as a Chetnik with a crab-filled beard drunk as never before what came over me instead of crossing over to the Ghetto as I came out of the bar I went in the opposite direction, to the north, I arrived at the Square of the Two Moors, in front of the bas-relief of the little camel, stumbling I bounce against the walls I have a rifle in my hand my cap on my head bent double like in the war I go forward I come out onto the quay I see the tall brick façade of the Madonna dell'Orto what the hell am I doing here I live on the other side all of a sudden I have a flash of inspiration I have come to die I have come in front of this church to put an end to it it's the middle of the night what idiocy I make a u-turn what could I have been thinking I missed the bridge, I missed the bridge and I ended up in the canal, aquatic silence, desperate movements of my arms, my legs, my clothes inflate like a trap my shoes get heavier the taste of water in my mouth no air, no air my feet in the black mud I'm going to die, that's what you wanted well it's a success, you're going to croak, I suck in air on the surface I'm freezing my lungs are tiny my arms are abandoning me everything is heavy, the Scamander is going to carry me away, everything is heavy I'm sleepy and I've had enough I'm going to sink the river has won I let myself sink to the depths, I have the precise memory of letting myself go into the darkness, of stopping struggling, what happened then, Saint Christopher came down from his pedestal, the good giant of Chaldea put the child he was carrying on his shoulder down to come to my aid, he held out his immense hand, he dragged me out of the water, half unconscious, I don't remember a thing, I woke up soaking sitting against the church door my shoes muddy my mouth full of salt my cap still glued to my skull bells were ringing in my head and my eyes were burning, with a fine bronchitis as my only viaticum for the new life

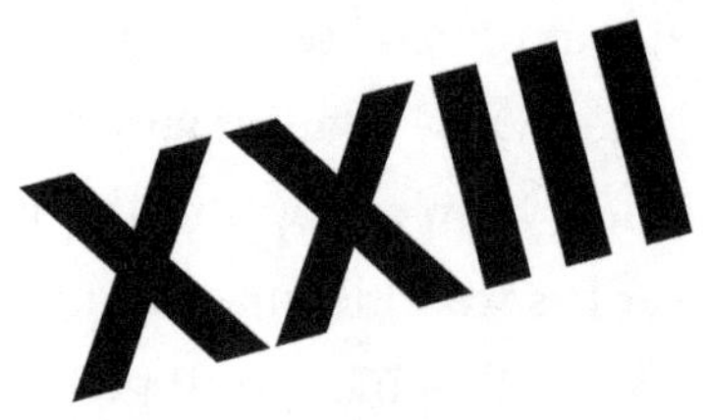

the icy water of the canal, I had a fever when I reached my place trembling like anything it was light out I took two aspirin a scalding shower and I went to shiver right up against Marianne still wondering who could have dragged me out of the water, my clothes stank of old fishing nets, Marianne asked me jokingly if I had fallen in a canal, without meaning it, I didn't say anything, she was afraid when she saw my face, sick exhausted and frightened, it was one straw too many for her personal camel's back, I wasn't going to tell her on top of that that I was practicing swimming with the rats in the waterways of La Serenissima, in the middle of the night, I had pity, I kept this story to myself, I coughed for two weeks, I was surprised at having wanted to die, at having stopped struggling, so it was that easy then, you just had to stop floundering, let yourself slip to the bottom, the way you entrust your body to a train, more tunnels, *Sette Bagni* says the signpost, Seven Baths station, funny coincidence, we're a few kilometers away from Rome, not far to go now, I'm a little afraid of arriving, I'm afraid that Sashka the blonde won't be able to do anything for me, it's too late, she is far away, far away in the midst of her saints, in the whiteness of the *levkas* you soak the wood of icons in, she thinks that Francis Servain is a respectable entomologist who wouldn't hurt a fly, I'm going to have to confront the world alone, alone, having gotten rid of the weight of the dead, Yvan old pal I have a strong feeling that we've made something of a mess of it all, drinking like fish slapping our thighs avenging each other for centuries, the gods have toyed with us, they've tricked us, and now we're going to die alone with no hope of resurrection, in Jerusalem the Holy Sepulcher is bathed in incense, Golgotha and the tomb gleam, among the priests' squabbles and all the liturgical languages, men patiently filed down the mountain and rock to build their house around the tomb, John the Eagle of Patmos writes that Joseph of Arimathea, a secret disciple of Christ, asked Pilate for permission to take down the remains from the crucifix, and Pilate, surprised that the Nazarene was already dead, gave his assent, so Joseph of Arimathea came, removed the heavy body in the company of Nicodemus who brought a mixture of myrrh and aloes, about twenty pounds, they took the emaciated Christ and wrapped him in strips of cloth with the aromatics, according to the way the Jews are buried: in the place where he had been crucified there was a garden, and in the garden a new sepulcher, where no one had been placed, and that's where they put Jesus, wrapped up prepared his body protected from putrefaction by the aromatic resins, like Sarpedon valiant son of Zeus washed in the Scamander and anointed with ambrosia, fathers can do nothing to save their sons, neither the One God nor thundering Zeus, all they can do is prevent corruption, rot and flies, just as Thetis fills the nostrils of the divine Patroclus with red nectar to protect his body from the myriad worms, Jesus son of God carried away by Sleep and Death far from mortals, embalmed like the animals in the Cairo museum, wrapped in strips of cloth in a rock tomb, which Nathan Strasberg regarded as one of the treasures of Jerusalem, one of the tourist attractions, among the gleaming mosques, the Western Wall and the Damascus Gate, Jerusalem was an accumulation of histories, dead people, destructions and reconstructions, ever since the cannibalistic Crusades the Knights Hospitaller with the fine tunics Saladin and his ponies, all great killers of infidels, Jerusalem thrice holy shone like a beacon in the depths of the Mediterranean, waiting for the Second Coming and the Apocalypse, about which the three religions present were pretty much in agreement, the whole thing was to know when, and how, and who would preside over the Last Judgment, when they all return, Matthew of Ethiopia, Mark of Alexandria, Luke of Antioch, John of Ephesus, they will all come, the saints the madmen the angels the bellringers the corpses hacked by swords scimitars arrows will rise up in a perfume of spices, Mohammed the bearded mounted on Buraq the eternal mare will travel across the heavens, Bilal the Abyssinian voice of Islam will sing, Omar the Wise, Ali with the his two-bladed sword, all will rise in a fine commotion, the severe prophets, Abraham the sacrificer, beautiful Hagar the humiliated, Ishmael the predestined,

Isaac the blind, Jacob the fighter, Esau in love with lentils, the gods will feast on the smoke of rams and ewes that all these lovely people will offer them, on the Temple Mount three times promised, there where the heads of Palestinian suicide bombers take off for the skies, corks of divine champagne, during the celebration of the end of days, the last fireworks, prefigured by the explosions of war, and it's no doubt only a question of patience before the universe decides to become infinitesimal again and sucks all these burning memories into nothingness: in Jerusalem you met lots of messianic lunatics, fanatics of the ineffable God, of Christ or Allah the transcendent, with bells in their hands homespun robes or immense beards, ready to preach to you and announce the Last Judgment, in the world capital of eschatology, land too of hatred of the other of resentment and mystical illusion, where Nathan the son of survivors from Łódź looked at this whole circus with amusement, it's folklore, he said, you know, it's the folklore of Jerusalem, Megève has skiing, here we have religions, Jerusalem has lived on this income for millennia it's not going to change overnight, the tomb of the Crucified One seemed very small in the end in the midst of this huge debauch of Faith, I brought back to my mother some holy oil blessed by some patriarch or other, a little icon and slides of the Sepulcher, the glass flask began oozing in my suitcase and I had a pair of socks that could have cured quite a few plague victims or convert the most perverted of atheists they smelled so strongly of the balm, which didn't at all amuse Marija Mirković the serious, *one day you'll pay for your impiety* she had said to me, *you who had the luck to visit Jerusalem*, and a great fear came over me, an infantile fear that she was right and that I'd end up stricken down by the wrath of the All-Powerful, before I came to my senses, pouring a little oil even holy onto some cotton was not the worst thing I'd done, far from it, does everything you do get paid for some day, maybe, Nathan Strasberg spoke to me of his parents survivors from Łódź city of Jews, now living by the blue sea, his father great fighter in the Resistance and his mother a *Volksdeutsche* from the city of three cultures, renamed Litzmannstadt by the Nazis, named for an obscure general who had won fame there in 1914, Łódź was a city of red brick, industrious, where Jews comprised over half of the population, Nathan's mother a German whose family of Prussian stock had settled there in the 1880s, during the textile explosion, a militant communist who fought too for women's rights, afterwards converted to Judaism and living in Palestine, land of the gods, in Łódź they spoke Yiddish, German, and Polish, in the spring of 1941 the ghetto is formed, 160,000 Jewish inhabitants under the orders of King Chaim Rumkowski the ambiguous, the first convoys of useless people are sent to Chełmno to die in the gas trucks—as in Belgrade that same year they use specially equipped vans to rid the Wartheland of Jews, SS drivers carry the naked corpses into the countryside to mass graves dug in the middle of the woods, revenge, revenge, that's what Nathan Strasberg's father has been shouting since 1942, miraculously escaped from imprisonment thanks to his German wife he joins the Polish Resistance and fights against the Nazis in the forests next to Lublin, without knowing that hundreds of thousands of his co-religionists are exterminated nearby between Sobibór and Majdanek, without knowing that the children of Łódź are gassed all together, thousands of kids emaciated and crying given to the Germans by Rumkowski the tragic, *give me your children*, he said, *I need 20,000 children under ten*, Rumkowski shouted into his microphone *I am sacrificing the limbs to save the rest of the body*, all the toddlers went that way, the German ogre knew how to twist the arms of the Jewish leaders convinced that work would save them, that *productivity* would save them, they hadn't understood, they hadn't understood that the monster was not rational, that its head was in other spheres, in the black clouds of destruction, and the Jews were destroyed, Strasberg the courageous wounded at the end of 1943 returns to Łódź in 1945 to realize the extent of the disaster, revenge, Nathan didn't know exactly when his father joined the avengers of the Nakam group, after having settled his wife and sister in a safe place, the night was long, in 1946 the day has scarcely dawned, the Jewish Brigade of Palestine is billeted to Northern Italy, on the border with Austria, and secretly murders all the Nazis and fascists that fall into its clutches, with a bullet in the back of the head, Abba Kovner the partisan poet who organizes the secret emigration to Palestine wants more, he wants *six million dead Germans*, revenge, real revenge, with the craziest plans, he imagines poisoning the water supply of Nuremberg, he imagines killing the prisoners of war in the Langwasser camp: in the end they will manage to kill a few hundred German prisoners with arsenic, impossible to know how many, the Americans in charge of these captives being little inclined to acknowledge the massacre, before they went to Palestine for good to devote themselves to winning the independence of the

State of Israel by fighting, this time, the British—revenge is sweet at the time, my fury after Andi's death, the cataclysm I set off, we set off, in the villages around Vitez, the houses that burned, the screams, the unhappiness, and that group of civilians opposite me, no great warriors with weapons in hand but rather men in their forties in work clothes terrified by the rifle butts raining down on them their homes in flames humiliated tearful we threw them shovels to dig trenches in the middle of mines and bombardments I thought of Andi dead in his own shit his body lost taken away without our being able to fight to save it I thought of Vlaho with his arm cut off of Sergeant Mile killed with a bullet in the middle of his forehead, revenge, one of the prisoners was smiling, he was smiling the bastard, he thought we were funny, we were making him laugh with our rage, why was he smiling, why, he doesn't have the right to smile I gave him a huge clout, he laughed, his face was dirty, his eyes half shut by bruises he kept laughing and stuck out his big black tongue at me, the other guys were looking at him, terrified, this madman was going to draw divine vengeance onto them, he was making fun of me, the retard was making fun of me, making fun of me of Andi of Vlaho of Mile of all our dead and even his own Athena breathed an immense strength into me, all the gods were behind my right arm when I took Andi's bayonet out of its sheath, found behind his pallet, behind me as they had been behind Seyit Havranli the Turkish artilleryman and his 400-pound shell, behind Diomedes son of Tydeus when he wounds Ares himself, I let out a shout worthy of Andrija the furious I brought the long blade down on the laughing Muslim, with divine power, the power that comes from the belly, from your feet in the earth, a wave of pure wrath a perfect movement from right to left that doesn't stop at obstacles of flesh a gesture that continues into the sky where my cry of rage rises along with the victim's blood an inexplicable red column, his body gives a jump his shoulders stiffen his monstrous head is still laughing on the ground his eyes blinking before his torso collapses, accompanied by the incredulous murmuring of the spattered witnesses, I still have the strength to send the vile head rolling with a huge kick, not even surprised by my own power, beside myself, outside myself outside the world already in Hades paradise of warriors, for you Andi this bloody head rolling down the hill, this atrocious slicing through the soft flesh before brandishing my weapon at the sky, everyone moves away from the butchery, everyone moves away from the miracle, one of the prisoners faints and falls into the black blood of the village idiot, of the saint maybe whom I've just decapitated so cleanly that it's a wonder, a medieval fresco, the martyr beheaded lies on the Bosnian soil without anyone hurrying over to recover his head on a golden platter, we go on to something else, another fire other rapes other pillages other carnages until dawn, until dawn we go back to our barracks exhausted despite the drugs our fingers a little numb because of the alcohol sitting on my pallet I bend over to take off my boots the laces are sticky with blood, the laces and the tongue, it's disgusting, it's disgusting my stomach contracts, that's it, the gods have left me alone, alone in the blood and bile, to choke with disgust fatigue and remorse—I didn't decapitate Medusa the terrifying like Caravaggio, just a poor madman, a simpleton, his thick blackish tongue pursues me, his surprised eyes, his laugh, the madman at the Milan train station had something of the same gaze, he held out his hand to me, I refused it, too bad for me, *erbarme dich, mein Gott, Herz und Auge weint vor dir, bitterlich*, I think of Leon Saltiel the man from Salonika, he took revenge too, he tortured the man who betrayed him to death and strangled the woman he loved, crying, he abandoned their bodies and went to a crowded cabaret to listen to Roza Eskenazi sing *To Kanarini*, Leon Saltiel ordered ouzo, to the sound of the *rebetikas*, the violin the lute the exciting voice of Roza the irreverent with her Constantinople accent, there were no more Greeks in Smyrna, almost none in Istanbul, there were no more Jews in Salonika, almost none, Agatha was dead, her eyes wide open were slowly clouding over in Stavros's café, next to the corpse of her lover, farewell, the cabaret customers think stupidly that Leon is crying because of the music, *bitterlich*, the head of the Muslim madman is decomposing in my memory, next to that of the Baptist, and of the seven Tibhirine monks, *erbarme dich mein Gott, erbarme dich*, for death and despair are stretching around me like Ahmad's brain on the wall in Beirut, who dragged me out of the canal in the Venice night, why, to what purpose, to go serve the forces of shadow and fill this suitcase that's becoming heavier and heavier, the train accelerates, the train wants to arrive at its destination, like Achilles's horses, like Achilles's horses the train is whispering my fate into my ear, tataktatoom, tataktatoom, the train is predicting that my bloody karma will send me directly to dung beetle, directly to dung beetle without passing ape

when Stéphanie shouted *you are a monster* I should have guessed, she knew all that of course, she knew, since when I don't know, since the beginning maybe she wanted me to tell her to confess to her to admit everything to her sobbing on her shoulder, she wanted me to ask for her compassion to reveal my mortal sins to her, she wanted to forgive me, she thought she had the strength to forgive me, but it was necessary for me to confess, the burden had become too heavy, I imagine it's curiosity that spurred her to find out, after the business of the British documentary probably, after the violence of that night, she asked one of her high-placed friends for my personal file, she must have voiced anxieties, she must have moved them, manipulated them, Stéphanie couldn't imagine being affected herself by the shadows she handled, couldn't imagine being contaminated by Hades where the lower-echelon spies live, I imagine her expression, her tears, her sadness, is anyone prepared for official truth, for cold reports on the well-guarded Table of the gods, Stéphanie was too much like me, reading the conclusions to the investigation on Francis Servain Miković she saw herself, she saw herself living beside this life, jealous frightened and disgusted, Dream had told her too much, I imagine she must have made some efforts, as she waited, as she waited for me to tell her, to confess the unsayable to her, without daring to speak to me about it, out of fear, at the same time, of making the monster rise up, seeing without seeing, knowing without knowing, and I myself was particularly idiotic for not guessing, not understanding that my fate was weighty, that the shadows had swallowed me whole and that it would not be easy to get out, if you can get out, in Istanbul the sublime a few days on the Bosporus between two worlds, the journey of the last chance, between two or even three worlds, the Ottoman capital was the center of the Mediterranean for so long, the Bosporus scarcely wider than the Danube, the city divided by the waterways floats beyond the well-guarded Dardanelles, beyond Troy the martyred, on the lips of the Black Sea that bathes Sebastopol and the Caucasus, from Tangiers to Stamboul there were cubic meters of corpses, corpses ruins and fates, in Constantinople Roza Eskenazi the Jewess was triumphing in the 1930s, Roza was born around 1900, her real name was Sarah, she spoke Ladino, Turkish, and Greek, her father wore a handsome tarboosh and was the owner of a warehouse in Scutari, Stéphanie wasn't interested in the life of Roza Eskenazi the great diva, singer of *rebetika*, songs of the tavern, of hashish opium alcohol love solitude and despair, she did not even care that we had first met in Constantinople, New Rome, she was tormented, irritable, and alternated very somber moments with a great tenderness, an almost desperate love for my person, I thought of Roza Eskenazi the provocative, of Leon Saltiel and of that song where Roza talks about the pleasure of having a hookah in your mouth, the twofold excitation it provokes, that of the drug and that of love, Stéphanie preferred Christ Pantocrators Byzantine churches Sinan's mosques to smoke-filled *meyhanes*, she was desperate because I always signed to the musicians to come over and play at our table, and immediately her face shut down, she scowled into her glass of raki of course I didn't understand why, the fiddler and his assistant played "When You Go to Uskudar" or some other song I didn't understand a word of and I was delighted, Stéphanie groaned, *I can't bear this screeching*, true it wasn't Paganini, it was a nice fat bald mustachioed Turk, but the repertoire and the place suited him perfectly, *how can you bear this music?* or else *I wonder what your mother would think of this*, what did Marija Mirković have to do with it, I didn't understand what she was leading up to, I didn't say anything in reply, then we went back on foot from Beyoğlu to our hotel in front of the Hagia Sophia, she coiled around me like a snake to escape the cold as we crossed the Golden Horn, the floating bridge moved a little underfoot and emphasized the effects of the raki, I imagined the Turkish boats right up against the outsized chain that closed access to the harbor of Byzantium, the bombardes and the Greek fire shot by panic-stricken Greeks from the hills, the night streaked with flames, a beautiful clear night, the dawn of

May 29, 1453, the naval diversion to prepare for the final attack on the city walls, at that hour the Janissaries were coming to open a breach near the postern of Blachernae, the attack lasted from midnight on, the old Emperor Constantine the nobility and the clerics had prayed for a long time in Hagia Sophia, prayed to the Lord, that He have pity on the second Rome, the Lord and his Holy Mother, *Áxion estín os alethós*, everyone terrified everyone reconciled to the end, to destruction death or slavery, Constantine the Last dies at the ninth hour the next day, he takes off his purple and descends the walls to fight in the street, in his city, he knows all is lost, he is not trying to flee, he throws himself into combat to die, on his shoulders he has the weight of his ancestors since Constantine the Great since Augustus since the powerful Achaeans and the conquered Trojans, Priam prods him in the back with his example, Constantine is pierced in the side by a Turkish spear, then by an arrow, then by a sword and the black veil falls over his eyes, he does not know that Apollo is carrying his body far away from the fury of combat, to wash it in the sweet waters of Europe and entrust it to the White Island, at that instant the Ottomans reach the magnificent Hagia Sophia, among the tears of families who have taken refuge there, with Stéphanie I look at the illuminated basilica from the window of our room, an oil tanker is going down the Bosporus, it is coming from the Black Sea, it will cross the Sea of Marmara, slip through the wild Dardanelles, pass by Kilitbahir the impregnable, go down to the south, follow the shores of Troy, pass the Morea peninsula and steer for the west, due west along the pelagic plain smooth as a tombstone, in three days it will be within sight of Messina, a strait just slightly wider than the Bosporus, if it's going to Marseille or Barcelona, otherwise it will cross in front of the Barbary coasts over to Tangier or Gibraltar, where the apes of the Rock will give it a final salute before it's lost in the Atlantic frontier to the world—Stéphanie stood right against me, I smelled the perfume of her hair, gazing at the lights of the blue Mosque and the twinkling glimmers from the ship's stays, the *kamances* of the taverns still ringing in my ears, relaxed by the raki and the warm presence of the woman beside me, sometimes there are instants held suspended, between two moments, in the air, in eternity, a dance shoulder against shoulder, the movement of a hand, the wake of a boat, humanity in pursuit of happiness, and everything falls down, everything falls down, Stéphanie became savage again, moody, I know why, she saw in the cupolas the perfumes the hookahs the violins a barbaric side, my barbaric side, she imagined the deadly savage refinement of the Orient, stakes, decapitations, she was afraid of me when I summoned the violinists, of what there was in me that escaped her, the inexhaustible other, and she identified with my mother guardian of Western order, with Louis-Ferdinand Céline the cowardly sworn enemy of otherness, she glimpsed like a romantic Orientalist the deleterious influences of drugs and violent cruelty, I thought of the poem by Cavafy the living-dead, the civil servant of Alexandria, "On the Night of the Fall," cities fall so often, the world spins so often, is there room for sorrows, is there room to miss Dionysos when you're no longer drunk, the Turks had made Constantinople the greatest city in the Mediterranean, a beacon, a miracle of beauty and culture,

Stéphanie was sad because she saw in me the warrior the murderer she locked me up in my violence with no forgiveness, I know what she had read, Lebihan the bald with the Wepler oysters also had a gift for me, he was about to retire happily, Lebihan, anxious but happy to be able to devote himself to biking to oysters and to café conversations, he looked at me kindly, after thanking me for the 7.65 Zastava that touched him especially, he said to me Francis I took these pages out for you, read them, it's instructive, and take note of them, it was my personal file, the preliminary investigation, my various grades, my assignments, my requests for leave, my absences, my parents, my teenage political friendships, my stages of military service, my life, including the Croatian and Bosnian activities, words like *war crimes*, *violent acts, torture*, the names of my superiors at the time, the parts of the file from the International Court of Justice about the valley of the Lašva that concerned me, these notes were dated long after my entry into the Agency, the forces of the shadows are never wrong, *to be supervised*, a psychological profile defined me recently as *tending towards alcoholism and depression, to be spared from responsibilities*, nevertheless I was credited with fidelity, patriotism, and integrity, not liable to be manipulated from outside, not interested in money, only known hobby: amateur historian, that was ironic, the last investigation was dated last year, who had authorized it, I knew of course what code I was going to discover on the bottom of the page, what excuse could she have found, *for a possible assignment*, she had pretended to want to recruit me, the cunning one, to learn as much as possible about me, the request was initialed by her and bore the number of her department, all was fair in love and war, all was fair in love and war she couldn't bear any more she wanted to know, was she going to be able to bear the result, in Istanbul she alternated between passion and disgust, in Paris she discovered she was pregnant, one last chance and farewell, farewell Francis the terrible, I took note, as Lebihan said, I checked that the results of the investigation didn't mention Yvan Deroy the mad, lost in my adolescence, I easily usurped his identity, liquidated my apartment and farewell, now I'm in a train approaching Rome, approaching the end of the world and Sashka the golden, she is not interested in the truth, she is not affected by the outside she is detached, she is floating tenderly in the practice of sacred illumination, desirable and unreachable, a magical body for a soulless presence, one more illusion, Sashka never went to the Bosporus, *Nikogda ja ne byl na Bosfore, Ty menya ne sprashivai o nem*, her eyes so blue that they don't need it, she has the Tiber the churches and the memory of the white sea, and today Stéphanie is working somewhere in Moscow, is she thinking about Yesenin in the city of the thousand and one bells and the thousand and three towers, farewell, I have a suitcase full of dead men a borrowed name a few kilometers before me and farewell, the calm after revenge, I salute you, Andrija, even in the innermost depths of Hades, I'm going to join you, everything flees like the colorful houses in the Roman suburbs, yellowed by the sad December streetlights, the last lights Yesenin sees before hanging himself or before being hanged, the cathedral lit up like the Hagia Sophia opposite his hotel room, *Ya v tvoikh glazakh uvidel more*, there is nothing to see in Sashka's eyes, hopeless as the sea, *Polykhaiuchee golubym ognem*, I know where I'd like to go back to, now, far from the cold night of Russia, I would like to find a warm day between Agamy and Mersa Matruh, a few kilometers away from Alexandria, on the immense beach, it's evening the Mediterranean is metallic the sky rosy the sand soft, I look out to sea the pure phosphorus of the sea makes your eyes blink in the slanting light, two shapes slip out of the water, they leap one behind the other and sparkle, two iridescent sprays of water come towards the coast in little leaps, two dolphins, two dolphins are playing in the lukewarm sea not far from the shore, I've never seen them before, I get up, they're so close you can see their backs sparkling, they are leaping in front of me, there is no one else, so of course I run they seem so real seen just above the waves, I have tears in my eyes, never have I seen such a sight, a sight for no one, they were gamboling for me alone, in the evening on a deserted coast, a gift of chance or of Thetis the generous, I threw myself into the water, a shroud of coolness covered me, the two silver shapes were outlined against the pink sky, the taste of salt filled my mouth, I swam slowly toward them, it was beauty calling me, beauty calm and pure happiness harmony of the world, I swam toward the two dolphins, slowly so as not to frighten them, I wanted to follow them, I wanted to follow them, I would have followed them to the home of Poseidon with the azure hair, it was a fine sunset to disappear, a fine evening to die or live eternally in the wake of marine mammals, they sensed me coming, perceived my vibrations in the waves, I was not worthy of them, I was not worthy of them they moved away with a leap, one last flash in the dying sun and I was alone again on the infinite beach, we are going to get out soon, Yvan, but not in the kingdom of the god of the sea, get out of the train, the passengers are already restless, they are looking out the window seeing Rome approach with lights in the darkness, I know now, Yvan, it's time to organize a funeral, a pyre for Francis Servain Mirković whom his mother and sister will miss, everything is more difficult once you reach man's estate, everything rings falser, but sometimes the gods offer you flashes of clairvoyance, moments when you contemplate the whole universe, the infinite wheel of worlds, you see yourself, from high up, for a few instants truly before leaving, propelled into the next thing, toward the end, propelled toward the woman waiting for me there, the one who opens the door to me, in front of whom I stagger with shame and drunkenness, my eyes blinking, my breath fetid, my head beating like a decapitated sun, the woman who looks at me without seeing me, so profound is the fracture, my chest open deep, the one who doesn't seem to recognize me, for life has little weight, as little as the bodies struggling in it, this woman is doubtful about me in the alcoholic fumes my clothes give off, and I, who have crossed the sea to join her, who have crossed without feeling it the space that separated me from Paris, I for whom a stewardess on the Middle East Airlines had to come outside for an instant of drunkenness to help me get into the plane, I whom a flick of a finger could push out of the world, I who desire nothing more, not even sleep whose awakening I fear, not even the woman who is not waiting for me and whose presence I wanted so strongly, before engulfing myself in drink and flight, stiff, dead drunk man entrusted to the heavens like an angel, sleeping a leaden sleep, snoring probably at 30,000 feet up, far above the clouds where the night is always clear, there where you can contemplate the star clusters and the galaxies, one July 14th, one night of national celebration when I am crossing the Zone by plane, one night of leaving the embassy, as one must, almost on all fours I was so drunk: I had to be driven to the airport, I had to be driven to the departure area, I had to be awakened to be driven to the plane, I dozed off dead drunk in the international airport of the Lebanese Republic, I say it without vainglory, with a certain shame, I had to be awakened later when we arrived in the Roissy airport, I saw nothing of the mountains of Cyprus, the mountains of Italy or the coastal plain, I saw only a scoffing taxi that thought I was arriving at least from China or the other side of the world, to look so awful, and I was arriving from the end of the world, I was arriving from the end of the world as if from hell, which is in me, that's what the woman who opens the door to me is thinking, and she is disappointed: she is disappointed, she looked at me like a wounded man, a sick man with my chest open, the Prophet in Dante's *Inferno*, drunk the day before I shouted the *Marseillaise*, I think of it as I see her, I shouted *qu'un sang impur* and the genius of Berlioz, who did everything he could to rescue this military tune, Berlioz loved *poor Ophelia* as I love you, those are the thoughts of men still drunk in the morning, those are embassy celebrations, full of alcohol drunkards and cheap patriotism, the gardens were large, beautiful, there was champagne, wine, anise, and uniforms, the ambassador shouted *long live France!* Berlioz rang out and with him Rouget de Lisle and I heard *Harold in*

Italy, I saw Harold, *Romeo and Juliet*, and the little Roman wood where Hector went to shoot at crows with a pistol to dispel the boredom of the Academy, of France, while now I'm crossing the Tiburtina train station, Berlioz describes the suffering of the proud Trojans and the wanderings of Aeneas, Berlioz despaired of Rome, he preferred the mountains of the Abruzzi and the brigands you find there, you needed a few days on horse to reach that region, I didn't know what to say to Stéphanie I was still drunk I should have spoken to her about Berlioz and his Ophelia about his Trojans today what would I say to her I would say to her I loved you more than anything don't be mad at me I would tell her the story of Intissar the Palestinian saved by Marwan's ghost, all that is very far away, Stéphanie is very far away the child we didn't have is very far away in limbo Astyanax thrown from the ramparts of Troy, Hector is dead, Hector tamer of mares is dead and it's already Rome, it's already Rome, in the midst of the beautiful gardens of the French Embassy in Lebanon I was lost, lost between worlds, floating in space without knowing it, already departed for Rome, for the missed plane, the documents, the databases, the lists in my briefcase, the cardinals and laymen the secretaries of the dicastery who are waiting for me, I am in the same state as when I left Beirut or when I arrived in Paris before the woman who opened the door to me, drunk from so much train-travel from so many kilometers and from the dead heaped up on the roads, the tracks, the memories of war, of Trieste, of Paris where Stéphanie opened to me, I had just awakened her, I could see her breasts under her T-shirt, her legs were bare, like Marianne's in the hotel in Alexandria, like those of the Dutch women in Harmen Gerbens's photos, like those of the corpses in the river in Jasenovac, those of Andrija covered with shit, the spread filthy legs of the girls in Bosnia, the legs of Intissar under Ahmad's violence hundreds of bare legs, we're already in Rome the last meters before Termini, the train is moving at a walking pace over the thousands of bodies placed one after the other, the wood of crossties, bodies are wood that's what Stangl said in Treblinka, that's what my father said too in Algeria, wood duty, crossbeam duty, noble wood that you make icons from with the logs of funeral pyres, line up the memories in a ditch to burn them, like goat thighs whose smoke makes the gods salivate, Stéphanie's curves make me salivate in the early morning hours of Paris: it's the beginning of the century, of the millennium, you have to rebuild everything and ride, ride with a train exhausted tense trembling aching swaying from shunt to shunt, revenge consummated, the dead accumulated and neatly lined up, Stéphanie's legs were bare in the early Paris morning it was my turn to arrive at her place unannounced, back from a quick mission to Beirut, a few days before that she had informed me that I was a monster and that she never wanted to see me again, I'm trying my luck, I present myself at her place in the early morning with my eyes burning from sleep and alcohol, drunk and dangerous like Lowry in Taormina, like Joyce in Trieste, she looks at me, she looks at me without saying anything there's no need she doesn't sigh she just has to look at me in silence and I understand, I understand that the door is going to close, that Stéphanie's legs are going to disappear behind it, farewell, the tomb closes again, farewell, I didn't know what to say to her, didn't know what to ask her, it was up to me to hold out my hand, now we're going alongside the Roman aqueduct we are penetrating the walls then the dead end of the Termini station the travelers are thrown into turmoil, animals disturbed in their sleep, they all get up at the same time recover their luggage put away the books and newspapers I discreetly get out the little key I free the briefcase the suitcase that's so light and so heavy, the train is coming up to the platform, it's wheezing, it's taking its time, I grab my bag now I'm standing in the aisle between my traveling companions we are going to separate, each will pursue his own fate, Yvan Deroy too I am going to go on foot to the hotel life is new life is alive I know it now, farewell wise Sashka, I can stand up all on my own, I don't need this suitcase any more, don't need the Vatican's pieces of silver, I'm going to throw it all into the water, the wood accumulated for Hector's pyre, on the tenth day, on the tenth day I will go by foot to the fatal Tiber right next to the Sixtus Bridge to throw these dead into the river, so it will take them to the sea, the blue cemetery, so everyone will go away, names and photographs will be eaten by the salt, then evaporated they will join the clouds, and farewell, Yvan Deroy will join the sky too, the New World, farewell Rome too eternal, by plane, in the Fiumicino airport I'll wait for the last call for my flight, the passengers, the destination, I will be sitting there on my deluxe seat without being able to move anywhere there is no one else I belong to the space between to the world of the living-dead finally I have no more weight no more ties no more attachments I am in my tent near the hollow vessels I have given up I am in the universe of grey carpets of television screens and that will last everything will last there are no more wrathful gods no more warriors next to me the planes are resting the seagulls I live in the Zone where women are made up and wear a navy blue uniform beautiful *peplos* of a starry night there is no more desire no more flight no more anything a great floating a dead time where my name is repeated invades the air it's the last call the last call for the last passengers for the last flight I won't move from that airport seat, I won't move anymore that's it for journeys, for wars, next to me the guy with the sincere look will smile at me I will return his smile he's been there for years suspended him too chained to his seat years he's been there since long before the discovery of aviation he has a nice face, he's dark-skinned, a giant, a giant from Chaldea who looks like he has carried the world on his shoulders, for centuries and centuries he has been between planes, between trains, as they are dispossessing me of my new name by breathing it into the loudspeakers, I think of the arms of the steel bird waiting for me, 150 companions in limbo have already boarded but I refuse, I am Achilles quieted the first man the last I have found a tent for myself it is mine now it's this fireproof rug and this red plush it's my name they're shouting my space I won't get up my neighbor is with me he's the priest of Apollo he's a demiurge he has seen war too he has seen war and the blinding sun of cut necks, he is waiting calmly for the end of the world, if I dared, if I dared I would perch on his shoulders like a ridiculous kid, I would ask him to take me across rivers, rivers three times three times round and other Scamanders lined with corpses, I would ask him to be my last train, my last plane my last weapon, the last glimmer of violence goes out of me and I turn to him to ask him, to beg him to carry me away he looks at me with infinite compassion, he looks at me, he suddenly offers me a cigarette he says so my friend one last smoke before the end? one last smoke before the end of the world.

This book is full of all those who have entrusted me with their stories, Vlaho C., Ghassan D., Imad el-Haddad, Youssef Bazzi, Sandra Balsells, Sylvain Estibal, Igor Marojević, Alexandra Petrova, David Blumberg, Patrick Deville, Alviero Lippi, Hugo Orlandini, Ahmet Riyahi, the late Eduardo Rózsa, Yasmina Belhaj, Hans B., Mirjam Fruttiger, Manos Demetrios and all the others, witnesses, victims, or killers, in Barcelona, Beirut, Damascus, Zagreb, Algiers, Sarajevo, Belgrade, Rome, Trieste, Istanbul. I also have an immense debt to journalists, historians, filmmakers, and documentary makers whose work I have used, during the years spent in the Zone, as well as to those who have accompanied me on those long journeys. Thank you to Jean Rolin for having generously allowed me to entitle this book *Zone*, as I had planned. Thank you to Barbara, to Peter the Great, to the whole Rat Pack, and to Claro who, along with friendship, shelter and food, offered me the two pages of the discovered journal by Francesc Boix.

To confess wrong without losing rightness: Charity
have I had sometimes, I cannot make it flow thru.
A little light, like a rushlight
To lead back to splendour.

—*Ezra Pound*

Mathias Énard studied Persian and Arabic and spent long periods in the Middle East. A professor of Arabic at the University of Barcelona, he won the Prix des Cinq Continents de la Francophonie and the Prix Edmée de la Rochefoucault for his first novel, *La perfection du tir.* He has been awarded many prizes for *Zone*, including the Prix du Livre Inter and the Prix Décembre.

Charlotte Mandell has translated fiction, poetry, and philosophy from the French, including works by Proust, Flaubert, Genet, Maupassant, Blanchot, and many other distinguished authors. She has received many accolades and awards for her translations, including a Literature Translation Fellowship from the National Endowment for the Arts for *Zone.*

Open Letter—the University of Rochester's nonprofit, literary translation press—is one of only a handful of publishing houses dedicated to increasing access to world literature for English readers. Publishing ten titles in translation each year, Open Letter searches for works that are extraordinary and influential, works that we hope will become the classics of tomorrow.

Making world literature available in English is crucial to opening our cultural borders, and its availability plays a vital role in maintaining a healthy and vibrant book culture. Open Letter strives to cultivate an audience for these works by helping readers discover imaginative, stunning works of fiction and by creating a constellation of international writing that is engaging, stimulating, and enduring.

Current and forthcoming titles from Open Letter include works from Argentina, Catalonia, Peru, Poland, South Africa, and numerous other countries.

www.openletterbooks.org

Printed in the USA
CPSIA information can be obtained
at www.ICGtesting.com
JSHW080805051124
72997JS00002B/2

9 781934 824269